ATHENA VOLTAIRE

PULP TALES

From the Library of

_____

ATHENA VOLTAIRE

PULP TALES

Edited by
Chris Murrin
with
Steve Bryant

Illustrated by
Steve Bryant

Cover by
Steve Bryant & Jason Millet

FOR ACTION LAB ENTERTAINMENT:
Bryan Seaton: Publisher/ CEO
Shawn Gabborin: Editor In Chief
Jason Martin: Publisher-Danger Zone
Nicole D'Andria: Marketing Director/Editor
Jim Dietz: Social Media Manager
Danielle Davison: Executive Administrator
Chad Cicconi: Typewriter Ribbon Repair
Shawn Pryor: President of Creator Relations

Book Design and Layout by Steve Bryant

ATHENA VOLTAIRE™ PULP TALES

Published by Action Lab Entertainment

November , 2017
First Edition
ISBN

1 3 5 7 9 10 8 6 4 2

CONTENTS

INTRODUCTION 9
   Paul Malmont

JUST A QUICK PICK UP 13
   Mike Oliveri

THE CURSE OF DESTRUCTION ISLAND 28
   Eric Trautmann

THE PLOT TWIST PERIL 54
   Steve Bryant

THE HEAVENLY ABYSS 61
   Caleb Monroe

THE GODDESS OF FILTH 84
   Genevieve Pearson

THERE IS AN EXPLANATION FOR WHAT I AM ABOUT TO DO ...114
   Tom King

OFF THE MAP 130
   Corinna Bechko, Story by Corinna Bechko & Gabriel Hardman

A SONG IN THE NIGHT 147
   Brad Keefauver

HAKKŌ ICHIU 163
   Chris Murrin

A MAGICAL MURDER 175
   Ryan L. Schrodt

WELTSCHMERZ or "ATHENA VOLTAIRE AND THE GOD OF
FLESH AND BONE" 188
   Dirk Manning

THE GUNS OF KERR 197
   Marc Mason

THE KISTE, THE KASTE AND THE KYKEON 223
   October Crifasi

LAND, SKY AND SEA 244
   Elizabeth Amber Love

THE FORBIDDEN ISLAND 259
   Michael May

THE AUSTRIAN PRISONER 281
   Ron Fortier

CULT FILM 302
   Will Pfeifer

AFTERWORD 313

CONTRIBUTORS 316

INTRODUCTION

Paul Malmont

Our heroine's adventures begin with the word.

Certainly not enough ink has been spilled on behalf of our women of action, but though the line is slender, it is straight and strong. Like most modern adventure writing, it has its roots in the totally false true frontier stories of America's creation. The trend began perhaps in the hands of the rich and famous Davy Crockett, whose insistence on appearing in his own adventures would ultimately doom him, thereby making him the Steve Irwin of his time. His wildly popular Crockett Almanacs told tall tales of women—shemales, he called them, and oh, if he only knew what that would end up meaning—who would rather fight than love, in stories with such creative titles as "The Flower of Gum Swamp" and "The Mississippi Screamer." Soon, the Wild West was creating women whose real lives were at least as interesting as their dime store counterparts. The tales of Martha Jane Canary, now known to us as Calamity Jane, would be popularized in the Deadwood Dick series, and Myra Maybelle Shirley, whose crime-spree may have included a run with the Jesse James gang, would be turned into the legend of Belle Starr, the Bandit Queen in the pages of the "National Police Gazette." At the same time, our heroine is finding her fully fictional feet across the Atlantic in the penny dreadfuls written by James Malcolm Rymer, featuring the Victorian-era cloaked avenger, the White Mask, secret identity of the beautiful heiress, May Dudley. By the turn of the century, Elizabeth Cochran has taken matters into her own hands, both putting herself into adventures such as going under cover in a lunatic asylum or racing around the world in an attempt to mythbust Jules Verne, and then writing about her exploits in Joseph Pulitzer's papers under the fanatically wonderful name, Nellie Bly. Women seem poised to take their place alongside men as full partners in action.

But then something happens.

She becomes an accessory. A sidekick. In other words, she loses her character and becomes objectified. While real women are taking on more and more responsibility for civilization's progress, their fictional counterparts are stepping to the margins. Pat Savage may go on the occasional adventure with her cousin, Doc Savage, but spends most of her time managing an upscale Manhattan beauty salon. Margo Lane spends as much time being rescued by The Shadow as she does snooping for him. By the time the classic Pulp Era has come to an end, women haven't become bad, they're just written that way. Fishnets gartered on, cigarettes dangling from ruby lips, they've become symbolic of something darker; the Femme Fatale has taken over the stage, and women are not to be trusted again in pulp for a long time.

Fortunately, by this time, our heroine has found a home in the comic books, where she fights on under many guises—as Diana of Paradise Island, Lara of Krypton, and Silk Satin of Central City. There she thrives for decades, every once in awhile making the leap back to great success on the written page as, for example, Modesty Blaise did. But even that was back in the sixties. It's been far too long since our heroine kicked ass between the covers of an actual book. Maybe she's been on a quest while her sisters have been shopping for shoes and handbags.

Which is why I'm particularly pleased to see that Athena Voltaire is making the leap from line drawing to sentence. Actually, she's making the leap from digital line to prose, which shows you just how far our heroine has come to get back to the beginning. Created over a decade ago as a serialized webcomic, Athena Voltaire has expanded into print media, and under the guidance of Steve Bryant, become a regular series of traditionally published comics. Now Steve, his editor Chris Murrin, and a group of talented cohorts he's assembled are expanding the world of this character as a tribute to the pulp roots that are part of her origin.

Of course, the transition fits her like a sleek pair of riding boots. After all, the Pulp Era of the '30s and '40s was a golden age of adventure. There were more than enough Nazis, lost worlds and Artifacts of Power around to keep the heroes busy, so why shouldn't a heroine fly her plane into the mix? Athena Voltaire, raven-haired beauty, seeker of adventure, possessor of wry wit, is right at home on these pages, as you're about to find out in this collection of short stories.

As they used to trumpet in the old movie trailers, you'll be thrilled as modern master of the pulp genre, Ron Fortier (seriously, check out his credits at Airship27. com and tell me he's not one of the keepers of the true faith), plunges her deep into Reich-held territory in "The Austrian Prisoner." You'll be chilled by the attack of the harpy-creature in Brad Keefauver's "A Song in the Night." And you'll find yourself laughing along with Will Pfiefer and his secret movie studio history story, "Cult Film," an idea so clever I wish I'd had it.

Marc Mason takes her on a trip to what's left of the Western Frontier, Corinna Bechko and Gabriel Hardman take her to the Pacific in search of another famous female pilot, while Mike Oliveri takes her to, well, I won't spoil the surprise, but a shadow lies over her destination. Other stories in this collection will take her from a supernatural tour of Greece, to fighting assassins in old Tokyo, to the Native American mysticism of the Pacific Northwest and to the site of a deadly air disaster. One thing that becomes clear from these stories, you couldn't ask for a more attractive travelling companion.

It's good to see our heroine in print again. In prose, you're not constantly reminded how hot she is, but rather, are drawn to how cool she is. Athena Voltaire carries with her, like a sidearm, the tales of those who've gone before. The fact that she survives and thrives time after time, medium after medium should be a warning to those that count her out. There's life in the old girl, yet! Welcome back, our heroine, and welcome home, Athena Voltaire.

Paul Malmont is the author of The Chinatown Death Cloud Peril, Jack London in Paradise, *and* The Astounding, the Amazing, and the Unknown. *He works in advertising and lives in New Jersey with his wife and two children. His Web site is PaulMalmont.com.*

For Mom—
Thanks for teaching me not only how
to read, but why. I love you.
—Chris Murrin

For Kerrie—
I'm so glad I'm on this adventure with you.
—Steve Bryant

JUST A QUICK PICK UP

Mike Oliveri

"If they haven't cleared that landing strip, there's not going to be enough of us left to bury," Athena said.

She pushed the yoke forward. The plane's nose dipped toward the dirt.

"Just try not to bang up my face too badly, dear. I want to look good for my last photos." Carter Charles sat in the co-pilot's seat. He put on a good show, but even his acting chops couldn't hide the death grip he had on the edge of the console.

The night landing didn't bother Athena, nor did the overcast sky and dark runway. She'd made riskier landings look easy, and she had good maps and instruments. No, it was the unfamiliar plane the client insisted she take and the unfamiliarity with the ground crew. The beat-up, old cargo plane handled like a brick with cardboard wings glued to the top. It felt like if she pulled any sudden maneuvers, the whole thing would just fly apart.

She had better planes available to her, but the client insisted it had to be this plane on this night. He identified himself only as Mister Smith, and he'd offered a fat wad of cash to alleviate her concerns. He claimed the people in this remote coastal town valued their privacy, and this one plane ferried certain goods in and out on the same day every month. If any other plane attempted to land at any other time, it would be "firmly turned away."

"At gunpoint?" she asked him.

"One could hope," he replied. Then he took out his handkerchief and dabbed the sweat from his brow. He was a peculiar fella, with bulbous, wide-spaced eyes and a high forehead. He dressed like he had just walked off the set of a Victorian stage-play, complete with a too-large top hat, a frock coat, and a gem-topped cane. He sweated like a cool pint of beer on a hot summer evening, and the handkerchief would hardly leave his hand before he took it out again to dab, dab, and dab some more.

"Understand, Miss Voltaire, it's not your prowess as a pilot I want to hire." He paused to lick his lips with a fat, lumpy tongue. "I can find a pilot anywhere. It's your reputation and... discretion... that I require."

Fair enough. Now she just had to survive this landing.

The landing strip rose up to greet her, a somewhat-less-dark patch of darkness in a sea of darkness. She rolled back the engine speed, pulled back on the yoke to level out, and used a distant shack to find her horizon and ground level. Carter let out a half squeal, half grunt beside her, and the right wheel touched down.

Hard.

The plane rocked to the left and slammed onto the left landing gear. The whole plane shuddered. The wings bounced and the struts groaned, then the rear wheel touched down and the plane started to fishtail around to the left. Athena corrected the steering and hit the brakes.

"Kill the engines!" Athena shouted. "I have my hands full!"

"What? How!?"

"The two big red switches in front of your left arm!"

It only took him a second to find them. The engines sputtered into silence, leaving only the rumble of the earth below them and the groaning wing struts. The plane slowed, then rolled just past the small outbuilding Athena had steered toward. She used the rest of their momentum to turn the plane around and point it back up the runway for takeoff.

"That wasn't so bad," Carter said. "I seem to recall a rougher landing back when I worked on Barnstormin' Beauties."

"Yeah, well, as they say, any landing you can walk away from is a good one." Athena unbuckled her safety harness and went to the back. She touched the revolvers holstered on her hips, just a quick reassurance they were still with her, then opened the side door.

A man hustled a lantern from the outbuilding to the plane. Tangled white hair spilled around his head from beneath a fraying golf cap, and an array of coarse stubble jutted out from his chin. Baggy, blue coveralls draped from his lean body.

"Miss Voltaire! Thank God!" he proclaimed. "With all that's happened, I feared the worst!"

"Are you Lee?"

"Aye, Roland Lee, Miss, at your service. But please, we must hurry. There has been a change in plans."

The old man turned, put two fingers to his lips, and blew a short, sharp whistle. "Jared! Miles! Get out here!"

A clank and a creak sounded from the darkness, and a second later two men appeared at the periphery of the lantern light. They wore coveralls similar to Lee's, and they pushed a large cart toward the plane. Cumbersome hoses crisscrossed the fuel tank atop the cart.

"What do you mean?" Athena asked him. "Where's the package?"

"We have to fetch it, Miss. Mister Smith's plan was almost undone! But there's still time. We can be to the house and back before the plane is refueled."

"Slow down a moment. Undone how? I was told to pick up a package. If it's not here and ready to go, I don't see how that's my problem."

"I'm sorry, Miss, but Mister Smith was quite clear in his direction to me. You are not to leave without the package. Until we're on our way, my men will not fuel this plane."

He snapped his fingers at the two crewmen. They set down the refueling hoses and backed away from the engine.

"I see." Athena rested her hand on her pistol. "And what's to stop us from taking it ourselves?"

"You could do just that, Miss. But if you return without the package, you forego the rest of your fee. Further, your reputation says a lot of things about you, but I see no suggestion you're a killer, and that's the only way you'll get the fuel."

She turned to Carter, who crouched in the open cargo door behind her. "What do you think, Carter?"

"It reminds me of the double-cross in The Jade Dragon."

"And?"

He chuckled. "Things didn't go so well for the protagonist. That's why I didn't take the part."

Nobody paid the kind of money Smith offered just to pick up a trunk of clothing. It had to be contraband, probably antiquities or family heirlooms of some value. Smith had assured her Lee would have made all the proper preparations on the ground, which suggested they were either smuggling or thieving. Both suggested some possibility of a hostile reception.

She did not expect she'd have to leave the plane.

Lee stood calm and cool as he waited for her answer. The ground crew fidgeted and whispered behind her. The tank on their wagon had an old hand pump on it. It would take them some time to prime it. Add the refueling time, and they weren't taking off anytime soon.

"How far to the package?" she asked.

"Five minutes," Lee said. "It's right downtown."

"All right, then. Carter, hand me one of the shotguns."

"Sure thing." He disappeared into the plane and returned with the two 12-gauge pump Winchesters. He passed one out to Athena. "Do you want me to come, too?"

"No, you keep an eye on the plane, make sure these guys get their job done. I want to take off as soon as we get back."

"Will do. You just be careful, hear?"

She shot him a wink. "Always."

"Don't you worry none, Miss," Lee said. "My nephews will keep him safe."

Athena tried to find reassurance in that.

Lee led her around the building to a modified Model T pickup that had seen better days. She felt a pang of regret as she climbed into the passenger seat. Maybe she should have left Carter in Chicago with her own plane. She had just accepted this job when Carter surprised her with his time off between films, so they decided they'd spend some time in the Windy City and on the Lake when the job was done.

Then he insisted on coming along. She couldn't be sure whether he did so out of a desire to spend more time with her or out of some chivalric obligation, but she should have told him to stay put. Though it reassured her now to have someone she trusted watching the plane, she didn't want his pretty face to get busted up.

Or worse.

The T's engine coughed and wheezed, and finally roared to life. The transmission groaned, but engaged smoothly and the pickup whisked them away from the airfield. Athena set the butt of her shotgun on the floor and tilted it back to conceal the barrel along her left arm. It wouldn't pass close scrutiny, but passersby wouldn't panic.

A coarse gravel drive wound through an overgrown field toward the town proper. Athena could make out roofs and structures in the distance, but there were few signs of life. Dim lamps dotted a few windows, but she could see many more roofs and structures that were left in darkness. The rumble of the T's engine drowned out everything but the noise of the distant surf.

Lee muttered to himself and chewed his lip, but offered no real explanation or conversation. He'd lean forward to peer around her from time to time, or crane his neck around to the left to watch their backs, but otherwise ignored her.

The T bounced onto a cobblestone street at the end of the gravel drive. The houses around them had obviously been here for some time, most constructed of lumber and wooden siding in varying states of disrepair. They would drive past three or four with peeling paint or boarded windows, then pass one with flickering firelight showing through tattered curtains or the rim of a window.

They passed an inn with an old gas lamp out front, and a tavern with an open front door but no patrons that she could see. Lee took them through a square surrounded by shops and with a fountain in the center, but several of the shops stood empty, and someone had broken the head off the angel in the fountain. The water was still and quiet, and as they drove around the edge Athena could see the algae spread across its surface.

Lee steered them out the south end of the square and down a gradual slope toward the coast. "We're almost there," he assured her.

It struck her then that she had yet to see any citizens out and about. A town square should have some life, even at this late hour, and she'd have expected any number of people wandering the streets or carousing in the taverns. A church appeared on the corner to her right, but a large chain dangled from the door handles and the windows were shuttered tight.

There, a figure in the shadows down the street. A dark figure in a heavy cloak, walking with a peculiar, hunched gait. Then the T crossed the intersection and he was gone.

Athena leaned into her seat. More houses, another dark tavern. She almost missed the Masonic Hall ahead on the left, and the plaque mounted out front with its crude, scratchy text: The Esoteric Order of D--. Dragon? Dagon? She missed the rest behind Lee's body as they passed, and could not read it behind them without the headlamps.

"We're here," Lee said. He slowed the car in front of an old house with a high, sloped roof and a turreted tower on one side.

"What is this place?"

"Mister Smith's ancestral home."

"And the package is here?"

"Follow me, Miss."

"O'Fallon!"

Carter jumped at the sound of the booming voice. He stepped away from the plane's fuselage and looked under the wing for the source. Jared and Miles stopped pumping the fuel.

"O'Fallon, damn it, where are you?"

A fat man ducked under the wing and approached Carter. His old suit strained to contain his bulk, and a thick wattle of flesh unrolled from beneath his chin. Peculiar folds of skin marred the sides of his neck. He breathed in great gulps of air as he set a large valise on the ground near his feet.

"Good evening, sir!" Carter flashed the man a wide, toothy smile and took a step to the left to hide the shotgun leaning against the side of the plane. "How can we be of service?"

The fat man tilted his head back and regarded Carter through narrowed eyes. "Where's O'Fallon? I need him to deliver something for me."

"Ah, that's no problem! Plenty of room, sir, plenty of room. If you'll just leave your satchel with me, I'll be sure to get it aboard right away."

"Who's he?" The fat man thrust a stubby finger at Jared standing by the fuel tank. His voice rose to a bellow. "That's no crewman! You're not O'Fallon's man! What's going on here?!"

Where had Miles gone? Carter wondered. He took a half step back toward the shotgun. "Now now, sir, no reason for alarm. O'Fallon had urgent business in town. I'm sure he'll be back momentarily."

A movement caught Carter's eye. He looked past the fat man's shoulder and saw Miles creeping up behind him. Carter gasped as Miles raised a heavy aircraft wrench high.

The fat man turned, then bleated out a peculiar croak as he got one hand up just in time to block the wrench. His left hand darted into his coat, then came back out with a long, gleaming dagger.

"No!" Carter hurled himself onto the fat man's arm and grabbed his wrist with both hands. The man's flesh was soft and flabby, and Carter's thumbs slid across something slick and viscous on the back of the man's hand. Miles struggled to pull his wrench back, but the fat man had a firm grip on it with his right hand.

The fat man belted out a loud, watery croak, a half cough, half grunt unlike anything Carter had heard before.

"Shut him up!" Jared shouted.

Carter pushed a shoulder into the fat man. He was more worried about the dagger and keeping the man's arm immobilized than the noise. Miles grunted and pulled the opposite direction, and the fat man stumbled, then lost his footing. He took another awkward step, and the three men tumbled to the ground in a tangle of limbs.

Athena followed Lee through the front door and into a small foyer. The air inside felt cool and clammy, and the place reeked of mildew and rot. She could not see into the room to their left or down the hallway straight ahead, but a dim lamplight spilled through part of the sitting room to their right. A long divan and several ornate, high-backed chairs circled an empty fireplace. A dark sheet covered a statue in the corner except for a pair of arched, bat-like wings swooping up from the back.

Lee took her across the sitting room and through an archway into an adjoining library. A chandelier dangled from the ceiling, though only one of its five bulbs cast any light. It flickered as though it, too, would die at any moment. Built-in shelves bursting with books covered the walls to the right and directly ahead, and a large desk rested at a diagonal where they came together. A young woman sat in an old leather chair behind the desk, and a barrel-chested young man stood beside her.

The young man had a hand inside his waistcoat.

"Put your hands up!" Athena aimed her shotgun at him. His eyes went wide and he threw both hands into the air. The woman stifled a shriek and clutched a small bundle closer to her chest.

"It's okay!" Lee assured her. He stepped out in front of her and held his arms wide. "Let's not do anything to hasty, Miss."

Athena lowered the butt from her shoulder, but kept her hand on the grip and her finger alongside the trigger guard.

"Thank you. Miss Voltaire, this is Irwin Poole and his wife, Elizabeth."

The couple had the same bulging eyes Mr. Smith did, and Irwin pursed a pair of thick, puffy lips. At a closer look, his chest seemed more swollen and bulbous than muscular, and his upper back hunched forward, making it look as if his neck were mounted to the front of his shoulders rather than the top. Elizabeth could be pretty if not for those eyes. Her pale skin looked yellow in the soft light, and wispy tufts of stringy hair stuck out from the side of her head.

"Are you the pilot?" Irwin asked.

"That's right. I understand you have a package for me?"

"Yes, ma'am. Right here." Irwin set a hand on his wife's shoulder. Elizabeth stood, and something inside the bundle fussed.

"Oh, no," Athena said. "This wasn't the deal."

The couple looked at one another. Lee rested a hand on her shoulder, but she threw it off and took a step back.

"Please, Miss Voltaire, this is a desperate family."

"I'm not a kidnapper."

"I assure you, ma'am, this is no such thing," Irwin said. "You are reuniting a daughter with her father, and a child with her grandfather."

"No. We're going back to the plane. Now."

"Please, be reasonable!" Irwin pulled open a desk drawer and reached inside.

Athena brought up the shotgun.

Irwin's hand came out holding a tall tiara. The arms swept back in a long, elliptical arc, and its metallic surface gleamed in a mix of gold and silver. He reached into the desk again and slapped down a necklace of fat pearls and a broach inlaid with the same metals as the tiara.

Athena relaxed her grip on the shotgun, but did not lower it.

"Do you need more?" Irwin asked. "I can get more!"

"Mister Smith is a very rich man," Lee said. "Please, just get his daughter to him!"

"This isn't about the money," Athena said.

"Then please, do it for the child." Elizabeth spoke in a calm, clear voice that dominated the others despite its soft volume. She stepped around the desk and approached Athena with caution. Just a few feet from the muzzle of the shotgun, she opened a layer of the baby's swaddling clothes and held her out toward Athena.

"This is her only chance at a normal life."

The fat man kept barking out that harsh bleat as Carter slammed his hand against the ground over and over. At last his grip on the dagger broke and it bounced into the grass several inches out of reach. He bucked in panic, and Miles let out a shout as he thumped the man across the chest with his wrench. The fat man let out a loud woof and stopped his cry, but then rolled toward Miles with such ferocity he took Carter with him.

Carter's back hit the ground. The fat man grabbed the front of his shirt and pressed him into the dirt. His ribs crackled under the pressure and he could hardly draw breath.

The fat man snatched the wrench out of Miles' grip and threw him to the ground. He raised the wrench high over his head. Carter winced in anticipation of the blow.

"That's enough!" Jared shouted.

The wrench blow did not come. Carter opened one eye and saw Jared standing above him. He pointed the shotgun right at the fat man's chest.

"Get up," Jared said.

The fat man did as he was told. Carter and Miles stood, and Carter took the wrench away from him.

"This is about the girl, isn't it?" the fat man demanded. "Old Jeb Smith sent you, didn't he?"

"Who are you?" Carter asked.

"His name's Deacon Marsh," Jared told him.

"And he's trouble," Miles said. "Just shoot him."

"No!" Carter said.

"You'd do well to listen to him, boy," Marsh said. "If you kill me--"

Clank! Carter thumped him across the temple with the wrench. Marsh hit the ground like a bag of sand.

"The shotgun would have been too loud. Go ahead and tie him up, then let's finish getting this plane fueled up."

The baby girl fussed at the sudden exposure to the cold air, her little arms flailing. Downy brown hair clung to her scalp, and she had a small, button nose beneath a pair of beautiful blue eyes.

Could that be what Elizabeth meant by "normal?" Athena wondered. Had this little girl been spared some genetic deformity passed down the generations?

"Her name's Lillian," Elizabeth said. "Please, give her a chance."

Athena frowned. This had been a setup from the beginning. There wasn't much she could do about it now, and if she had to fly back anyway, she may as well complete the job.

"Let's go," she said at last.

Lee let out a long sigh of relief.

"Thank you!" Irwin said. He grabbed his wife and gave her a long hug. "Now go. Hurry!"

"You're not coming?" Lee asked.

"No, it's too late for me. Get her to safety. Both of them." He stroked the baby's cheek, then planted a kiss on her forehead.

"Be safe," Elizabeth told him. Tears trickled down her cheeks.

"I will," he said with a sad smile.

"I hate to interrupt," Athena said, "but I don't have all night."

"Of course. Go. Go!" Irwin shooed them with his fingers.

The three of them hurried through the sitting room and out the front door. Athena looked up and down the street as they raced down the walk. As Lee helped Elizabeth into the back seat, Athena noticed a sparse fog rolling up the hill.

"Is that normal?" she asked.

Lee followed her gaze. "Is what... oh, no... Quick, get in!"

Athena jumped into the passenger seat. The fog swept in even closer, and thicker fog rolled in behind it. Lee started the engine, then wrenched the wheel all the way around. The car lurched away from the front walk and Lee let it roll up onto the opposite walk before getting it righted, then raced up the street away from the fog.

Elizabeth muttered something in the back seat. It sounded a lot like a prayer, but not one Athena was familiar with. She concentrated on the streets ahead, and kept the shotgun across her lap and at the ready.

"I'm sorry, Miss," Lee said. "It was never supposed to be this way. In and out, that's all. In and out."

"Just what have you people gotten me into?"

"A curse. It's the plainest way to say it. A curse has befallen this town."

"And my little girl has dodged it," Elizabeth said. The baby let out a soft cry. Elizabeth cooed to her, rocked her gently.

"Damn..." Lee muttered.

Athena looked up to see two men standing in the street at the end of the block. They walked toward the car, right down the center of the street. Lee started to let off the gas, but Athena pushed his knee down.

"No! If they don't move, go through 'em."

Lee winced as the T accelerated. Athena reached out the window and held onto the edge of the roof. Elizabeth prayed again, with more urgency this time.

The men kept coming. The car closed the distance faster and faster. One of the men looked at the other, uncertain. At the last second, he dove clear. The other tried, but the front bumper on Athena's side clipped him. The impact made a soft crunch, and the man spun away from the car and toward the gutter. Athena looked back and watched him roll to a stop. He didn't get up.

The T barreled into the town square. Lee spun the wheel, almost putting them on two tires as they careened around the fountain and up the next street. Athena heard a dull roar carried on the air, the surf crashing against the beaches with a greater fervor.

Then she heard the growl.

Not a dog, though. More like a frog's croak, only rougher. Louder. Another sounded, then another, all from their right. Either something kept pace with them, or there were several of the barking things. Neither was any more appealing an explanation than the other. She twisted in her seat and scanned the houses and side streets with the shotgun.

The fog began to close in around them, flowing across their path like the tide. Wispy tendrils broke across the front of the truck, only to coalesce again in their wake. Cool condensation settled on the shotgun barrel and across Athena's face and hands. More croaking and barking sounded from the streets and alleys they passed.

Then the frog-thing leapt out at the car.

"You're doomed." Marsh squirmed onto his side like a fat worm on a hook. "All of you."

"You just keep quiet or I'll give you another thump." Carter shook the wrench for emphasis.

The fat man scowled, but didn't say another word.

"We're about done here," Miles said. "You'll be ready to take off as soon as she gets back."

"Suits me. This place is even creepier than the sets in Transylvania when I worked on Lair of the Vampire. You boys ever see that one?"

Miles shrugged. "We don't get talkies here."

"Are you kidding? Boys, film is the great art of the Twentieth Century! You should--"

A distant shotgun blast rolled across the field, followed closely by a second.

"Boys," Carter said, "I think we best start the engines."

The squat creature walked on two legs like a man, but hunched so low its arms hung to its knees. Its wide, flabby lips curled into a snarl, and its wide-spaced, bulging eyes flashed in the headlamps. It wore a loose black cloak and clutched a barbed spear to its chest.

Athena gasped and brought the shotgun to bear on it. Lee cursed and swerved, throwing Athena's first shot wide. The baby Lillian screamed and cried. The creature raised its spear as Athena pumped the shotgun.

"Stop swerving!" she shouted.

"Look out!"

The creature threw the spear. Athena drew a bead on the creature as they raced toward it. The spear clattered across the roof, just above Athena's head. She pulled the trigger and shot the creature square in the chest. It flew backward and disappeared into the mist.

Lee slammed on the brakes and took the next turn to their left.

Athena grabbed the doorframe so she wouldn't be thrown through the window. "Where are you going? I thought the airfield was that way!"

"We need to get farther from the coast, Miss. We're just going to have a bumpier ride."

"I knew this was a bad idea!" Elizabeth said. "I told Daddy maybe it's not so bad here! Maybe they would have left little Lillian alone!"

"Don't start thinking that way," Athena told her. "All we have to do is make it to the plane and you're home free."

Lillian's cry suggested she had her doubts.

The cobbled streets gave way to dusty tracks weaving through a collection of run-down homes on the edge of town. All of the doors were closed, all of the windows shuttered tight. No signs of lamps or fires. The croaking fell farther behind them.

Then a roar erupted from out toward the coast. It sounded like a chorus of demons dropped into a vat of boiling water. Elizabeth screamed behind them.

"What is that?" Athena asked.

"Never mind it, Miss. I hear the plane ahead."

"Shoggoth!" Elizabeth shrieked. "Shoggoth!"

"Shut up!" Lee snapped at her. "That's a tall tale to scare away the sailors."

"What is it?"

"Just think about the plane, Miss, and keep that shotgun at the ready. It's better that way."

Carter had just set down the pre-flight checklist when he heard Jared let out a short, sharp shout. He grabbed his shotgun and jumped out of the plane, and saw four men standing near the opposite wing. Their leader drove Jared to the ground with a pitchfork. Jared tried to crawl away, but they kicked him to the ground and stabbed him again. He stopped moving.

Carter fired, pumped, fired again. The leader spun and fell, and the other three scattered. They all wore shabby clothing and had the same flabby features Deacon Marsh did. Relatives? Carter wondered. The engine noise must have masked their approach.

Miles tackled one of them around the legs and beat at his back and head with his wrench. Carter rounded the back of the plane as another of the attackers ran toward Miles. Carter shouldered the shotgun and fired. The blast swept the man's leg out from under him and he went down screaming. What remained of his leg bent and lay at an unnatural angle.

The last man ran at Carter. He pumped in the next round, but the attacker was on him too fast, swinging a large club overhead. Carter raised the shotgun and blocked the blow. The blow made a mighty crack that stung all the way down Carter's arms. The stock cracked at the grip, but it held. Carter stomp-kicked the man in the gut, sending him sprawling backward. He started to rise, but Carter shot him in the chest.

Miles screamed, still beating the motionless man beneath him. Gore covered the end of the wrench.

A light broke the darkness across the field. It bounced and rolled, and soon resolved itself to twin points moving in tandem.

Carter pumped the next cartridge into the shotgun's chamber and aimed it at the car.

Lee stopped the car just twenty feet from Carter and his shotgun.

"Hold your fire!" Athena shouted as they all piled out of the car. Lee ran toward his nephews.

"Athena! Am I glad to see you." Carter lowered his shotgun and nodded toward Elizabeth and her crying baby. "What's going on? Who's this?"

"This is our package. Get on the plane, I'll explain -- look out!" Athena raised the shotgun. Carter ducked and spun, and saw Deacon Marsh barreling toward them, his dagger in hand, with bits of cord still hanging from one wrist.

Athena shot him in the chest. He stumbled, slowed, but kept coming, and she shot him again. This time he pitched forward and fell flat on his face.

A roar sounded from down the hill, audible even over the plane's engines.

"What in God's name was that?" Carter asked.

"Shoggoth!" Elizabeth screamed.

Athena grabbed her arm and rushed her toward Carter. "Get her on the plane and strap her in! I'll be right there!"

Carter nodded and took Elizabeth by the other arm. She ran with him toward the open cargo door.

Athena ran around the tail of the plane and found Lee and Miles struggling to pick up Jared's body. Four other men lay on the field around them.

"We need to get on the plane!" she said.

"Not us, Miss! We'll take the car."

"Are you sure? We have plenty of room!"

"Go," Lee said. "We've other plans."

The roar sounded again, closer this time. No time to argue.

"Good luck," she said. She ran for the cargo door as Lee and Miles carried Jared to the T.

Athena slammed the door shut behind her, then locked it. Elizabeth was already sitting in the cargo seat, shuddering but strapped in. Lillian's bawling echoed through the small space. Athena dropped the shotgun in the locker behind the cockpit and slid into the pilot's chair. She allowed her fingers to dart across the controls as she checked gauges and dashboard lights. She didn't bother to strap in before releasing the brakes and opening the throttle.

"Here we go," she said. The plane rolled across the airstrip. She saw only darkness ahead and did some quick math in her head. How long was the strip again? She started counting as she watched the speedometer climb.

Carter did strap in beside her. He crossed himself.

"Get ready to pull back on that stick," she said.

"Say the word." He grabbed the steering yoke.

"Six... seven... eight... PULL!" They yanked back on the twin yokes. The ground fell away, and their guts seemed to sink down into their seats. Athena could just make out the tips of trees streaking by below them.

"Ha-hah! We made it!" Carter whooped.

Athena banked left. As the plane rolled into its climb, she leaned and looked back at the airstrip. The T's headlamps darted through the trees. Behind them, a lumbering, black shape rolled past the supply building. She could not make out shape or form, but it seemed to writhe and pulse as it slipped onto the airstrip.

Seconds later, the night and the distance enveloped the whole scene. Athena sank back into her seat. Whatever it was, she vowed she wouldn't be returning to Innsmouth to see it again any time soon.

Smith met them on the runway. Athena fought the urge to slug him as she stepped out of the plane.

"Daddy!" Elizabeth cried.

"You made it! Thank you, Miss Voltaire!"

Athena helped the young woman out of the plane, and she immediately ran into her father's arms. They held one another for a moment, then he gently unwrapped the swaddling blanket from around Lillian's face.

"Oh, she's so precious," Smith said.

Athena's anger cooled as she watched the family's tearful reunion. She could see now the resemblance between Smith and Elizabeth, the strange eyes and the flabby facial features, and wondered how Lillian had managed to avoid the same.

"I apologize for the subterfuge, Miss Voltaire, but I couldn't take the chance you would refuse the job."

"I've got no problems getting children out of nasty situations," Athena said, "but if you'd warned me, I'd have brought more men and more guns."

"Of course. Now if you'll excuse us..."

"Not just yet. Lee said you'd compensate us for the surprises." She almost let it go, but hitting him in the wallet would be a close second to hitting him in the face.

"Very well," Smith said. "I'll double your fee. I'll attend to it right away."

Smith led his girls to his waiting Packard. The moment they closed the door, the driver sped off down the runway. A moment later, the ground crew showed up to tend to the plane.

Carter put an arm around Athena as they walked toward the terminal building.

"Well. That wasn't so bad, right?" he asked.

She chuckled. "Let's just say I'm suddenly not too keen on visiting the Lake."

THE CURSE OF DESTRUCTION ISLAND

Eric S. Trautmann

1. When The Dead Man Came Knocking

HOLLYWOOD, CALIFORNIA
1937.

The last time Athena Voltaire saw Kimber, he coughed blood, expelled a single ragged gasp, and died in her arms.

The first time she'd seen Kimber, there had been music.

Benny Goodman, playing "Moonglow." It wasn't Athena's favorite — she preferred Artie Shaw, ever since she caught his show at the Imperial back in '35 — but she couldn't help but tap her toe. Howard Hawks always put on a hell of a New Year's bash, and as he prepared to film his latest opus—"Only Angels Have Wings," a picture about pilots, mining Hawks' love of flying—he made sure that he pulled out all the stops. Lured by the chance of some film work, the creme de la creme of the Hollywood aviation community had assembled, and as the band played on, roughneck stunt pilots rubbed elbows with movie starlets and matinee idols. Shutterbugs prowled the ballroom, and the flashbulbs popped almost as frequently as the champagne corks.

They'll run out of reporters before Hawks runs out of the bubbly, she mused, a wry grin tugging at the corner of her mouth, a welcome moment of distraction from the annoyance that had been gathering around her like a storm cloud.

A clutch of news-hawks had been orbiting Athena ever since she entered the ballroom. She was no fool; in the white, clinging evening gown she'd donned for the party, it was no surprise that she'd turned heads. That was the point, after all, but one particularly pugnacious stringer from the Tattler was so insistent on getting a picture of her cleavage that he was on the verge of a good, sharp pop to the nose.

Her hand was gathering into a fist, straining at the silk of her gloves when she spotted Kimber.

He was young and dashing, fair of hair and blue of eye, with a strong chin and a single dimple on his left cheek. He was also quite clearly a gatecrasher at the affair, with his ill-fitting tux and occasional nervous glances at the bouncers. When she spied Kimber, he had been staring at Athena with undisguised admiration—specifically at the slit that afforded a view of her white stockings. His eyes widened when he caught her smirk and arched eyebrow.

It was her obvious amusement that left Kimber just one choice: up the ante.

He marched directly over to her, gently elbowing past the scribbler, who harrumphed in outrage before waddling off to find an easier mark. Kimber looked her dead in the eye and said simply, "Let's dance."

Without pausing for a response, he whisked her out into the swirl of tuxedos and ball gowns, leaving the photographers and gossip columnists in the dust.

She cradled Kimber's head, trying hard (and failing) not to notice his wide-open, glassy eyes and the stream of blood that leaked from his mouth. It was wrong, like a terrible nightmare, adrenaline giving the entire tableau an acid-etched quality.

Kimber's eyes were supposed to glitter with mischief, not stare, empty and unseeing, at the ceiling.

"Oh, Kimber," she whispered, "you sweet, silly man. What did you get yourself into this time?"

She gently ran her fingers across his face, closing Kimber's eyes.

The second time she saw Kimber, there'd been laughter and the clink of glasses.

The speakeasy was nestled far outside of Hollywood, and the rumor was that one of the matinee idols from the Hawks bash was the silent owner of the joint. The drinks weren't watered, they weren't too pricey, and there wasn't a chance you'd go blind downing a shot.

Not much of a chance, at least.

She hadn't been in Hollywood long, but had already fended off a dozen offers of work as a stunt pilot. The idea of flying for the movies did not lack appeal, and her time behind the stick with Keefauver's Air Angels—not to mention her various wins at any number of California air races—made her a "name."

Still, she'd turned down all the offers. Something about flying for the movies rubbed her the wrong way. Her father had always hated cameras, and only occasionally deigned to be photographed for publicity purposes in his days as "The Great Voltaire," prestidigitator extraordinaire. When she had chided him about being camera shy, he invariably looked her square in the eye and said, "The lens makes a cheap toy of my art, dear girl."

Always the showman, she thought, a wry smile briefly playing across her lips. That "cheap toy" paid his bills now; "The Great Voltaire" was now one of the most sought after makeup and effects men in Hollywood.

Instead of flying on camera, her entrée into Hollywood had come when she'd agreed to help choreograph and plan the aerial stunt sequences for a handful of low-budget Great War serials. It paid the bills, and more than that, she found she enjoyed coordinating and controlling the scenes, like a general moving men on the battlefield.

In a few short months, she'd become a Hollywood fixture, a welcome addition to various productions. She knew friendships among the film crews happened fast. People ebbed and flowed through that world, drifting together for a job before dissipating like morning fog as soon as the director called a wrap.

Despite the transient nature of such social groups, certain bonds were forged which outlasted the normal film-land associations—adamantine connections between professionals that shared the passions of their professions. Camera operators, for example, tended to gather near West Hollywood, congregating in the grandly-named Coconut Heights (though inside was a different matter; the one time Athena had set foot in the Heights, she found herself in a dank, dimly lit one-room "club" that was notable only for the smell of stale beer and the muttered conversations about f-stops and film stock).

Athena had heard of the speakeasy—the Cloudtop—and its reputation for discretion and calm, as well as the bar's legend as a favorite hangout of pilots. As her eyes adjusted to the subdued lighting, she heard a loud voice, brimming with good cheer, somewhere in the back of the bar.

The barman eyed her for a moment, frowning. She'd heard of him: a taciturn Greek named Stavros, who kept a length of pipe beneath the bar, and was quick to use it at the first sign of some fool rube violating the unwritten rules of the bar.

He nodded abruptly, and with a curt jerk of his thumb, pointed her to the source of the jocularity.

Athena found the spot, a large, round oak table in the most isolated corner of the speak. It was nicknamed the Aces' Stable, and only the best of the Hollywood pilot community drank there. There would be little fanfare, she knew; these were top-notch flyers who had invited her into their midst. She didn't fly on camera, but they knew she was one of them—all brothers in the sky. She took a seat, looking around the table and waving for a drink.

There was surly, acid-tongued Macken, who'd left Chicago, it was rumored, under something of a cloud involving bootleggers and a lost shipment of Canadian whisky.

Next to him sat lazy-mannered Hollis, nicknamed the "Sky Cowboy" due to his Texas drawl.

Beyond him was Doakes, a Tulsa mail pilot who had headed westward and who hated the too-obvious nickname applied to him by the other pilots: "Okie Doakes."

Finally, there was Kimber. The young pilot was holding court, gesturing expansively and habitually spilling drops of gin with each wave of his hand. He gave her a welcoming nod as he continued his monologue.

"—was sure that damned bird was gonna auger in. A goner for sure," Kimber said, grinning, "I was dead stick, dropping like a brick, all for a silly bit of stunt business for an even sillier bit of film. Dead at 22, thanks to a turkey titled 'Wings of Passion.' One hell of an epitaph, eh, fellas?"

Athena chuckled. "I'm pretty sure you didn't die on that film, Kimber, or else I wouldn't be sitting through this story. Again."

"Well, of course I didn't, Athena, thanks to me being the best pilot flying," he shot back, his expression mock-wounded.

"Second best, Kimber," Athena replied. "But go on."

"Oh, like you could stop him," Macken groused. "You couldn't shut up Lindbergh here if you gagged him."

"If I may continue," Kimber said, waving aside Macken's comments and grinning like a madman. "There I was, falling from the sky. Fire-walled the throttle, and got the prop turning again — " his hand carved a glittering arc of gin droplets through the air, the big finish to the tale "—and got that kite's nose up and whoosh! Perfect landing. Textbook, y'know?

"And the director rushes over, asking me if I'm okay, if the bird's okay, and wow what a close call. 'I was terribly worried for you, dear boy,' he told me. Looked like he was going to seize up right then and there.

"Of course, the grips told me a different story. I asked one of 'em why the crash wagons hadn't been rolling. The director should've sent 'em out the second the bird's nose dipped, but I didn't see 'em anywhere. 'Why didn't the director send out the medicos and firefighters when he saw I was in trouble?'

"And the assistant director just sighed and said, 'He was too busy yelling at us to keep the cameras rolling. He didn't want to miss the shot.'"

Cue laughter, and the clink of glasses.

She stood, Kimber's blood still wet on her hands. The shakes hadn't hit yet, but they were coming, and soon. More blood leaked from him, slowly pooled below him, almost black against the oil-stained concrete.

Athena could see that Kimber had been stabbed several times, a short blade perforating his abdomen in a cruel line. The cuts were designed to be lethal, but not instantly so. Whoever had killed Kimber wanted him to suffer first. That he'd even made it all the way to her private hangar was a miracle.

There would be police soon, blasé detectives cracking wise over the cooling body of her friend, beat cops roping off the scene, probably a reporter catching the scent of a big story in the form of a corpse turning up on the doorstep of Athena Voltaire. There would also be questions, dozens of them repeated ad nauseum, and she had no answers.

The trembles hit at that moment, as mounting anger slammed through her, both at the monster who had butchered Kimber, and at Kimber, too, for being stupid enough to get into a situation that was clearly over his head, for dumping this mess on her doorstep, and for the last words they had spoken to each other.

"What the hell were you thinking?" Athena stood on the sandy landing strip, hands clenched as fists, fists balled on her hips. "Damn it, Kimber, you could've gotten yourself killed! Not to mention the guys flying with you!"

Kimber stared back at her, his eyes blazing with angry defiance. "I thought I was doing my job. You know, dazzling displays of aerial derring-do for our half-sauced director to immortalize on film."

Athena's eyes narrowed, her voice quieting. "Don't even try that with me. You were showboating."

"You just can't stand it, can you?" he snapped. "That maybe somebody out there knows more about flying than Miss High-And-Mighty Athena Voltaire."

Athena's answering bark of laughter was involuntary, and served only to infuriate Kimber even further. "What's that supposed to mean?" he growled.

"It means you're a fair pilot, kid," Athena shot back, "and you've got some skill. But you're also behaving like a schoolboy who's acting out in class because he wants everyone to pay attention to him.

"One foot," she continued, jabbing him in the chest with her index finger, "just one foot out of position and everyone has a very bad day. And you? You were three feet off your line."

"The hell I was."

"The hell you weren't. It's all on film, you jerk."

Kimber's handsome features had reddened, and the easy charm he displayed had been replaced by frustration and barely-contained anger. He struggled to modulate his tone, but succeeded only in biting out his words. "Look, maybe I cut it close. Maybe I want to be noticed. I need this, Athena."

"Need what? The limelight?"

"No," he snarled. "I need the cash. I'm running on an empty tank, Athena. I need something to kickstart my career. We can't all be Athena Voltaire."

"Causing a midair collision is a damn poor way to get noticed, Kimber," she said, her voice filled with steel. "But you've got my attention, now. And you're off the picture."

Kimber's head snapped back, as if he'd just been slapped. "You can't be serious."

"Deadly serious, Kimber. I'm sorry, but you're dangerous, and you're careless, and you're going to get someone killed."

"Well, pardon me, Miss Perfect. "

She sighed, rubbing the bridge of her nose as she tried to manage her anger. This conversation was giving her a headache. "Shut up, Kimber. Just shut up. You're not helping your case."

"So that's it? You're going to ground me? You know what that means, right?"

"What choice have you given me? I can't use you on the picture. Maybe the director doesn't care if a stunt pilot buys the farm, but I do. When you cool down, you're going to realize I'm doing you a favor."

"Don't do me any more favors," Kimber yelled. "My career won't survive it. You know this means I'll be blackballed. If you sack me, no one else will touch me."

"And you'll have no one but yourself to blame, Kimber," she said.

She regretted the words, but she also knew they needed to be said. She didn't truly have the power to get someone like Kimber blacklisted, and she certainly had no desire to. He was young, and brash, and loved to fly—and he had real skill, she had to admit. The truth was, though, she was a name, and in Hollywood, reputation was currency. If—or rather, when—word got around that she fired Kimber, there was almost no chance of another director taking him on.

Kimber's jaw clenched. He stared at her for several long moments.

"Have it your way," he said at last. He paused, as if considering his words, and then looked her square in the eye.

"You're a block of ice, Athena Voltaire…and you can go directly to Hell. Maybe that's what it'll take to thaw you out."

He turned on his heel and strode away.

She inhaled sharply, steeled herself, and began to search the body.

There was precious little to find. Kimber had no jewelry save a battered watch with a scratched crystal, his billfold was down to a mere two bucks, and aside from some pocket lint, she could only find an address book with very few names in it.

She winced when, as she thumbed through the address book, she noticed her name had been laboriously scribbled out. She spotted a few other names, mostly women on the lower rungs of an upward climb of Hollywood's ladder, and among them several others she recognized: Macken, Okie, Cowboy.

One name stood out, penned in Kimber's blocky handwriting: Prof. J.W. Ballantine. Beneath the name was scribbled the word "Antiquities" and a telephone number. Kimber had never been the academic type. The fellow pilots and wanna-be movie starlets in his little black book made perfect sense, but an antiquities professor?

Athena stuffed the watch and the address book in the pocket of her battered leather flight jacket and made her way to the airfield control tower, calling the police on the office payphone. A bored-sounding policeman responded, perking up only when he heard the words "dead body."

The murder detectives would arrive within ten minutes, she knew. Even out here on the outskirts of town, the words "murder" and "Athena Voltaire" would make even the most hardened policeman hustle.

Just enough time, she thought, to make a few more calls—to Macken, Doakes, Hollis, a few others. Each sounded horrified upon learning of Kimber's fate. Macken cursed under his breath and hung up without another word. Doakes just sighed and muttered, "It's a helluva thing." Hollis thanked her for the call, and added, "Y'all let me know who's behind it. I got a rope could maybe hold up to a hangin'."

Athena dialed the mysterious Professor Ballantine's number last, and it rang until the operator indicated there was no answer.

She hung up, and walked back to the hangar.

Athena weighed her options, none of them appealing. The police would question her all night, but the facts in her possession were minimal at best. She could see it all before her, repeating endlessly that no, she had no idea who killed Kimber, nor why he had come to her in his dying hour.

"Damn you, Kimber," she whispered. She sighed, then began gathering a few things she'd need for an out-of-town trip. The small leather satchel with extra clothing, stashed beneath the workbench in case of emergencies. The keys to her silver coupe, gassed up and parked outside.

Her gun.

2. Things Being Equal, I'd Rather Be In Philadelphia

The Professor lived on a quiet, slightly shabby cul de sac on the northwestern outskirts of town. His single-story house — white stucco in desperate need of a wash — was small, with a gravel drive. It was also dark; no lights burned within.

Athena parked on the street, softly shutting the car door before creeping toward the house. Despite the mundane surroundings, she felt an overwhelming sense of dread, the hairs on her neck and arms standing upright as if she'd been connected to a mild electrical current. She wiped a drop of sweat from her brow; the evening heat was stifling.

She made her way around the perimeter of the house, her movements careful and deliberate. With each footfall, the unwatered grass crunched and crackled, and she bit her lip in frustration. The tiny noises sounded like gunshots in her ears.

The sense of foreboding continued to weigh on her, that humming current singing discordant notes. She swore she could actually hear the humming of her nerves.

Athena mounted the creaky wooden steps to the house's back porch and stopped short. The sound wasn't her imagination; there was a definite buzzing noise coming from within.

As she stepped forward, hand raised to knock, she noticed the shattered, splintered wood near the door's lock and the scuff marks of a heavy boot— someone had smashed their way into Professor Ballantine's home.

She drew her pistol, thumbed back the hammer, and pushed open the door with the toe of her boot.

The buzzing noise swelled in intensity, and Athena found herself cloaked in a smothering, metallic blanket that swooped out of the inky interior of the house. The noise was all around her now, so loud it seemed to rattle inside her skull. She covered her face, and dropped into a crouch, fighting the urge to scream as the cold, writhing cloud of flies enveloped her.

She struggled forward, eyes tightly shut, mouth covered. Athena had never been squeamish, but the feather-like feeling of insect wings fluttering on her skin and in her hair was almost too much to bear.

Athena dropped to a crawl, trying to get clear, and for several uncomfortable moments, swore to herself that this was the worst feeling she'd ever experienced. At last, the cloud dispersed through the open back door, and she frantically brushed and swatted at her coat, her pants, her hair. She'd be hearing that buzzing in her nightmares.

She pulled herself up on one knee, her eyes adjusting to the gloom slowly. She was in a cramped kitchen at the back of the house. A small pile of clean dishes was neatly stacked near the sink, papers and books organized into tidy piles on the battered but serviceable kitchen table. The weathered wallpaper—with an unusual spotted pattern—caught her eye; it took a moment for her to realize the spots were more flies, lazy in the oppressive California heat.

Athena found a light switch and with the flick of a finger, dull yellow light fought a losing battle against the gloom.

The Professor's house was—insects aside—well-ordered. Everything was tidy and organized to a near-pathological degree.

She moved into the small sitting room at the front of the house and stopped short when she nearly tripped over the body on the floor.

"Professor Ballantine, I presume," she muttered, stifling a shiver of disgust.

Ballantine lay face-up on the sitting-room rug, his hands curled into claws; the blast-furnace heat had, over several days, desiccated the man into a shriveled husk. Paper-thin skin had pulled taut across his skull, giving the corpse a ghoulish aspect, an effect not greatly improved by the presence of a lone fly squatting on Ballantine's wide-open eye.

Athena grimaced as she examined the body. Ballantine had been stabbed several times, the wounds visible through the torn and disheveled clothing—a series of incisions calculated to kill slowly, just like Kimber. His right wrist appeared to be broken, and his wallet and watch were missing.

She stood, looking carefully around the room. Unlike the kitchen, the sitting room was a shambles, save for a halo of empty floor around the Professor's supine body. The room's three small bookcases had been upended, spilling history texts onto the floor. The leather couch had been shredded—based on the blood smears on the cushions—by the same knife that had finished Professor Ballantine.

"What were you looking for?" she muttered. The killer had torn the place apart in search of something, but Athena had no idea what. She made her way through the small house; the bathroom had been rifled, as had the Professor's bedroom. More journals, books, and sheaves of typewritten pages had been tossed about. Whoever the killer was, Athena thought, he had a lot in common with a tornado.

A small leather-bound book caught her eye; bloody fingerprints dotted its battered cover; the killer had spent time examining it. Athena flipped open the book—a treatise on ancient Indian folklore, pausing where blood smears seemed the most pronounced. She read:

The Misp (also referred to as "Musp") is a "transformer" legend of the Salish and Quinault tribes of the Pacific Northwest—powerful, heroic beings that were believed to be agents of change—altering monsters into benign animals, for example. Though traditionally viewed as benevolent entities, some tales have survived of Trickster-Transformers, who created mischief or outright evil through their actions.

The Hoh Indians, a small tribal offshoot of the Quinault, occasionally refer to "Innouyashii," once a revered hero of their community, who did battle with ancient forces, shape shifters similar to the Navajo "skin walker" (akin to a European lycanthrope, or "werewolf"). Innouyashii, according to the legend, successfully ended the shape shifters, but in the process had become corrupted by them. Driven out by the tribe, he took residence upon a nearby island, where his howling spirit—often appearing in the form of a large wolf—is believed to prey on those foolhardy enough to set foot upon his territory.

Athena closed the book, a frown creasing her forehead. The description of a fallen hero and his howling ghost made for a good campfire story, but why murder two people over it?

She tucked the book away, and glanced at her watch—almost midnight. She would have to summon authorities again, and there would undoubtedly be more questions for her—

Her eyes widened slightly. She looked down at her watch, as if seeing it for the first time.

Watches.

The Professor's watch was missing, taken by whoever had murdered him

Kimber's watch, still on his body because the murderer hadn't finished the job on him, was still in her pocket.

A faint, lopsided grin tugged at the corners of her mouth as she retrieved Kimber's battered timepiece. Her eyes blazed with curiosity.

She studied it intently, turning it over in her hand. The watch itself was battered, of little value, with faux gold flaking away at her touch. The crystal was scratched, but upon closer examination, there was something familiar about the appearance of the scuffs and marks.

Her grin turned into a luminous smile.

"I'll be damned," she said, "Kimber, you were one clever son of a bitch."

Athena Voltaire raced to her car, her boots crunching on the gravel driveway, and sped off into the night. The police could wait.

She had a few more calls to make.

3. All The Daring Young Men In Their Flying Machines

"Y'all don't do anything halfway, do you?" Hollis quipped.

Athena Voltaire gestured at the massive airship that loomed above her, moored within a titanic hangar. "You're a Texan," Athena replied, "so I figured this would be right up your alley."

The airship's envelope was painted a bright crimson, and the gondola slung beneath it was large and ornate, with art deco patterns formed in polished aluminum, brushed steel, and luxurious, exotic woods. The name Pegasus was emblazoned on the side of the ship. Behind and beneath the gondola, cabled to a complicated crane mechanism, festooned with safety netting, hung Athena's battered biplane.

Hollis, standing with his fingers hitched in his belt, stared up at Pegasus, nodding. "Reckon so."

Macken shot him a sour look. "You're both nuts. These damn things are flying bombs." Next to Macken, Doakes shrugged. "Maybe they are, Mack, but what the hell? Got anywhere better to be?"

Athena's eyes wandered across Pegasus and past it to survey the hangar. She was at home in such structures, but this one was enormous, constructed from huge wood beams that formed a lair cavernous enough to house a behemoth. Unlike the hangars she was accustomed to, this one was almost supernaturally spotless. No telltale oil or grease stains, no dust, no engine parts in various stages of disassembly. It was a fourteen-karat setting for the jewel that was Pegasus.

"So what's the story with this crate?" Doakes asked, staring up at the airship. "You can't just hire one like a taxi, right?"

Athena nodded. "It's an…experiment, I guess. Hawks wants to try it out as a camera platform for his next picture."

As if summoned by the mention of filmmaking, one of Howard's lackeys, a nervous, bespectacled stick-insect named Smythe, materialized. He waved a sheaf of papers at Athena.

"Miss Voltaire, I must reiterate," he stammered, "this aircraft is the property of Columbia Pictures and Mr. Hawks. Should it fail to return to this hangar in pristine, I say, absolutely pristine condition, you are solely financially responsible—"

"Understood," Athena snapped, cutting the bureaucrat off with a sharp glare. "If I don't bring it back, you can bill me."

Mr. Smythe did not find this answer fully satisfactory. "I assure you, that is exactly what will happen."

He insisted on dozens of forms signed in triplicate before making his exit, never once losing his air of a man grossly wronged.

"Friendly fella, ain't he?" Hollis muttered.

He adjusted his Stetson. "Now that the bean counters are happy," he drawled, "you kinda got me wondering where exactly we're fixin' on going."

Athena started walking toward the rope ladder that led to the gondola, preparing to board the Pegasus. "That'll all become clear soon enough. What's more important is why we're going."

"We're going because we're a bunch of idiots," Macken groused.

Athena paused, her hand on the ladder. "Two people are dead, Mack, and one of them is—was—one of us.

"So ask yourself: why do people kill?"

"Love," said Doakes, shrugging.

"Aw. Ain't you the romantic?" Cowboy said.

"Sure," Athena replied, ignoring Hollis, "Murder's usually a crime of passion, and Kimber was certainly in and out of various…passions, married and unmarried alike. Jealousy could explain why he was killed, but unless Professor Ballantine is an extremely well-disguised Lothario, that doesn't explain why he was killed."

Macken stopped in his tracks and said, "Then it must be money."

Athena nodded. "Kimber didn't have any, but he was always on the hunt for it, and I think we all know he has—had—the persistence of a bloodhound. So that's the connection. As unlikely as it is, somehow the Professor, either knowingly or unknowingly, stumbled onto something valuable, something Kimber wanted in on. It's the only explanation that makes sense.

"So that's where we're going," she said. "Somewhere out there's something worth killing for. And we're going to find it."

Doakes expression darkened. "I'm all for making some dough," he said, "but I don't see what that'll do for poor old Kimber."

"Simple. The killer didn't get what he needed from either the Professor or Kimber. So we find it first, and we grab the prize, whatever it is. The killer will have to make a play it."

She started to climb the ladder. "And when he does, we shoot the bastard."

Cowboy whistled appreciatively as he surveyed Pegasus' flight deck. Okie's eyes widened as he entered. "Wow," he said with near religious awe. Even Macken seemed impressed.

The bridge was spacious, and the windows that ringed it afforded a magnificent view. Every instrument gleamed, the controls perfectly placed. Comfortable seats—upholstered in red leather—for the navigator, the radioman, and the pilot were spaced throughout the bridge. At the pilot's station were control wheels in mahogany and brass, reminiscent of the steering wheel of a tall ship from the age of sail.

Athena sat in the pilot's seat, enjoying their reactions. "She's something, isn't she?"

Macken studied the bridge. "That she is. Good radio, good instruments. I guess all she needs is a destination."

"All in good time, Mack," Athena said. "Toss your gear in the staterooms, and we'll get underway."

Half an hour later, Pegasus soared.

A row of engines, mounted along the airship's midline (three to port, three to starboard), growled like tigers and pushed the crimson airship forward with surprising grace and speed. Pegasus was derived from German designs, with a metal superstructure supporting hydrogen cells within the envelope, providing lift. Smaller than the Teutonic passenger zeppelins, she still could lift a tremendous weight—including Athena's own aircraft and a large supply of food, fuel, and other essentials. Unlike the German airships, Pegasus outmatched them in raw horsepower. The engines, developed by engineers from Pratt & Whitney, made Pegasus live up to her namesake's legend.

Athena steered the ship northward, putting Los Angeles behind them, and opened up the throttle. The thrum of the engines filled the cabin, as if they were in the gullet of a leviathan.

"We've got a few hours to kill, so get some rest. I'll fill you in over dinner."

"Now wait just a second," Macken said. "I don't know about the rest of these rubes, but I want to know where we're going—"

"Dinner," Athena snapped, her tone inviting no further discussion, "will be at six o'clock. Sharp."

She turned back to her navigation charts as the three men reluctantly beat a hasty retreat.

Athena sipped her champagne and smiled.

The smile did not reach her eyes, but none of the men in the dining room seemed to notice.

The dining room—more of a large wardroom—was as luxuriously appointed as the bridge and staterooms, despite its small size.

Macken, Hollis and Doakes took seats opposite her. Macken toyed with the food on his plate—picnic fare, cold sandwiches and egg salad—with little enthusiasm. "How can a joint this nice have food that lousy?" he muttered.

Athena chuckled. "I must've forgotten my apron, with all the distractions."

"Distractions?" Doakes asked.

"You know: flying the aircraft, which doesn't leave one a lot of time for baking."

Hollis pushed aside his plate, his gaze steady. "Well, then. Let's rope that steer right now. We're flying where, exactly?"

The others looked on, as Athena propped her feet up on the table, savoring her champagne. The food was terrible, but the not-quite-legal alcohol she'd found secured in the galley was world-class.

"We're going hunting."

"It used to be called the Island of Sorrows," Athena began. "In the 1880s, the place got a bad reputation when three ships all wrecked near the island. The Spanish hated the place, which is how it got the name.

"The stories don't get much better. The local tribe, the Hoh Indians, have an old legend about a mythical hero who turned evil and basically kills anyone who sets foot on the island.

"It sounds like a fairy tale, but it turns out, a lot of people have turned up dead there over the years. Shipwrecks, murders, animal attacks.

She paused for effect. "The island is supposed to be cursed."

Macken slapped his palm down on the table. "Oh, come on! Ghosts? Curses? Quit pulling my leg, Athena."

Athena's expression darkened. "I've seen stranger things before, Mack," she said, her voice almost a whisper. She blinked, taking a moment to rid herself of the ghostly afterimage of long-dead creatures, swathed in rotting bandages. They'd smelled faintly of old paper and dust—

Doakes cleared his throat, snapping Athena out of her reverie. "How'd you find out about this place?"

Athena held up Ballantine's journal. "The other dead man. The Professor from Kimber's address book."

Hollis cocked an eyebrow. "I would'a swore on a stack of bibles that Kimber and schoolin' only had a passin' familiarity."

Athena nodded. "Exactly. He was smart, but can you imagine him sitting in a classroom? It's ridiculous."

Macken stared at the journal in Athena's hand. "And that's what's in the book? This ghost story?"

"Among other things.

"Ballantine was an expert in folklore, specifically Indian myths and legends, the more obscure the better. He heard about this curse, and the spirit of the fallen warrior who had turned evil, and wanted to know more.

"Especially," she continued, "when he did some research and learned that the deaths and mishaps have continued over the years. A drowned child in 1911, a murder in 1929, and so on. They call it 'Destruction Island' now, but it's still the same bad place."

"My god," Doakes said, his expression incredulous, "he wanted a field trip. To find a damned ghost."

Athena smiled. "Enter Kimber, stage right. He needed the job, so he offered to ferry the Professor to the island."

"And died for his trouble," Macken said.

"Then I have one more question," Hollis drawled. "It's a whole island. How are we gonna find whatever it is we're lookin' for?"

"That," Athena said, "is the best part."

They stood at the navigator's desk on the bridge, peering at a survey map of Destruction Island. The map didn't have a great deal of detail; aside from normal maritime shipping hazards, there simply wasn't much to map in the first place. The island, 30 miles off the Washington coast, was uninhabited.

Athena switched on a long-necked lamp, positioning it so that the light shone straight down onto the chart. Her comrades looked on, hunched over the map table and deeply puzzled.

"Ain't nothin' to see," Hollis said. "If I'm readin' this map proper, it's a speck of nothin' smack dab in a great big empty."

"This is just the patter before the magic trick, Cowboy," Athena said. "Here comes the hocus pocus."

She placed Kimber's watch on the table, face up, and held out her hand. "I need something to pry this apart," she said.

Macken handed her his pocketknife, and she quickly popped the crystal from the front of the watch. She held it up so they could all see it clearly. "Nothing up my sleeve," she quipped, before holding the crystal in front of the lamp bulb.

The scratches in the crystal cast fuzzy lines of shadow on the map, crisscrossing at the edges, and coalescing into a more coherent shape near the northwest corner of the island.

"Holy crow," Doakes breathed, "it's an 'x.'"

"As in 'X marks the spot,'" Athena concluded. "Whatever's worth killing for is right there."

The men paused, exchanging glances, before Macken finally stood up straight, his fingers still trailing absently on the map. "We best get moving, then."

Destruction Island was barely visible. A light drizzle obscured visibility, but thin moonlight found gaps in the gloom, just enough for Athena Voltaire to spy the island's edge against the inky blackness of the Pacific.

She adjusted trim and velocity, and began the descent toward the island. She stretched, cracking her knuckles, fatigued from several hours at the wheel. The boys had been asleep for a significant portion of the flight, and she savored the quiet and solitude, but it was time to get things moving.

She stood, stifling a yawn, and strapped on her pistol belt before exiting into the companionway that led to the staterooms.

She knocked on Cowboy's door, and was surprised to receive no answer. She pushed the door open, and saw only an empty room. Puzzled, she continued further aft, calling out, "Let's go, boys. Rise and shine."

No response.

No one in Macken's stateroom. Same, too, with Oakes' quarters. Where the hell was everybody? she wondered.

Her hand dropped to the butt of her pistol.

She was almost to the galley when she smelled smoke.

The description of Pegasus as a flying bomb had been accurate enough; fire was the great enemy aboard an airship. One errant spark finding it's way onto something flammable, and from there to the hydrogen cells, and everyone's day was well and truly ruined.

She spotted black tendrils of smoke creeping from beneath the galley door; another was further aft. She exhaled, took a deep breath, and pushed open the galley door.

Smoke boiled out, and a wave of heat slammed into her. She shielded her face with her arm, moving deeper into the galley.

Despite the smoky haze, she could see the source of the fire—the galley oven.

She quickly grabbed the extinguisher and flung open the oven. She squeezed the trigger, and sent pressurized water blasting inside, blotting out the angry orange and yellow licks of flame that burst from within.

The fire was out in moments, and she looked closer, her jaw set in an angry line. Someone had placed wads of discarded newspaper into the stove and turned it on.

This was sabotage.

Someone on board was trying to kill her.

Athena Voltaire's anger flared. She drew her pistol, and she turned to exit the galley.

She crumpled to the floor, her vision blurred by dancing sparks, when a wrecking-ball fist slammed into her face.

Get up, she thought. Get up now, stupid girl.

She couldn't see. Her breath was ragged.

One thought burned in her mind: find the gun. Find the gun and shoot the man trying to kill her.

She yelped in agony as a heavy boot crashed into her side. One rib gave out with a sharp pop. Her mouth filled with copper.

She rolled, and could feel the passage of the attacker's follow-up kick, narrowly missing her.

Athena shook her head, trying to clear her field of vision. The blurs resolved into cloudy, indistinct slashes of shadow and light, and she realized with a start that one of those slashes was streaking toward her.

She ducked, dodging the brunt of the attack. A burning sensation creased her upper cheek.

Someone was trying to stab her.

With a roar of anger, she charged forward and grappled with her assailant, who barked in surprise. Her elbow slammed into what she hoped was the side of his head, and her foot connected with his midsection.

Adrenaline and anger coursed through her, and her vision finally began to clear.

"You," she growled, staring her attacker in the eye. "Of course it was you. You always were a bastard."

"It was the knife gave me away, wasn't it?" Macken sighed.

"Showing me the weapon you used to kill my friend wasn't the smartest move, no," Athena snarled. "But the real newsflash was when you punched me in the face."

"Couldn't resist. You always were too uppity for your own good." His knife licked forward again, forcing Athena to step back until her back hit storage racks on the far side of the compartment. Pots and pans rattled from the impact. "You always have to be the one in the spotlight. Well, you've got my undivided attention now, Athena."

He stepped forward, keeping his knife hand moving, the blade bobbing and weaving like a cobra. "After you, there's Okie and Cowboy. And then I'm free and clear."

She locked eyes with him. "So this is your big plan? Stab me, kill the boys, and…what? Go back to Hollywood and pretend none of this ever happened?"

"Something like that. When I'm finished with you, I'm going to head on back to where the boys are trussed up, and I'm gonna shoot 'em with your gun and toss 'em in the drink. Then I figure I'll take your plane and fly away, after I set this overgrown balloon on fire.

"But don't worry," he added, his tone mock-conspiratorial, "I got plenty of experience killing people so they go slow. You'll get to see it all before you die. Just like Kimber."

He stalked forward, the fake playfulness gone, his knife smeared with her blood.

The blade darted forward again, right for her gut.

Macken was a top pilot, which meant he had speed, hand-eye coordination and fearlessness in spades. Athena Voltaire, on the other hand, was a much better pilot.

In an instant, Macken's look of grim triumph flashed into one of surprise, then immediately to panic, when Athena's hand whipped forward, blocking the knife strike with one of the brass-bottomed pans she'd plucked from the racks behind her. Sparks flew from the impact, and a resounding "clang" reverberated through the galley.

Macken yanked his hand back, a hiss of pain escaping his lips. The knife flew from his grasp.

Athena was on him a moment later, the pan slamming Macken in the face. Blood poured from his ruined nose and his eye began to swell shut. He reeled backward, fumbling for the knife.

She kicked him, hard, then dived past him. Her hands scrabbled beneath the stove.

Macken pulled himself up on one knee, wobbling and cursing Athena with an impressive array of profanity. He reached for the knife.

Athena yanked her fallen pistol from beneath the stove, and pulled the trigger. "You don't dodge bullets," her father had once told her. "They either miss…or they don't."

Athena snarled as the bullet pinged from the edge of the galley door, and the hornet-whine of the ricochet echoed throughout the airship.

Macken ignored the knife, yanking himself up and out the door before Athena could fire a second shot.

She bolted after him, answering Macken's curses with some colorful language of her own.

Macken moved further aft, towards the engine room and the exterior walkways, Athena Voltaire in hot pursuit. If he made it to the engines, he could doom them all.

Blood drops on the deck-plates painted a path that was easy to follow, and she paused to catch her breath a moment. Her ribs ached like hell, and her right side movement was restricted, which was the only reason she could think of that her shot had missed. That or Macken had more lives than a cat. If that were the case, she promised herself, she'd see just how fast she could burn through those lives.

She kept moving to the rear of the Pegasus, following the drops of blood, relieved when the trail led past the engine room, and not inside.

Finally, she reached the hatchway into the aircraft launch bay, though "bay" was perhaps too grand a term. A narrow metal catwalk led ten feet or so into a small boxlike cabin, little more than a shack, with a rope ladder that descended down to her plane. She slammed open the door, gun held in front of her, her finger tense on the trigger.

"Stop right there!" Macken cried.

He had Cowboy in a chokehold, and as the Texan struggled, Macken muscled him forward, threatening to shove his captive through the wide-open gap in the deck and into the nothingness below. Okie was unconscious and bound, lying at

Macken's feet.

"One step more," he yelled over the roar of the wind, "and they both go for a stroll."

Athena raised the pistol, Macken's head square in her sight picture. "And if they die, you think I won't kill you?"

Macken shrugged, his mashed, swollen eye strangely monstrous. "I guess we'll see."

He shoved Cowboy, who stumbled, fell, and disappeared into void.

"NO!" Athena screamed. Some part of her believed the man she considered a friend wasn't this far gone, that he wouldn't kill another friend with casual ease.

By the time she recovered from the shock, Macken had hauled Doakes to his feet. Okie was groggy and confused. Blood trickled from his scalp from where Macken had cold-cocked him. "We clear, Athena?" Macken called out. "We understand the rules now?"

"I understand," she said, holding her hands out in front of her, the gun pointed up and away from Macken. "Just calm down."

"Calm down? The hell you say," Macken screamed. He was enraged now, and his hatred for Athena was a palpable presence in the windy bay. "You have any idea what you're doing to me? What that imbecile Kimber did?"

"No," she replied, slowly placing the gun on the deck. "But I can guess."

"Right, right. Athena Voltaire always has everything all figured out."

"It's the money, isn't it?" she shot back. "I've heard the stories, Mack. You skipped out of Chicago with a bucket of mob money, and they want it back. What I don't get is why you didn't just keep going."

"That's right. The mob wants their money back," he yelled, tightening his grip on Okie. "But I didn't have it. My partner stole it."

Athena's eyes widened in realization. "You were the getaway pilot?"

Macken nodded. "My partner was the thief. I was the escape. I got us out of Chicago, and all the way across Canada. We split up, and were supposed to rendezvous in Vancouver to divvy up, but the jerk left me high and dry, holding the bag, with the syndicates hunting for us.

"So I laid low. I made my way south, because my partner had family connections in Los Angeles. I tracked him down easy enough, but he jumped me.

"You killed your partner."

"No choice. Him or me. But he died before I could beat the location of the loot out of him."

Athena, her hands still in the air, paced back and forth, slowly, trying to draw Macken off balance. "So you stayed in Los Angeles, looking for his family connection. And leave it to Kimber to figure out who and where they were.

"Ballantine." Macken growled. "He was my partner's uncle. And Kimber figured out that the Professor knew where money was stashed."

"There." She pointed roughly downward. "Down there on that island.

"It's a good spot," she continued. "The spooky stories keep people away, but the curse legend was like catnip to the Professor. He started poking his nose into it. You couldn't have that, could you?"

"No!" Macken replied. "It's mine. I earned it."

"Yeah, Mack," Athena growled, "you sure as hell did."

"Enough talk!" Mack was losing control, his eyes wild. "Step over to the opening. Let's see how well you can really fly."

Athena nodded and slowly moved closer to the gap. Cold air slammed into her, chilling her to the bone. She looked down, and could just barely make out the water below. Her biplane, swaying slightly in its moorings, seemed very far away.

"You can step out," Macken hollered, "or I can push you out."

"I've got a better idea," Athena yelled back, her eyes as wild as Macken's.

She leaped forward and grabbed Okie by his lapels, yanking them both backward, hard. Okie's eyes widened in alarm when he realized what was happening, and Athena heard his scream, muffled by the gag.

They tumbled, backward, into void as Macken looked on, astonished.

Okie was still screaming when Athena untied the gag. "Are you crazy?" Doakes cried, his words drowned in the rush of icy air. Up here, at this speed, the seemingly calm drizzle spied from the cockpit felt like a torrential downpour, battering at them and making the rope netting dangerously slick.

"Quiet!" she barked. She pointed up at the opening. With the rain, the wind, and the darkness, she could barely see it, but if Macken managed to spy them, he'd have all the time in the world to shoot them with her own gun.

Athena untied Okie's wrists. Fortunately, Macken hadn't had time to secure Doakes with a complicated knot. The rope dropped free and whipped away into the darkness.

They crawled along the netting slung beneath the bay's exit hatch, moving closer to her plane. Doakes' panic was subsiding, the closer he got to the relative safety of the plane.

The biplane was a two-seater training aircraft, a Boeing Stearman she'd purchased after a student pilot pranged it off the runway. A few months of TLC, and some additional modifications and refinements, and the bird was dependable as hell.

As Athena reached the cockpit, Hollis' hands pulled her up and inside, and then, together, they drew the shaken Doakes in, as well. "Nice to see you," she shouted. "Good thing I saw you hit the net."

"You're just lucky it didn't rip clear when I came down," Hollis shouted back. "That first step was a doozy.

"I assume," he continued, grinning, "you have a half-baked, lunatic plan?"

"Hey," she shot back, "look who you're talkin' to. Of course I have a half-baked, lunatic plan."

She clambered back along the fuselage, and into the training pilot's seat, situated behind the front cockpit. From here, a teacher could seize control of the plane if the rookie made a near-fatal mistake.

She grinned as she watched the men squirm into the front seat, which was awkward and uncomfortable but, in her view, was also a damn sight better than plummeting a couple thousand feet into the drink.

Athena strapped herself into the trainer's position in the rear, and grabbed the stick. "Ready!" she called out, then reached up, and yanked a long metal lever.

The Stearman fell free, dropping like a stone.

Athena counted to three, ruddered right, banked, then fired up the engine. It coughed and sputtered, and for a sickening moment, she was convinced they'd splash down before the engine caught.

Seconds later, the engine growled to life, and she pulled back on the stick, arcing them back upward.

Pegasus was already descending toward the island. Athena brought the plane up behind the airship, maintaining position above and to the rear. "I could use your help, boys," she shouted, pointing.

Hollis looked confused, but Doakes had regained his composure. He realized what Athena needed, gave her a thumbs-up, and squirmed his way around Hollis.

Pegasus hovered one hundred fifty feet above Destruction Island.

The rain had given way to a thick mist, and the airship drifted slightly, ghostly and unreal. A rope ladder dropped from her undercarriage.

One hundred feet.

Fifty.

The rope ladder was just starting to scrape the muddy ground, when a lone figure began a frantic, breakneck descent.

Macken nearly lost his grip three times before forcing himself to slow down. He was within minutes of securing a fortune in cash, and making a clean getaway. Visions of putting Hollywood behind him, settling someplace the syndicate could never reach him—Bora Bora, maybe—beckoned him on.

He didn't notice the rattle of the aircraft engine until he was a dozen feet from the bottom of the ladder. By the time he looked up, trying to spot it in the overcast and gloom, Pegasus exploded.

Doakes cheered as he fired a final burst from the plane's machine guns. Pegasus' envelope sagged, fell into itself, and spectacularly burst into flame, sending burning wreckage tumbling and lighting the swollen clouds a sickening orange.

Athena winced; Pegasus had been a beautiful ship, but using it to kill Macken seemed a fitting send-off for Kimber. She arced the plane into a wide loop and circled around, watching the airship die in graceful slow-motion.

When the envelope went up, Macken was flung from the rope ladder. The pressure wave from the blast hit him like a truck, swatting him to the ground. He hit the soft mud and tumbled to a halt.

He struggled to his feet, reeling. He realized with a start that his jacket was on fire. He tossed it aside, staring at the heavens.

The sky itself seemed to burn and plummet toward him. Pegasus' envelope was rapidly burning away, and the airship's superstructure reminded him of a giant, skeletal hand, clutching at him.

Panic filled him, and he tore off at a dead run, slogging through the muck and mud.

Behind him, the world burned.

Athena brought the plane lower, buzzing mere feet above the treetops.

The wreckage left this corner of the island a flame-wreathed hell-scape. Macken had to be dead. If the fire and explosion didn't kill him, the fall would have, she thought.

As she banked to starboard, she scanned the tree line beyond the crash site, and her eyes widened as she saw a shadowy figure crashing into the woods.

"This place must be cursed," she muttered.

Macken swore under his breath. The airship was gone, which meant he was stuck out here, at the mercy of the elements and whoever was behind the stick of the plane that was hunting him. Maybe it was the mob, finally tracking him down, or simply waiting for someone to make a run for the cash.

It didn't matter. He would find the loot. He would build a raft and sail the thirty miles to the Washington coast if he had to, or bribe or buy his way aboard a passing ship.

He had won. The plane couldn't land—the island was too heavily wooded for that—and in the dark and poor weather, they'd never spot him. They'd run out of fuel and turn back long before they'd catch him. He laughed to himself, on the verge of mania.

At last, he found the location Athena had scrawled on the map.

He began to dig, his hands plunging into the thick, wet soil.

Athena circled the island, desperate to find a place to put down. There were only a handful of clearings on the tiny island, and none of them were big enough to use as a landing strip, unless she planned on making their stay permanent.

She yanked the stick and banked to port, briefly considering a foolhardy landing attempt on the largest open space she could find, and damn the consequences.

A series of dark shapes glided across the clearing, melting from the tree line and disappearing into the shadows, startling Athena Voltaire. Dread caressed her skin, raising gooseflesh.

She arrested her descent, and continued to orbit the island.

Macken's voice, hoarse from exhaustion, echoed madly as he screamed in triumph.

He clutched a mud-slick burlap sack, reaching in to draw forth several bundles of neatly wrapped bills. Thousands of dollars, and finally, at last, all of it his.

He laughed, and sobbed, and hugged the sack close to his chest.

Professor Ballantine wanted to come out here to examine the legends of a curse, and at the thought of it, a bitter laugh exploded from Macken. Cursed? As far as he was concerned, this place was blessed, like a mythical paradise.

Curses and ghost stories, he thought. Nonsense.

He stood and turned to make his way back toward the crash site, to find any supplies that might help sustain him until he could get off the island. He knew, with the plane overhead, he should stick to the shadows, but he couldn't help but feel urgency. He charged into a small clearing.

Macken stopped short, gasping, as a pair of yellow eyes gleamed at him out of the dark. He fell to his knees when he saw a dozen more draw closer.

He looked up at the heavens and saw Athena Voltaire's biplane glide by overhead. Macken shook his head, convinced he'd seen Voltaire looking back at him. Crazy, he knew, but he was certain she could see him.

He laughed. "All right," he said. "You got me."

He dropped his head, still hugging the money bag, and only began to cry when the growling started.

"My God," Athena whispered, her eyes wide in horror.

She kept the plane banked, hypnotized by the tableau playing out below her. Macken sat in the clearing, defeated. She could've sworn he looked up at her, that somehow, despite the darkness and fog, he saw her.

Then the wolf pack struck.

She was too far away to hear, but she was relieved that Macken's screaming didn't seem to last long.

For a moment, she remembered the legend of the Misp, and the comparison to werewolves, and it chilled her blood. Whoever set foot on Destruction Island was doomed.

Just ask Macken.

She leveled out, and sent the plane east. They had enough fuel to make Seattle, and enough cash to find the nearest speakeasy. She would put her money on the bartop, and she, Hollis, and Doakes would drink one hell of a toast to Kimber.

That would be the last memory of him, she decided, one far warmer than the last time she'd seen the young pilot. No more anger nor blood— just laughter and the clink of glasses.

She put Destruction Island and all its ghosts behind her, and opened up the throttle.

THE PLOT TWIST PERIL

Steve Bryant

Athena Voltaire sat at the conference table, facing Harry Warner, who was, as always, flanked by his lapdogs. Harry hadn't bothered to introduce either man to her by name, and since their contribution to the conversation invariably consisted of nodding and interjecting insights such as "Great idea, Mr. Warner," she didn't exactly feel that she was missing anything.

"Tell us about *you*, Miss Voltaire. Who is *Athena Voltaire?*" Warner eyed her curiously, puffing on his cigar, trying to figure out if the young woman in the smart suit and hat sitting across from him had really accomplished everything he had heard. She was a knockout, to be sure, and those gams…but an amazing pilot? A crack shot? An adventurer who had braved jungles, deserts, and the Orient?

"What is it you'd like to know, Mr. Warner?" she responded, with slight trepidation. Sure, the deal could yield a tidy sum—enough to get her Tri-Motor out of hock, repaired, and maybe enough for a down payment on a Farman 190—but at what price? How much did she want to reveal about herself?

"Harry, please. Call me *Harry*. Everyone does, Dollface. Isn't that right, Barton?"

The lapdog on the left, excited to be addressed by name, immediately responded, "Yes sir, Mr. Warner!"

Athena hoped her smirk wasn't apparent. She opted for the cautious approach. "Alright, *Harry.* You already know plenty about my background with my father, *The Great Voltaire - -* "

"Old news, Sweetheart! And besides, stage magic is dying! People want action, adventure, and exotic locales!"

Okay, so that's how we're playing it, she thought. All in, just tell 'em everything and let them pick and choose what parts of her life would be the most exciting to motion picture audiences. She had once stood naked amongst a cannibal tribe in the Amazon, yet felt far more vulnerable right now.

"Gotcha," she said, "I think I have something that will fill the bill for you." With that, she launched into an anecdote:

I was assisting an expedition near Patagonia. I had flown the famous psychic Hereward Carrington and his associate to a remote location to investigate some scientific anomalies in the area. Banished from the dig itself, I passed time outside while Carrington and his assistant, Doctor Van Elk, frantically jotted notes in their journals, documenting the psychic ebb and flow of the dig.

"Miss Voltaire! Come quickly! Dr. Carrington would like you to see something!" called Van Elk, interrupting my twentieth crucial solitaire hand of the afternoon.

"Really? Now I'm allowed at the site? I thought my 'negative energy' was disturbing his work? Of course, after two days in a plane with Dr. Hocus-Pocus, who wouldn't develop some negative energy?"

"From what I've heard about your adventures, you're the last person I'd expect to be skeptical about the paranormal," Van Elk chided.

"And based on your reputation, Doctor, I'm just as surprised you'd hire me to cart the author of Your Psychic Powers and How to Develop Them halfway around the world. Just because I know zebras exist, it doesn't mean I start looking for them every time I hear hoof beats."

I wasn't in the mood to be patronized.

As we descended into the tomb, Van Elk was bound and determined to make his point.

"Ten years ago I would have agreed with you, Miss Voltaire, but studying the Sickles magnetic phenomenon has prepared me to look outside the conventional scientific disciplines. If Hereward Carrington's psychical theories can shed some light upon the mysterious disappearances, radar failing, and compass malfunction that plague this area - -"

"I think you're going to be disappointed, Doc," I interrupted. "I grew up around

men like Carrington. They're excellent showmen, but the act is always designed to amaze—not to explain. How else do you get people to buy another ticket? And frankly, it worries me that his need for secrecy has kept my backup on the other side of the island."

I was just getting started. The longer we walked along the carved-out corridors, deeper into the tomb, the greater the head of steam—pent-up frustration—I let out. "Crackpot or not, I don't like being responsible for a bunch of eggheads out here in the jungle without decent protection."

My rant was suddenly shushed by Carrington himself, kneeling, head cocked and close to the floor, examining God-knows-what.

"You wanted to see me?"

"Watch your step, Miss Voltaire," Carrington said patronizingly. "I believe that you are standing before a portal to a world undreamed of by man. Its power--"

I heard the hammer click back right before the gunfire started, giving me enough time to shove Carrington and Van Elk out of the way. Barely.

"Carrington! Stay put! I'm going to lay down some cover fire!"

"I prefer to stay close, Miss Voltaire."

I've got to hand it to him. Carrington wasn't about to be intimidated. But I wasn't going to leave the topic open for debate. "That's like painting a target on your chest," I told him. "I don't think Astral Projection stops bullets."

"But--"

"Stay put!" I punctuated my point with a shot from one of my Colt Peacemakers. One of our unseen attackers let out a yelp that trailed off into a whimper.

But Carrington wouldn't let me have the last word. "Do be careful, Miss Voltaire! The gunplay may upset the balance of the portal! We haven't had time to fully examine--"

I turned to see what cut off Carrington mid-lecture. Grinning back at me was one of the locals, Vazquez, a man with glassy eyes and bad teeth. Carrington's people had hired him to head-up the diggers.

Right now, though, he held a revolver of his own to Carrington's temple.

"Drop your guns, woman! The game is over." Vazquez flashed his crooked smile at Carrington.

"Shouldn't you have seen this coming, Doctor?" I couldn't help but make the joke, but before I could hear Carrington's response, the butt of a rifle to the back of my head made everything go black.

When I awoke, I found myself and Van Elk bound and dangling high over a pit. Below us, I could make out a dozens of spears pointing upward in the inevitable event that we fell.

"I think Vazquez has seen one too many movie serials; he's made this awfully dramatic. Or he has a soft spot for yours truly. Is it my eyes, Doc?"

"Miss Voltaire, this is no time for levity! What we need is an escape plan!"

"Patience, Doc. I can pull off a little Hocus Pocus of my own." I keep a few tricks of the trade stowed on my person, just in case. It comes with the territory when you're the kid of a stage magician, I guess. *"Nothing up my sleeve…"*

"I know! And then we could have a savage Ape Man swing in to your rescue!" Harry Warner beamed with pride behind a cloud of smoke.

"Excuse me? Do I *look* like I need rescuing from an *Ape Man?!*" Athena exclaimed. She tried to regain her composure. "Not to mention the fact that I've never met a primal foundling raised by indigenous animals.

"And Ed Burroughs would slap a lawsuit on your ass so fast your head would spin."

She couldn't resist taking that last shot, but immediately regretted it, as Warner's face reddened a bit. In contrast, any trace of color drained from the faces of "Barton" and Lapdog Number Two.

Athena cleared her throat and prepared to smooth things over. "Pardon me. I just thought that story might not end up where you'd like." She punctuated that with subtle turn of a smile on her lips.

Warner, a red-blooded American male with a pulse, reciprocated, grinning broadly, "Quite all right, my dear! What else do you have?"

"How about something with pirates in the South China Sea?"

Off the coast of Burma is a band of Malay cutthroats whose leader goes by the handle "The Pirate Queen." I'm pretty sure she's self-appointed, but you can never tell with any number of these small-time warlords and gangsters…some of them really do pass such ridiculous titles down.

Anyway, she and her boys had gotten the best of me, swiping an artifact called The Helm of Nabu out from under me. I wasn't about to let her get the best of me, so I swam out to where her junk was anchored and slipped aboard the ship.

I managed to take out two of her lieutenants before the alarm was sounded.

In such close quarters, I didn't have the opportunity to draw my guns, and their sheer numbers overwhelmed me.

"Athena Voltaire," the Pirate Queen glared at me as she drew her dagger--

"Where's the male lead in this scene?!" Harry Warner grew impatient.

Frustration built in Athena's voice. "There is no 'male lead' in the story. I fought the Pirate Queen solo and recovered the helmet. We tangled a few times after that, too."

"You can't ask us to believe that you did all of this by your lonesome, Miss Voltaire. I mean, really," puffed Warner behind a fresh cigar.

The incredulity was contagious. Barton the Lapdog added, "And, besides, Miss Voltaire, every motion picture needs a male lead—especially an action picture."

Emboldened, even Lapdog Number Two piled on. "We're taking a huge risk as it is. Conventional wisdom says that a female lead can't open an action picture."

Athena Voltaire furrowed her brow and reminded herself how much she missed her Ford Tri-Motor, and how she longed for that speedy new Farman 190. "How about this one…"

I was hired to lead an expedition to recover water from the fountain of youth; water that could not only prolong life, but reanimate the dead--

"Please, Ms. Voltaire!" Harry Warner had heard enough. "I appreciate your desire to get involved in the creative process, but you don't need to embellish. We have screenwriters who are paid top dollar to do so, and I'm sure what they can think up will top all of the daydreams in that pretty little head of yours."

Athena Voltaire was stunned. "But," she started, "I'm not making it up. You wanted to know about what I do; *this* is what I do."

"Of course, darling. We'd never accuse you of lying! I'm just saying that the motion picture business is pretty complicated, and you don't need to worry about any of these niggling details."

"No, really. It's on the level." Maybe it was the "daydreams" comment, maybe it was the "pretty little head" remark, or maybe it was the cumulative effect of trying to explain herself to these sedentary know-nothings who couldn't tell a Mayan temple from the Mayan Movie Palace, but Athena needed to be believed then and there.

"Of course, Doll. We believe you. Right, Barton?" said Harry Warner in a patronizing tone.

Eager to bark in assent with his master, Barton readily agreed, "Yes sir, Mr. Warner!"

Empowered by his subordinate's affirmation, Harry Warner reclined, put his wingtips on the conference table, took a long drag on his cigar, and spoke, "I know what this picture needs. Cowboys are hot these days. We'll pair you up with a cowboy!"

Athena sat in stunned silence, realizing that she had had her say, and that time was now over.

"Not just a cowboy! We'll throw in an Indian, too! A faithful Indian guide! The kids'll eat that up!" Warner was on a roll now, and the lapdogs were on the edge of their seats.

Nothing to do now, Athena cradled her head in her hands and listened as the great Harry Warner rewrote her life and times, as only he could.

"And a detective! Not just any detective, an occult detective! You see what I'm doing here, Sweetheart? *This* is how we make a *picture.*"

Athena Voltaire closed her eyes and thought of flying, "Whatever you say, Harry. Whatever you say…"

THE HEAVENLY ABYSS

Caleb Monroe

George Vane adjusted his glasses and cast another surreptitious glance at the woman in the driver's seat.

"Yes, Mr. Vane?" Well, he'd thought it was surreptitious. Athena Voltaire turned her eyes on him for a moment before returning them to the road, which he realized is what he'd been half-hoping would happen when he first looked her way. His mind invoked a line from Yeats: "*The blue and the dim and the dark cloths/ of night and light and the half light.*" Eyes blue like hot summer sky. Dark cloths of hair. The half light of skin dusked by long hours in the sun.

For George, beauty was philosophy, theory, golden ratio, and poetry—captured by words, contained on pages, and transmitted through books from one mind to another, heedless of time or distance. But Athena reminded him how ineffably more beauty was than language. She made the time and distance of a shared front seat matter immensely.

It was incredibly unsettling.

He also realized, far too late now to avoid awkwardness, that she had asked him a question and he still hadn't answered. "We're quite close now. Thank you again for agreeing to come."

She smiled, ignoring his momentary lapse of manners as if it hadn't happened. "I just hope I'll be useful. I know Mr. Winters intended for you to bring my father, but no one knows when he'll be back. Do you think your employer will be upset?"

"He insisted on urgency."

"But he wouldn't say what, exactly, was so urgent?"

"He's like that. All I know is what I shared: he wanted to put some questions to Mr. Voltaire about his, um, fortune-telling."

"Fortune-telling *act*."

"Of course. Mr. Winters has been writing a monograph on the history of scrying and divination. The anthropology of folklore is a particular passion of his. He seemed peculiarly interested in your father's expertise, though I don't know why. He doesn't share works-in-progress with me."

"Well, I've been in or around Dad's 'Great Voltaire' show most of my life, so there's a good chance I can help. Why didn't your boss just phone, instead of putting you on a train and sending you all the way to L.A.?"

"Mine's not to reason why."

"Ha! I think he and Dad would get along famously. 'A magician never tells' is practically the family motto."

They arrived at Library House just as the sun kissed the horizon. It and the thousands of pieces of it spreading blindingly across the ceaseless steel ocean drifted from their left to their rear as they turned off the coastal highway onto the manor's gently hilly drive. Their shadow was long and easterly; the one cast behind the sprawling western-facing mansion was so large it looked like a patch of night come too soon. They swung around the corner of the house and parked near the side entrance, parallel to that line between fading day and arrived night. "Can I get your bag, Miss Voltaire?"

"That'd be lovely, George."

Athena's single bag was half the size of his own—a scarred, tan-green rucksack that looked like it'd seen action in the Great War. Once they'd decided she would return with him to Cambria, she hadn't even packed. She'd simply grabbed the bag from a front closet and walked out the door as if it—and she—were always prepared to leave.

As he straightened under their luggage, he noticed her looking up, taking in the mansion. George was accustomed to the House, but Athena's expression reminded him how spectacular it was, how fortunate he'd been to be selected as Mr. Winters' personal librarian. "What do you think?"

She grinned. "You know, there are giant homes everywhere you look in

Hollywood. Everyone fancies themselves royalty and tries building a palace to match. But this place puts the lie to all of them, makes them look like dollar-a-night beach bungalows. Winters' father made his fortune in railroads, right?"

"And guns. He married a Remington heir."

Athena's grin took on the quality of a kid's at a candy counter. "Is there a collection?"

"Afraid not. Mr. Winters sold the entire lot to a museum to make room for his own collections. I doubt he's ever so much as held a gun."

She sighed and switched her gaze from the house to the grounds. As those summer eyes swept past him they suddenly froze, and her expression changed in a way he didn't understand. "I need my bag, George."

"No, it's fine; not heavy at—"

"*Bag*, right now." Her previously friendly tone suddenly carried such authority that he handed the rucksack over before realizing he'd done it. She opened it and reached inside without taking her eyes off the yard behind him. He turned to see what she was staring at.

It was standing several feet from the House, half in and half out of the manor's deep, black shadow.

At first he thought it was one of the ponies got out. It was about the right size.

Then his mind, half a second behind since Athena's sudden change of character, adjusted. It was nothing like a pony. Something was...wrong...with the shape of its head. He'd call it vulpine if forced, but that didn't quite capture it. And its eyes were too large and wrongly placed. They were like mirrors, reflecting the disappearing light behind George and Athena. Two discs of twilight in a midnight face.

The thing's entire body was pitch black and sleek as a cat's, but its shoulders and forelegs were thick and ropey like a gorilla's. Something akin to gills flexed on its neck. As they dilated, they seemed to emit a sickly green glow, but it must have been a strange trick of the light. The sun was almost beneath the horizon now; the gloaming had played tricks on his eyes before. Which had to be what was happening now. The animal (what else could it be?) must be a bear. Or a cougar.

Then it opened its mouth. That same sick glow rolled down over its restless tongue like something viscous and tangible. It barked. Or growled. It was hard to know what to call it. George was reminded of ravens, of hyenas, of the bull elephant seals fighting each year on the beach. It woke something primal in him, hot tremors of adrenaline and a chill of fear rippling across his back and arms simultaneously.

He heard a muffled thump and a click directly behind him. He glanced over his shoulder just long enough to see that Athena had dropped her bag once she'd retrieved what she wanted: a Colt New Service revolver. Her voice was soft, but clear as a diamond. "Is the door to the house locked?"

"Yes."

"Do you have the key? Can it be unlocked quickly?"

"Yes. A...as quickly as any other door, I suppose." There was the briefest pause. He didn't dare take his eyes off the thing in the yard again, but he could practically hear her calculating the distance and angles between them and the door, them and the creature, the creature and the door. The sharp huff of air through her nose signaled a summary dismissal of that course of action. A bead of sweat tickled his lower back. "Do you know what it is?"

"No, and I've seen more than my share of strange."

"The car?"

"When I say. As quickly as possible."

George tensed and the beast in the shadows cocked its head slightly, as if it could hear the change in muscles and heartbeat.

"Now," Athena said, and George sprinted for the car. At least, that's what he assumed she said. He only heard the "N—" before the sound of the Colt's first shot drowned everything else out. He was surprised how loud it was.

Then there was only the running. He heard Athena's feet pounding behind him between two more shots. He thought he might make it.

But he could see the thing in his peripheral vision, coming far faster than any being subject to gravity should be able to, and he knew this was his last moment on Earth.

Athena suddenly changed direction, cutting at an angle toward the car's hood, directly between George and the thing, emptying the last three shots in the creature's face as she passed. The beast swiveled its baleful gaze to follow her, pulling its heading just enough to save both their lives. As George reached the rear passenger door, the thing plowed into the front door with enough force to lift the vehicle onto two wheels. Athena just managed to vault over the hood, the creature's claws rasping across her boot. She already had the Colt open, expelling the spent cartridges, the flying brass forming a fleeting halo.

Hail Athena, Angel of Death.

George slammed his door shut and, lunging forward, threw the driver's door open for Athena as she tossed the gun from her right hand to her left and loaded a new bullet from her pocket into the cylinder. She threw herself inside, snapping the gun shut with a flick of her wrist while her right hand emerged from her coat pocket with the keys.

The beast's monstrous arm burst through the front passenger window. Athena fired across her body with her left hand while starting the car with her right. The arm disappeared, the engine roared to life, and George was rocked back in his seat as Athena floored it and the car surged forward.

For a moment, through his window, George was face-to-face with the creature, and he realized all his categories and definitions of evil were too small and unimaginative. This thing lived and moved and had its being in a depth of depraved atrocity that made George numb. Whatever classification one might create for a book, that thing was demon—a foul cosmic malignancy taken flesh.

Then it was gone. George adjusted his glasses and shuddered from the soul out.

He was thrown against the door as Athena cut the wheel. Her revolver thudded into his stomach. "Here!" she reached back, her fist holding five more bullets. He felt a panic attack rising. Hands vibrating with fear, he took the bullets and concentrated on trying to get them, one by one, into the gun's open cylinder. There was a squeal of tires, a sudden change in direction and the demon's hell-voice rang out sharply, followed by an impact that made the car shudder. George did not look up. He exhaled as each bullet slid home, inhaled as he reached for the next.

Six breaths and he was finished, but he kept his head bowed. His vision seemed to have come unanchored.

"George!" There was another swerve and thump. The Colt slid to the floor and he snapped out of it. He fumbled in the dark by his feet, his hands responding sluggishly.

"George!" He glanced up, saw her eyes in the rearview mirror by the light of one of the House's windows as they swept past. She didn't meet his gaze, but she didn't have to for him to see the tightly-wound fear there.

The revolver! He handed it over the seat and she grabbed it left-handed again even as the car sped up. George realized the demon was now hanging off the hood of the car. Athena stuck her arm out her own window, which had also somehow been shattered while George was in his haze, and emptied the Colt into the thing in less time than it had taken George to load it.

The entire time, the car kept going faster. He realized they were driving over grass, that the unseen ocean must be somewhere to his right, because the north end of Library House loomed in all its brick and stone impressiveness directly ahead. The sight of his long-time home seemed suddenly ominous at this speed. They whipped past several tree-like blurs.

One claw buried in the hood and one sunk into the roof, the demon, completely unfazed by the bullets, rammed its misshapen skull into the windshield, spider-webbing the glass.

Library House seemed twice as large as it had ever been.

"Brace!" Athena shouted. He saw her bow into the steering wheel and wrap her arms tightly around it and he threw himself to the floor between the seats.

Then the impact, the loudest thing he'd ever heard, including the Colt.

As soon as he could breathe, his terror of not knowing what just happened overrode his terror of knowing and he pulled himself back upright. The front half of the car was crumpled and half-buried in brick where Athena had driven it straight into the building.

The demon shrieked and lashed about, apparently pinned between the collapsed stone and the car's heavy, compacted engine. George had seen a kid pin an angry snake under a rock when he was a boy, and that's what the demon looked like now: furious, boneless, and fast. Its claws churned the car's steel into screeching, twisted ribbons, but to no avail. It remained wedged fast, Athena still flooring the sputtering engine to keep it there.

"Up here, George, now!" He clambered into the front seat. "Put your foot on the gas, and don't let up." It was an awkward exchange, but he managed to ease his foot onto the pedal as she eased hers off, keeping the car in constant forward motion and the demon pinned.

Then she was gone, the driver's door hanging open. Athena ran, half-limping, back to her rucksack, upended it onto the driveway, and ransacked the pile, throwing clothes and other items in all directions. George was growing queasy, and the demon's angry squeals felt like blows to his temples.

Athena hurried back with a metal box. She pried it open and started thumbing its contents into the revolver. More bullets. "We should get inside."

"Windows won't keep it out. We only have a moment before the thing gets free again."

"But bullets haven't done a thing to it!"

"These might." She handed him the metal box, stepped forward and fired. "Silver."

It didn't seem to have any more effect than the previous shots. The car's engine was sounding less certain by the second.

She cocked the gun and fired again. "Cold iron and St. John's Wort." The demon screeched and thrashed a bit harder.

"Blessed by a priest." This shot caused a flash of yellow light when it hit. Puffs of black smoke escaped the thing's gills and its rage sounds took on a slight note of pain.

"Bone of a Chinese qilin." The bullet tore straight through the demon, splattering green-black ichor across the stones behind it.

"Inscribed with the Tetragrammaton." The demon shuddered, grew still, and retched across the front of the car as if it had ingested something unimaginably foul. The hood sizzled wherever its chyme fell. There were things moving in it. The engine coughed and nearly died.

"Cast in running water." This final shot received no reaction at all. "Okay." Athena held her hand out. "Bone bullets, please." George opened the box and saw it was divided into six compartments, a different type of bullet in each. It was easy to tell the ones made of bone from the others, and he handed her six of them, his hand trembling as he did. He was really starting to feel ill now.

Athena loaded them with practiced ease, her eyes on the demon the entire time and its eyes on her. As the engine died and the demon finally began to lurch free, she raised the gun and fired the full complement into its face. Its head burst under the impacts like a rotting melon and, about a minute later, the rest of it finally stopped moving.

"Next time," Athena said, taking the bullet box from his hands, "I'm making sure these are packed on top."

George felt light-headed. If he hadn't just emptied the contents of his stomach onto the driveway in the adrenaline comedown from the encounter with the demon, he would certainly be doing so now. He removed his glasses and wiped his brow with his sleeve. When he instinctively began to return the lenses to his face, he stopped himself. His poor vision was actually a mercy at the moment.

Mr. Winters had not died easy. Knowing firsthand how fast the demon moved, it had probably been quick. But it certainly hadn't been easy.

They were in the Occult Room. Library House was exactly what it sounded like: the entire house—every room, nook, cranny and hallway—had been converted into a library and divided into rough subject categories. And even that was not enough to keep Mr. Winters' bibliophilia in check. There were piles of books everywhere, on every surface, on the floor. George's job title, "Librarian," obviously meant much more than in the common usage. He was part majordomo and part card catalog. His eidetic memory had been the main reason for his selection to the post. It was among his duties to walk through a room every time Mr. Winters left it, so later he could recall with precision where, exactly, Winters had left each and every one of the volumes he'd been reading in a particular session.

Having near-perfect visual recall had certainly given him an amazing opportunity for employment beyond his station in life, but today made him long for forgetfulness. The demon in the driveway had obviously already been inside the house by the time they encountered it and had had its way with Mr. Winters. The Occult Room was soaked in blood, seemingly more than a human body could contain. The ragged and dismembered Winters was spread everywhere. The pulpy pieces were so small they seemed like they couldn't possibly add up to a human being.

George looked at the nearest stack of blood-drenched volumes, the fluid soaking entirely through some of them. Apuleius's De Deo Socratis. Abulafia's

Chayei ha-Olam ha-Ba. Zoroastor's Yasna Haptanghaiti. Ibn Hayyān's Kitab al-Sab'een. He mused how the blood would actually increase the value of many of them for collectors, then realized his mind was trying to escape its present circumstances and wrenched it back to the situation at hand.

"You say this is the Occult Room. Could Mr. Winters have accidentally done this to himself? Summoned something, invoked something?"

"I...I don't think so. As fascinated as he was, he considered demonology a byproduct of our cognitive growth as a species. Survival patterns as superstitions."

"Well, I didn't just sacrifice my car to kill a superstition. I can't say for sure it was a demon, but if it was and Mr. Winters read the wrong passage from the wrong book out loud, especially if he didn't fear the result..."

"I can't see him having the imagination to even try. As for reading out loud, accidentally or otherwise, he was a very interior person. Sometimes I'd go days without hearing his voice when he was absorbed in his books."

"Well, in my experience, no one runs into these sorts of things accidentally. It takes real effort to even get one onto the material plane. If that effort wasn't your boss', then we're looking at a third party. Was anyone else in the house today?"

"I'm the entire staff, and I was in Los Angeles fetching you."

"Appointments? Does he keep a calendar or date book?"

George pulled up the kitchen wall calendar in his mind. "Just the family lawyer, at four. He was bringing some investment papers for Mr. Winters to sign."

"Was he new?"

"No, Mr. Hathcock's been Mr. Winters' representative since before I worked here."

"Wait. Hathcock? What's his first name?"

"Victor." He could tell it was bad news. "What's the matter? Does that name mean something to you?"

"My father." He waited for the connection. "This trip he's on, the reason he couldn't help you. He was engaged by a lawyer named Victor Hathcock to investigate a series of paranormal occurrences in Eastern Europe. Which usually means debunking them. There's surprisingly good money to be made in keeping gullible heiresses away from predatory illusionists at the behest of their wealthy relatives. Did Mr. Hathcock have other clients?"

"No, his practice was dedicated entirely to the Winters estate. He mostly verified book provenances, secured items from private auctions, negotiated with archaeologists and other collectors."

"Does Mr. Winters have any relatives in Europe?"

"No."

Athena pinched the bridge of her nose like she was coming down with a headache. "I need a phone."

"The Antiquities Room. Two doors down, on the left."

"While I'm gone we need that photographic memory you were telling me about. Go over every square inch of this room. Don't worry about items that have moved; a lot of that's bound to have happened in a struggle like this. Look for what's missing."

He did as she asked while she made her calls. "Hey, George, what does your Mr. Hathcock look like?" she yelled once down the hall.

"Medium height, portly, bald on top, gray on the sides," he shouted back. The room was in complete disarray. It took him longer than he expected to match each book's current location to his last visual inventory of the room. He moved slowly, carefully.

Despite his best efforts, he stepped on pieces of Mr. Winters twice. He only retched once, though.

A single manuscript was missing: an illuminated eleventh-century edition of Firdausī's Shāhnāma. The title obviously meant nothing to Athena. "Which is...?"

"An epic poem telling the history of Persia from the creation of the world to the Islamic conquest of the 600s."

"That narrows it down. Have you read it?"

"Portions. Nothing worth killing over."

"Everything's worth killing over if you're the wrong type of person."

"I just mean nothing seems to set it apart from any other historiographical epic."

"Something does, though, if you're someone with a pet demon."

"Who were you calling?"

"My father."

"What did he have to say?"

"I couldn't reach him. He never took the flight he was ticketed for and he never checked into his hotel in Prague. So the one person Mr. Winters wanted to speak to regarding his monograph disappears after being sent on a trip by the last person scheduled to see Mr. Winters alive. Where is this monograph?"

"Not written yet, but Mr. Winters' working notes should be on the pad in his desk in the Composition Room."

"Get them. You can read them on the road."

"Where are we going?"

"To find Mr. Hathcock. If he kept his appointment and left at, say, five, that means he's got about a four-hour head start on us. He's either the killer or the next victim, so we need to find him one way or the other. Have another car we can use?"

"Yes, several."

"Make sure it's fast."

George was reaching for the keys on the peg in the mud room, the ones to the Audi Front UW 225 roadster, when he suddenly became very ill. Nausea, a severe headache, muscle tremors, and a fever seemed to roll over him in a single wave. He gasped and fell to his hands and knees. There was movement to his left and he attempted to raise his head. "Miss Voltaire," he gasped. "S-something's..."

He froze. The movement wasn't Athena. It was a demon like the one from the driveway. Smaller, about the size of a large dog. Its gills flexed, its eyes narrowed. Its mouth opened, then kept opening, its lower jaw seeming to unhinge. It took a step toward George, and he suddenly felt even worse. There was a throbbing, rushing sound in his temples. One of his arms gave out from under him. Another step, claws clicking on the tile, and George vomited for the third time that day. His leg muscles cramped and spasmed.

The Colt roared. Inside, this close, the sound was painful. Greasy ichor splashed across his cheek, there was a howl and the demon bolted through the side door with enough force to crack it right in half. Athena's arms were around him, helping him up, but he already felt like himself again. The illness had departed with the monster. He wondered why the first one had not had the same effect on him, or why this one seemed not to have affected Athena. Perhaps she'd been out of range.

"I've only got five of those bullets left," she said.

"Then let's leave. Now." If there were two there could be more.

"I assume you're a book-lover, being a librarian and all?"

"Very much so." She was trying to put him at ease, and he knew it, and she knew he knew it. But he appreciated it nonetheless.

"Favorite type?"

"Tragedy."

"That so?"

"They're just hero stories, really. But with flawed heroes. In the traditional hero tale, the hero makes all the right decisions, takes all the right actions, and that's why they're the hero and why they come out on top. A tragic hero takes all the right actions but one, and that's their undoing. I don't know, it just seems to me hero stories teach you not to make mistakes, but tragedies teach you which mistakes to avoid. Or how not to exacerbate them once made. I think I'm more likely in life to be the guy who makes a mistake, and I just hope it won't be a life-ending one."

"What about sacrifice? Sometimes the right action's still a tragic one."

"What do I know?" he said. "My life experience is all on paper."

"It's sweet. I'd wish paper loss over real loss for anyone."

Reading Winters' monograph notes by moonlight in a speeding car was making George motion sick but, compared to the sensations he'd experienced earlier, motion sickness seemed rather inconsequential. He adjusted his glasses and pressed on. "Okay, let's see...scrying, fortune-telling, divination...catoptromancy, using mirrors; psychomanteum, mirrored rooms; sensory deprivation... macharomancy, by swords...lychnomancy, by candles...batrachomancy, using frogs.... Hm. He seems to spend over half his notes discussing divination by water. Hydromancy, dowsing, bletonomancy, lecanomancy.... Scyphomancy, using cups...let's see, Joseph in Genesis, Pausanias' Description of Greece, Occult Sciences by Smedley, Taylor, Thompson, and Rich...Ah, this may be it. The Cup of Jamshid as described by, among other sources, the *Shāhnāma*. Mythological predecessor to the Nartyamonga and the Holy Grail. Said to be a seven-ringed cup in which the entirety of the seven heavens are visible. Carries the elixir of immortality and gives its bearer unparalleled knowledge, wisdom, and dominion. There's a note in the margin: 'Consult Voltaire re: secret text.'"

"There's our connection. Now what does it mean?"

"I'm not sure. The rest of the pad is empty. I wonder what secret text he's referring to, and what your dad would know about it?"

"Beats me. Dad's never been much for research outside the history of illusion, and he invented most of his techniques himself. Not exactly a bookworm."

"Well, as a bona fide bookworm I can say a lost or hitherto undiscovered work would be irresistible to a man like Winters. He'd be unable to rest until he located and verified it."

"Verified? Like what Hathcock does? Do you think he found some forbidden tome and unleashed an ancient evil?"

"There's nothing secret about the *Shāhnāma*. It's been around for centuries. There are multiple copies, translations, and editions. And why would your father be missing?"

"That's what we're here to find out." Athena parked the car in front of a small, tasteful office. They were on Main Street in Cambria. The businesses were all closed, including the office with its small brass plaque reading MR. VICTOR A. HATHCOCK, ESQ. ATTORNEY AT LAW.

"Looks empty."

"Do you know where he lives?"

"No."

"Then we start here."

The office was two stories: a comfortable reception area and conference table downstairs, with Hathcock's personal office upstairs. Athena bent over the office door, picking the lock. The longer it took, the more nervous George became.

There was a clack and the door swung inward. The office was very well appointed. One client was more than enough when that client was as rich as Winters. Athena moved immediately to the first filing cabinet. "Check the desk."

He did. He found nothing of import and was about to help her with the files when the sound of a key in the front lock downstairs echoed through the empty office. George and Athena both froze. She was the first to move, drawing her gun, padding to the office door and closing it almost all the way. George joined her and they watched as a heavy-set woman in her forties stepped inside and flicked on the lights. "That's Hathcock's assistant, Mrs. Copeland," George whispered.

He heard a faint scraping sound as Athena opened her gun, began removing bone bullets, and replaced them with normal ones.

"Are you going to shoot her?"

"I hope not. But if something happens I don't intend to waste the only bullets we have that kill those demons." She snapped the cylinder shut as noiselessly as possible, but it still seemed incredibly loud.

Downstairs, Mrs. Copeland was whistling to herself. George recognized Louis Armstrong's "Heebie Jeebies." She hung up her coat, then walked over to the hearth and started a fire. Still whistling to herself while it crackled to life, she began sorting through several documents and books she had brought in with her. Starting with the papers, she began throwing them into the fire, piece by piece. George physically cringed at the thought of the books being burned.

"Burned means important," Athena hissed. She emerged onto the landing and cocked her gun. "That's enough of that."

Mrs. Copeland looked up with less surprise than one would expect. "Now how did you get in?"

"A magician never tells."

Mrs. Copeland made an amused sound and returned her attention to the rest of the books and papers, picking up the entire stack at once.

"Don't do it." Athena's voice brooked no argument. Then again, Mrs. Copeland didn't argue: she simply tossed the books to the flames.

Or mostly tossed, because Athena shot her through the hand the moment she moved. The books landed half in and half out of the fire. George let out a sound of anguish, drowned by Mrs. Copeland's cry of pain, and rushed downstairs to save them. He snatched them away, stamping and blowing out the flames. Mrs. Copeland vainly tried to impede him with her good hand, her wounded one clutched to the breast of her floral sweater, slowly turning all the flowers red.

"Was that really worth a bullet?" Athena joined them on the first floor.

George looked at her. "This top one's the *Shāhnāma*."

"Leave it alone!" Mrs. Copeland seemed devastated they were looking through things she was supposed to destroy.

"The missing copy?"

"No, it's a modern edition. And not the best translation. These others are the *Avesta* and the *Yasna*. Zoroastrian scriptures. They mention the mythological Persian god-king Jamshid, first owner of the Cup bearing his name."

"I'm detecting a pattern. Why were you burning these, Mrs. Copeland?" The older woman was unresponsive, rocking back and forth and shaking her head forlornly.

"Talk to us, Mrs. Copeland," George said gently. He'd known her for years and she was always so gentle with him. "What are you mixed up in?"

"I can't," she moaned. "He'd be so angry."

Athena crouched next to George. "Are you really more scared of an estate lawyer than of me?"

Mrs. Copeland gave a strangled laugh. "Not a lawyer, not afraid of a *lawyer*. But the new god-king of the earth—" She suddenly doubled over in pain, the color draining from her face and beads of sweat appearing on her forehead and nose. "I don't—" The rest of her words became groans of discomfort.

Now it was happening to George: that full-body, full-symptom sickness he'd felt earlier in the mudroom. "Demon...here," he wheezed before gagging and dry heaving. Athena spun around, Colt-first. The beast was crouched malevolently on the conference table, its reflection in the polished wood's surface an unbroken extension of its black form. This one was smaller than the other two, though it still looked like it could rend a man to pieces in seconds. Where it had come from was a mystery.

Mrs. Copeland didn't even notice it. She just writhed, emitting glottal sounds of pain.

"Front door, George." Athena grabbed him by the collar and pushed him in that direction. He began crawling. The ambient sickness was far worse than it had been in the mud room, but he crawled because he didn't want to die. After he got a foot or so from the creature, he began to realize his affliction lessened with each inch closer to the door. Athena, again, was strangely unaffected and stared at the thing without blinking.

Then the demon sprang without telegraph, as if the laws of physiology like tensing and contracting of muscles to create motion were optional to it. Athena fired, and there was a burst of plaster from the wall. It was the first time George had seen her miss. "Athena!"

But the creature hadn't sprung at her. It landed on Mrs. Copeland and, with a casual twist of its hindquarters, split her open from shoulder blades to front hip. George's aural memory was not as acute as his visual, but he would never forget that butcher-shop sound.

Athena took an instinctive step toward the other woman to help, even though she was beyond help...and the most peculiar thing happened.

The demon hopped back a foot with a cry that might have been a yelp of pain echoing through a tunnel of hatred and broken glass. Athena, George, and the hell-thing all froze in surprise. Then Athena took another step.

The demon slunk back an equivalent distance.

Two quick steps, then a third. The creature convulsed and hacked up more of the wriggling vomit they'd seen from the first demon before it backed swiftly under the conference table. Every time it backed up, George felt that much better.

For another moment, no one moved. Then the demon let out a chilling screech and leapt through the room's back window. George felt recovered even before the shattered glass had settled onto the carpet.

And in that moment, he began to suspect what was happening.

They were outside, by the car, still wary, when Athena finally let herself react. She released a shuddering sigh and her eyes lost focus for a moment.

"Being a deluded fool doesn't mean she deserved *that*."

"No."

"Or even being shot in the hand."

Before he could respond to that second part, she got in the car and started the engine.

George looked at the note. Athena had had the presence of mind to take Mrs. Copeland's purse when they left the office and the note had been inside. It read, simply, "The *Atlantis – midnight*." They were assuming it referred to the Atlantis Hotel, about thirty minutes up the coast. They still had an hour until midnight. For a long while neither of them spoke. There was just the rushing of ocean air through the car's open windows and the hum of the tires on the asphalt.

It was Athena who finally broke the silence. "Why was it afraid of me? I seemed to have the same effect on it that it was having on you and Mrs. Copeland."

"I have a theory, but it will sound strange."

"Stranger than demons that can only be killed with the bones of flaming Chinese unicorns?" They both laughed. Not really at the joke, but because they needed it.

"I suppose not. Do you know what a cambion is?"

"No."

"It's the offspring of a human mother and a demonic father."

"That would make family reunions awkward."

"The most famous one's probably Merlin, from the King Arthur tales. In the earliest sources, his mystical powers were said to be inherited from his demonic father."

"Okay, I'm following so far."

"One of those powers was an uncanny knowledge of the future. And some sources give as the reason for this that Merlin aged backward. If he did, and there is a lot of 'if' to that statement...that would have come from his demon side as well."

"You're saying—"

"I think. I think these creatures we keep encountering tonight are actually the same demon, moving backward through time, or at least time as we perceive it. You may have killed it in that first encounter, but for the monster it was the final encounter. And as that event gets further in the past for us, it gets further in the future for the demon."

"You know, my headache was almost gone. So, what? It keeps getting smaller because it keeps getting younger?"

"Exactly. It's really an incredible rate of growth. It must have been very small when it was first summoned, an event which, based on the rate it's growing, must happen tonight or tomorrow."

"So when it first charged us in the driveway, it was running backward to its own senses?"

"Even moving the same way through time as us, demons are supernatural beings with a powerful bag of theoretical tricks. I'm guessing this one can sync somewhat to our time as it moves through it. Like a diver holding his breath. But it's imperfect, or impermanent, which is why it seemed to leap without using its muscles, or how it entered a room without open doors."

"And the sickness?"

"That's when I got the idea. In the office. The demon may violate nature as we know it, but not without side effects. See, you made the creature sick when you drew near because in your past, and its future, you killed it. Cosmically-speaking, I just don't think you can get that close to someone who's already killed you without feeling some sort of effect. Mrs. Copeland felt sick in its presence, see, because in her future, brief as it was, it had already killed her."

He didn't mention the obvious about his own violent illness in its presence and neither did Athena. They lapsed back into silence.

Several miles later, she spoke up again. "Nothing's set in stone, you know. That's what makes the future the future."

Yeah, he thought, *unless it's already someone—or somet*hing—*else's past.*

The bone bullets were back in Athena's gun.

The Atlantis was quiet. Deserted, actually. They had parked down the road and approached by foot. Athena had given George's hand a reassuring squeeze as they got out of the car, and he could still feel the touch long minutes after she'd let go.

There were lights on behind the main building. They had almost reached the parking lot when Athena stopped. George looked down and saw what she'd noticed: starting a foot in front of them and stretching all the way to the hotel, all vegetation was completely dead. The once-decorative trees around the parking lot were black clutches of rigor mortis, their leaves in brown piles blown against their trunks.

With a crunch of dead grass, they resumed their cautious approach.

Their painstaking route finally brought them around the corner of the hotel where, crouching behind a dead hedge, they could see the source of the lights. Between the bulk of the hotel building and the beach was a large courtyard area. On one side was a cafe with patio tables and on the other was a tennis court. In the center was a huge pool. All the lights around the pool had been turned on.

There were four figures framed by the light. One wore a ridiculous black robe that made him look like a freshly appointed college dean. "That's Hathcock," George said.

Athena pointed to the man on his knees on the concrete before Hathcock, hands tied behind him. "And my father."

Neither of them knew the other two. Both were tall and thick, wore black suits, black gloves, dark overcoats, and matching Homburgs, brims pulled low over their faces. "What do you think?" asked George. "Hired muscle?" Athena shrugged. Hathcock plucked a book from a lounge chair and held it before Louis Voltaire's face.

"Winters' *Shāhnāma*," George whispered.

"Everyone who's still speaking to you agrees how clever the Great Voltaire is. Before he died, my late employer went on at great length about your various areas of expertise. Including invisible inks and secret writings, which are of particular interest to us here tonight." He flipped the book open to a specific page and held it up for Louis to see. "See this? This page tells of the storied Cup of Jamshid. But I have it on good authority there's far more than that written here. And you're going to tell me how to read it."

Oh, thought George. *The 'text' part of 'secret text' wasn't a book at all. It was hidden writing.*

Louis simply looked at the page. "Don't try my patience, Voltaire. If you won't do it, I'll simply kill you and find another candidate."

"After all the trouble you've gone to? Wouldn't dream of it. What's this 'far more' that's hidden here?"

Victor Hathcock grinned. "Godhood. I know it's a cliché, but you know, when it becomes actual possibility…"

"What a man like you considers godhood is always so pedestrian. You should have just bought some new golf clubs." Hathcock's face turned bright red and his hulking companions both laughed without the motions normally accompanied by the act. They quieted themselves when the lawyer turned his furious gaze on them, but the moment had revealed something important. Those were not human laughs.

Hathcock focused on Louis once again, and after a few seconds of huffing, finally worked up enough violence to slap him. The silence grew long and uncomfortable. "Well!?" Hathcock finally burst out, jabbing the priceless manuscript like it was a phone book.

Louis bounced his bound wrists. "Can I have the use of my hands?"

"No."

Athena laughed, but George didn't get the joke. "What?"

"His hands aren't really tied," she replied. "There isn't a knot on earth that can hold Dad."

Back by the pool, Louis was inspecting the vellum pages as closely as he could from his position. "What's the provenance?" he asked.

"Rome, eleventh century. Translation from Persian."

"Well, anything pre-Renaissance is going to be organic. Probably tithymalus sap, but it doesn't really matter. Just run a flame over it."

"What, like kids do with lemon juice?"

"Hey, it was cutting-edge technology a millennium ago."

Hathcock motioned to one of his human-shaped things, which lit a match and waved it under the page.

No, not a match. Its finger.

Soon the page's margins were full of char-brown new verses. "You know, when Winters first told me why he wanted this particular manuscript I thought he'd finally cracked. Now look at him. And look at me!" Then, his voice heavy-laden with what only someone who'd never encountered gravitas would believe was gravitas, he began to read aloud.

"What language is that?" Athena asked as they appraised their situation.

"Latin," George replied. "Sounds like pretty standard alchemy stuff."

There wasn't a way to approach the pool under cover. They'd be exposed and well-lit before they ever got close.

"Can you shoot them from here?" he asked.

"With a rifle, no problem. With the revolver, it's less certain. With Dad between us and them..."

The pool's surface began to roil. "We may not have a choice."

"Stay here. That demon thing's still out there somewhere."

"What if it kills me while I'm alone back here, waiting? Plus, if I start to get sick you'll know it's coming and it won't be able to catch you by surprise."

She gave it some thought, but not much. The pool water was sinking at the edges and swelling in the center, a diffuse, sourceless light emanating from within. "Fine, come. But when things get hairy you grab my father and you get him out of there. Leave Tweedle-dee, Tweedle-dum, and the Dodo to me, understand?"

He nodded, but she repeated herself. "Understand?"

"Understood." This time it was she who nodded, quick and business-like. Then, with the faintest scent of faded sweat and even more faded perfume where she'd been, she was gone, running across the courtyard. George did his best to keep up.

Hathcock was intent on his incantation, but his companions noticed the charging man and woman almost immediately. Their heads moved to track the duo's progress, but they remained otherwise impassive.

Louis noticed their shift in attention and followed it. His smile upon seeing his daughter was automatic, and while her face remained calm and ready, he saw the corners of her lips twitch up involuntarily in response. He had no idea who the uncertain spectacle-adjuster behind her was, but he was used to that: Athena tended to sweep men up in her wake. Her first shot was for the suited man-thing on the left, her second for its partner. Neither reacted. Her third was for Hathcock. His hands suddenly free, Louis dove out of the way to give her a clear shot just as she pulled the trigger but, shooting on the run like she was, she missed the lawyer.

Hathcock stopped incanting at the sound of the shots and looked up to see what was happening. He glanced at the first suit Athena had shot and flicked his head toward the interlopers. "Take care of that, will you?" Then he picked up the recitation where he'd left off. The suit waved its hand casually in their direction, lifting Athena and George off their feet and flinging them into the fence surrounding the tennis court.

George realized the sentinels hadn't been waiting for orders. They were just utterly unconcerned by any threat the humans could muster. He couldn't imagine what it had taken for a middle-aged estate lawyer to summon such power.

Athena used the last two bone bullets, taking head shots at both the suits. One ricocheted off. The other simply shattered.

Hathcock's voice rose as he neared the climax. He shouted the final couplet at the top of his lungs, then there was nothing but the steady pulse of the ocean, lost in the black night behind the would-be god-king. The rising swell of glowing pool water should have been making sounds, even gentle ones, but it was eerily noiseless. Slowly the mound resolved itself into a pedestal approached by sweeping stairs clear and silent as crystal, their surface in constant motion like water.

The light radiating from below drew itself together, forming a single bright shape in the water directly below the pedestal. Then the light-form ascended upward through the column and pushed its way out the top. At first it was too bright to discern any shape, but as the light faded they could all see what it was: a cup.

A cup too beautiful to comprehend. Their eyes quickly filled with tears.

For an eternity there was nothing but the Cup.

Then Hathcock stepped out onto the water's surface. It held his weight like it was solid, but the hem of his robe sank through the surface and whirled in eddies of its own making behind him. He mounted the rippling steps and slowly, reverently, reached out his hands to grasp the Cup. His eyes closed with a shudder of pleasure when his fingers finally made contact.

There was another eternity as he simply stood there, unmoving. The others waited. They knew there was no stopping him and no escaping, not with the things in the suits watching them.

Then Hathcock raised the Cup to his lips and drank.

"Immortal," he whispered. He turned and descended back to the edge of the pool.

George suddenly didn't feel so good. Without seeing where it came from, there was something on four legs beside the sorcerer: the demon from Library House, no bigger than a squirrel. It shied away from the side of the pool where Athena stood.

"Lady and gentlemen, meet the Curse of Jamshid." He knelt and scratched under the demon's chin. It tolerated it. Barely. "It protects the Cup, and will forever obey its rightful owner." He made a hand gesture over the demon like he was giving a benediction. "You will come with me earlier today to kill Mr. Winters and secure the manuscript, and you will end anyone who would stop me from making tonight a reality."

He stood up. "It was four o'clock this afternoon when I realized I'd already succeeded tonight. Because the Curse here was waiting outside Library House. Waiting to follow my orders as rightful owner of the Cup. And, my, how he'd grown!

"Now, you three get a choice. You've seen me achieve godhood firsthand. Bow to me here and now and I'll spare your lives. I'll even bless you and favor you in my new world." He made the benediction gesture again.

Athena spoke for all of them: "Go to hell."

"In that case, allow me to introduce you to my other companions. In this new world I think they'll be my royal guard." He waved the Cup at one, "This is Zarizel Zarich, Daeva of Poisoninous Death," then the other, "And this is Taurizel Tawrich, Daeva of Destruction." George knew those names, and when he heard them he went numb and resigned himself to death. "Daevas, I'd like you to kill these three. Please make it last. A week, let's say."

The daevas stepped forward and George realized their faces weren't shadowed by the low brims of their hats. Their faces were shadows. Solid, palpable darkness. Anti-light. Athena knelt and hugged her father close.

Then the daevas turned to face Hathcock.

<No,> Taurizel Tawrich said. <I don't think we will.> It had no mouth or vocal cords, but there was no way not to hear it. Comprised of something more unearthly—and far more frightening—than sound, its voice slid across the humans' forebrains; oily and deep, a physical presence.

"What?"

<You did not summon us. You could not possibly. You simply managed to catch our attention. Unfortunately, now you have it.>

"Obey me!"

<We allowed you to mistake our patience for the Cup as obedience,> said Zarizel Zarich. <Now, instead, I will kill you.>.

"I'm...immortal."

<Precisely,> the daeva said, picking Hathcock up by his neck.

<If you truly knew us,> Taurizel Tawrich said, <you would never have dared speak our names. We are of the six anti-emanations, progenitors of all horror. We exist solely to oppose the Amesha Spentas, the six divine sparks of creation. My brother is created to undo the work of Ameretāt, the Immortality.>

<Which means I desire nothing more than to kill the unkillable.>

"But...I'm the king of the earth."

<Which I do not belong to. Do you realize most of this earth you claim is made of molten fire? Perhaps we will visit it. All of it. We have forever.> Zarizel Zarich's face blossomed, dilating open in uncountable sets of interlocking, flexible jaws, each revealing even more toothed blackness behind it. Hathcock screamed.

Then there was a folding, a tesseract of air, and they were both gone.

The Cup remained. It caromed off the ground and began to roll, but didn't make a single sound, as if its substance couldn't fully interact with three-dimensional matter. The remaining daeva stooped to retrieve it, but George snatched it up first. It made his hands feel...*divine*. He knew what touching the Cup meant: the waves of pain and nausea were almost instant. But he just needed a second. He fell to his knees, offered up the Cup, and got his plea out to the daeva before the Curse could reach him.

"You can have it. Of course you can have it. But please spare my friends." Taurizel Tawrich cocked his head, then the Curse was there and George was disembowled. It felt both far, far worse and not as bad as he expected. Distant, somehow.

"George!" Athena screamed.

George had the sensation of the courtyard standing up and smacking him in the face. Athena was a split-second too late to catch him. She rolled him onto his back and tried to put pressure on his stomach, but there was nowhere effective to press. His organs were protruding, and his blood was spreading across the concrete so, so fast. Dark, dark blood.

A final jumble of sensations: Athena's eyes were that perfect summer afternoon when George was five, the picnic before Dad died in the accident and Mom started drinking. Her hair was the first night he hadn't been afraid of the dark. Her skin was his first girlfriend's belly button, back of knees, neck, corner of mouth. Her tear was the warm rain the day he bicycled furiously to the hospital, the day his sister's baby, his goddaughter, was born. Her hands on his chest were his mother's hands, warm and dry on the covers, crinkled like used paper, her final touch of love.

Leaving Athena here, his life made flesh, he slipped away.

She adjusted his glasses for him one last time, but he was no longer looking through them. She wanted to cry; she wanted to kill the little demon again with her bare hands. But Taurizel Tawrich was still there, so she stood up.

Louis had stood between the daeva and his daughter while she was with George, holding the final bone bullet before him like a talisman. Athena hadn't missed Hathcock earlier because she'd never aimed at him. Louis had caught the bullet, as he had in the act that first made them both famous. It was their unspoken backup plan, their last-ditch ace in the hole. Of course, that was before they knew what the daeva truly was. Whatever kept it from acting, Louis knew it wasn't the totemic bullet. But he held it up anyway. He didn't know what else to do.

Finally, Taurizel Tawrich moved. It picked up the Cup.

The Cup's guardian dutifully slunk forward, claws clicking on the tile lining the pool's edge, but the daeva simply glanced at the demon and it squelped and ran into the night.

<My brother must kill what can't be killed. I must destroy what is whole. There is almost nothing whole the way the Cup is Whole. We are both blessed tonight. I have chosen to bless you as well. With your lives.>

The endless black depths of its face angled toward George. <There's still meaning to blood sacrifice. And you are both so good at destruction. You destroy everything you touch. In return for this favor, I will one day claim a favor from each of you. You won't want to do it. But you will. Or I will unmake you.>

It turned from them.

<The bullet could not have hurt me. But daring to threaten me with it bears consequences.>

Taurizel Tawrich broke Louis Voltaire's arm in eight places with a thought, then was gone.

Somewhere Victor Hathcock's screams go on and on and on.

Somewhere Taurizel Tawrich waits to ask his favors.

Somewhere George Vane still ascends the heavenly abyss.

But here, now, it's a long, painful stumble back to the car.

THE GODDESS OF FILTH

Genevieve Pearson

"Nice kitty, soft kitty. You don't want to muss up your lovely coat, do you?"

Athena's words were lost on the beast. Silken, black fur, gold eyes shimmering in the fire, the jaguar paced back and forth, an easy pounce away. Athena used to like house cats. She imagined her opinion would change after this. It would be hard to like something after discovering its cousin was willing to disembowel you for the fun of it.

Attempt to disembowel, Athena reminded herself, leveling her makeshift spear between herself and the beast. It was important to keep a positive mindset in situations like these.

Something like thirty-six hours earlier…

The sun was the worst kind of bully, the kind that just kept hitting you over and over again without giving up or getting tired. Hoping for some relief, Athena pulled at the collar of her flight jacket, making a slight ack noise. She was hot.

Really hot. That in itself was odd. This high up, "hot" was not normally a word that came to mind. There was a reason pilots wore a lot of layers.

She sneezed. A rain of snot splattered the windshield. Uh oh. Squinting, she leaned forward to wipe off the windshield, leaning back heavily when a wave of dizziness struck.

Dang it. She should have stayed home and slept this off with soup and crackers in her childhood bed. But summertime was when the lion's share of filming happened along the Gold Coast, and there was money to be made and fun to be had in the lights of Hollywood. This was the time Athena's ledgers typically inched across the thin black line and into the land of "solvency." Instead, she'd had to turn down a gig and go haring off to Arizona to answer her father's desperate telegraph that he had an emergency.

The emergency being that he was being kept in hock at a local gambling hall until he paid down his tab. And just like that, her little black line inched farther away, as Athena had to spend her hard-earned gains on making sure dear old dad kept his right hand.

At least I make a profit out of stirring up trouble, Athena thought to herself, don't know why dad always has to take a loss.

She'd blithely told her manager on the phone she'd be landing in Los Angeles by tonight, ready and waiting to be part of another fight—this one, at least, staged and from behind the camera. Except sometime during the process of bailing her dad out and taking care of business on the home front, she'd stopped to wipe the nose of a wayward child. Damn children, contagion carriers every one.

The dizziness, the fever, the cough—sounding like the tuberculoid cough of some Dickensian orphan—she couldn't keep flying like this. Reaching down, Athena pulled out a map. To the north lay Joshua Tree. Farther south was San Diego, at least an hour's flight and off course to boot. But slightly south was another town, a town on a lake she'd never heard of, San Elaina. At the least it should be quiet, and they said the high desert was good for sickness. Athena changed course.

As she climbed out of the cockpit, Athena felt a wave of heat hit her. High desert was right. She stripped off her jacket and looked down at the pit stains rapidly growing on her white cotton blouse. Lovely. Ladylike, even. Sighing, she poked her head into the office of the manager of the airstrip and dazedly made arrangements to park her plane for a day or two.

"You need me to call someone for you, miss?"

Athena shook her head. "Just point me in the direction of the nearest hotel, please."

"Hotel?"

"A place to sleep," Athena explained.

"Of course, a hotel." The portly man looked at her over half-moon glasses, happily unaware of the oil smudged on his cheek. "Of course." He had a habit, she noticed, of repeating himself. "No hotel here."

"Excuse me?"

He gestured to the cluster of buildings that made up San Elaina. The airstrip was located on the edge of the small mission village. From here Athena could see a small square bordering a fountain, a picturesque little red-roofed church with a bell, a cluster of adobe buildings and a few storefronts that looked straight out of the Wild West. It was a rustic and interesting combination, and she wouldn't have expected the set builders at Paramount to pull together a more iconic Southern California town.

Unfortunately, that didn't quite explain his point.

"I need a place to sleep."

"Ah, well, too small for a hotel. There's a boarding house that way, though, over the drugstore. Mrs. Anderson will fix you up. Sure you don't wanna ride?"

Athena glanced out the window. The town wasn't so far away; maybe a walk would do her good. "Nah," she said, "I'll be fine."

The manager nodded, but she noticed as she closed the door that he was already reaching for the phone.

Right foot. Left foot. Ten steps, Athena bargained with herself. Ten steps and she would take a rest. That was about how far she had to make it to the picket fence ahead. Nothing like leaning on a four by four to make a girl feel healthy and hale again. The dirt road wavered underfoot, and the dust from the road irritated her already itchy, drippy eyes. Athena sighed. She should have known the town was farther away than she'd thought; everything was farther away in the desert.

A Ford rumbled up next to her and idled the engine. The window rolled down.

"You don't look too hot. Or maybe too hot is your problem. You running a fever?"

Athena grunted in response to the driver, "I'm fine."

"I'm happy to give you a ride to town, miss. Or to the doctor. I'd say you have more need of the latter."

"Look, Mr.—" Athena turned. The brown car bore a familiar starred logo, that of a sheriff. The man beaming out at her wore a khaki uniform and a tall cowboy hat. "Officer. I thank you for your concern, but if there is one thing I have learned in life, never, ever, accept a ride from a stranger. Now if you'll excuse me, I'm just going to sit here one second and catch my breath." She'd reached the fence post at last and sat against it gratefully, resting her elbows on her knees.

"Certainly, miss. I understand completely."

Nodding, Athena waved "good bye." The sheriff remained, tapping his hands on the steering wheel, humming along to a song in his head. She got up and started walking to town, expecting him to drive off. Instead, he remained, slowly following her. A few more steps and Athena turned to glare, planting her hands on her hips: "I said I don't want a ride."

"And I said I understand completely. I'm not going to give you a ride, but miss, to put it kindly, you look about as healthful as something my old cat Charlie barfed up. Three residents out of the five residences you've passed have called me in concern for your health, and if I drive off without doing something, I'm going to have the Ladies' Bunco League down my throat. And quite frankly ma'am, the Ladies' Bunco League scares me a hell of a lot more than that glare of yours. So you don't have to take a ride, but if you don't mind a little supervision I'd mightily appreciate it."

Turning to glare once more, Athena found herself facing a young man with a moon face, a freckled, upturned nose, and a complexion clearly not intended for a climate like this. The kid couldn't have been more than twenty-four, too young to be in his position, certainly. But far from being a smart ass, he had the attitude of someone who'd, well, already heard every insult you could lob at him. She sighed, walked around to the passenger side, and climbed in, tossing her knapsack on the seat next to him.

"Thank you, miss, I do consider this a favor to me."

Groaning, Athena laid back, shielding her eyes from the sun.

"Not to bother you, miss, but I swear I've seen you somewhere before?"

Dang it. Was this a come on or small-town chit-chat? Did it matter? Either one was an irritation she didn't want to deal with while she was busy just trying to keep the mucus from running down her face.

"—wait, wait—I got it. Hang on, hang on just one second!"

Athena didn't bother to move as the sheriff dove into the backseat of his car. Paper cups, files, and used oil canisters went flying as he dug through the mess that was the back seat. Finally he emerged in triumph.

"That was substantially more than one second."

"Yeah, sorry," he panted. "I just, I just—hold up."

The young sheriff handed her a much worn, bent up magazine, the kind they sold for a few cents at the drug store. This one was titled Amazing Tales of Derring-Do!, and on the cover was... her. Well, sort of her. A skinnier, bustier version of herself whose hair seemed like it probably cooperated better on a day-to-day basis, but her nonetheless. "Well, I'll be."

Athena paged through the magazine. Sure enough, page ten, there was her name and illustrated self, shown next to her plane. And with it, the story of how she'd fought off fifty Bedouins in a battle to save a Sheikh's young daughter from being a sacrificial victim to some sand god or another. She read the account, snorting softly in amusement.

"Isn't it true?" he asked. "My wife loved this issue. It sure would break her heart if it's not true."

"I'll give it credit, it's more true than you might expect. There were Bedouins, and a Sheikh's daughter, but it was more like five and I was saving her from being sold to a house of ill repute, nothing mystical."

"Nothing supernatural then?"

"Not that time…"

"But you have had experience with supernatural stuff in the past, right? This isn't just a case of 'right place at the right time'?"

Athena shrugged. "More like right place, right time, right hook."

The sheriff laughed and extended his hand. After wiping her own clean on her shirt, Athena took it, and he shook vigorously. "Wonderful, just wonderful. My wife would be so jealous, if she found out I met the famous Athena Voltaire."

"My name's Rick, Rick Goodman," he went on enthusiastically, "and this seems like it's my lucky day."

His lucky day was going to turn out to be one of her worst, Athena wagered as Rick put the Ford into gear and peeled off.

"This doesn't look like the boarding house over the drug store." Athena looked out the window at a low brick building. The sign above the door read "Sheriff's Office."

"'Cause it's not." Jumping out of the car, Sheriff Goodman rushed around to open Athena's door for her. He looked perpetually happy, like the kid in the Pep cereal ads. Now that he was standing, Athena couldn't help but notice that his uniform was both too big and too short at the same time. It hung oddly on his long-limbed frame, like it really belonged to someone bigger and fatter than he was.

"You are an actual sheriff, aren't you? You're not just play-acting while your dad's out of town?"

Sheriff Goodman, and the smile on his face, froze. After a second he coughed, and his face dropped. Athena felt guilty. Then again, the guy had asked for it.

"Nah, I'm really the sheriff. I just wanted to ask your opinion on something,

Miss Voltaire," he said, digging his toe into the rough floor board. "Had a situation I wanted to run by you. Of the supernatural sort. See what your take might be on a little bit of an unusual goings-on in town."

"Is it a jackalope?" Athena asked. "If so, it's just kids. Jackalopes only eat birds in real life."

"No. No it's definitely not a jackalope."

Athena followed Sheriff Goodman into headquarters. At least, she figured, it was a good deal cooler than anything outside, which had to be up in the triple digits. Or maybe that was her forehead. She trailed Goodman past a disinterested secretary who half-heartedly waved at his cheery greeting and request to bring them both something to drink. Athena couldn't help but notice that on the door, under "Sheriff" the name "Goodman" had been written on a piece of paper and taped over, presumably, someone else's name. Inside, Rick motioned for her to take a seat. She sat down in one of the wooden chairs. Reaching into a box next to the desk, Rick pulled out a file and sat down in the chair next to her.

As he flipped through the file, organizing some papers, Athena looked around. The office was barren, almost empty. Yet here was Rick, operating out of a box. He only had one personal item in the office, a framed wedding photo of him—about eighteen or twenty, they must have married right out of high school—with a lovely young woman.

The secretary came in with two glasses of lemonade. As Athena took a sip, Rick placed a pile of photos on the desk. Athena made the mistake of looking down at them and immediately regretted it, as what little she'd ingested tried to reverse course out of her stomach and through her nose. She shoved the photos away.

"Warn a girl, why don't you?" Athena said, choking.

"Sorry." Rick said. "That was my reaction first time I saw one of those bodies, too. Then the second one was even worse."

"Why?"

"This one," Rick tapped the second photo, "was my boss. The actual sheriff. This might surprise you, but I'm, well, I used to be the deputy. Emergency promotion. I'm a little green, but no one else wanted to take the job. The responsibility or the, the ah, risk."

"Can't say as I blame them." Having gained control of her stomach, Athena dared a second look at the photos. Even in black and white, they were horrific. She couldn't imagine what it might have been like to see them first hand, the three bodies flayed and skinless, chests ripped open.

"Are you sure it's not a wild animal? These look like big cat claw marks."

"That's the thing, whatever, ah, ate their hearts," the sheriff gulped, "did it like a wild animal, just digging in. But the skinning, that was human. Knife marks, according to the local doc who acts as our coroner when we need one. Which, until now, we didn't."

"A serial killer with a pet tiger?" Athena mused, "A magician gone mad? What do the Feds say?"

"That they ain't gonna care until I got more than five deaths. At this point, they think we're a small town making a bogey man out of a wildcat. We ain't worth their resources." Rick spun his chair to look out of the double-glass windows and into the main square of town. Athena followed his gaze, seeing a mom walking her two kids, a man on his way home from work and a few other residents about their business, shopping, picking up laundry.

"This town, these people—I grew up with them. I know every one of them." Rick's voice grew hard, determined, "I don't wanna wait and wonder which two have to die before I can pull the Feds in. I want to figure this out now. And Miss Voltaire, I know you're sick, but I believe you have experience with this kind of thing. And I gotta admit," he leaned forward to whisper, "I'm a little out of my depth with this."

"No kidding. I think Dr. Frankenstein would be out of depth with that," she said, indicating the photo. She looked at the photos and sighed. Sick or no, she couldn't just let this kid stumble through the dark. Not when he needed her help. "Tell me more, then," she said. "When did this happen?"

"Once a month, these three months past. Each on a New Moon," he said. New Moon. That was, by Athena's calculation, tomorrow night. Oh, well, this just kept getting better and better.

"Anything connecting them?"

"Not really. Gary was the sheriff, married with two kids. This one is Albert Daniels, he worked the gas station, has a wife and baby now fatherless. And this is—was—Stuart Greendale, a local lawyer, pretty wealthy family. They'd be acquaintances at best."

Athena closed her eyes, thinking. Three men, three different worlds. The question was where did those worlds intersect? Where would a gas attendant, a sheriff and a lawyer all be welcome?

The local bar.

Compared to Los Angeles, this town was a haven of respectability and domesticity from what Athena could see. They crossed through Main Street just as the sun squatted over the church steeple that marked the end of the square, a whitewashed adobe building.

Sheriff Goodman stopped in front of a store with a striped awning called The Toolbox. At first glance it looked like a hardware store.

"Hardware 9 to 5, hard liquor 5 to 2," Rick explained. "Small town like this, the owner decided maybe his place could do double-duty after the Depression nearly put him out of business."

Inside, the store was half-lit. Shelves lined the right side, packed with everything you'd expect to find in a hardware store. But a polished wood counter ran the length of the left side, stocked with everything you'd expect to find in a bar. A friendly looking man with white, slicked-back hair and a blue jumpsuit with a nametag reading "Frank," smiled. "Can I help you, miss?"

"Don't suppose you have chicken soup on tap?" Athena asked, sliding onto a stool and melting onto the counter.

"I'll see what I can do. And you, Sheriff, the usual?"

Sheriff Goodman nodded, and the bartender headed off. Two men sat in the corner. One raised his beer with a friendly salute, "Hey-there, Deputy Goody-Two-Shoes. How you doing?"

Rick turned red: "That's Sheriff, Jansen. And I'm fine, thanks."

"Sheriff Goody-Two-Shoes, that's right, forgot. You want a beer? Or, oh wait, should you call your mommy and ask her first?"

Rick sat down next to Athena, "Keep running your mouth, Jansen, and you'll be sleeping it off in the drunk tank."

"Sure, sure, my apologies, Sheriff," Jansen said, making a "zipping my lip" motion, "No hard feelings."

"Here's your Italian Soda, Rick." The bartender slid a drink in front of the young sheriff, whose red shade deepened somewhere to maroon.

Athena snickered a little. "You know," she whispered behind her hand, "it might help your reputation if you at least pretended to drink whisky or something a little harder."

"Yeah, well, if I cared what they thought, I wouldn't—I wouldn't be Sheriff, now would I?"

Shrugging, Athena turned back to the bar in time to see a mug of hot broth placed in front of her, along with some oyster crackers and seltzer water. "Oh, Frank, you know just what a girl needs," she said with a sigh, digging into the soup. Next to her, Rick looked at his soda, watching the whipped cream melt.

"It always this quiet?" Athena asked. She glanced at the clock. It was closing in on 7 p.m. "It's Friday, isn't it?"

"It's been pretty quiet 'round here lately," the bartender said, answering for Rick.

Rick nodded. "Used to be, the local bars, every Friday and Saturday night seemed like Gary—that's the old sheriff—and I would be getting called out to settle fights or answer noise complaints. This is a small town, and there ain't much to do on the weekends except hang out and get drunk. Except it's been quiet lately."

"Maybe word's out that men are getting skinned alive."

"No. No, actually, things got quiet before that, almost four months past, now."

"I know, Sheriff Goodman." A young woman, pert and pretty, sat down next to Rick, placing her head on her hand in a sign of dejectedness. "It's getting so a girl's gotta pay for her own drinks, and that's never a good sign."

Athena looked at the young woman with interest. Rick smiled. "Want a drink, Annie?"

Annie twirled a wayward curl round her finger. "Only if you'll have one with me, Sheriff. Unless you're still on duty?"

In an unconscious echo of Annie's gesture, Rick twirled something around his own finger, his wedding ring. "I'm afraid I am, Annie. Working on a case with Ms. Voltaire here."

Leaning around Rick, Annie's eyes widened. "You don't look so good," she said, genuinely concerned for Athena. "Did someone beat you up?"

"Yeah, about a million little bacteria," Athena replied.

"Well, I hope you catch them," Annie said, clueless, before grabbing her pocket book and sliding off of the stool. As she did, she was intercepted by a newcomer who'd just come in, a man who suited the definition of "tall, dark, and handsome," to a tee.

"Awfully forward, considering you're married," Athena said.

Turning bright red, Rick looked down at the Italian Soda. He still hadn't drunk any: "Don't be too hard on her, Annie's a nice girl. We have a lot in common, and she, she's just trying to be friendly."

"Yeah, I can see that," Athena said.

In the corner, Annie giggled, quite loudly. The newcomer leaned in close, whispering something in her ear.

"You know that man?" Athena said.

Rick looked over and shook his head. "Never seen him before in my life."

"Could be he's just new in town?"

"He's brand new," Rick said. His frown grew dark, suspicious. "You saw for yourself how long it takes me to get to know the newcomers."

"Well, Annie sure seems to like him."

Rick shrugged, dismissing Annie as quickly as the girl had dismissed him. But still, something rubbed Athena the wrong way. Sure, two people could hit it off at a bar, but the way these two were, it was almost like the man'd zeroed in on Annie.

He whispered something in her ear again, and Annie nodded eagerly.

"Let's have some fun!" Athena overheard as the two slipped out the door.

"Oh boy," Athena said, "Let's go."

"Where?"

"You wanna solve the mystery?"

"Yes."

"That means following your leads. A stranger appears out of nowhere and leads the pretty and clueless young woman off to have some 'fun'? Trust me, that's a lead." Athena felt the world swim as she straightened. Soon, she promised herself, soon she'd find herself a nice soft bed, some aspirin, and a long sleep. But in the meantime, she had a town to help. Luckily, the familiar thrill of danger filled her, giving her a bit of a pick up. Rick nodded and double-checked his pistol before leading the way out the door and down to his car. They slid into the front seat, and Athena pointed to the couple getting into the sleek roadster. "Don't let them out of sight." Leaning against the headrest, she felt her eyes slide closed. She peeled them open with difficulty, "And wake me up if you hear me snoring."

At her instructions, Rick flipped off their headlights as they followed the slick, green roadster out of town and down a winding road that led to the desert floor. The slivered moon cast little light, but the stars made up for it, the sweep of the Milky Way reminding Athena why people liked to live in places like this, despite being miles from anywhere. The Joshua trees stood guard along the road like spikey soldiers, silently armed and waiting to strike.

Ahead of the roadster, a small flicker materialized along the horizon.

"There, up ahead, the lights, that's where they're going." The lights seemed to bob, like lamps on the shore. The highway curved to the right, away from the lights.

"I don't see them," Rick said. "You said they're ahead?"

"Yes, right there." Athena pointed. Rick looked at her, raising an eyebrow.

"Just turn off the highway."

Rick obeyed, pulling onto the barely-visible dirt road that materialized. It should have bumped and jostled them along the way, but instead their trip was smooth, the road well maintained.

"Athena, I don't see the roadster. Are you sure this is right?"

"I'm sure this is the way." She couldn't say how she knew, just that something was pulling her, a curiosity, a sense of intrigue. Suddenly, a number of palm trees of all sizes seemed to rise up from the desert, like an oasis emerging at a genii's wish. They passed under a canopy formed by the palms and approached a man-made arch bridging a short wall made of desert rocks and adobe. Ivy climbed over the wall—or rather, conquered it—in places, heaps and heaps of ivy, and a wrought iron gate beneath the arch was propped open to welcome visitors.

"Did you know this place was out here?" Athena asked, slightly awed. Beautiful, magical even.

"What place?"

"This, this mansion?"

Rick pulled the car to the side of the road and looked at her curiously. "Are you sure you're all right?" he asked. "Do you think maybe someone slipped something in your drink? Your fever still runnin'?"

"I'm pretty sure I'm all right. Can't you see it?"

Rick looked right at the mansion and shook his head.

"Ok, my turn to drive."

"I'm not sure that's—"

"Get out." Grabbing Rick's ear, Athena hauled him out of the driver's seat and slid in. "Pay attention." Carefully, slowly, she drove through the iron gates and into a large courtyard paved with cobblestones and lined with moss. Inside she saw a number of vehicles of all types, arranged in a circle around the fountain. Bordering the courtyard was a mansion, sprawling and immense, with a red-tiled roof, adobe walls and wood shutters. Bougainvillea climbed the walls, lending an intoxicating smell. Oil lamps hung over porticos, and potted plants spilled lush vegetation onto the patio.

"Holy moly," Rick gasped. "Where did this place come from?"

Getting out of the car, he walked a short way up the driveway, through the gate. Then back. He shook his head, an expression of wonderment: "Now I see it, now I don't. How does it work?"

"What I want to know is why I could see it, why they could see it, and you couldn't," Athena said.

"Either way, I can't believe this place was here, right under my nose, this whole time."

"To be honest, see it or not, I'm surprised you couldn't hear it from town."

The mansion throbbed to the beat of the jazz flowing out from the open double doors ahead, the tempo giusto of the human heart. Laughter and chatter flowed with it. As they watched, a nicely dressed couple passed them by, and the woman shot Athena a scathing look. Athena was used to evil looks from other women, but this one was different. Turning, she caught a look at herself in the reflection of the car's mirror. Oh. That was why. She still wore her old blouse, and her hair hung, lank and sweaty. This would never do for fitting in, though it might do for getting a free lunch from the back door.

"Give me a second. Don't look."

Disappearing into the backseat of the car, Athena was happy to see the black knapsack she'd brought along from the plane was still there. Rifling through it, she pulled out her all-purpose little black dress. Checking again to make sure the sheriff wasn't looking—and, living up to his name, he was very conscientiously not looking—she slipped out of her aviatrix uniform and into the dress and some pumps. Then it was just a matter of throwing on some lipstick and running a comb through her hair.

"How do I look?" she asked, emerging from the car.

Rick smiled. "Uh, better."

A little lipstick might not hide the flu, but at least the flush in her cheeks might pass for artificial blush. It would have to do. Grabbing the sheriff's hand, Athena pulled him forward, into the club-hotel-whatever it was. They stepped into a lobby dappled with shadows and lantern-light. Couples passed around them like fish in a stream, dancing, kissing and, well, frolicking. Yes, Athena decided, frolicking. That seemed to be the best word. She looked back at Rick, whose eyes were as wide as saucers.

"You had no idea this was here?" she asked again, skeptical.

"I don't even know who most of these people are. I think there are fewer people living in my town then are in this building at this moment."

Athena could fully believe it. Every second it seemed a new group was coming or going, most stopping by a front concierge desk on their way in or out, all relatively the same age. All seeming to be having the time of their lives, drinking, carousing, some even in various stages of undress.

"May I help you?" A fastidious man in a white bow tie and cummerbund arched an eyebrow with a warm smile. "First time?"

"His," Athena said, punching Rick on the arm playfully.

"Ah, so you already know the lay of the land." Had she not be semi-undercover, Athena may very well have slapped the concierge for the tone of his entendre. Instead she smiled and slipped her hand around Rick's arm.

"Sheriff, I'd never have expected you to have the taste for vice required for entrance. I see I underestimated your…appetites. As this is your first time, and as a courtesy to law enforcement, all drinks will be on the house tonight, though don't go spreading that 'round." The concierge winked, a disturbingly slow change in expression. "Or we'd have everyone asking for favors. I suggest you begin in the lounge, down that hallway, and when you're ready to take a break, come back here and we'll find you a key."

As the concierge welcomed Rick, Athena glanced around the lobby. Scanning the room, she couldn't help but get the feeling of being caught in a vortex, a typhoon of vice and splendor. Everything spinning, round and round an axis…it took some effort, but Athena traced the movement until she found the one object at rest, the center of the axis—another woman. Short and voluptuous, the kind of body one expected to find on an ancient fertility totem, with enormous eyes that glimmered like pools of gold and dark brown hair cascading down her bare shoulders, once Athena found her, she wondered how it was possible she'd missed her in the first place. Now it did seem like this little universe revolved around the one person who seemed not to participate, but simply watch.

"What do we do next, Athena?" Rick asked. Blinking, Athena looked to the sheriff and then back to the center of the room—but the woman was gone. Here we go, Athena thought with some resignation. If she'd doubted before that supernatural forces were at play, well, now that she stood in the magical half-way house to hell, Athena knew that Rick had been on to something. Or else her flu was acting up. Way up.

"Ok, so, this normally goes a certain way," Athena explained. "I show up, stuff happens."

"Stuff happens."

"All right, maybe it's a little more involved than that. But look, you're going to have to do the heavy lifting on this one. Do you think you can handle it?"

Rick looked around. He nodded, about eighty percent convincingly. "Yes. Yes I can."

"Good. You just have to do the leg work, I'll do the rest. Don't worry. Supernatural stuff's drawn to me like a flame."

"Then let's get you a drink." Extending his arm, Rick led the way to the bar.

"I don't suppose they have any Alka-Seltzer?" Athena asked hopefully.

Armed with her Alka-Seltzer, Athena found a comfy chair in the corner of the lounge and settled in. Rick sat down next to her, but she shook her head. "No, no, no. You're doing the heavy lifting, remember?"

"So what's that?"

"That means recon."

Rick stared at her blankly.

"Mingle. Drink. Talk. Drink."

"You already said drink."

"I know. Look, put something in your hand, try to look natural—for the love of god, just look natural."

Rick's expression became pained. "But Athena, there are women dancing on tables."

Athena looked; indeed there were. Attractive women, wearing little more than appropriately placed tassels. Funny how she hadn't noticed that earlier, but she'd been so eager to find a place to sit that tunnel vision must have set in.

"Then go talk to them. You heard the man up front, this is a place of vice, engage in a little vice."

Rick shook his head. "I'd rather not."

"C'mon," she said, "You want to fit in, don't you? See anyone else without a drink here? One whisky, please." Athena said to a nearby busboy. He nodded and rushed to get Rick the drink.

"Ooh," a voice purred over Athena's shoulder, "A bad influence. I like you already." A finger stroked down Athena's arm, and for some reason, Athena didn't punch the interloper. Something about the perfume, the purr, the softness of the gesture just…she couldn't. Instead she turned to see the woman from the lobby, the axis, staring up at Rick with those big brown eyes.

"An officer of the law, are you?"

Rick nodded mutely, his mouth gaping open and closed. "I. I do law. I mean I practice law. No, enforce. I enforce laws. Sheriff."

"Hm. Brave and strong. I like it." The two stared at one another, until the woman pouted. "Well?" she said.

"Well, what?"

"Aren't you going to ask me to dance?"

"Oh, oh, of course! Yes, would you like to dance?"

"I most certainly would."

Athena grabbed Rick by his arm, pulling him aside. "Ok, I know I said blend in, but I didn't say to leave your brain at the door."

"What do you mean?"

"Hello, this chick has femme fatale written all over her. I lay odds at nine to ten that she's the one behind this."

"All right, then how better to stop her than to go along for the ride?"

"Rick—"

"I can handle myself around a woman, Athena. I'm not that inexperienced."

"Sure. And the Mississippi's not that wet."

"Look, Athena, I'll be fine. You told me I'd have to do the heavy lifting." He slid a glance over to the beautiful woman. "Here's me doing the lifting." Looking back at Athena, he flashed a conspiratorial smile at her. Athena stilled. It was the first time she'd seen Rick even hint at an ulterior motive. She wasn't sure she liked it.

"Okay," Athena said. She felt woozy again, so she settled down, cuddling into the couch. "I'm watching your back."

And she did, as the clock ticked on. She watched as he awkwardly tried to look at his date and not the nearly-naked women on the table, she flinched as he tried to be smooth and charming at the bar (and failed), cringed as he attempted to dance. But whatever interest he'd seemed to inspire in the woman, it soon wore off. Not even fifteen minutes after introducing herself, she gave him the slip. Rick went to the bar to get her a drink and when he returned she was gone. He stood there with her champagne in hand, alone in the crowd.

Under normal circumstances, Athena might have felt badly for him. Instead, she felt a little relieved. Rick turned to look back at her, at which point she gave him an awkward "thumb's up." Heartened by this, he dove back into the war zone, a crowd full of cavorting adults all ready and eager to behave badly. Most certainly not Rick's crowd, they were all so enthusiastic that even Athena felt like a fuddy duddy watching them play drinking games, throw down shots, and gamble away hundreds of dollars on the roll of the dice.

Over an hour had crawled by when she saw that, for the first time, Rick seemed to be comfortable speaking with someone. Athena was hardly surprised, though, when another party guest stepped aside and revealed that someone as Annie.

Athena wasn't worried. She'd been in situations like this before. All she'd have to do was wait. Wait and everything would fall into place.

"Now, now, you're much too pretty to be a wallflower tonight."

Right on cue, Athena thought to herself. Looking up, she smiled at the tall, dark and handsome stranger, not so strange, though, the same man she'd seen leaving with Annie.

"Hello there," she purred. Or rather, tried to purr. Unfortunately, in the middle of the "there" her voice caught on some phlegm in her throat. Athena coughed, holding her finger up in a "wait for a second" motion while trying desperately to regain composure and hide the fact that snot was dripping down her nose.

When she finally regained her breath, she looked up. The handsome stranger was gone.

Maybe this isn't going to be as easy as I thought, she mused to herself. Hopefully Rick was doing better. She glanced out at the lounge. Nope. Still exactly where he had been, and still talking to Annie. Goodness, the man was terrible at this. Bor-ring with a capital B. And since when had clubs become so loud? And the smell of smoke so obnoxious? And the dancers, with their twirling and their tassels, it was all so, so, dizzying. Leaning back, Athena closed her eyes, promising herself it would just be a moment.

It was more than a moment. Athena came awake with a jolt. She had no idea how long she'd been out, but she had a surreal moment as she wondered where she was and what was happening. She was in the same club, but everything felt different. Different dancers, different music, different drinks. Trying to shake the cobwebs loose, she stood. She'd like to think her drink was drugged, but she had to admit it was the flu that had dragged her down. Maybe she wasn't as up to this

night as she'd assured Rick. It would be best, she reasoned, to just find him and go, to wait until she felt better and try again.

Except she couldn't find him. Athena slipped through the crowd, looking for that familiar mop of ginger hair, but saw nothing. She left the lounge and headed to an outdoor patio, low-lit with flickering lamps. Nothing, nothing…no, something, there…Annie, Athena recognized the other woman's hairdo as she was locked in an amorous embrace behind a potted palm.

The polite thing to do would be to wait until the kiss was over. Athena was not in the mood to be polite. Firmly, she grabbed the other woman by the shoulder and pulled her aside, expecting to find Rick. Instead, though, a bespectacled stranger glared at her, offended, "Do you mind?"

"Yeah!" Annie said, "Do you mind?!"

"Where's Rick?" Athena asked.

Annie shrugged. "I don't know."

Athena wiped her nose and held it up to Annie. "Do you see this? Do you? I'm warning you missy, I mean business, and if you don't tell me where you last saw Rick, I'm wiping this hand all over your pretty dress."

"Ok, ok!" Holding her hands up, Annie took a step back into the arms of her lover. "We danced a bit, but he kept going on about his duty and responsibility to the town, so I found someone else. The last I saw, though, he was with that woman. She must have wanted a challenge. That man's still married to his wife in his heart." She sighed. "He's never moving on."

Still married to his wife? Athena wondered. She filed that remark away for later and zeroed in on the more pressing issue:

"That woman?"

"That woman, you know, the woman."

As though she didn't need a name. Athena cast her mind back and a face came to mind, the woman in the middle of the crowd. No, no of course she wouldn't need a name. She was, after all, the woman.

"Tell me where I can find her."

Annie shrugged, genuinely clueless. "Sorry. I do know they were going at it pretty hot and heavy."

Muttering, Athena didn't bother to respond. Serves me right for helping someone when I feel like dirt, she thought to herself, he wanders off to get lucky. Goody for me. And I guess he's not such a Goody Two-Shoes after all, cheating on his wife.

His wife.

The station attendant, the banker, the sheriff—that's what they all had in common. By Rick's description, they were all happily married. But if they were so happy, Athena wondered, why come here in the first place? Something wasn't quite right. According to Rick, his boss wasn't the type to come to this place for fun. And Annie, she hardly knew the man she came with, and she'd certainly not wound up with him. It was almost like they were being lured here. Brought here by a secondary force. Like that feeling she'd sensed in the desert, the tug, the draw. A mansion only visible to some, a siren's call to come play, a place that seemed part and yet apart from the desert where it was located. Magic was in force here, definitely.

Looking up at the sky, Athena tried to find the moon. Instead, she saw only a dark shadow. It was the new moon, and Rick was with the woman, the one at the center of this place.

Oh no.

"So you can't tell me where he is?"

The concierge stared at Athena blandly. "No Madame, I'm afraid not."

"But he may be having an affair, right under my nose." Athena sniffled for effect, for once not having to fake it, and blew her nose on a handkerchief, playing the aggrieved wife—she hoped.

"Pardon me, Madame, but considering the locale, I do not understand your surprise. If you are lonely," he said, "surely that will not be difficult to remedy."

"I don't want just any man, I want my man. I want the sheriff." Lightning fast, Athena's fist zipped out over the counter and she grabbed the concierge by the collar, yanking him over so his nose was just inches from her. "Now tell. Me. Where. He. Is."

"You think you scare me, miss? You have no idea, the things I've seen these years. These many, many years."

His eyes darkened, a well of pain and something else becoming visible for a split second before turning blank once more. Athena let loose his collar, and he slid back to his feet, straightening his jacket as though nothing'd happened.

"Now miss, if you'll excuse me."

The concierge strode away. Crossing her arms, Athena tapped a toe. Rick was in here somewhere, she wagered, and she'd be damned if she was going to let that sweet boy get skinned alive.

"'Scuse me, miss." A busboy passed, pushing a cart of room service.

Ah ha, Athena thought.

After a quick stop at Rick's car to change back into her regular clothes and grab her two Colts— which, let's face it, Athena would have to be idiotic to leave behind at this point—it didn't take too long to track down the kitchen. Even supernatural dens of vice and evil needed a place to cook. Everybody's gotta eat. There was so much going on, so many comings and goings, no one noticed as Athena slipped in, grabbing a white chef's coat. From there, she was able to track down a trashcan full of receipts for completed room service orders that various bell hops were bringing down.

It ain't always a glamorous job. Athena grabbed the little trashcan and ducked back out into the hall. Heaven knew it was a long shot, but next to knocking on every door around, or bribing one of the supernaturally possessed, she didn't see many other options. Athena reached into the can and pulled out a handful of receipts, reading them quickly, waiting for something to catch her eye. All standard fare, wine, champagne, hard liquor, the odd order of ice cream or oysters, Italian Soda—wait a second. Athena looked at the order sheet again. One bottle of extremely expensive champagne, one Italian Soda. Both delivered to the penthouse.

Oh, Rick, Athena thought, you stuck up little teetotaler.

The room number led Athena to the top floor of the mansion, down a long hallway to the west wing until she stood in front of a large wooden door with hammered iron hinges. Athena tried the knob, locked.

"Rick?" she whispered, "Rick, are you in there?"

In answer, she heard a groan of pain. Trouble, definitely in trouble. Reaching into her jacket, Athena pulled out a lock pick. It always came in handy, having a lock pick. The door lock was pretty standard, and in a matter of moments she heard a satisfying click as the pins slid into place.

"You're not supposed to be here."

The stranger materialized from the side hall, his tall, dark and handsome taking on a more foreboding air. Athena straightened up and sighed as she realized he was still, unfortunately, quite large. And now he'd managed to place himself between her and the room where, by the sounds of it, Rick was being tortured.

"Look here, Handsome Dan," Athena snarled. "I've had it up to here with being told where to be—you want to know what? I don't care." Her punch caught the uppity man right on the jaw, and he stumbled backwards. She smiled, shaking out her hand. Until he stood back up, same uptight smile on his face, still blocking her way. Ok, take two. This time it was a left jab, hard, to his kidney, a blow that would have sent a normal man to the floor, vomiting. Instead, Tall, Dark and Handsome took one step back and shook his head. And man, now her hand hurt. What was this guy, an automaton?

"Sorry, miss, but you need to leave."

Athena drew one of the Colts from her jacket. "I wanted to keep this simple," she said, trying not to reveal the slight shake of her hand that betrayed her illness.

"Me, too," he replied. Moving quicker than she would have expected, he whipped forward, knocking the gun from her hand.

"Good thing I carry backup." Athena withdrew her second Colt, but no sooner was it pointing than he'd knocked that from her hand, as well.

Athena watched the Colt go skittering down the hallway and out of her reach. Damn it, she thought, I knew I should have invested in a third.

"Ok, ok, white flag. You've got me." Athena put her hands up and turned away.

Holding his arms out, the tall man shepherded her back down the hallway. Pretending to acquiesce, Athena turned away from the room. But as she passed a side table, she kicked it hard, breaking lose one of its wooden legs. Spinning, she slammed the table leg into the side of the handsome man's head like a she'd just hit a home run in a baseball game. The man went stumbling backwards down the hallway. Growling, he lowered his head, preparing to charge her like a bull. As he came rushing towards her, Athena ducked down, this time swinging the wood leg down and around, hitting him square on the shins. He landed hard on his stomach, sliding past her.

"See you." Athena turned, running towards the room where Rick was being held. She turned the doorknob. "Don't worry, Rick, I'm here to—oh—"

"Whoa, whoa, whoa!" Rick grabbed a sheet, covering himself. For a moment it seemed like not one, not two, but four dark haired, dark eyed women looked up from the bed where they surrounded him. A ménage a cinq? Shaking her head, Athena blinked, and the four women manifested into one. Swaying slightly, heat and blood rushing to her head, Athena retreated to the hallway.

"Sorry!" she said as she left. "Sorry, sorry, I thought you were in trouble." She beat a hasty retreat down the hall, back towards the Tall, Dark Stranger, but felt her legs go all wobbly. It was the flu, the flu making her see things that weren't right…weren't normal. He wasn't in danger, just doing what any man might do in his position.

"Wait!" The voice rolled through Athena like molten lava, hot and fluid, with a rough edge of grit. Gulping, Athena turned around slowly. The woman, the woman as Annie had aptly called her, was now wrapped in an elegant dressing gown. A head shorter and perhaps twenty pounds heavier than Athena, with smudged makeup and bedroom hair, the woman shouldn't have seemed like a threat.

And yet she did. Something about the woman strummed with power, possibility. No wonder Rick succumbed. Alarm bells ringing, and maybe her ears, too,

Athena took a step back. "Are you all right?"

Athena nodded her head, "yes." "I'm fine," she said.

The woman tilted her head. "You are not. Your flu is progressing to pneumonia. If you don't get some rest, soon, you might not recover."

"I've dealt with worse," Athena said.

"A disease is not a man with a gun. A disease is more clever, more insidious. It sneaks up on you in the night and drains your strength. Like the frog in the pot, you ignore the growing heat at your own risk."

Lady had a point. Athena breathed heavily, feeling the fluid in her lungs. She coughed, feeling her temperature rise, the world swim. She leaned against the wall, trying to move, to go forward, but her feet felt like lead weights. The woman approached, looking concerned. She placed the back of her hand on Athena's forehead. It felt cool and refreshing.

The world began to narrow. The woman smiled at her, reassuring, as Athena slid down the wall, the dark curtain of unconsciousness drawing closed.

Athena woke groggily to find herself propped in the corner of a couch. The same couch where she'd been before...wait, before what? She'd fallen asleep on the couch, that was all. The flu must be messing with her, the heat and humidity of the packed bodies, the volume of the music, all combining to make it impossible to think.

So then where was Rick? His was one figure she couldn't make out in the crowd. Just like before.

Like before?

Her mind sought backwards, past the feeling of déjà vu, sifting through fever dreams that—wait a moment—Athena reached into her pocket, pulled out a crumpled piece of paper. A room service receipt.

It had been real, not a dream at all.

Standing shakily, she tried desperately to orient herself. Someone was going to die tonight—wait, oh no, was it still tonight? Was she too late? Slipping from the club, Athena rushed outside, looking up at the moon, only to remember, belatedly, it was a new moon. No help there. A cool breeze wafted past and she could smell the soft scent of gardenias in the air, mixed with the heady smell of liquor.

Wait, smell? Athena sniffed experimentally. She could smell again. Her nose was still clogged, but she could breathe through it. And her aches were, well, less. She wasn't her best, but at least she was better. She could stand up for more than thirty seconds without getting tired. Maybe she did just need a little rest, though it came at the worst time.

That woman, that blasted woman had done something to her, made her brain all wonky. And Rick had slept with her, the moron. She had to find him—again. Damn it. Teaches me to let the strange lady put her hand on my forehead, Athena thought. Speaking of which—what kind of person can do that kind of magic? A witch? There were powerful forces at work here, Athena realized. Much more than a simple witch could manage. Not on her own, at least.

First thing's first. A brief search revealed that her pistols were gone. That alone was enough to signify that this was villain territory. Bad guys typically took things like weapons from you when holding you prisoner. Good guys usually let you retain your property.

It took an embarrassingly long time for Athena to find her way back to Rick's room. Wading through the crowds of revelers was no picnic. She made it, though, and leaned against the door, panting. She knocked. "Rick?" No answer. "You in there? If you're having…relations, that's all right, but you should just know that common courtesy demands you leave a sock on the doorknob."

Tentatively, Athena reached for the knob.

Of course the door was locked. And her lock picks were gone, taken along with her weapons. But that was why one wore steel-toed boots, was it not? Taking two steps back, Athena lifted her foot and slammed her heel into the doorknob. The force reverberated through her bones. Another step back, another slam into the wood. Knowing her knees were going to hate her in the morning, Athena kicked one more time. This time the deadlock gave, breaking through the frame. The door hung loose on the hinge.

"Please be decent, please be decent." Athena gingerly pushed the broken door all of the way open. But there was no call of protest this time, no shout of surprise. No noise at all, in fact.

Gingerly, Athena peaked through her hands. The room was empty. Stunning, immense four-poster bed—empty. Bathroom—empty. Armoire (yes, she checked there)—empty.

That was a bust. Athena crossed her arms, tapping her toes. What next? The concierge probably knew where they were, she mused. Maybe she could interrogate him. As she moved to the door, though, she saw what she missed before—another door, hidden in plain sight next to a potted plant.

"Or I can look in there," Athena said to herself. She opened the door. A set of narrow stairs wound down. "Secret stairs, that's a good start." And now she was talking to herself. Great. Sure sign of lunacy, there.

Looking around, Athena found depressingly little in the room to act as a weapon. Deciding it had worked well enough the first time, she broke off the leg of another end table and hefted it in her hands. Better than nothing. Thus armed, she descended the stairs…

Ten steps turned into twenty turned into, well, she lost count. She did notice, however, that as she went lower and lower, things began to feel warmer and warmer, more humid, until a thin sheen of glossy sweat stood out on her forehead and she began to worry she was running a fever again. As she was beginning to wonder if she'd somehow crossed through a Hellgate and was descending to Dante's First Circle, she hit bottom. Literally, not figuratively speaking. She stepped out onto rough stones, in a hallway lit by flickering torches. The walls here were different than the adobe upstairs, more like heavy limestone blocks. A hot breeze flowed through the passage, smelling of damp earth and tropical plants. A strange noise filled the air—a monkey? There weren't monkeys in Southern California!

"Somewhat odd," Athena admitted quietly to herself. Not the weirdest thing she'd seen, but surely not normal by far.

"Oh, Athena, is that you? Hello there." Rick's chipper voice was not what she'd expected. Athena spun on her heel to see an open passageway leading to a small room. Lit by a brazier in the center, the room was filled with rough-hewn furniture of a very old fashioned sort, lots of rugs and an odd, low couch. Or bed, perhaps. Whatever it was, Rick lolled across it in a silky robe, seeming awfully smiley.

"Rick! What are you doing?"

"You're mad at me! Are you upset that I had sex?"

"No, I'm not upset that you had sex. I'm upset that you had sex with the one single woman I told you not to have sex with. What's wrong with you?"

"Well, Maria and I are both consenting adults. And it's been a very long time," Rick admitted, not at all embarrassed. "Almost two years."

"First of all, too much information. Second of all, three men in your town have been murdered under mysterious circumstances. We tracked their last known whereabouts to this, a magical hotel of magic, and you decide that now, while investigating, is a good time to have sex with a mysterious woman?"

"I did. I, I mean, I thought I'd be bait," Rick said, "And you told me to investigate and loosen up."

"I told you to investigate, not be a moron! Bait? Are you kidding me? Let's get you out of here before she comes back."

"Oh, she's going to kill me," Rick said. "She is definitely going to kill me. You should probably leave so she doesn't kill you, too."

"Then why are you just waiting? Come on, let's go!"

"That's a nice thought," Rick admitted. "It's very nice of you. But you see, I drank this sort of hot chocolate concoction and I can't exactly move or feel anything below the neck. But thank you anyways."

"You're kidding me."

"Nope!" he said, "Look." He laid there, head still askew, not moving. "See?"

"Nothing happened."

"Exactly!"

Great. Fabulous. Moving forward, Athena hoisted one of Rick's arms behind her neck, preparing to lift him up. Just then, however, she heard the muffled sound of voices.

"Oh Richard, darling," the woman called, "are you ready for your confession?"

Rick rolled his eyes towards Athena in a Look. She had no idea what it meant. She did, however, know she had no chance of taking on anyone while dragging a 165-pound man around. Gently, she set him back on the lounge where she found him. Looking around, she decided that simplest was best and dropped to the ground, rolling underneath the couch.

"Kenny, will you take him in hand, please?" The voice, soft and seductive, rolled through the room.

The tall, dark stranger's name was apparently Ken. How dull. Athena held her breath as Ken kneeled to pick up Rick. Luckily, neither Rick nor anything else gave her away.

When they were safely gone, Athena rolled out from under the bed. Confession was normally said to be good for the soul, but Athena had a feeling that in this case, it meant death for Rick. She'd have to do something. What that would be, she had no idea. But it would definitely be something. Athena crept along the torch-lit passage, keeping close to the wall, until she reached the door. The area led outside, into another courtyard. Unlike the others Athena had visited in this labyrinthine building, however, this one had an older flavor to it. Gone was the Spanish Mission style. This courtyard had been lit all around with old-fashioned torches, and ancient pinnacles of limestone stood on every corner, carved with square-headed gods and winding maze patterns. Bordering the courtyard, the barren vegetation of the Californian desert had been replaced with unnervingly lush, looming trees with dark, heavy fronds and dense vines.

It was like stepping into another world, or at the least another continent.

Situated in the middle of the courtyard was a large, raised stone dais with elaborate designs carved into the side and grooves cut into the top. A sacrificial altar, she guessed, having seen a few before.

Good to know what genre of bad guy I'm dealing with at last, Athena thought.

Kenny and Maria argued as they arranged Rick on the altar and undressed him down to his underwear, the comfortable bickering of siblings who'd known each other far too long. Rick smiled at Maria as she laid his hands out above his head, not bothering to tie or restrain him.

"I'd like to be here this time," Kenny said. "I think I'm ready."

"Now, Kenny, you know you make too tempting of a distraction. It can be difficult steering her in the right directions."

"But Maria, I want to see."

"I know," Maria said, stopping to touch Kenny's cheek, "but is it worth risking your life over when you're only barely competent?"

Seeing Rick properly laid out on the tablet, Kenny retreated to the shadows, returning with a bucket of soapy water that sloshed over the cobblestones as he set it down next to Maria, getting the bottom of her robe sopping wet. She arched an eyebrow at Kenny.

"Oops," he said. "I guess I'm only barely competent."

"You've only done this for the past fifty years. I've been doing it at least two hundred years longer, since the first Spanish conquistador…"

"…Betrayed your mother and she taught you the dark secrets, yes, yes, I know. But think of all the innovations I've added to this place. I've streamlined your process. I modernized the operation. Don't I deserve at least some kind of promotion?"

"Fine. You can watch, but stay out of the way. Don't want her getting any ideas."

"How are you going to kill me?" Rick interrupted, sounding more curious then afraid.

"Oh it will be perfectly refreshing," Maria said, "like a release of pressure. And then it all will be over."

"Ok," Rick said. "But you've got to stop killing guys from my town. I'm fine, no one cares about me, but some of these guys have families. They need to stick around."

"Don't worry, we don't draw from one town too heavily," Kenny said. "One year and then we move on. We have a very fair system set up."

"Yes," Maria purred, "I do." She knelt next to Rick, stroking his forehead. "Now that you're feeling nice and loose, it's time to confess." She took out the sponge and began soaping Rick down.

"Confess? To what?" Rick said, confused.

"Why, confess to your vice. As you confess, I can purify your soul and you can go on to the next life unburdened."

Don't do it, Athena silently told Rick, don't do as they say.

"Ok!" Rick said cheerfully. "Let's see. When I was four, I stole a toy car from the drug store. My mother made me return it."

"Hmm… A good start, but not exactly what we had in mind, dear."

"Once, when I was in high school, I snuck out of my room and picked my girl up, and we went driving."

"Getting better. What did you do on the drive?"

"We just looked at the stars. Awfully pretty from the mountaintop. Then I took her home. We were so tired the next morning!"

"That was it? Surely you've done more. Especially recently. Like that lovely companion of yours, Athena. Surely she got you to engage in some vice. Drinking, gambling?"

"Oh, well, I took that whisky she gave me and when she wasn't looking I dumped it in a potted plant," Rick said, sounding guilty. "Was that wrong?"

"Damn it, Rick!" Maria said. "This is not what we're looking for! Surely you have secrets, deep dark sins you need to confess!"

A pause. A long one.

"I once lied to my mom about breaking one of her porcelain figurines?" Rick said. "Oh, except I told her the truth the next day."

"Damn Goody-Two Shoes," Kenny snapped.

"I know!" Rick sobbed. "I know, I know. I'm the most boring man on the planet. I can't help it. I was just born that way. Tonight's the first night I've ever done something crazy, if only so I could prove I wasn't such a straight edge. And now I've gone and betrayed my wife."

"Now look what you've done, Kenny, you made him cry. He's confessed, hasn't he? We have what we needed. Thanks to me this boy has sinned enough in one night to make up for a lifetime. Now do you want to see the ritual or not?"

She began to speak in a strange language, but as she did, she stopped periodically to translate for Kenny: "This man calls upon Tlazolteotl. He calls for her to cleanse him of sin. To make him pure and grant him life anew." Maria dropped down, picking up an ancient looking blade from the ground next to the pedestal. Faster than Athena could react, the woman slid the knife along Rick's abdomen. A dark line of blood sprang up.

"Hey!" Athena stepped into the courtyard. "Not so fast!" Ok, no time for a plan, so, here's to winging it. She hefted her table leg, which was looking pretty flimsy compared to the ceremonial machete-blade that Maria held.

Maria looked at her, arching an eyebrow, mildly curious. Blood dripped down Rick's chest, mingling with the soapy water, collecting in small grooves cut in the tablet, flowing to the ground.

"Why, I wasn't planning on going fast at all," Maria said.

"You're not going at all." Athena said. "I won't let you sacrifice him to some imaginary—whatever a Tlazolteotl is—"

"Whatever I we am are?"

The voice, young and old, sweet and harsh, washed over Athena. She looked towards the noise. From deep in the shadows, four women of varying heights stepped forward. They spoke at the same time and yet the voices were unique.

"I we are a Goddess. The Goddess."

"Tlazolteotl." Maria prostrated herself at the feet of the four women: "I beg your forgiveness for this intruder."

"Forgiven." The women—woman?—at once they seemed four and one, turned to look at Rick. Athena shook her head, wondering if it was the flu or there really were four women standing there. "Is this our sacrifice?"

"He is, my Mightiness, that you might dine and grow powerful, and in turn bestow some of that power on your humble acolyte."

"Acolytes," Kenny chimed in. He prostrated himself in the corner.

"And you? Are you not an acolyte? You seem ideal. Vice and righteousness, sexuality and purity, a wonderful contradiction if I we say so."

It took Athena a moment to realize the Goddess was speaking to her. Gulping, she stepped forward. "Sorry, hon," she said. "I prefer not to worship things that take sacrifices. Seems a thing like you isn't fit to eat the dirt off of my boots."

The Goddess-es waivered again, and then they laughed, a noise that rang in Athena's ears so strongly it almost brought her to her knees. "That is as I do."

"She is the Goddess of Filth," Maria said, voice reverent. "The eater of Sins. The purifier of Adulterers."

"And we are hungry," The Goddesses said. The figures waivered again, coalescing into one woman once more and then seeming to disappear. Until a dark, liquid creature emerged from the shadows and into the ring of light cast by the torches. Athena gulped. A black jaguar easily twice her weight eased across the courtyard with languid grace and ferocious potential, making a beeline for Rick.

So that was why the hearts had looked as though they'd been devoured.

"Is this when I die?" Rick said.

"Not if I can help it," Athena said. She crossed the courtyard in a few steps, vaulting over the pedestal to land between Rick and the jaguar.

"Nice kitty, soft kitty. You don't want to muss up your lovely coat, do you?" she said, lowering her makeshift spear between them.

"Step aside. I shall devour his sins. We will eat his adulterous cravings and make him pure that he may have the gift of a blissful eternity."

"That doesn't sound too bad," Rick said.

"It does, it definitely does, Rick," Athena said. That explained it, then, why all the men were married, why everyone had taken an interest in Rick's wedding ring and his wife…his wife.

Who he accidentally spoke about in past tense.

Who Annie thought he should be over by now.

"Wait, you're wrong, it's wrong. He's not an adulterer, not technically!" Athena said.

The jaguar snarled. "I weary of technicalities, vaguely entertaining mortal. The adulterer will be made clean."

"But he's not an adulterer," Athena insisted.

"That's not true," Maria said, speaking up for the first time. "I was there my-self. I participated in his sin. The man spoke of love, of adoring his wife, he wears the ring of commitment, and yet he engaged in sinful acts with me."

"It's true," Rick said. "I love my wife so much. So so so much. And I did en-gage in sinful acts." He giggled. "Very sinful."

"You're not helping, Rick!" Athena said. "Look, he wears a ring and he talks about her like she's alive, but she's not. She's dead, isn't that right, Rick?"

For the first time, Rick's expression changed, darkened. He looked sad. That was the confirmation Athena needed. "Till Death Do Us Part, so it doesn't count for adultery if the wife's dead. Right?"

"Oh it counts," Rick sighed. "It counts for me."

The jaguar sat on its haunches. If Athena didn't know better, she'd say the Goddess was confused.

"Just ask him. Ask him outright. Rick, where is your wife?"

"In a better place," Rick said.

"NO! Is your wife alive?"

"In my heart."

"Rick, do you live with your wife?"

"I live with her memory every day."

"For the love of—Look, " Athena addressed the jaguar, trying to tell herself she'd done weirder things than talking to sentient animals. "Can't you do some kind of Goddess-vision and see for yourself?"

The jaguar leaped up onto the pedestal. Athena spun, ready to attack, but the jaguar was still, simply looking into Rick's eyes.

"He is true in his heart," The jaguar snarled. "This offering is clean. He has never sinned in his life."

"Ha! See, I told you—I—" Athena's voice trailed off as the jaguar looked at her, with endless, deep moon eyes, drawing her in, overwhelming her. Gulping, she took a step back. Now might be a good time to keep her mouth shut, she decided, since the Goddess was after all.

"Oh, merciful Goddess, I beg your forgiveness. I did not know," Maria said.

"I grow weary of your mortal requests. I shall not return to you again. Con-sider my favor, and your powers, revoked." With a swish of her tail, the jaguar turned towards the jungle.

"No, wait, your Goddess!" Maria said, her voice a wail of despair, "Please do not withdraw your favor! I have another offering. This man, here, Kenny, he is rich in sin—"

"Wait, what?" Kenny said.

"Shut up, Kenny," Maria hissed.

"I did not agree to this!"

The jaguar looked back and, Athena swore, sized Kenny up and down. Kenny turned on Maria. "You backstabbing bitch!" he yelled. Grabbing the ceremonial knife, he rushed towards Maria. Maria screamed and covered her face, but the face was not what Kenny was aiming for. Instead, he stabbed her in the stomach. Maria crumpled onto the cobblestones, blood pooling around her, her lovely skin turning ashen.

Taking this as her cue, Athena rushed over to the pedestal. The wound down Rick's stomach was just a flesh wound, she was happy to see. He'd have a scar, most certainly, but would probably live. With a grunt and some effort, she managed to slide the sheriff over her shoulder, quickly heading back towards the passage, only to find herself face to face with the Goddess once more.

"Oh, sin. Blood. Yes, indeed I shall feast." With a snarl, the jaguar leaped forward. Scrambling backwards, Athena yanked Rick aside, but it wasn't them the Goddess was interested in. The big cat fell on Kenny, and the echoes of his screams and Maria's filled Athena's ears as she stumbled, fast as she could, with Rick down the passageway.

The hotel faded. Without Maria's power holding it up, the building began to lose its hold in reality. Athena could tell by the way the walls dappled in and out of vision—one moment she would be looking at stucco, the next the night sky. Her calves and hamstrings screamed as she climbed the stairs, but she kept going, kept climbing. Heaven knew where they'd be left if the hotel died before they could escape. Athena didn't want to be trapped somewhere in between the jungle of whatever place that had been and the California where they should be…

…don't think about that, she told herself, just think about getting back. About bringing Rick home. She crashed through the hotel bedroom and into the hall, grateful to see familiar geography. The hotel was empty, the patrons having already fled as she stumbled at last out of a hallway and into the lobby. Then, abruptly, the hotel flickered and was gone, like a burned out light bulb, leaving her and Rick standing alone in the middle of the desert next to his car.

Almost alone. A moan behind her alerted Athena to another's presence. Turning, she spotted Annie, dressed in a negligee, lying on the ground and seeming very surprised. Sheepishly, the woman got up and dusted herself off. She looked around.

"I don't suppose I could have a ride home?" she asked, voice soft.

"Of course," Athena replied.

After two days of sleep, Athena was ready to head back to Los Angeles. When Rick got back from church, she asked him for a ride to the airfield. He nodded. "Time for one last lunch, though?" he asked, looking at his watch.

"Sure, I'm about ready to graduate to solids, I think," Athena agreed.

They went back to the Toolbox. It wasn't where most families ate on Sunday, Rick explained, but it had the best burgers in town. Sure enough, the bar was packed for lunch with wayward souls who cared more about how crisp their fries were than sending the right image. There were only two seats open, one next to Jensen, who, Athena was beginning to guess, was an ever-present fixture at this place. Sitting down, Rick waved down the bartender.

"I'd like a beer, please," Athena said, "and a burger, too. Beer, Rick?"

"Nope. I'll have an Italian Soda, Frank. Just like usual."

"Just like usual," Jensen sneered, "Deputy Goody--" Rick slammed his money onto the bar. He leveled an ice-cold stare at Jensen. Everyone in the bar fell silent, watching.

"--I mean, Sheriff. Sheriff Goodman," Jensen said, hastily amending his statement.

Rick grinned brightly in response, accepting his Italian Soda from Frank. "Great."

"Look at that. I guess you have a little bad boy in you after all," Athena said under her voice.

"Yeah, well, I can't deny I've done some things. Been some places." Rick winked at Athena. "Ladies like a dark and mysterious past, right?"

"Drops 'em dead," Athena said, "every time."

THERE IS AN EXPLANATION FOR WHAT I AM ABOUT TO DO

Tom King

"Chance is a word void of sense; nothing can exist without a cause."
—Voltaire

Before the story begins, let us praise God. His wisdom is all that can be known. His power is all that can be done. His will is all that is and also all that is not. God is the first cause. God is the last effect. He created the sky and the stars that fly there. He created the earth and the men who wander there. He created what we call good. He created what we call justice. He created a man named Rashid Hassan Mahmud who, in the cruel summer of 1934, in the back room of a small house in Peshawar, India, stood in front of a beautiful woman, ready to cut her throat, ready to watch her bleed then die.

"Please, please, you must let the girl go." This was the voice of the Britisher, Algernon Lewiston. He spoke from the side of his den, near a wall decorated with the heads of animals great and small. Both he and the woman were kneeling, their hands bound in front of them, tied tightly with rope Rashid had purchased that morning. Behind each stood one of Rashid's cousins, a rifle in his hand, the muzzle pointed into the neck of his prisoner.

"Be quiet," Rashid said, his eyes still on the woman. "Just watch."

"My friend, listen to me, listen to reason, please. Let the girl go; she is uninvolved."

Rashid drew the knife from his belt and looked back at Lewiston. This Britisher was a young man, handsome of face and body. It is well known that he had to that point lived a life of remarkable accomplishment. The fourth son of an ambitious earl, he had traveled to India and earned an enviable reputation as a courageous man of arms, a leader among his generation, marked with the promise to perhaps one day ascend to the viceroy, to become keeper of the Jewel in the Queen's Crown. Generally, he was known to his friends as Algy, or at least this is what Rashid had always called him.

"Please," Lewiston said with tears now forming in his eyes. "The girl, please, it is not right, Sahib. You know that it is not right."

Rashid wiped sweat from his nose. He cocked his head to the side. "No, no. You are wrong. It is right." Rashid turned to the woman. He ran his finger over his knife, hooking his fingernail on its edge. The blade was warm, almost hot, capturing the heat of the day, the dry, breathless air that clung to all things that day.

"I have money, my friend. I have more money than you have dreams, Sahib. Allow me to buy the girl. You may still have me. I know that I might not have a price; I understand that, of course, but surely the girl, surely some level of kindness can be arranged here."

"How much money do you have?" Rashid's nail reached the tip of the knife, and he pushed forward lightly, cutting into his finger. He felt no pain, and he pushed the blade in a bit farther. "Tell me about your money. How much is there?"

"Enough. For whatever this is, surely there is enough."

"Enough, yes. And you give it for the woman? All of enough for the woman."

"Of course, yes, of course. Allow her to leave this place, and you shall have riches, all the riches a man in your position would need. You would never wash a floor again, or bring a man tea, or have to beg a richer man's favor. Take the money, let the girl go, and you are the servant no more. The world will serve you, my friend."

Rashid grunted, then nodded. "This is very generous."

"I can be very generous," Lewiston said. "As you well know, old chap. Have I not treated your family well over these years? Have I not met my obligations? What were you before me, you and your family? What are you now? What could you be?"

Rashid removed his finger from the knife and inspected the blood coming from the tip. He wiped the blood across his lip and looked at the woman. Her long hair and skin were darker than most of the Bristishers. With her blue eyes, she almost could be a Pathan. She was sweating from the heat, sweat running down her forehead, dripping from her eyebrows into her eyes. From behind the sweat, it was clear she saw Rashid's stare, but her expression remained passive, almost uninterested. While Rashid looked, she stretched her neck back into the gun pointed down at her, rubbing her neck against the barrel as if she was scratching an itch.

"Please," Lewiston said. "There's a fortune for you."

"All this," Rashid said, stepping forward. "For a woman. She is important to you?"

Lewiston laughed lightly. "No. No, I can't say that she is. I can't say I even know her, if that is what you want in all of this. We only met tonight. I only just invited her here, for a drink, a small ending to a night out. You have been here for years; you would know, Sahib, she is no one I know."

"But you give a fortune for her." Rashid continued to stare at the woman. Though her eyes filled with the sting of sweat, she did not blink. "I do not think I believe you."

"She is my guest, Sahib. Certainly you must have some understanding of that. I have invited her here, to share my wine and my company. As such, she is under my protection. And I will protect her! This is my honor. Of course, you understand this, of all people I know, I'm sure you at least must understand that. And in the light of honor, money is meaningless here; to me it is meaningless. But to you, Sahib, to you it can mean everything. Just let the girl go."

Rashid reached the woman and squatted down. The woman kept her eyes on his. She remained calm, unaffected. "What is your name, please?" Rashid asked.

"Do not talk to her!" Lewiston yelled. "Talk only to me. I am the one negotiating. I am the one who can pay. She is no one. She is unimportant."

"What is your name?" Rashid asked again.

The woman kept her silence, only acknowledging Rashid's question through a slight tilt of her head. She looked at Rashid the way a newborn babe looks at her father, with the lost wisdom and ignorance of one so recently torn from God's grace. Rashid rotated the knife in his hand. He brought the blade up to her neck.

"Talk to me!" Lewiston continued to yell. "Let me pay you! Let the girl go!"

Rashid ignored the Britisher and spoke instead to the woman. "I am here to kill you. I will try to do it quickly. Please know that I have killed many animals. I have practiced." Rashid pointed the tip of the knife to the top of the woman's throat, where her jaw met her ear. "I will start here, and I will continue across." He lightly dragged the blade beneath her jaw line, across the top of her throat and up to her other ear. "I will be quick with it. You may not even make a noise. Some of the animals I have killed, they made no noise at all."

"You're a bloody savage!" Lewiston yelled. "You're all bloody savages!"

"I am sorry for what I am about to do." Rashid reached out and ran his finger across the woman's cheek. The cut from his finger still bled, and he left a small trail of red from her temple to her chin.

"Don't you dare touch her, you savage!" Lewiston screamed. Rashid turned and looked at the Britisher, and Lewiston lunged forward, stretching his bound hands out toward Rashid. Rashid's cousin slammed the gun down into Lewiston, knocking his neck forward, flinging his head back. Lewiston grunted and fell to the floor. The cousin used the gun to whip the side of Lewiston's face, opening up a gash on his cheek.

Rashid chewed on his tongue and watched Lewiston bleed onto the floor. "You should not move. It is not very good for you to move."

Lewiston twisted his head and looked at Rashid. The cousin used the rifle to push Lewiston's face farther into the floor. Lewiston grunted, then laughed through red teeth.

"It is all funny to you?" Rashid asked. "I will do what I have said. You will see. You will watch. Then I will do the same to you. Then you will not watch anymore."

Lewiston kept laughing. "You little ignorant savage, you poor thing. My God, man, I gave you a way out. You might have had money. You could have run, you poor boy."

Rashid stood back up and turned to Lewiston. "I do not need your money."

"You ignorant little chai boy." Lewiston spit more blood through his teeth. "I liked you. I always liked you. You were mine. I would've given you the money. But you touched her, you stupid little boy. Now there's nothing that can be done."

The cousin spoke in Pashtun, asking if he should hit Lewiston again. Rashid nodded, and the cousin battered Lewiston's nose and eye, using the sharp metal of the gun's front-sites to gouge into Lewiston's face.

"You should be quiet," Rashid said. "Just watch."

Lewiston grunted and arched his chin and smiled again. "Now they'll come for you. No matter what you think you can do here. There's an army out there, Sahib. And they will be at war with you." Lewiston breathed deeply and looked at the floor. "They will find you. They will find the family that helped you. And they will line you up against a wall. And they will kill you. Then they will kill your family. It is an army, Sahib. I tried to save you. But they're coming now."

"You should be quiet," Rashid repeated. He spoke in Pashtun to the cousin standing over Lewiston, and the cousin again whipped the Britisher, cracking the front of the rifle into the Britisher's nose.

Lewiston grunted and spit and rested his head against the floor, pushing his nose into the wood. Again he laughed. "My friend, I'm sorry, but I can hear them.

Their footsteps. The Empire is marching to you, my little boy. Mercy, eh? Mercy!"

The cousin asked if he should hit the Britisher again, and Rashid told him no. Rashid wiped sweat from his eyes. "First you offer the money. Now you offer the death. Please hear me. I accept both. I refuse both. I ask only this. You will watch. Then you will also have your turn with the knife."

"Why don't you get me another cup of tea, chai boy?" Lewiston continued to speak into the floor. "I could use another cup of tea."

Rashid stared for a while at Lewiston, then turned back to the woman. Her face was awash in sweat, and Rashid ordered the cousin holding her to wipe her dry. The cousin removed a soiled kerchief from his pocket and rubbed it over the woman's face. She closed her eyes briefly as the kerchief crossed her face, then she opened them and once again stared at Rashid with the same empty glare.

Rashid squeezed his knife and stepped toward the woman. He began to whisper a prayer his mother had taught him, an old prayer spoken by old women that praises of the indivisibility of God, that begs to be taken into that oneness, absorbed in its depths, buried in its warmth, and to take from this warmth the power needed to greet the sun each day and recognize that it too glows with the warmth of God, then from behind Rashid heard a small scuffle, then a grunt, a scream, and the loud pop of a gun being fired.

Rashid turned and saw Lewiston now on his feet wrestling with the cousin, trying to tear away the cousin's gun. As they pulled and pushed, the gun went off again, firing into the roof. Rashid shouted to his other cousin to hold the girl tight. Do not let her go. Then he rushed forward, toward the struggle, but before he could take more than two steps, Lewiston jerked back quickly, throwing the muzzle of the rifle under the cousin's chin. The gun went off, and the bottom half of the cousin's face flew away. The cousin released the gun and fell to the floor.

Rashid rammed into Lewiston, throwing him back into the wall, forcing the gun from Lewiston's hands. Rashid stabbed at him with the knife, and Lewiston jumped back, avoiding the blade. Lewiston butted his head forward, slamming his forehead into Rashid's, opening a gash in Rashid's head from which blood began to flow freely.

Dazed, Rashid dropped his knife and stumbled back, grabbing at the wound, trying to stop the blood. Rashid looked through his fingers, trying to find Lewiston, and Lewiston came around with his tied fists clamped together, slamming his knuckles into Rashid's temple, sending a blinding blast of white through Rashid's head. The room shook, then tilted, and Rashid fell to his knees, choking on blood and bile.

The cousin holding the woman screamed out in Pashtun, saying that he would kill the woman, kill everyone. Though his hands remained bound, Lewiston easily picked up the free rifle and leveled it to Rashid's forehead. Rashid looked up the barrel and watched Lewiston confidently play with the trigger, squeezing it a bit then letting it go. From so close, Rashid could see Lewiston's cuff links, decorated with the brass faces of two elephants, one male, one female, or so he always claimed.

"So sorry, Sahib." Lewiston sniffed in blood and bile. He spoke between rough gasps for breath. "But I imagine we both knew it would turn out like this. It always does, I suppose." Lewiston laughed. "In all the best books."

The cousin screamed out, yelling threats and curses in a language Rashid knew Lewiston couldn't understand. Rashid yelled back at him in Pashtun, telling him to be calm. Please, please, by God, be calm.

"Tell your man to walk away from the girl," Lewiston said. "Tell him to do it or I will kill you, and then, well, then I will kill him. And then the girl will go free anyway." Lewiston nudged the gun a few times into Rashid's forehead. "Go ahead, Sahib, tell him."

The cousin continued to yell in Pashtun, and Rashid screamed at him, demanding he be silent. The cousin allowed some gaps in his shouts, and Rashid explained that all would be fine, that God was still here, even in the middle of all of this. Trust in God, please, remember His justice is in the room with us.

"He needs to get rid of his gun and move away from the girl," Lewiston said. "Quickly, quickly." Lewiston pushed hard on the gun, forcing the tip into Rashid's open wound, grinding pain into the bones of Rashid's skull. Rashid yelled out, slamming his open hand onto the floor, hoping to feel something besides the burn in his head. After some time, Rashid calmed and coughed and spoke to his cousin. His cousin objected, and Rashid yelled at him, reminding him of things he needed to be reminded of. His cousin yelled back, but conceded nonetheless. His cousin threw his gun to the side of the room, and stepped back from the girl.

"Well done," Lewiston said. "Now tell him to come here, sit here next to you. Again, quickly, Sahib. Lives depend on it, really." Rashid yelled to his cousin; his cousin yelled back then came over and squatted down next to Rashid.

"Do not worry, my dear," Lewiston said to the woman kneeling on the other side of the room. "Just relax for a moment. I will have you free fairly shortly. And there's still wine, I believe, good wine, if you'll have a cup after all of this nonsense."

The woman did not respond.

Lewiston moved the gun from Rashid onto the cousin. The cousin mumbled a prayer and spoke of his wife and daughter, reminding Rashid that he had said everything would be fine, that there was no danger here. Rashid told his cousin to be calm. God would care for them all. "There is no worry," Rashid whispered. "Believe in His righteous justice, and I will free you. You will see your family, I promise that. I swear to God, I will save you. Just be calm, please, please."

"Now, Sahib," Lewiston said, "take that good knife of yours off the floor and cut away this silly binding. All right?" Lewiston whipped the gun into Rashid's face, scratching again at the wound. He pointed the rifle back at the cousin.

Rashid grunted as a fountain of pain grew inside his head, dribbling down his neck to his body and heart. He stared at the Britisher and nodded slowly.

"Make an untoward move," Lewiston continued, "and your man here will be as dead as your poor sister is, and then you will be dead as well, obviously. So just be quick and loyal, and you'll be fine. Please, I am a man of my word. Whatever has happened, even all of this, you know that my friend, surely."

Rashid stared up at the Britisher's stolid, carved face. It was a face that held no hesitation or fear, the face they put on the advertisements for the Colonial service, the man abroad, seeking adventure, finding glory. Rashid reached across to the floor and reclaimed his knife. He stood up and approached Lewiston slowly, each movement of his hands made to be clear and obvious.

"Fine, fine." Lewiston tapped the side of the rifle with his thumb. "Do it quickly now."

Rashid carefully put the knife at Lewiston's wrists and began to saw into the rope. As the knife moved up and down shredding bits of golden string, Rashid looked down at the cuff links, at the twin elephants, at the tiny brass waves that wrinkled their skin.

"Good," Lewiston said. "Thank you, my boy, thank you."

Rashid hummed the end of a prayer, then tilted the knife and pulled the blade down and into Lewiston's wrist, cutting deeply into flesh and blood. Lewiston fired the gun, putting a hole in the cousin's head, then Lewiston screamed and whirled the gun around, bashing it into Rashid's ear, folding the ear back into Rashid's head. Rashid continued to hum, letting the music carry the pain out of this little house, through the window, out into the desert. Rashid pushed hard on his knife and cut a little more into the Britisher's wrist.

Lewiston jerked backward, trying to swing again, and Rashid swiftly moved the knife up and into Lewiston's neck, pushing it past the small bump of bone. Rashid released the knife, and Lewiston gargled and coughed, firing the gun into the roof. The handle of the knife sticking out of his neck, red coming freely from the wound, Lewiston stumbled backward; he dropped his rifle and fell.

Rashid watched Lewiston shake and gag as death took him. Rashid bent down and grabbed Lewiston's swinging wrists, holding them tightly. Rashid removed the cufflinks and placed them in his chest pocket, then he let the hands go, let them struggle to remove the knife.

Rashid heard something, a small sigh, and he looked across the room, peering through a haze of blood. He saw the woman. She was standing now, her hands free of their restraint. She looked down at her wrists as she rubbed them lightly.

"Athena Voltaire," she said, not looking up.

Rashid wiped at his eyes. "What?" he asked. "I do not understand this. What is this you say, 'a thing of all terror'?"

"You asked me my name," she said, her voice calm, her head still tilted down. "My name is Athena Voltaire. Two names. Like the god and the writer."

Rashid again wiped at his face, mixing blood and sweat. He grunted and hummed his prayer. Keeping his eyes on the woman, he bent down and picked up his cousin's rifle and cocked it. Tonight he would go back and tell his aunt that her sons were dead.

"The god and the writer. Yes." Rashid pointed the gun at the woman. "The god writer, of course, of course." Rashid could feel the cuff links in his pocket, the two elephants mixing, mating, pressing against his chest. "I am sorry, god writer, I am very sorry, but now I will kill you."

Athena Voltaire looked up. "No. No, you won't."

Let us pause to consider the hero God has granted us. Rashid Hassan Mahmud was the first and only son of Hassan Mahmud Ashem, who worked for his livelihood as a porter in the service of His Majesty's army, living mostly off of small tips handed out from the impeccably dressed officers who forever adventured across our country in those old days. The father was a good man, not strong or handsome or brave like some, but good in the way that all fathers whose hands bleed in the day so that children may eat in the night are all good, are all, ultimately, God's most blessed.

Rashid's few memories of his father come from the times when, though not much more than a babe, Rashid would accompany his father to work, watching his father beg the soldiers to let him help, let him carry something, let him get you something. Yes, sir. Please, sir.

On one such occasion, Rashid saw something sparkle inside a bag his father was hauling. Rashid picked it out quickly and stuffed it in his pocket. Quickly, yes, but not quick enough for his father not to notice. His father took him behind a train and beat him for some time.

"My son is not a thief. To steal from any man is to steal from God. To commit injustice against His creation is to commit injustice against Him. Promise me you will not be this way. Promise me you will love justice as God loves you."

"Yes, Father, yes, I promise."

His father took back the thing in Rashid's pocket, returning the sparkle to the Britisher. Rashid never found out what it was.

Rashid was no more than five when the men came to tell his mother that the father had died. They were local men, an Imam and a retired soldier who sometimes played cricket with the father. An accident, they said; the Britishers were very sorry, they said. The Britishers were offering a small amount of compensation, they said. Rashid asked what had happened, and the men remained silent. When he asked again, his mother slapped him.

"You are the leader of the house now," the old military man explained, rubbing his hands down his white mustache. "You must behave yourself. You must listen to your mother and care for your little sister."

"And you must remember the power and joy of God," the Imam added. "Your father knew this well, and he would want you to know. We are all the moved, and God is the unmoved; you must remember this, take comfort in this."

Rashid looked at his mother, watched her shrink and shrivel into the widow she would now always be. Rashid looked down and thought about God, about the unmoved, then he thought of his father. He wondered what it was that had sparkled.

The money ran out soon enough, and his one baby sister cried for food that never came. She cried day and night as his mother retreated into dark scarves and darker shadows. One hot summer night, Rashid sat up and walked to his sister's crib. He watched her cry, listened to the pattern in the screams created by her small attempted breaths. He stuck his finger in her mouth, felt her toothless grip grind on his knuckle. He watched her quiet, satisfied for a few seconds with this kind fiction. Then she saw through it and cried and cried, and Rashid left the house and started to steal whatever he could.

He was a good little thief. Bread from the blind man preparing his dinner. Sugar from the storeowner flirting with the young boys. Meat from the old Imam who needed only the help of God and perhaps a boy to carry such a heavy load home. He told his mother he had a job, a porter, begging the Britishers for tips. Yes, sir. Please, sir. And when she was gone he would hold his sister, dipping his finger in the thick, red sauce his mother had prepared, allowing her to suck it off his finger, and he would confess to her: "I steal from God, I commit injustice against God; He is the unmoved and I shall always move. I am Rashid Hassan Mahmud son of the porter, Hassan Mahmud Ashem, and I will never stop moving." Sometimes he said it proudly, arrogantly, and sometimes he wept with the shame of his words.

Years passed. Children grew. Rashid stole all that he could. When he was caught, he would run, and he would hide; and when he was found, he would fight, and sometimes he would kill. And always he would return to his family, his sister and his mother, and he would lie and he would confess, and years passed, and children grew.

When Rashid was a lad of only fourteen, he stole from Haji Naseem, a local leader and warrior. Haji Naseem, who was very famous long ago, had his people catch this little thief. Rashid was taken to the desert and beaten for two weeks, then he was brought forward for inspection.

"Why do you steal?" Haji Naseem asked.

"I feed my family, Sahib. My sister. My mother."

"Every man feeds his family. Every man has a sister. Every man has a mother. Not every man steals."

Rashid looked down at the ground, looking at the long wounds covering his naked legs. "I steal from God. I commit injustice against God. He is the unmoved, and I am always moving. I will never stop moving."

Haji Naseem considered this carefully. "My people provide work for the Britishers. There is always need for more workers. You will work for my people. You will be a servant and you will be paid and you will feed your family, your mother and your sister."

"Yes, Sahib."

"You will not steal from the Britishers. You will live a just life in service to them and to God. For now and for always."

"Yes, Sahib."

"Thanks be to God."

"Thanks be to God."

Rashid worked for a kind Britisher family for three years, mostly as a kitchen helper, slaughtering the animals, preparing them for the cook. He did not steal or commit crimes of any kind. He was known to all as a hard, good worker. He brought home food and money to his sister and his mother, and he enjoyed many days of quiet pain and quiet pride.

When he was seventeen, he was recommended as a house and tea boy for a handsome young man of immense promise named Algernon Lewiston. This was a welcome promotion, and Rashid enjoyed his raise in status and income. He began to provide money not only to his mother and sister, but also to his younger cousins living nearby. Oh, how his reputation grew in his village. Here was a boy blessed with the Love of God, the Love for God, truly his father's son.

Lewiston and Rashid became friends in that easy way that Britishers often befriend their most loyal servants. Rashid was a man Lewiston could trust, a man who would listen to Lewiston's moans and boasts as he climbed the Asian ladder. Rashid laughed at Lewiston's jokes as he shined Lewiston's shoes. Rashid cried at Lewiston's pains as he dusted Lewiston's jacket. Rashid nodded quietly at Lewiston's stories as he served drinks to Lewiston and his latest guest, the next beautiful colonel's daughter Lewiston had brought home for an afternoon tea and whatever else might strike her fancy.

Yes, sir. Please, sir.

Generous and grateful, Lewiston offered a fine, respectable job to Rashid's young sister when a servant girl was needed to help with the laundry. Rashid shined with pride as Farah started work at the house. With their two salaries together, they would surely be able to secure enough of a dowry to ensure her a marriage of respectability.

A few months later, brother and sister sat in their home after a day of hard work. Rashid lit a cigarette and sat back and enjoyed his own exhaustion, feeling the connection between his fatigue and his father's, letting that connection extend to the whole world, a strand tying every man to every other man. God is the unmoved, and we all move, but we move together. We dance. Then his sister giggled and reached out and opened her hand and revealed two brass cuff links, elephants, one male and one female, or so Lewiston always claimed.

"My God, my God, girl, what have you done?"

"The Britisher will not notice them gone. He has hundreds. He is such a foolish man."

"No, please, no."

"With them I will have the money to marry. I will marry well. A good man. A Godly man. It is my dream. It was father's dream."

"No."

"I have done what you have always done. What you did for so long. What you always told me. I listened. I learned."

"No. You will return them. You will go to the Britisher and you will confess and you will never do it again. Never!" Rashid hit her. He told her that to steal from one was to steal from God. To do injustice against any is to do injustice against God. Then he left and walked into the desert and cried and thought about something from long ago, something that once sparkled.

The next day, with Rashid standing with her, Farah confessed. Lewiston took back the cuff links and said he would consider what it meant, what the punishment should be. These things happen, everyone understands. He loved Rashid, and he loved Rashid's family, and everything would be fine in the end. Rashid thanked him again and again for his kindness and mercy. Thank you, sir. Yes, sir. Please, sir.

Lewiston invited Farah to meet with him later in the day, alone. After the meeting he called Rashid into the back room and told him things had not gone well. Farah had resisted her punishment, had become rude, then violent, attacking him, if Rashid could believe it. Lewiston had no choice in the terrible matter, no choice at all. Tragic though it was. But these things happen, everyone understands. "Now please, my friend, my Sahib, can you please clean this up. The General's wife is coming for dinner, and all this mess just won't do."

Rashid returned the body to his mother, who cried for days and days. He saw his sister buried, and he rubbed the tip of his finger over the dirt above her grave, and he remembered her toothless grip, her unformed lips sucking desperately, then he went back to work. Yes, sir. Please, sir. A week later, he went to Haji Naseem and asked a favor.

"Your men guard Lewiston. For one night. For one hour. They must look away."

"This is not possible. The Britishers will find out. They will kill us all."

"An injustice has been committed. I will see it answered."

"My poor friend, justice? What is justice? Justice is known only to God. Who can know the will of God? Who can answer for God?"

Rashid hesitated, but he did not look down. "I do not know God," he said, talking quietly. "So I try to stand still. I try to be unmoved. I try to be like Him and understand. I stand as still as I can, I try and try, and still God moves me."

Haji Naseem bowed his head. "You will have one night, one hour."

"Thanks be to God."

Haji Naseem looked at Rashid. "Know this, remember this, if the Britishers find out what you have done, what I have done, I will kill you and your family, your mother, your uncles, your aunts, your cousins. I will deny you; I will conspire with them against you. No one must ever speak of what happens in that house."

"Yes, of course."

"Do you understand my friend, by God do you understand?"

Yes, sir. Please, sir.

Rashid gathered his cousins, two young men who had grown up with Rashid's bread in their mouths. He had taken care of them as a father would, and he loved and trusted them both. They were young, but they would do.

"We will go quickly. Lewiston often has visitors. He is almost never alone. We will capture them all. We will kill them all and we will make him watch, then we will kill Lewiston, and we will leave, and we will never speak of this again."

"Everyone must die?" the younger cousin asked.

"I am sorry. I am sorry for it all, but there is no choice in this. Our hand is guided now, and by God, I swear, there is no other choice."

The boy looked scared; his eyes began to tear and the water caught the midday light. Rashid looked at the sparkle of it all, then he looked away.

The woman charged, and Rashid fired. He hit her in the side and fired again and missed. She reached him and threw her shoulder into his chest, shoving him back and off balance. Rashid tumbled backwards, the woman falling with him, falling on top of him.

Rashid hit at her with the gun, bashing the wood and metal into her neck and head. She reeled back, and Rashid tried to get the rifle straight, to aim it into her chest, to pull the trigger. The woman hit Rashid in his throat, and Rashid forgot the gun and gagged on nothing. The woman reached forward and pushed her thumb into the new wound on Rashid's forehead, inviting a convulsion of pain to claim Rashid, a horrid pulse that sent his arms and legs moving out of his control, twitching with unexplained urgency.

The twitch, though, was enough, bucking the woman from his body, creating enough room for Rashid to kick out at the woman, to kick her where the bullet hit, enough to allow him to squirm and slide away as she cried out, enough to get him to his feet. The gun was still in his hand, and he turned to fire, but she reached out, grabbed his ankle and yanked, and Rashid again fell back into the wood, knocking his head against the hard wood, losing the world for a second and dropping the gun.

His breaths hurt him now, betrayed him, and the woman was on top of him, and she held the gun, pointed it into his chest. She screamed at him to surrender, to stop, to stand still, and she pushed the barrel into his chest, into his pocket, scratching up against the elephant cuff links. Rashid swung at her head and hit her hard enough that she fell to the side. Rashid was on his feet again, scrambling away, looking for another gun, another weapon.

He tripped over Lewiston and fell to the ground, dirtying himself in Lewiston's blood. The girl yelled something from behind him. Rashid reached up to Lewiston's neck and pulled out the stained knife. He looked up and saw the woman a few feet away, the rifle in her hands, pointed forward, shaking lightly. Her face was bruised and swollen, and when she limped, blood from her side dripped onto the floor.

"It's done," the woman said between heavy breaths. "I have you. Don't move."

Rashid stood up, the knife gripped in his hand. He wiped the back of his hand across his eyes, clearing away a mess of blood and sweat.

"Drop the knife," the woman said. "Don't move."

Rashid pointed the knife out. His arm hurt for a reason he did not understand. The knife seemed to carry all the weight of life; all he could do was hold it out there, watch it tremble in his cracked hand.

The woman stopped just out of Rashid's reach. She tried to talk, then she bit her lip and closed her eyes and opened them again quickly. "Don't move. Drop the knife."

Rashid poked his knife out a few inches farther. With his other hand, he touched his pocket and noticed that the cufflinks were gone; they had fallen out somewhere in all the fighting. Though nothing touched him, a sudden pain kicked into ribs and stomach and he fought the urge to bend over and wretch. The pain passed soon, and he looked up at the woman and smiled.

"Drop the knife," she said. "Don't move."

Rashid laughed. He laughed and laughed. "My dear god writer," he said between laughs. "Please god writer, can you not see? Can you not see it? I cannot do both. I cannot." He laughed and laughed. "But I will try; I will try for you, by God, I will try!"

The woman watched him for a while, then she started to laugh too, long and hard, and Rashid rushed forward, striking out with his knife, and she fired into his chest and face, and Rashid Hassan Mahmud fell backwards, falling back over Lewiston. As he died he searched the floor, looking for brass elephants.

Athena Voltaire fell to the ground, holding her wounded side. She bowed her head and cried. She wiped her eyes and sat for a while among all the dead, as if she were waiting for something, then she picked herself up, moaning only lightly, and limped over to Rashid.

She moved Rashid's body away from Lewiston and put her hands in Lewiston's pockets. She found Lewiston's keys and walked to the door and walked out to the front of the house. Outside she found the car Lewiston had driven her in, though all the guards and servants who had greeted them then were now gone. She got in the car and went off, back to the city proper, back to the airport, to the plane, to the sky above.

Later she would ask those who might know, what happened to Lewiston? Who was this man who killed him? Why was it done? She found no answers, only sad looks and a few mild jokes. No one knows. These things happen. This is the price of the life of adventure, I suppose. Then someone would ask her why she wanted to know, what it meant to her. Nothing, she would always say, it means nothing.

And so we reach the end of our story, my friends, and you may rightly ask, why it is told, why now on the edge of this new battle does Rashid Hassan Mahmud's small life and small death have any meaning? But, ah, what answer can be given?

Perhaps Haji Naseem is right, and justice and wisdom reside solely with God, and the stories we tell each other are but that, stories, small distractions from the burden of a man's odd wonderings. Yes, there is perhaps truth in that.

But here I am reminded of another story, one that preceded all the prophets of our God. Let us recall what men once said of the god Zeus, how he mated with a powerful goddess, but feared the potent progeny of such a union and so ate the goddess whole, consuming her and their unborn child. Ah, but the child was then born and lived inside the god. Over time it grew stronger and stronger and stronger until the child became the woman and the woman took an axe and cut through her father's head, bursting fully formed from his head, a newborn god capable of bringing wisdom and strength to her true followers.

My friends, the world fears the story of Rashid Hassan Mahmud. They attempt to repress it, to hide it away, to consume it and hope it dies. But the story is alive still, and it grows stronger and stronger and stronger, and someday it too will take up the axe, it too will burst from its oppressor fully formed.

And they will feign ignorance, and they will ask where this has come from, how could such strength simply appear, and they will wait, and they will listen for an answer, and instead they will hear the laughter, Rashid Hassan Mahmud and his god writer, standing wounded in the den of a small house in Peshawar, India, their weapons in hand, laughing still.

OFF THE MAP

Corinna Bechko, Story by Corinna Bechko & Gabriel Hardman

God, it's good to be in the air again.

Travel by ship is so damn boring. Nothing to do but eat nimono. Pork nimono. Potato nimono. Fish nimono. I have to admit that the IJN was awfully generous to give me a lift all the way out here. And there's no doubt that the Kamoi is a fine ship. But, still. I wish I never had to see another bowl of nimono.

Being on a boat for so long does have one upside, though. It makes getting into the air this much sweeter. Even so, I'd happily be stuck on a ship eating nothing but nimono for another month if it meant finding Amelia alive somewhere down there.

I think the key here is to be methodical. It's been ten days since the Electra was last heard from. Ten days of searching by the navy, the coast guard, American research vessels, battleships, and Japanese seaplane tenders like my dear Kamoi. Ten days without any trace. And yet, all of them must be missing something. Amelia Earhart is tough. Resourceful. In short, a lot like me. I can't imagine her going down without a fight.

So far they've been hunting for her near Howland Island and the Phoenix chain south of there. Which makes sense if she and her navigator Fred were where they thought they were. But as any pilot knows, thinking and being are sometimes two entirely different things.

That's why I'm heading towards the Gilbert Islands instead. One of the crewmen on the Kamoi told me that they'd had random bursts of radio transmission from near there. It wasn't on Amelia's frequency, but who knows? A lot of things can go wrong when you're out in it. I just hope I'm in time. There've been storm warnings for this whole part of the Pacific. We've been lucky so far, but these are treacherous waters. Obviously. Which reminds me…

"Kamoi? This is Athena Voltaire. Flying at 1,000 feet on line north and south. Do you read?"

"Voltaire? Please repeat. Your signal is breaking up".

Great. Perfect. It's like this whole stretch of ocean is one big radio sink.

Am I seeing islands? Damn the tiny volcano-birthed nubs that litter the ocean around here. Amelia could be on any one of them, and they're almost impossible to spot from any distance.

"Voltaire? Still not reading you. Repeat position please".

"Approaching first of the Gilbert Islands, I think. Running on line north and south. Do you copy?"

"…"

"Kamoi? Do you copy?"

"…"

Fantastic. It's just me, myself, and I then. Into the breach and all that. It is odd, though. I didn't expect to hit the Gilberts for a while yet. And there aren't any other land masses mapped through this region. Maybe I should get a new navigator. The old one is showing some signs of stress. Good thing the pilot is still fresh.

Even so, these little rocky islands play tricks with your eyes at the best of times. They seem to shrink and grow with the rhythm of the waves. They move, rotate. Sometimes they disappear. That's when you know you've been fooled by a reflection. That, or maybe you've been in the air too long. Is that what happened, Amelia? Was Fred fooled by a reflection? Did he send you off course, thinking he'd seen the stub end of Howland Island when really he'd just seen the shadow of a mare's tail?

Speculation. What I need are facts.

"Kamoi? I know you probably can't hear me, but I'm going lower for a closer look. Voltaire out".

Some people say that flying over open water is disorienting. That lack of landmarks makes it easy to get lost. Those people are right. Am I really over the Gilberts, or are these islands uncharted? Time to find out.

Well, the first one is real. Real boring. Nothing but rock. Nothing green, no room for so much as a sea lion. Certainly nothing like a protected bay for a water landing. There must be some sort of upwelling nearby, though; that's the third whale I've seen breach in this little patch of ocean during the last ten minutes.

Coming up on the second island now. It's a little bigger, hint of a crescent shape, probably a lot of barely submerged reef just below the surface completing the circle. The dry part poking out above the waves doesn't look too promising, though. It's hardly above sea level. Looks like it might even submerge at high tide. And the green I saw from farther back? Just kelp. Probably a whole host of crabs and snails too, but nothing that looks the least bit like wreckage. Nothing that could support two humans for ten days.

Ah! Now, this third island. This looks more like it. Or should I call it the fourth? I'm writing down third in the log. That last one, after the atoll, hardly qualified. More like a big rock or maybe a sleepy whale getting a suntan than an actual island. This one, though, it looks big enough to hide a plane and a couple of people. Big enough to hide an airstrip even, now that its full extent is coming into view. And what's that, on the western tip? A semi-protected bay? Jackpot!

"Kamoi? Can you read me Kamoi? Found promising hunting ground. Over".

Can it be? Am I really this good? I'd swear that's sun-sparkle off metal down there. I shouldn't get my hopes up. Lots of ships go down around here, run aground, break up and wash ashore. Like that island just south of Howland. Looked like Amelia and Fred might have been there, what with the lean-to set up next to that perfect natural harbor. But next to the bay, just another broken-backed cargo ship, and no humans left alive to tell their tale. That crew wasn't lucky enough to have me on the case, though.

"Kamoi? I'm preparing for a possible water landing. And I apparently like talking to myself, because I know you aren't hearing me".

Okay: methodical. Circle once. Circle twice. Yes, definitely the flipped-nickel glint of a plane down there. Signal. Once. Twice. Wait a minute. Two planes? Four? This isn't right. Pulling back now, putting some space between us. What is this place? It's not on any map that I've seen.

Now, think. If Amelia landed here, we'd have known. Whoever's down there would have told the world. Unless…

Unless they didn't want the world to know they were out here. Looks like they're ready to make my acquaintance, though. Problem is, that's no welcoming committee. That's a full-on Gladiator. Hey, buddy, don't mind me. I'm not looking for your secret base. I'm just passing through, okay?

Holy crap! Gunfire without so much as a warning shot. Now that's just rude. No way you're getting the drop on me in that bucket. Just no damned way. Unless…

Unless you brought friends. Two shooters and a destroyer, just to give little

old me lead poisoning? At least now I know who you are, you bastards. No one but Nazis would be dumb enough to bring a bomber out to the middle of the ocean and use it to run off one tiny plane.

Is this what happened to you, Amelia? Are you captive, right now, down on that island? I could let them ventilate me, fish me out of the drink, but that seems like a harsh way to find out. Maybe I'd be better off getting the hell out of here and bringing back reinforcements.

Damn, that was too close. These boys know their stuff. That Gladiator, I guess that one was mostly bluff. But these two, they're not playing around. Blue sky above, green ocean below. Gunfire all around. Let's see if you're scared of getting your tail feathers full of salt spray. Follow close now. Nice. A little closer and we could reach out and touch the waves. Maybe get a fish to jump in and copilot. But I'm not here to make friends. Now, tight corkscrew up, and see what we've left behind. Just how good are you? Good enough to bring your tail up, to not counter-dip and bury your nose in the Pacific?

Ha! One of you is that good. And one of you is having a meeting with Neptune right about now. Still hanging on after what happened to your friend, eh? We'll see about that.

Not much in the way of cloud cover today. Too wispy to provide any place to hide. What about that island over there, though? It's got a peak to it, and a bit of vegetation. Might be just the thing for playing hide and seek if this Nazi drone is still game.

C'mon, you goon. Ring around the rosy. Oh, you know this game? Let me get just one good shot in. Just one. Now you've had it! Say hello to those whales for me, won't you?

I'm sorry, Amelia, but I'm going to have to bring back some friends if I'm going to explore that base. Guess it won't do any good to radio the Kamoi now, but they'll hear all about it as soon as I get back there.

Except, I'll never get back on this amount of fuel. Crap. I guess I must have been hit after all. This is going to be rough if I can't find anywhere to set down. And I don't like the look of that horizon. The sky there looks bruised. Damn!

Okay, options: I try to beat it back to the ship and hope that my fuel lasts longer than it looks like it will, with a storm cloud riding my tail the whole way. Might get a little extra boost from the wind, come to think of it. Or, I try my luck with one of these little lumps of rock. Not a pretty picture in a high tide. Maybe the one with the peak, where I ditched my Nazi pal? No thanks. I'll take my chances with the weather. I don't like the company around here.

Holy! What was that, a bird? Damn near shattered the windscreen. Goddamn, another escort? Where the hell did you come from?

Oh. Not good. Not good at all. But that cloud of smoke from your nose tells me I'm taking you down with me. At least I can still steer, which is more than I can say for you. Looks like that island with the peak is going to play host after all.

Did I mention that this was going to be rough? I did? Well, that's the wrong word then. I'm flying straight into a storm, barely able to steer, almost out of fuel. Hopefully, if I can reach that island I'll be able to radio for rescue. That is, if the Nazis don't find me first. Let's say "practically impossible." That's more accurate than "rough."

All right. Peak's in sight. Wind is rising, trying to beat me back, but if I make for that little bay I should be able to get a bit of protection. Good. Very good. Almost down now. Coming in fast.

Too fast! No chance of an elegant water landing. Only chance is to curve into that little beach. C'mon, c'mon. Keep your nose up just a little longer…

And… I think I'm in one piece. Everything seems to work. Bit woozy, leaving some blood behind, but definitely alive. Time to see what's become of my crate.

Oh god. How the hell am I going to patch you up? Palm fronds and seashells? I need to plug that monster hole in your fuselage, put in a new strut, get that propeller blade straight. At least! And now, rain. Where the hell were you clouds when I needed you?

I hope that little shadow up there is a cave. I'm exhausted, and there's nothing I can do in this storm. I just pray to whatever gods might be watching over this little fleck of rock that you're sitting above the high water line now. And that this rain washes away the blood I'm leaving behind. The last thing I need is for some overachieving German to follow my trail and catch me asleep. You hear that, little gods? A blood sacrifice for you, in return for a bit of luck. Because I really need some right now.

All right, so far so good. This little hole is dry at least. But I should have brought more of my gear. I must be more out of it from that bump than I thought. I didn't even grab the first aid kit.

And it's so hard to stay awake. There's nothing I'd like better than to lie here in the dark for a bit. It's not a good idea, though. They say a little dirt never hurt anyone, but a grimy wound can be damned annoying if it doesn't outright kill you. I need to patch this up right away.

Speaking of patching things up, I doubt the Germans will fly in this storm, but what about afterwards? They're bound to spot my plane. Is it too much to hope they believe me dead? Either way, they're sure to come looking when none of their boys make it home.

Bloody hell, I forgot about the Gladiator. So they won't even waste time searching for their people, they'll have an eyewitness report about the first part of that dogfight at the very least. They'll know their boys are lost but that I'm still around. That can was too heavy to dance with me, but I'm sure it was keeping tabs on everything. Maybe they don't know exactly where I am right now, but they'll know I'm close. So much for a clean getaway.

What to do? First step: clean these cuts. The one on my shoulder's deep. I can tell even without looking. It's going stiff already. I wouldn't worry if I was back in the States, but out here infection can finish you off fast. I once knew a man who died from a scratch he got on a barbed wire fence. Big burly guy, laughed it off right to the end. No way was a thing like that taking him down. Except that it did.

Step two is hiding the plane. Palm fronds to break up the outline maybe? She'll still glow in the sun, though. Maybe I'll get lucky and this storm will last until nightfall. Never mind. First things first. I can hear water dripping somewhere farther back in this cave. Maybe I don't have to go out in the storm right away.

It's odd, but this depression seems to get deeper the more I look at it. I suppose my eyes are just adjusting. The floor is so smooth that it almost looks carved. If I were more given to fantasies I might be worried. Lava tubes are strange things, though, and I'm guessing that's what this really is. Follow it far enough and it might tunnel right to the hollow heart of this mountain. I'm not going any farther than the light penetrates, though, which is happily right about where the dripping noise is coming from. Clean, clear water, filtered through all that rock above. Perfect.

The wind is still howling out there, but it's blowing the rain away from my little nest. I suppose it wouldn't hurt to wait here for a bit. Wouldn't want to reopen this cut. Yes, that's an excuse, but damn it, I need sleep. Just for a little while. Just long enough to get my head together…

Where the hell am I? It's dark. Darker than it ever gets at sea. And I'm stiff, full of shooting pains, dunderheaded. Feels like the worst hangover ever. Oh, yeah… Search and no rescue. Nazis. Crash landing. Tiny cave… And me, dumb enough to fall asleep after a knock on the head. No wonder I'm not thinking right. It's a miracle I didn't just sleep forever. Now, what really woke me up? Hard to hear anything over my beating heart. Nothing quite like waking up in the pitch-black on what you thought was the loneliest island in the Pacific to what sounds like footsteps.

"You… Do. Yes. You do!"

Jesus, what the hell?

Ooof! Whoever this is, they pack a mean punch. I almost caught that one in the face. What's going on here?

"You. You!"

Don't think. Just get out of the way. Out of the way of what? I can't see a thing! No matter. Zigzag it close to the ground, towards the entrance. Can't be any worse off there.

"You will. You will!"

What is this? No German accent, that's for sure.

Christ! That kick almost took me down. I need light. I need to see what I'm up against.

"Where? Come back! You. Back!"

He's panting now. Sounding a bit more like a man and less like an animal. I can't hear the rain any more. Maybe there's a bit of moon rising. If I can just position him between me and the mouth of the cave...

"I'm here, you buffalo." Damn. He was closer than I thought. Almost paid for underestimating him. Even so...

Bingo!

"I'm warning you, I've got a gun and a clear line of sight." Does this guy even understand what I'm saying? What a scrawny rag of a thing. Completely mad, I suppose.

"Step towards the wall, into the light." How did he get here? Shipwreck? A tussle with those air dogs, same as me?

"Closer to the wall. Now face me." From the looks of him, he's been sleeping rough for quite a while. From the smell of him, too.

"Okay, let's have it. I want to know who you are and why you attacked me. And no sudden moves. Unless you've got something better than a gun on you, you'd be wise to play nice."

"Gun. Ha! Something better. Better than a gun,"

He really is mad. His pupils look like quarters sunk in a fishpond. And that smile belongs on a spider. It doesn't look right on a human.

"So, are you going to tell me your name so we can have a chat like two civilized people?" As if this guy could see civilized with a spotting scope. I'm guessing it's been a while since anyone spoke to him using full sentences.

"Name? Might be Fred. Of course... Fred."

Fred. Fred! Good God, could this be Fred? Amelia's navigator, Fred Noonan? What could have put him in this state?

"Mr. Noonan? Is that who you are? Where's Amelia?" To see a man this changed in just over a week is horrible.

"Mr. Noonan... Yes. Amelia, she's gone. But you should be gone instead. You should meet the monster."

"Are you saying that Amelia died? Where's the Electra?" He's not even looking at me. More like looking through me, that horrible wolf spider expression frozen on his face. But if the Electra is nearby, maybe it can be repaired. Or maybe I can cannibalize it, get one or the other of the crates in the air. God, could this rescue get any more pathetic?

"Amelia's gone to the monster. Told you already."

"Well, how about you show me where? How about that?" This is getting old fast. Maybe I should have him trussed up just in case. No, that won't work. He'll never be able to explain where I should search. Gotta let him actually lead the way. Poor guy, it's like there's nothing of the old Fred left at all.

"This way. Farther in. Farther, deeper, in."

"But there's no light, Fred. How will we see where we're going?" Deeper into the cave? What the hell? Was he in here the whole time I was asleep? Ug. I don't even want to think about that.

"Light soon. Brought flashlights in. But he doesn't need them."

I wish he'd stop with this monster jag. It's starting to make me nervous. Most of these little islands don't have much terrestrial life on them at all. Biggest thing living here is likely to be a wild boar or a seabird, neither of which is a match for a bullet. Unless he's talking about a sea creature. Or maybe just a big ugly rock?

I must be as daft as he is, since I'm following him into the dark. This cave really goes a lot farther than it looks. It comes to a little dogleg just after the pool, then widens out. The floor's almost as smooth as the walls and ceiling. It only tilts a little, not enough to worry about losing my footings. And it's easy to keep Fred in sight since he gave me one of the flashlights. I should be watching for loose rocks, but I'm keeping the beam trained on his back instead. He makes one sudden move and I'm putting him on the ground.

Jesus, what's that noise? Earthquake while we're this far under the mountain? Not good.

"Bombing run. They don't like you."

"It feels more like a tremor to me."

"No. Nazis have a Gladiator. They're bombing to make sure you don't leave here."

Well, that's one mystery solved. Fred and Amelia must have run afoul of that hidden base too. First time I've heard Fred speak any sense at all. Maybe he's coming around.

"We almost there yet, Fred?"

"Just ahead. Gotta crawl."

Lovely. As if knowing there's a whole mountain on top of us, complete with bombs falling on it, wasn't claustrophobia-inducing enough.

"You really think it's a good idea to crawl into this little opening while there are bombers out there? What if it collapses?"

"It won't".

Well, maybe I trust he's really taking me to whatever's left of Amelia, and maybe I don't. Why the hell did they come this far in anyway? All the same, I can't back out now. I've got to know what happened.

"Fred, you know that I'm here to help you and Amelia, right? The whole world is worried about you. You've got to tell me if Amelia is hurt, or worse, so I can help. You understand, right?"

"Through here."

Now, this is a tight fit. This isn't even crawling. This is inch-worming, maybe. Elbow-foot pushing, perhaps. I only wish we were crawling.

The floor feels sticky-soft all of a sudden. I'd shine my flashlight over it, but it's clamped between my neck and my shoulder and I can't use my hands to reach it. Maybe I can angle it down a bit. Damn, wrong way. Now I'm just illuminating a bit of ceiling up ahead. That's not going to help. Or…

Centipedes! White, semi-translucent, almost luminous. They're as long as my hand. And they're everywhere, now that I've noticed them. Fred's even got one on his back. Are they attracted to the dampness in this tunnel? Or a food source near here somewhere? Oh, no. I'm not thinking about that. No. Eyes down, no thoughts about what these guys are eating. No more looking at the ceiling.

Okay. Deep breath. The floor isn't muddy. No, it's covered in centipedes too. The sticky part is their carapaces popping open as Fred inches over them. I'd scream, but I'm afraid of getting one in my mouth. Breathe deep, ignore the chemical, injured-insect smell. Eyes forward, on Fred. Don't scream. Don't scream. Say something instead. Anything. Keep breathing.

"Fred? Why did you bring me into a tunnel full of monster centipedes?"

Monster? Monster! Maybe these are Fred's monsters. Which means that Amelia… No. No thinking. Not until we get out of this tunnel.

"What monster? Keep going. Almost there."

It looks like Fred's unbending, his body and feet distorting from my perspective. His voice is muffled too. Are we through? I just see his feet now, his shoes scuffed and stained with white bug juice beneath ragged cuffs. One is untied, missing the lace in fact. No sock either. How did he lose the sock and not the shoe?

I'm almost out of the passage now too. I feel cooler air against my face and smell the open space beyond. The scent is clean in that way that only places deep underground can be. My arms emerge and I lever myself forward with my hands, wriggling to free my shoulders and hips from the last tight turn of the tunnel. When I'm finally out I look around and notice Fred leaning against a rock pillar, propped up by his shoulder, contemplating the far wall. He doesn't turn around to help me, seems to have forgotten that I'm here. I do a quick check. No live centipedes in my clothes, no obvious wounds besides the ones I already had, and no gun. Damn it! It must be back there in the tunnel where I first shimmied in. Hard to imagine going back to get it. Also hard to imagine continuing on without it.

"Fred? Why don't you tell me what's going on? How did you find that passage in the first place? Someone chasing you?"

"Not chasing. No. Not that."

"Well, then why?" He's facing me now, the desperate spider-smile gone from his face. In my carefully aimed flashlight beam his features are sharp and hungry, but his eyes are sad. He seems to be returning to himself more with each passing moment, little bits of Fredness swooping in like swallows returning home.

"What did you say your name was?"

"Athena. Athena Voltaire. I'm part of a huge search to find you and Amelia and bring you home. It was a valiant effort, what you two did, really one for the history books. But we have to get off this island before your story can be told. Everyone else is looking for you far south of here. I'm your best bet."

"Yes. That's true."

"So, where's Amelia?"

"She's… Not herself. But I think she could be again now that you're here."

Well, well. Maybe this wasn't just a trip for biscuits after all. Fred's already moving again, and I'm right behind him. I can pick up my heater on the way back. Chances are the centipedes won't use it against me anyway.

"Let's catch our breath for a minute," Fred says, shocking me with his sudden concern. Finally, a glimpse of the Fred I had heard about, the gentleman adventurer who was so trustworthy that Amelia Earhart picked him to enter history with.

"Is Amelia hurt? How are we going to get her back through that corridor with all the centipedes?"

"Funny thing about those bugs," he says, looking a bit dreamy again. "They don't seem to bite. Or is it sting? It's like they're just echoes. But I'm not worried about those little ghosts anymore."

He's moving again, but I'm slowing my pace. We're back to talking about monsters and I'm feeling a lot less confident all of a sudden. What the hell am I doing? I'm stiff and sore, covered in insect ick, exhausted, marooned, hunted by Nazis, and seemingly miles underground. I could use a bath, a nap, maybe even a bowl of nimono. Instead I have a madman and a slim hope.

"We're here," he says without inflection, and I almost bump into his back. "See?"

I see nothing, even after playing the beam over the walls and floor. Is he hallucinating?

"Amelia! I've found a replacement!"

Replacement? Whoa, hold on. What is this? I'm backing away, trying not to think about the centipede tunnel and how to get through it quickly. Because this is not right. Curiosity killed the cat, and maybe the aviatrix.

"Amelia! Are you listening?"

I'm running now, no longer caring about being quiet. But Fred is faster. And despite his ten days of isolation, he's stronger. I don't think he could have dragged me all the way here, but the final few feet are a cinch.

Falling through darkness is a terrible thing. For a second I think I may fall forever, straight to the molten center of the earth. A sharp pain against my hip and ribcage tells me otherwise. There's a warm trickle where the cut on my shoulder has re-opened. My flashlight has fallen just out of reach, its glass cracked but its bulb still illuminating a thicket of rocks. I grope towards it, testing my muscles and bones against the floor. Nothing broken, probably, but I'm not at my best either. And I can't fathom why Fred brought me all this way just to pitch me into a hole.

I reach the flashlight and train the beam upwards. Fred's still there, leaning over the lip of the depression, his eyes locked on me. Tensed and waiting. Is this what he did with Amelia? It seems like an awful lot of trouble to go to when he could have just left me to the Nazis.

I play the beam around, careful not to jar the fragile aluminum housing loose from behind the bulb. The thought of Fred still watching, his face hidden by the darkness but his eyes on me, gives me the shivers. It's all I can think about. Until I see movement from among the rocks to my left. An optical illusion caused by stress and shadow? No, there it is again. A shadow that's bigger than any that the rocks are shedding. An impossible shadow. A shadow made of light, cutting through the feeble flashlight beam. I watch as it gets bigger, growing taller, wider, more sinuous. Something big is approaching through a narrow tunnel behind me, a tunnel I hadn't even noticed before. I hesitate a moment, unsure of what I'm seeing. And then I hear it. And turn to run. But there is nowhere to go.

The thing is nearly in the chamber with me now. I feel it more than hear it, a thrumming almost below the threshold of the audible. It's like standing on the edge of a cataract, that sensation that falling water creates, the feeling of movement even when you know you're standing still. It's uncurling into the larger space now, a thing not unlike the centipedes I'd seen earlier, but also not like them. It's translucent to the point of shining in the darkness, huge, slippery-looking. I can't see how far it extends back into the tunnel, but it gives the impression of great mass. And now, improbably, it's gingerly climbing the wall.

I feel the weight of its gaze on me. And yet I can't find its eyes. I search for any sign of a vulnerable area, an eyestalk, a mouth, seeing nothing but segmented rows of appendages. The thing is built like a tank. A horrible, graceful, unbelievable bit of battlefield equipment. Fred's monster is indeed a monster. I suppose it's no wonder he went mad. Poor Amelia. I don't think she stood a chance.

I reach for my gun, forgetting it's lost. Only when I come up empty do I remember the little knife hidden in my boot, but what good is that against this thing? I pull it out anyway; hold it before me more like a protective charm than a weapon. Somewhere above me Fred laughs as the beast rears up. I catch a glimpse of a circular pit filled with teeth between two of its spike-like legs, and a convexity that may be a simplified eye. Not everyone wears their face in the same spot, I think, and stifle a giggle. The giggling is a bad sign. It presages shock and hysterics, neither of which is useful. I recognize this in some dusty corner of my brain and try to regroup, to study the thing. It swings towards me, displaying its oddly offset face, and Fred lets out a whoop of joy. I gamble on the distraction and possibly the element of surprise.

The blade sinks deeper into the thing's body than I would have expected. It is less hard insect chitin than soft snakeskin, a detail that throws me off balance. I almost lose the knife as it throws its weight back onto the floor of the chamber. The bulb of my flashlight finally cracks when it hits the far wall, but my ability to see is undiminished. The beast itself is luminous.

I pull the knife away and spin around, ready to stab it home again, but the thing's nimble. I sense bewilderment from it more than pain as its final yard emerges into the chamber. I still can't quite comprehend how large it is. Coils slide past coils. Segmented legs seem endless. I duck beneath what seems to be its tail and end up directly below Fred. He's watching closely.

"Here, here!" he calls to it. "She's here!"

I pivot, almost fall, turn it into a dive and slide into a tight space between two rocks. My shoulder is on fire, but I can't spare time to think about it now. Fred tracks me with his outstretched hand, pointing and yelling for the thing to find me. He's contorted at the waist, leaning so far over the edge of the shaft that he almost succumbs to gravity, jerking back just in time. The beast lifts its body up, searching. I pull myself farther back into the shadow between the rocks, plotting my next vain move. It's impossible to remain hidden for long, though, with Fred's yelling. He leans forward again, gesticulating wildly. The spider smile is back. Fred the man is gone.

I'm on the move again, darting under a pair of stiltish legs and leaping over a low outcropping. Fred tracks every inch of my progress.

The thing is moving faster now, its body rising higher onto the walls as it whirls around. It seems confused.

"What are you waiting for?" Fred wails, reaching down and slapping at a tail segment as it whirls past. The heel of his palm is still coated with white bug juice and he leaves a cream-colored handprint on its supple skin.

The beast reacts as if it had been shot, standing still as a post but vibrating all over. Suddenly Fred is in the chamber with us, trying to get up from where he's landed flat on his back. I didn't see him fall, but he is at least as stunned as I was after he pushed me in. Without seeming to move, the monster is over him, it's complicated mouth finally revealed. I see whirls within whirls of serrated teeth set in a spiral as Fred screams. And then I'm somewhere else.

This new place is still underground, but feels closer to the surface somehow. A trick of airflow maybe, since I doubt I have a sixth sense for gauging depth. The chamber I'm in is narrow, smoother than the rocky pit containing the monster. I have no memory of getting here. I must have been knocked unconscious, moved, but I don't remember it. My eyes adjust and I pinpoint the light source: a small soapstone globe balanced in an alcove high above my head. It glows with a cold, pale light, illuminating the floor, the walls, and the other figure in the room.

At first I think Fred has followed me. I get up slowly from where I'm sprawled, testing each limb in turn. Nothing cracked, yet every muscle seems wrong, untethered. I feel as if I may disintegrate. And still the figure watches.

Finally convinced that I'm in reasonable working order, I pull myself to my full height. And suddenly Amelia Earhart is embracing me.

"You… you…" I stammer, sounding much like Fred did when I first met him back in the cave during the rainstorm.

"You're Athena Voltaire!" Amelia says, sounding delighted. "I should have known you'd show up, if anyone did."

"What… How…" I manage. "Does Fred…"

"Fred, yes, poor thing. And you, I think you're due an explanation. Come with me," she says, leading the way out of the dusky space.

I follow her along a short stretch of smooth tunnel, emerging finally on a table-like rock high on the side of the mountain. Surf pounds the beach far below us. The ocean spreads luxuriantly from horizon to horizon, its edges a distant memory. We sit in the sun and I realize how tired I am.

"I'm a little surprised you found us, to tell the truth," Amelia says. "But I guess it takes some time to hide an entire island."

I look at her, too exhausted to pass judgment on the extent of her insanity just yet.

"I'm going to trust you now. Trust you with a very big secret. One that I've traded everything for. Are you willing to trust me too?"

She's absolutely charming, and more than a little intimidating. No wonder she's done the impossible so often. She's smart and skilled, yes, but that's only half of the equation. The other half is the woman herself. I'm trying to remain skeptical, but it's hard. I nod, aware of the fact that I would follow her into a burning building at this point. Keep a secret for her? That's kid's stuff. Of course I'll keep a secret for her.

"Okay," she begins. "Forget whatever Fred told you about this place…"

I nod again. "All right," I tell her. "Consider Fred forgotten."

"No! Fred was a good friend and a good man. Don't let the world forget what he accomplished. What you saw here, that wasn't Fred, not really," she pauses for a moment, watching a gull wheel far out over the breakers.

And then she tells me her story.

Fred had indeed misjudged their position, just as I thought. And then they had run afoul of the Nazis, as I had. The important difference was that they'd reached this island first. This incredible island, this island that shouldn't be, that isn't really here.

Amelia and Fred had come down hard, a worse landing than mine. Amelia had been knocked around a bit, and Fred had helped her up past the tide line. There he had fallen asleep. When he awoke, Amelia was gone. Stolen, not by the Nazis, but by something far older. Fred had of course searched for her, and what he found sent his mind away.

Amelia, as far as Fred was concerned, had made a bad deal with the devil. And when I showed up, he became determined to perform a prisoner exchange. But if Amelia dealt with a devil it was a bargain she entered willingly. Her options were few, it's true, but I couldn't help but be impressed by her determination to keep her word.

"I know you weren't serious when you offered that blood sacrifice to the God of this island when you landed," Amelia says. "But it was a lucky thing to do. I might not be talking to you right now if you hadn't."

Fred's monster might not be a God in any conventional sense, but it had been worshipped once upon a time. People living on islands near here would bring it offerings, and, once every century or so, a companion. This was how it kept a link to the outside world. But the people on the neighboring islands had all been wiped out in the last couple hundred years by disease and colonization. Even the memory of what lived on this island was gone. It was preparing to leave its nest to find out what had become of the outside world when Amelia and Fred crashed here.

"And that," Amelia says, her hand grasping my wrist for emphasis, "would have been a disaster. You have no idea what the Nazis, or some other group of crazies, could do with it."

The creature can communicate after a fashion, and is learning all the time from Amelia. It can also pick things up from one place and instantaneously put them down somewhere else. Even big things like people, and planes. Or battleships. Or islands.

Here, for the first time, I became utterly incredulous. Amelia smiles.

"Do you remember how you came to be in that room with me?" she asks, and I have to admit that I have no idea. "You were moved," she says. "I wanted to meet you, to talk to you. Otherwise you might have been moved right into the middle of a rock wall."

I think about this, file it away to consider later.

"But it likes you. Because I like you. It's going to help you leave here, because

I can guarantee your loyalty. Right?"

I nod, and she continues. She tells me more about the creature's history, and why it can't fall into the wrong hands. If its power could be harnessed, it could win a war for whomever controlled it. Armies, ships, bombs… All of them could be moved instantaneously behind enemy lines.

"So why not move you and Fred off this island?"

"I have to stay. That's part of the deal. It doesn't mind isolation if it has someone to share it with. And I knew Fred would talk, send others after me." She shakes her head.

"But you're going to let me leave? And you're still staying, after what it did to Fred?"

She sighs. Fred had sealed his fate when he had slapped at the creature with a hand still covered in centipede goo. Were those smaller beasts its children? A different but similar species? Amelia is unclear. All she knows is that Fred committed a terrible sacrilage. And that she needs to mourn for him. But not just yet.

"You," she says, giving me a sly glance, "need to tell the world not to forget Fred and me. Because I'm vain enough to want that." She looks at me seriously now. "And, you need to keep an eye out for my replacement."

"Isn't that what Fred was doing?"

"Not like that. I know I'm stuck here, probably forever. There are worse ways to make your retirement mean something. But I won't live forever. You just keep your eye out, start really looking around a couple of decades from now. Find someone who's… Well…" she looks out over the water, then back at me. Shrugs.

"Someone who's a lot like us?"

"See, you do understand." She stands up and leads the way down a narrow path towards the beach, and the broken outline of my plane.

The storm and the bombers have done nothing to fix any of the problems I arrived with. No way I can repair this much damage, even if I scavenge half the Electra. I feel hot pinpricks behind my eyes, blink back tears of frustration.

"Get in," says Amelia. "Think you can steer this thing?"

"In my sleep," I say, meaning it. "But I don't know how I can get in the air."

"Let us worry about that."

I do as I'm told and climb in. And I'm somewhere else. Not just anywhere, though. I'm right above the Kamoi, my long-suffering bird just barely flying level. I fumble for the radio, but they've already seen me and are clearing the deck. I'm out of control, coming in fast, but not too fast to correct. The landing takes out part of a wing, a healthy chunk of Kamoi, and very nearly a crewmember. But I walk away from the wreckage, towards clean sheets and a warm bowl of nimono.

What happened? What did you find? Everyone wants to know. I shake my head, mumble about Nazis, and mime the need for sleep.

One year later, and still no sign of Amelia Earhart, Fred Noonan, or their Electra. One year later, and I've not told a soul about what really happened while I was out of radio range for those 24 hours. Oh, sure, I mention that nest of Nazis. And I listened for any word of an island with a single green peak somewhere south of the Gilberts. Either no one is talking, or Amelia's beast really does have the power to hide an entire island.

Oh, Amelia. I still wonder if I could have done more for you. Should I have stayed in your place? You certainly didn't need my help to keep your memory alive. I think the world is unlikely to ever forget you. They've even built you a marker out on the tip of Howland Island, that bit of sand and scrub that you never did make it to. They're even calling it the Earhart light, despite the fact that it doesn't shine. No, it's a day beacon, built to be unmistakably not-a-shadow to anyone flying past during daylight hours. In fact, that's where I'm headed right now. Some people might think it's too long a pilgrimage to make, just to light a candle to a memory. But I know better. I know there are some things you just have to do in person.

A SONG IN THE NIGHT

Brad Keefauver

Peter Mahr never watched the sunsets, even though he had the best view for a hundred miles.

After he had finished carrying the heavy five-gallon cans of mineral oil to the lighthouse's top floor at dusk, Peter always walked out on the observation deck to cool off, yes, he did. Climbing two hundred and three steps with forty-five pounds of weight in each hand was not something anyone enjoyed in the Florida heat, and cooling off in the ocean breeze, even for a single minute, could not be resisted. And his eyes had to go somewhere during that time, it was true. But the sunset was inland, to the west. To Peter's mind, the show in the opposite direction was much more intriguing.

To the east, away from the glorious red and gold skies, was the Atlantic Ocean, as far as the eye could see. And darkness creeping over that vast expanse of waves was what drew Peter Mahr's eyes every single night.

Something about that great, deep ocean. Something about the darkness.

During the day, the ocean kept its secrets hidden from the light, beneath layers and layers of cold, heavy currents. In the darkness, Peter felt as though those secrets might feel free to rise as the dark of the ocean blended with the dark of the sky. And the more anxious among the ocean's mysteries might even scurry to show themselves just as soon as the sunlight left the ocean surface some night. And just for an instant . . . a fleeting instant . . . Peter might catch one of them with his glance.

The lighthouse's head keeper delighted in what he called Peter's "fanciful yarns." But Peter Mahr was not an otherwise fanciful man. Somewhere in his soul, he actually felt like the ocean's dark mystery was going to come ashore one night. And so he watched dark oceans instead of sunsets.

Tonight the whitecaps were coming in particularly fast, and there were flickers of glowing sky on the horizon. A storm was coming. A sudden, chill wind whipped Peter's sweat-damp shirt and he could feel unseasonably cool days ahead in it. This storm looked big enough to cost him some sleep. As the last of the daylight fled not only the ocean, but the land as well, Peter gave a weary sigh, lit a lantern, and began his careful walk back down the wrought-iron spiral stairs. He made his way to the brick cottage he called home and prepared a simple supper. With head keeper Lindquist gone up to St. Augustine with his wife, there wasn't anyone expecting to chat over an after-dinner pipe, so he called it an early night and treated himself to some extra bunk time.

The storm woke him just before the mantle clock struck eleven. Three sharp cracks of lightning knocked Peter awake just enough for the loud booms of thunder that followed to finish the job. Rain was pounding the cottage roof with the sound of a thousand feet marching out of cadence. As he did during any storm of size, Peter lit a lamp, made barely necessary with all the flashes of lightning on this particular night, and went out on the porch to look up at the lighthouse beacon. Even though the storm would cut visibility for any ship at sea to near blindness, Peter liked the small reassurance that his job wasn't neglected. The great lamp still shone its warning far above him. He went back into the cabin.

It was hard for Peter to imagine the chain of events it would take for a storm to snuff that bright candle of his, but the world was full of wild and unpredictable happenings. You could just never be one hundred percent sure of anything.

Peter lit up the pipe he had skipped after dinner, built up the hearth fire, and settled down in his wicker chair to wait out the worst of the storm. He only had three reading books to his name: The Sign of the Four by Arthur Conan Doyle, The Three Musketeers by Alexandre Dumas, and Sir Percy Hits Back by Baroness Orczy. He saved them for times like this, when there was nothing to be done but wait. Some folks liked the Bible for such moments, but Peter saved his Bible for Sunday morning, the nearest church being forty miles north. Besides, God spoke in His Own Voice at the heart of storms, and Peter didn't feel he needed to be reading some ancient's dictation of the Lord when He was at full voice.

Tonight Peter picked up The Sign of the Four, as he was itching to learn how old John Watson met his blonde wife Mary one more time. Dr. Watson was a worn-out bachelor in the book, much like Peter himself, and the adventure that brought Mary to him was quite a tale, full of treasure, savage killers, and . . . oh, yes . . . Watson's great friend Sherlock Holmes. How great it would be to have a friend whose life was full of mystery and adventure, Peter imagined.

He was barely into chapter two, "The Statement of the Case," when a noise caught his attention – a sound, like the cry of a woman, in the distance. He thought it might be his imagination, but then . . . there it was again!

It wasn't a cry of fear or pain. It wasn't a scream. It was more like a calling, like a mother calling for a child whose name he couldn't make out. He carried his lantern out on the porch and tried to figure out which direction it was coming from, but by then it had stopped.

Peter stood on the porch for twenty minutes, straining to hear anything that wasn't rain, wind, waves, or thunder. For one odd minute, he thought he heard an airplane engine, but that, too, passed on before he could focus on a direction.

The chill in the air was actually starting to give him a shiver, so he went back inside, cursing the storm's tricks. Such was the life of a lighthouse keeper. A man with a good imagination could go crazy out here in the lonesome darkness. It took a man whose mind took in only what was there and didn't add anything to it to settle into this life. And that was Peter Mahr's gift.

At least he thought it was.

A few minutes after Peter had settled back into his reading, there was a knock at the door. He ran through the very short mental list of his coastal neighbors and their possible troubles as he got up and headed in the door's direction.

But when Peter opened the door, it wasn't a neighbor at all. It was a woman.

A beautiful, raven-haired woman in a soaking-wet evening gown.

"Can I come in for a bit?" the woman asked a bit testily.

"What . . . uh . . . yes, of course!" Peter exclaimed, recovering from the purely astonishing sight of her. Being soaked in rain and tossed by the wind didn't seem to dampen her raw good looks at all – dried out and dressed up, this woman had to be a stunner.

"How many of you are there? Is anyone hurt?" he said, ushering her quickly inside. Women in evening gowns didn't travel alone. Her party must have sent her for help.

"My pride is the only thing hurt, I'm happy to say," the woman said. "And it's just me, as usual."

He disappeared into the back room, leaving her by the fire, and was back in seconds with three towels and a paisley-and-blue quilt.

"Thanks," the woman said.

Peter couldn't seem to make himself stand still. "I'll put some coffee on. If you're hungry, I've got some bread and corned beef."

"Don't get a lot of visitors out here, do you?" the woman asked as she went through toweling off her arms and legs, then her hair, before wrapping in the blanket Peter had brought. She fidgeted around under the blanket, and soon an arm popped out holding the evening dress. "Could you hang this somewhere to dry. I think it's pretty much ruined for any society balls at this point, but I'll need to wear it tomorrow in any case. I've got regular clothes packed away in the plane, but I'm not going back out in this. The coffee and food sound great by the way. I don't think I'll be making the buffet at the Hotel Ponce de Leon tonight."

Peter started clattering around his small kitchen area, full of jitters he hadn't felt in years. He didn't have a clue why this amazing vision of a woman had appeared at his door, and he didn't much care. She obviously needed a haven from the storm, and even though he'd have given any stranded traveler the same treatment, just having a woman this beautiful in his cabin was a fair enough exchange for anything she might need.

"You were headed up to Flagler's hotel?" he asked. Henry Flagler was a Standard Oil millionaire who built a showplace of a hotel up in St. Augustine. "That's still a ways off, especially dressed like that."

"You have a name, friend?" she asked.

"Oh . . . sorry," Peter stammered, wiped his hand on his pants and stuck it out hesitantly, like he was afraid she might bite it. "Peter, Peter Mahr."

"Athena Voltaire," she replied, giving it a quick, rough shake. "You're with the Lighthouse Service, I take it?"

"That's right," Peter exclaimed as he went back to his fixings. He didn't say anything more until he had the coffee and a plate slid in front of her. She had been standing by the fire, but after taking the plate, she settled back in his basket chair. Her long, tan legs slid out of the blanket wrapping as she sat, and Peter tried not to stare. But he was a man, and he couldn't help where his eyes wanted to go.

"Go ahead, look all you want. This isn't the Folies Bergère, but I know men. I know what makes them tick, and I know how to put one down if need be. You seem like a decent enough fellow." Athena produced a pistol from under her blanket and set it on the little table next to her. "But trust me, this gun isn't the most dangerous thing I've got under this blanket."

The lighthouse keeper laughed, which seemed to surprise Athena Voltaire a bit.

"You are wonderful, if you don't mind me saying so," he said, "like somebody from a story. It has got to be one wild adventure that got you here, I'm sure of it." Peter pulled up a chair and leaned forward, eyes more eager for her story than anything else she might have been concerned about. "Pardon my manners, Miss Voltaire, but like you say, I'm a bit isolated and am glad to hear anything come out of a human mouth other than my own."

Athena nodded, dipped some corned beef in the gob of mustard he had put on her plate and ate it. After she had a long sip of the hot coffee, she seemed satisfied enough to start her tale.

"As a member of the Lighthouse Service, are you duty bound to report any and all infractions of U.S. law that you might hear of?"

Peter puzzled over that for a second. "Not unless it really needs reporting, I guess."

"Good enough," she replied. "Probably wouldn't do you much good to report it anyway, considering how rich the fellow is that I'm working for. He'd just buy off any judge who wasn't already on his guest list. He's certainly paying me enough to do something as blasted stupid as wearing a Jeann Lanvin gown to fly a plane."

Peter grinned at the word "plane." This was a story straight out of a dime novel. This girl was a regular Pat Savage.

"The job was to fly a seaplane out of Havana with a case of old Don Facundo Bacardi's private blend of rum. I was supposed to land the plane at the start of the cocktail hour in a private cove – put on a show for the guests on how old man Flagler spared no expense for their refreshment. Bet he was eight kinds of furious when his show didn't happen as planned. I'm not sure where this weather came from, but I've been fighting it all the way up the coast. Used up too much fuel, couldn't get above it, no part of this trip worked.

"Finally got to the point where I had to land, and I saw your lighthouse. Got the plane down in the inlet and actually drove it up the marshy side onto ground without dumping it over. Tied the thing down as best I could, and here I am."

"I heard your plane at one point," Peter said. "Think I might have heard you, too, yelling for something. But the order was wrong. Seems like I should have heard the plane first."

"Well, I sure wasn't quiet about having to put down in this mess," Athena admitted. "I'm a flier at heart, not a lander."

"Are you going to have enough fuel to take off in the morning, or are we going to have to get some brought down?" Getting fuel brought down might take a couple of days, and the thought of having her as a houseguest for that long didn't bother Peter at all. Not at all.

"That's for morning," Athena said with a yawn. She set the plate on the floor and curled up in the basket chair. "This will do fine for me 'til then. You might as well get some sleep yourself."

"Sleep would be a welcome thing," Peter replied. The loudest parts of the storm had moved on, leaving an easy howl of wind and a steady drum of rain, fine for sleeping. He took Athena's plate and cup, went out for one more look at the lighthouse beacon, and went to bed.

He let warm and cozy thoughts of his houseguest lull him to sleep. Athena Voltaire did that to men a lot, he imagined, filling their heads with dreamy thoughts that took the place of lullabies when the male of the species got its whiskers and sundry other grown man bits. And there, somewhere, on the edge of sleep, a female voice called to Peter. The voice called soft and sweet, like he always thought a lover would. His mouth began to form an answer, and as that answer began, the sound of his own voice brought him fully awake.

Peter jumped to his feet.

He heard the voice again. It was the calling he heard earlier, before the plane.

He pulled on his pants to make sure he had proper coverage and ran barefoot into the main room, where Athena was already upright, gun in hand, exclaiming, "What the Hell?"

"Sounds like someone else needs some help," Peter answered and got his lamp going.

Athena gave him a look like he was crazy. "What are you talking about?"

"There's a lady out there in trouble. You heard it."

"I didn't hear a lady, that's for damn sure. I'm not sure what in creation that awful sound was, but I know what human sounds like and that wasn't it!"

Peter headed for the door, and Athena followed, producing another pistol and still managing to hold the blanket around her by crossing her arms over her chest with a corner of the quilt wrapped around each gun handle. With the only male for miles safely in front of her on the porch, Athena took advantage of being behind him to stretch the quilt out like a cape and rewrap herself.

As the blanket swept out like great blue wings on either side of a definitely female form in all its glory, a shrill angry cry came out of the night.

"Crap!" Athena shouted. "What kind of things run wild up here?"

Peter was visibly shaken. "I've never heard anything like that before."

It sounded inhuman, like what Athena described before. It sounded female, if that made any sense, but surely not human.

The high, angry wail came again, only this time it was answered by a multitude of lower voices, syllables that sounded wet and sloppily spoken, like a thousand fat men with mouths full of soup, mumbled and indistinct. They seemed to be coming from everywhere. Not loud. Not as angry as the female thing. Just low, insistent, and determined.

"Back in the cabin!" Peter shouted.

"No, the lighthouse!" Athena shouted back, starting to run off the porch. "The lighthouse doesn't have windows on the ground!"

Peter ran after her, and from the edges of the lighthouse grounds dark figures started closing in on them. Dark legions were coming out of the brush, splashing through the rain-soaked grass as one dark, wet mass. Peter caught up to Athena at the lighthouse door, which they wrenched open together. As they slammed it shut behind them, throwing the heavy latch, a great thud of bodies hit the other side, seeming to jolt the door loose in its hinges.

"You piss off the local chapter of the Klan?" Athena asked as they put their combined weight against the door.

"I don't think those were people," Peter breathed in disbelief. He'd seen glimpses of their pursuers, like faceless hunchbacks in dark, shiny-slick leather cloaks of some sort. They seemed to have two legs, but they had ambled oddly in short strides, like their ankles were chained. Those were all the details he had picked up, and his mind just didn't know what to do with them.

After another token pounding or two, the assault on the door let up. A low chant took it's place . . . at least it seemed like a chant. The legion of flawed voices mumbling as one didn't really sound like anything human beings did as a communal activity.

Athena looked up the center of the high corkscrew of stairs that wound up the lighthouse's full height. "Is there any way to block the stairs up there?"

"We could close ourselves off on the lantern deck, but we'd be trapped there."

Athena laughed. "I have news for you, my friend, we're trapped right now."

The lighthouse keeper nodded and headed up the stairs. As they made their way up the great spiral of iron stairs as quickly as they could move, Peter heard the female voice again in the distance.

It was singing.

"What kind of thing makes a noise like that?" Athena shouted over the storm, the thudding of their feet against metal, and the sounds of whatever the small army was outside. "Sounds like a . . . well, I don't know what it sounds like, but it sure doesn't sound right!"

"It's singing!" the lighthouse keeper shouted back.

"Like Hell!"

On up they went, with the single intention of getting to the top. Just before they got to the lantern deck, however, Peter stopped and went out to the gallery deck where there was a railed, but otherwise unprotected walkway circling the lighthouse. It was wet and dangerous in a storm, but he had to go out, he had to try to look down.

He had to see where that singing was coming from.

"What are you doing?" the blanket-wrapped Athena yelled at him.

Peter didn't answer, just went to the railing and tried hard to make out details of the dark, moving figures below. It wasn't a moment before he saw the source of the mysterious song that drew his attention so – it was the porch of his own red brick cottage. It looked for all the world like a pale, beautiful woman was there, standing naked, except for a blue cape which hung from her outstretched arms like a pair of wings. And she was singing to him. What in the heck was he doing up here in the lighthouse? he instinctively wondered, getting a sudden and consuming urge to head back down the stairs right now.

He turned and left the gallery deck, only to run right into a not-so-pale, naked woman who was holding her blue blanket more modestly wrapped around her, with a gun in each hand. She transferred both guns to one hand, let the blanket half-fall away, and smacked him hard in the side of the head.

"Blast it, Mahr, what is wrong with you?"

Peter shook off the pain of the whack in the head, confused.

"Let's get up to the lantern deck and close it off," he said. But the singing . . . the singing was telling him otherwise.

They climbed to the next level, closed it off, and sat on the floor, underneath the beam of the great lantern and its first-order Fresnel lens whose prismatic surfaces spread the light so far.

"I get the feeling that you're in touch with something that I'm not," Athena said once they'd settled in, waiting to hear the sound of a breaking door far below and the clamor of feet pounding up the stairs after them. "What is going on?"

"There's a woman on the cabin porch, singing to me," Mahr replied. "That's the only way I can say it, even though I know it makes me sound crazy."

"There's a woman with that bunch? I could've sworn they were chasing me like they hadn't seen one in a long while."

"I get the feeling she's their boss. I think you riled her up when you came out on the porch, like she wasn't expecting another woman here."

Athena furrowed her brow in puzzlement. "Beats me how you keep thinking there's some woman here. All I've heard is some of the damnedest animal noises I've ever heard. I think maybe you've been out here alone too long."

"I'm not here alone most of the time. The head keeper and his wife are here, and we get a few visitors. And while Mrs. Lindquist isn't any young man's idea of a looker, she does stand as a reminder of what a woman does look and sound like."

"When you came off of that deck, you looked like a man possessed. Your eyes were wild like I've seen a fellow or two go on peyote or some exotic mushrooms. Something down there is working your brain, Mr. Mahr."

Peter believed her. The singing was still going on, trying to slip into the corners of his brain via his ears, but Athena's words were keeping his thoughts tethered to reality. His mind couldn't be lulled into the place the song wanted it to be as long as her voice distracted him with its own charm and her words kept his human intelligence from going to sleep on him.

"Keep talking, Miss Voltaire," he told her. "I think it's all that's keeping my mind together. But feel free to whack me again if'n you need to."

She smiled. "Think waiting here until morning will do the trick?"

"Your guess is as good as mine. I have no idea what or who that is down there. Never had its like show up here before, or even heard of such a thing. Florida's got a lot of swamp and wild country, but . . ."

Mahr shrugged.

"Florida," Athena said slowly, with each syllable taking its time on her tongue. "You know, I've heard stories about this place now that I take a minute. This wasn't my first trip to Cuba, and there are remnants of the original natives of Florida down there. Timucua is what we call them now, but not what they call themselves. The old ones that are left keep to themselves, but I managed to spend time with one of their last medicine men. He told me a lot of tales, but the one I think you'd be most interested in is about the chiefs who went what he called quana ibi."

"Those don't seem like any Indians I ever saw down there," Peter said.

"The Indians aren't down there . . . the one I'm talking about is up here. I think you're going quana ibi."

"You can call crazy 'crazy,' Miss Voltaire."

"Hold on, Mahr. You'll be calling me crazy in a second. I didn't think too much of the tale when I first heard it, because it's almost the same story any sea-going soul knows that came down from the Greeks and Romans. You've heard of the sea-sirens, haven't you?"

Peter was silent for a second, letting himself listen to the song that came rushing too-quickly back into his brain. He shook his head hard, trying to shake it out.

"I'm hearing a siren?"

"They were supposedly daughters of some sea god, women with wings, who used their songs to lure sailors to wreck on a rocky coast. But that's the Greek and Roman version. The Timucua version didn't have sailors and ships in it. It had strong chieftains who were lured to the beaches by the siren's song. And they were never seen again, being taken by the sirens to give her own people the chieftain's strength."

"Okay . . ." Peter replied incredulously.

"Guess they've run out of chieftains," Athena smirked.

"Did the legends say anything about a sea siren having her own army?"

The quilt-wrapped pilot pondered that for a second.

"Most ancient folks seemed to like leaving the naughty parts out of legends. They also like leaving out the things that made them make sense. Since there only seems to be one of those things close to being a woman down there, I'd have to figure they're like bees. One queen and the rest workers. But she seems more interested in you than them, so I think they're her brothers, all of them from a single parent, the last queen. And in order for her to birth the next generation, she needs a husband. This isn't an attack, it's a shotgun wedding!"

All Peter had to do was let the siren song fill his head, course through his bloodstream as it would, heading straight for his loins, and he knew she was on to something. He had thought it was just because he hadn't been around a pretty woman in a while, that somehow, through this whole nightmare, he'd been more than a little aroused. But as incredible as it seemed, the gorgeous Miss Voltaire, naked except for only a blue quilt, wasn't the one causing it.

"Goddamn," was all he could say.

"I think the storm is letting up," Athena observed. "Maybe I can get a clearer look at our situation. Can you hold yourself together long enough for me to get out on the gallery deck and back?"

"I'll make it," Mahr replied.

Athena headed down one level to the observation deck, leaving him alone. The voice of the siren, all high and sweet, female and sensual, settled on him like a warm fuzzy blanket of morphine, dulling his higher-level thoughts, giving his baser, male instincts more power. He wanted the siren down on his cabin porch. He thought about heading down the stairs and just giving her what she wanted . . . what he wanted. How could he do anything else?

Peter rose to his feet.

Then he heard the other song, belted out strong and loud.

"HIDEY HIDEY HIDEY HI!"

Peter didn't get out much, but even he knew the calling chorus of "Minnie the Moocher."

"HODEY HODEY HODEY HO!"

He jumped down to the gallery deck level, and looked out the door to see his blue quilt, being held out wide behind Athena. From behind, all he could see was jostling quilt, but it looked like the pilot was doing some kind of naked hoochie-coochie dance, and singing just as loud as she could.

All it took was one more "Hidey-Hidey" and the siren song stopped abruptly, replaced by an angry shriek the likes of which would cause even the most amorously inclined man to shrivel. It was the sound of the housewife from Hell in full-throated rage.

The sea siren had seen Athena, and it didn't like the idea of another woman on its turf. The low murmur of her brothers started rising up again in answer to the shriek, and a heavy thud hit the door at the base of the lighthouse. And a second thud.

Athena re-wrapped herself in the quilt and turned toward Peter, grinning when she saw him.

"That stopped her damn singing, at least."

"Yes, but we just traded that for--"

A splintering crash from far below interrupted Peter. The deep, inhuman mumbling that sounded so much like alien fat men with mouths full of otherworldly soup was now echoing up through the lighthouse's interior. The sound of heavy footsteps on the metal stairs began to beat a slow, formless percussion. Peter just hoped the things weren't used to much physical exertion and that the stairs would wear them out. Athena checked her guns.

"Don't suppose there's any other way out of here?" she asked. "Ladder on the outside or something like that?"

"Nope."

"Any other weapons up here?"

"A rope and a five-gallon can of mineral oil with about a gallon still in it. We probably don't want to set the place on fire while we're on top and they're at the bottom, though. It would probably work better the other way, even if I was willing to set fire to my life's employ. The smoke would kill us anyway. Mineral oil burns smoky."

Athena looked over the rail at the outwardly spiraling metal stairs.

"But you have a rope . . . I'd guess it's long enough to reach the bottom?"

"Sure. We use it to pull things up sometimes. But they'll be down there if we try to climb down."

"How long do you think it would take for that rope to burn through?" Athena asked as she started tying one end around the great oil container's handle.

"Not long."

"Can you lower the thing to the bottom of the lighthouse before that happens?"

"I can sure give it Saint Clement's best try."

"Light it and lower it, then, Mr. Mahr!"

Peter Mahr was a man who knew the sound of an order, and he automatically snapped to, getting the matches from the lamp room, setting the surface of the quarter-can of oil on fire, and hanging over the side. He let out the rope as fast as his hands would move, sure and steady so the thing wasn't flat-out falling. Dark, oily smoke billowed up in his face, and he coughed twice before craning his head to the side so he could breathe outside the fumes.

As the foully smoking five-gallon can of burning oil went down, the things on the stairs started bellowing at each other. Peter couldn't be sure what they were saying, but they sounded like they didn't like the looks of the fire. He slowed his pace as the rope ran out, then felt the big can set down hard at the bottom of the landing. The rope suddenly slackened after that, having burned through. He instinctively started reeling it back up.

"No time for that. Get up and seal the lamp room door. I'll get out on the gallery deck and keep them from getting out there. If we can hold the doors, the smoke will do our work for us."

"Do you think . . ."

"No time to think! Get up to that lamp room, Mr. Mahr!"

"Yes, ma'am, Miss Voltaire." He set down the rope and started climbing, only to see Athena pick up the rope and continue his efforts.

She looked up at him, saw him looking back at her, and shouted, "You never know! Go!" She dragged the bulk of the rope out onto the gallery deck and continued pulling from there.

Peter closed off the lamp room hatch and stood on it. Depending upon how much of a brain the leathery hunchback things had, they might not even see the hatch in the ceiling of the gallery deck as a door. That meant they'd put all their efforts toward the gallery deck's outside door, where Athena had chosen to hold them off. He felt like a coward, letting a woman take the most dangerous post. But she did have those guns . . .

The sound of dozens of feet pounding iron steps practically shook the whole lighthouse. They weren't moving fast, but they were moving. They'd be here soon. Peter began pulling every heavy thing that wasn't bolted down toward the hatch, lifting what he could and dragging what he couldn't. When he was convinced he'd weighted the door down so well nobody'd ever get through it, he unlatched one of the great windows that were the walls of the lantern deck and crawled outside into the storm, first stepping on the small ledge that ringed the windows, then carefully lowering himself down until he was hanging a few feet over the outside walkway of the gallery level. He let himself drop.

A swift, cloaked figure came around the walkway at him, and he had a gun in his face before he could recover from his jump.

"Dammit, Mahr! What are you doing?"

"I sealed the hatch and covered it with more weight than mine. Now I'm here to help you!"

"Men!" Athena cursed and charged back toward the gallery door, putting her back against it. Peter joined her, and they both braced their legs against the outer rail. Rain started to soak them both as they held their positions, no longer making any effort to stay clear of the storm.

"If this door budges an inch, I'm shooting through that inch," Athena told the lighthouse keeper. "We have to keep this closed."

As if in argument, something bumped the other side of the door, like someone was hammering it with his fist. Angry, mumbled voices came from the other side, along with more pounding. But the pounding wasn't focused on the door. It was all over the place. The black, faceless hunchbacks were pounding on the walls, pounding on the door, pounding on anything that might lead to the outside.

The unlikely couple pushed harder against the door, preparing for the inevitable ramming as the monsters focused their strength against the one true opening on the gallery deck.

"It's been a pleasure meeting you, Miss Voltaire!" Peter yelled over the rain and pounding. "I just wanted to say that, just in case!"

"That's me, bringing sunshine wherever I go!" she replied. "You're a good man, Peter Mahr! Keep it that way and hold that door!"

Their voices seemed to attract more pounding, but it was short-lived. In fact, it seemed like their attackers were losing interest. After a few minutes had passed, the other side of the door went silent. Neither Athena nor Peter relaxed. Both kept pushing.

"Either it's a trick, or . . ." she couldn't bring herself to say it. Luck had a way of turning back when you let too much hope creep in.

And then, the bat out of Hell came over the rail.

A big, black-winged, slimy harpy, half-woman, half-demon, screamed at Athena as it whipped around a sharp, spiny tail that the pilot caught in her left hand just as its stinger came within inches of her face.

Athena's right hand was still full of pistol, and she starting squeezing off shot after shot into the thing's belly. Her foot came up and kicked it solidly in the head, sending it back over the railing. The whole thing happened in seconds, and a moment after it was done, Peter already had trouble believing what he had just seen.

"AND STAY OUT!" Athena yelled, full of enough fire and spirit to match any demon-thing from some ocean Hell. Then she stuck her head over the rail and yelled down at the ground.

"I'M THE QUEEN OF THIS LIGHTHOUSE, YOU GODDAMNED BITCH!"

Peter looked over the rail and saw his lamp deck rope, tied to the base of the railing and dangling down to the ground. Athena's escape route. Apparently whatever that thing was had used it to climb up.

As he looked downward, the lighthouse keeper listened to the rain, much gentler now as the storm seemed to have passed, and he realized that was all he heard. No singing. No deep mumbling. No footsteps on the stairs.

Athena sat down on the deck with her back against the door and the pistol hanging wearily in her right hand. Peter sat down next to her.

They sat in the rain and looked out at the sheer blackness of night and ocean mingling into one. Peter could smell oily smoke creeping out the cracks of the gallery door. That was just fine, though. Just fine.

They were wet and tired, and they didn't talk. Just sat, shoulder to shoulder, and Peter realized he even dozed off a time or two. He didn't dream though.

Eventually dawn started to glow on the horizon. It was the prettiest time of the night, Peter thought. Still dim, but with your eyes adjusted to the dark, the fuzzy new bit of light seemed to light up the world.

Athena gave him an elbow.

"I don't know about you, but I feel like climbing down a rope."

The lighthouse keeper looked at her and the old blue quilt that never seemed to be able to keep her completely covered.

"I don't mean to be indelicate, but in that outfit, you're going to get some rope burns where you probably don't want rope burns. I have to open this place up sometime and let the smoke out. Just as soon do it while you and your guns are still here."

Athena had to agree on that point, and they both moved back on either side of the door. Peter reached over and pulled it open. They gave it plenty of time for the smoke to thin out, watching the open door the entire time. Nothing else came out.

The girl pilot headed in first, gun barrels ahead of her. She stepped over a big, dark something, the inside of the lighthouse still being far too dark to see in the dim light of early morning. Since Peter had boots on, he gave it a nudge with his foot. Part of it flipped back as he pushed it with his boot toe, and it seemed like something not all that unfamiliar to him. He pushed the edges of it around enough to see that it wasn't even close to alive, then grabbed what he thought was a good end for grabbing and dragged it out onto the gallery deck.

It was the biggest damned manta ray he had ever seen. Probably weighed eighty pounds or more. And it was on the gallery deck of his lighthouse. Peter jerked the big sea creature around, looking for anything un-manta-ray-like about it, but found nothing.

"You think one of those guys was wearing this thing?" he asked.

"There's another one in here," Athena reported from inside. "It's pretty dark, but I think there's more."

And there were more. As they carefully made their way down the spiral stairs of the lighthouse, it seemed like they were stepping around dead manta rays the entire time. Almost fifty, it seemed like, and it made Peter glad for the residual oil smoke. The rays seemed on their way to working up a smell.

When they got outside, Athena made her way back and forth across the yard, looking for something, looking up at the tower to orient herself, then looking some more.

"No way that blasted thing lived," she spat. "No way."

But they found no trace of the spine-tailed harpy that had attacked her up on the gallery.

When they got back to the cottage, Peter made coffee and heated water so his guest could get a hot bath. While she was enjoying that, he went to her plane to get her some clothes and then set to work dragging manta rays out of his lighthouse. It was like one of those rains of frogs or something, just a weirdness that came out of nowhere. The sun's full daylight made the events of the night before seem more and more like some kind of dream, and the hard work of dragging the mantas took his mind off it all the more.

Athena eventually came out, seeming quite pleased just to be in normal clothes again, and voiced the thoughts he was letting be.

"You don't think those things somehow grew arms and legs last night and came after us?" she puzzled, following it with a laugh so she didn't sound nuts. "Like mermaids or something?"

Peter just shook his head, clueless. "Not sure I want to know."

His guest stayed long enough to help him clean the place up, to get the fuel for her plane brought down, and even took him up for a ride before she left. And it wasn't until just before she left that Athena finally asked Peter Mahr the real question he didn't want to think about.

"If I hadn't been here, do you think the queen of the manta people would have had you for her royal consort? You seemed kind of taken by that song of hers." She grinned.

"Well," Peter replied at last with a grin of his own, "even with her pointy stinger tail and nasty disposition, I suppose, all things considered, that she was still probably a gentler choice than the dame that overthrew her."

Athena laughed and smacked him in the head. After she got in her plane, flew away, and he watched it disappear in the distance, Peter Mahr decided it was time to stop watching the ocean and start watching sunsets.

Somebody else could start keeping the damn lighthouse.

HAKKŌ ICHIU

Chris Murrin

Thousands of cheering fans greeted the steamship Suwa Maru as it docked in Kobe Harbor. On the main deck, a tramp waved to the crowd in appreciation of the warm reception. He danced back and forth much to their delight, pausing only to strike an occasional pose for them. Though not his usual garb, his white suit and hat accented his graying hair well and made his slight frame seem all the more delicate. Sidling up to his bulkier older brother, he smiled and said, "You were right, Sydney."

"I told you," Sydney said, "After this trip and our meeting with the premier, we'll easily get two hundred thousand here." As the tramp bounded away, Sydney shot the sleeves of his brown suit and took a drag of his cigarette. Coming over the horizon, several biplanes approached and began circling above the steamer. They dropped their payload. The wind whipped up, filling the sky with a cyclone of leaflets welcoming Charlie Chaplin to Japan.

Standing near Sydney, Athena Voltaire brushed a lock of midnight hair out of her eyes as she gazed at the aircraft. "Old friends?" Sydney asked. Still captivated, Athena answered with only a slight nod and a far-away smile. "Well, I'm glad you decided to remain earthbound for a while and join us for this leg of the tour."

Sydney moved in closer to her and followed her gaze. "I think your presence has helped both Charlie and the papers forget about that awful business in St. Moritz."

Athena shifted her eyes to him. "Finally, the truth behind the invitation comes out," she said with a smirk. "I'm to be the next May Reeves."

His face reddened. "Not at all. Not at all. Charlie was devastated by the word that your father couldn't join us for this tour, as he did the last few. His tales of life on the road take us back to our days in vaudeville. Seemed only right that his daughter come in his stead."

Athena decided to let Sydney off the hook with another jab. "I would think if anyone should be here with you to promote City Lights, Virginia should." Sydney couldn't help but laugh at that preposterous idea. Athena smiled for a moment, but her smile faded as she looked back toward the dock. "Sadly, since mother left, my father hasn't been in any condition to travel...or do much else," she said. "Still, I couldn't pass up a chance to see the Orient again."

Sydney turned to face her and placed a hand gently on the small of her back. "Well, Charlie is certainly glad you came along. Almost as glad as I am."

Once the ship docked and most of the other passengers had debarked, Sydney, Charlie, and Athena proceeded down the gangway, where Toraichi Kono, Charlie's valet, welcomed them to Japan with a deep bow, nearly losing his spectacles doing so. Kono had traveled ahead of the group to arrange for transportation to Tokyo and for proper hotel rooms there. Sydney took the lead as the four travelers forced their way through the mob of excited fans and toward the awaiting taxis. As they drove away, the tramp leaned out of the car window, doffing his hat and waving to the screaming crowd, his boyish smile never faltering. Once they had left the crowd behind, however, Charlie slumped down in his seat, frowned, and crossed his arms. "They all want a piece of me, of what's mine. I'm no more than a meal ticket or a piece of memorabilia to them," he said. Athena rolled her eyes. Aboard the Suwa Maru she had already been witness to Charlie's capricious nature and found it both arrogant and phony, even for a movie star.

Once aboard the train to Tokyo, the playful tramp would appear for the crowds that gathered at each stop on the route, but Charlie's plaintive side would replace him in close company. By the time the train arrived at Tokyo Station, the hour had grown late, and Charlie's mood had worsened even further, leaving him nearly sulking. Outside the station, two limousines awaited them. As the drivers loaded their luggage into the rear vehicle, Charlie sat in the front limousine, with Kono following behind. Sydney grabbed Athena's elbow and stopped her before she could join them. "We'll take the other car," he said to Charlie.

"But I thought we would all ride toge--"

Sydney closed the door on him. He offered his arm to Athena. "Thank you," she said, as he escorted her to their car.

"I apologize for my brother's poor demeanor," Sydney said as they pulled away from the station.

"It's all right. You know as well as I do: working the circuit, you develop a tolerance for grandiose personalities. Especially from family." The cars wound their way through the city and into a quiet neighborhood. Without warning, the limousine carrying Charlie and Kono stopped.

Athena leaned forward and looked through the windshield. "What's going on?"

"I'm not sure," said Sydney. He too leaned forward, next to the driver. "What's this all about?"

The driver shrugged. "Maybe Mister Chaplin want to see the Imperial Palace," he said, pointing out his window. In the distance, they could see the large gates and the uppermost tower of the palace. They could also see Kono and Charlie arguing inside their limo. Relenting, Charlie stepped out to the rear of the car, turned toward the palace, sighed, and gave a short bow. He turned toward the rear limousine and shrugged broadly—the tramp shining through for a moment—before getting back into the car with Kono.

Athena frowned. "Is that customary?"

The driver looked as bewildered as his passengers. "No," he said, shaking his head. The front car continued onward, and they proceeded to the Imperial Hotel without any further delays.

When they arrived, Athena guided Charlie aside, away from Kono. Sydney joined them. "What was that, Charlie?" she asked.

"I haven't any idea. Kono said it was some sort of tradition, but I've certainly never heard of such a thing. Bad enough I have to put on a show for everyone else, now I'm his puppet, too." With that, Charlie stormed off into the lobby. Sydney caught Athena's eye and shook his head. They followed him into the hotel.

After the long journey from Kobe, Athena welcomed the luxury of her hotel room. Charlie spared no expense on accommodations for his party. After changing into some low-cut, violet silk pajamas, Athena took a long look around the suite. Everything was of the highest quality. The lush carpeting felt wonderful beneath her tired feet; the stunning view of the reflecting pool captivated her for several moments; but what she appreciated most of all was the warm, comfortable bed. She fell asleep moments after lying down for the night.

The following morning, Athena awoke to the muffled sounds of arguing from Sydney's suite, next door. Throwing on a robe, she hurried into the hallway and knocked on Sydney's door. It swung open, and out stormed Charlie, red in the face. "Should you see that unreliable leech, tell him I must speak with him at once!" He hurried past Athena without even acknowledging her presence.

"What's all the ruckus?"

Sydney smiled to cover his embarrassment. "Ah. Kono has gone missing, as he's wont to do whenever Charlie's in one of his moods. Nothing to worry about." Athena noticed Sydney's eyes dancing over her body. She tightened her robe. "We have a meeting with the mayor of Tokyo this morning, but we're heading out for a bit of shopping later, if you would like to join us."

"Sounds like fun."

The three of them spent the early afternoon walking from store to store in an older area of Tokyo, window-shopping. Eventually people began to recognize Charlie, and a small crowd started to tail them, though at a respectful distance. Charlie repeatedly peeked over his shoulder at them, looking more uncomfortable each time. "Horrible urchins, hoping I'll give them some part of myself. An autograph, or perhaps a private performance," he said.

Athena decided to stop Charlie's rant before it began in earnest. "Let's go in here," she said, grabbing Sydney's sleeve and pulling him while pushing Charlie toward the door of a small art and antiques shop.

They wandered around the cluttered store, marveling at the beautiful craftsmanship and artistry of the wares. Sydney stared in wonder at the colorful woodblock prints of nudes hanging on the walls. The action of an antique pocket watch had Charlie mesmerized. Though she appreciated the pottery, artwork, and other antiques, the netsuke attracted Athena's attention most of all. She marveled at the small sculptures depicting laborers, demonic oni, animals, and even ghoulish skeletons in such beautiful, minute detail. After agonizing for several minutes, she finally selected an exquisite ivory carving of a hawk perched on a branch to bring home as a souvenir.

All the while, the shopkeeper had been trying to talk Charlie into buying the pocket watch, but Charlie wouldn't agree to do so, even though a sparkle in his eye confessed his admiration for the piece. "No," he said, walking away, "I have to think about it. I'll come back." With that, he fled the store.

"I guess we're meant to follow," said Sydney as he strolled out behind Charlie. Athena paid for the netsuke and thanked the storekeeper, who smiled and bowed slightly in gratitude as she left.

Outside, a mood had again taken hold of Charlie. "We must return to the hotel immediately," he said. "I find myself overwrought and must rest before dinner." Athena could feel her face flush. She turned her back on Charlie and took a few steps away from him, stopping herself from saying something in anger that she might regret. As Charlie rushed back toward the main avenue, Sydney and Athena walked in silence several paces behind him. Charlie hailed a taxi and they returned to the hotel.

That evening, they dined in a small but elegant restaurant. Charlie again donned a white suit, while Sydney wore a dark, pinstriped one. Kono—who had decided that he could now rejoin the party safely—wore a charcoal suit accented with a bow tie. Athena wore a sapphire ankle-length gown.

"A toast," said Sydney, raising a glass of wine, "to Miss Voltaire. You are a vision, if I may say so."

"Hear, hear," said Charlie as he and Kono raised their glasses.

"Thank you," she said, raising her own and taking a sip. "Actually, I wore this dress when I first met Charlie, at the premiere of The Circus. I'm glad I have the chance to wear it again."

Charlie said, "Ah yes, The Circus. Not my finest hour. Your father did splendid makeup work on that picture, though. That was his first time working with us, if I recall. I remember that evening well. After the premiere I joined Doug and Mary for …" His voice trailed off as he looked toward the door. Six Japanese men dressed in black wool coats and hats entered the restaurant. The shortest of the men pulled a chair up next to Kono. The other five stood behind their leader, who spoke angrily in Japanese. Kono turned pale. The scolding escalated and seemed to turn threatening. Athena looked at Sydney, who seemed to be as puzzled as she was. She began to reach into her clutch for the Baby Browning she carried, but Charlie shot up from his seat, his hand in his pocket, pantomiming a hidden gun. "What is the meaning of this?"

The six men looked at Charlie, bemused. Without turning away from the men, Kono said, "They—they are grandsons of the shopkeeper you met today. They say you were rude to him, and say you must go back tomorrow and apologize."

"What? Rubbish. I'll not be lectured in this manor! Kono, deal with this! Let's go," said Charlie. Athena closed her purse as Charlie nudged her and Sydney out of their seats. He led the way out of the restaurant, keeping his "gun" trained on the men the entire time. Outside, Charlie hailed a taxi and dove in, gasping from fear. Sydney held the door open for Athena. She looked back into the restaurant. Kono still argued with the men.

"Such excitement. You know, I think I'd like to take a little walk to calm myself down," she said.

"That's a fine idea," Sydney said, "but you shouldn't walk alone at this hour. Allow me to escort you."

Charlie looked out at them from the taxi. "But we should get away from here before they--"

"We'll join you back at the hotel soon, Charlie," Sydney said, slamming the taxi door on any further protest.

As the cab departed, Sydney and Athena moved away from the restaurant window and into the alley along the side of the building. "I take it you have the same idea as I," he said, lighting a cigarette.

They watched from the shadows as the six men left the restaurant, piling into two cars and speeding away. Soon after, Kono walked out onto the sidewalk. Sydney started to move, but Athena was on Kono in a split second. She grabbed him by the lapels, swung him around, and slammed him up against the alley wall.

Sydney took over, playing the heavy, looming over the frightened valet. "What the hell is going on here, Kono?"

"I—I can't..."

"Who were those men?"

Kono gave in. "The Black Dragon Society."

"What do they want?" Athena asked.

"I can't say. If I tell you, they kill my family!" Kono said.

"Preposterous. Your family is safe in America," Sydney said.

"No. I still have more family here in Japan, too."

Athena tried to calm Kono. She put a hand on his chest, smoothing his jacket where she had grabbed him. "Kono, whatever trouble you're in, we can't help you if we don't know what they want. Does this have something to do with our extra stop last night?"

Kono nodded. "It was a signal that I will go along with their plan."

Sydney moved in close to Kono. "SO WHAT'S THE BLOODY PLAN?"

Terrified, Kono blurted out, "They're going to kill Mister Chaplin and Premier Inukai tomorrow night."

Sydney and Athena looked at each other, agape.

"Taxi!" they shouted.

"Of course. People have been taking from me my whole life. Now they want to take my very life as well," Charlie said as he took off his dinner jacket. "I'm worth more to them dead than alive." Sitting in Charlie's suite, his companions were a captive audience, but Athena had heard enough complaining.

"Yes, that's terrible," she said, "but what do you want to do about it?"

Charlie thought for a moment and then sprang out of his chair. "There's only one manner in which we can dispose of this threat. We must be the heroes!" Charlie began to pantomime a swordfight. Kono had to duck to avoid being struck by a wild swing. "We must foil their plot ourselves!" He delivered the killing blow to his imaginary enemy.

Athena shook her head. "That's--"

"Brilliant!" Sydney said. "The press will eat it up. 'Charlie Chaplin saves Premier.' What a tremendous headline."

Athena couldn't believe her ears. "You can't be serious."

Sydney took her by the arm and ushered her out of her chair. He walked her toward the door, speaking over his shoulder to Charlie. "We'll double again our City Lights royalties. A tremendous plan! Athena and I shall go over the particulars." They left, stranding Kono with Charlie yet again.

As they walked down the hall, Athena yanked her arm from Sydney's grasp. "Have you gone whacky?"

Sydney dropped his façade of excitement. "Of course not. I'm not putting my brother in harm's way. I'll send word to the premier's staff. He can decide the best course of action. In any case, I'm certain he'll be grateful that we exposed this plot."

"All right. As long as we're giving them warning and not playing at being swashbuckling heroes." They arrived at Athena's room. She unlocked it, entered, and turned to face Sydney, who tried to follow her inside. She put a hand on his chest to block him. "Good night, Syd."

"It's still early," he said, taking her hand in both of his and caressing it as he subtly tried to move forward. "After all this excitement, I thought we could conclude the evening with a bit of a nightcap."

"I'm not in the mood."

He kissed her hand. "But dear Athena, I thought we had become quite close in our travels."

"We have, Syd," she said, "but that's as close as you're going to get." She pushed him backward gently and closed the door on him.

The following evening, Premier Inukai Tsuyoshi, joined by his son Takeru and a few guardsmen, met his four guests on the steps of his residence. The Premier was a short man with closely cropped hair and a gray beard. Yet despite his stature, he still exuded a powerful presence. The medals pinned to the chest of his ornate jacket told of a lifetime of service to his country. The visitors bowed deeply, showing respect to the Premier and to Takeru. Charlie then shook the Premier's hand. After this moment of friendly greeting, the Premier spoke in an embarrassed tone. "Mister Chaplin, I offer you my deepest apologies," he said in English. "Some important state business has come to my attention. Thus, I will not be able to spend the evening with you as I had hoped." Inukai placed a hand on his son's shoulder. "However, if you would like, my son had planned to see the sumo wrestling matches tonight and would greatly enjoy your company."

"I would be honored," Takeru said.

Charlie balked. "Well, I don't know…"

"Charles, this would be a tremendous opportunity to see one of the grandest of Japanese customs, and an appearance in such a popular venue could garner quite…valuable attention, if you get my meaning," Sydney said.

Confused by this sudden change of plans, Charlie acquiesced. "Yes. I suppose it could, couldn't it?"

"Excellent," the Premier said, smiling. He continued as they walked toward a waiting car, "You will have a wonderful time, I assure you. Mister Chaplin and Miss Voltaire, would you please come inside with me for a moment? I'd like to see if we can reschedule our dinner for some other time."

"Of course," Sydney said.

"But shouldn't I--" Charlie said, beginning to protest as he sat in the back seat. He thought the better of it. "Oh, never mind," he said, shutting the door on himself.

"Have fun," Athena said to Charlie through the car window.

Athena, Sydney, Kono, and Inukai all breathed a sigh of relief as the limousine whisked Charlie and Takeru away to the safety of the sumo matches. The Premier turned to his remaining guests and said, "Come this way, please." He led them up the stairs and into his home, then turned back to give orders to the guards stationed at the front door.

The guests entered a large parlor. The center of the room lay empty of furniture to accommodate the frequent greeting ceremonies held there. Numerous colorful paintings and framed newspaper articles adorned the walls. Sydney and Kono wandered the room, admiring the artwork. Premier Inukai joined them, closing the parlor doors behind him.

In the rear of the room, above a fireplace, sat several swords on an ebony rack. Though she couldn't read the inscriptions, Athena could tell that most of them were new, probably honorary gifts. One sword stood out, though, not only because of its beauty, but also because it was clearly far older than the others. Premier Inukai approached her.

"It's lovely," Athena said of the antique sword.

The Premier took the sword from its display and removed it from its sheath. "Thank you," he said, "It is a family heirloom. My ancestors were samurai. This sword dates back to the seventeenth century, when they first rose to power." With one hand on the hilt and one on the blade, he offered the sword to Athena. Pinning her purse under her arm, she accepted the sword and held it delicately, feeling its balance, admiring the intricate beauty of the etched blade.

"Amazing. I've never seen anything like it," she said, handing the sword back to the Premier. As he returned the sword to its sheath, Athena turned to the topic at hand. "I appreciate your help in keeping Charlie safe. Are you sure we can't convince you to leave as well and let your guards deal with the Black Dragons?"

Sydney, still admiring the artwork around the room, piped up. "Yes. Better to keep you safe, too, sir."

The Premier shook his head. "I cannot run from this threat. If I were to let my men deal with this situation while I fled, that weakness would be more subversive to our government than anything these Black Dragons could possibly hope to accomplish." Athena frowned; she couldn't argue with the Premier's sense of honor, but she still didn't have to like it. He continued, "You, however, should leave before--"

A great clamor arose outside the doors: men shouting orders and others shouting back just as loudly. A gunshot rang out. Another. More. Just as suddenly as the tumult began, all became quiet. Athena could see the fear in Syd's eyes. Still, he moved to the center of the room and drew a small pistol from inside his jacket. Kono retreated to a far corner. Athena stood next to Sydney and pulled out her Baby Browning, dropping her purse to the floor. The Premier, still holding his family's sword, stepped in front of them. "No," he commanded, "you will not shoot at them. Though they may be misguided, they are still my people, and I will deal with them."

Sydney said, "We understand and respect that. That doesn't mean we can't put forth a united front." Inukai smiled in agreement. He turned to face the parlor doors.

The doors burst inward. A dozen Black Dragons entered, including the six from the restaurant the night before. Except for their diminutive leader, they all had their guns drawn. Two of them had shiny patches of blood seeping through their black coats. Three others had the guardsmen's blood spattered across them. Athena and Sydney stood their ground. Unarmed, Kono crouched behind a sofa.

The Premier did not move. The scowling Black Dragon leader strode up to him and spewed something in Japanese. Sydney whispered back to Kono, "What's he saying?"

Kono began to translate: "Look at our brave leader. We thought you maybe have run."

The Premier opened his arms and spoke in a calm, soothing voice. Kono continued translating: "There is no need for further violence. I will listen to your concerns. If you would speak, I would understand."

The Dragon leader pulled out a pistol and fired point blank into the Premier's chest. "Dialogue is useless," he said in Japanese, looking into the Premier's eyes as he slumped to the floor. Sydney's jaw dropped. Even the other Black Dragons seemed stunned.

Athena fired twice, hitting the leader in the stomach both times. He doubled over, making a sound that Athena first thought was groaning, but soon realized was laughter. The laugh became louder, lower, more guttural. As the leader straightened up, he stood taller, and his face had begun contorting. He laughed even harder, baring sharp fangs. Continuing to grow in height and mass, his face twisted into a grotesque mask. His clothes started to tear, revealing reddish skin underneath.

The rest of the Black Dragons backed away from the monster. One of them shouted, "Oni!" The room erupted in gunfire as everyone tried to kill the demon. The creature laughed off their attacks. He turned his full eight-foot frame around to face his former accomplices. He struck the nearest man with a fist, driving him into several others. The Dragons closest to the door fled.

While the demon's back was turned, Athena eyed the sword lying beside the Premier's body. Dropping her gun, she ran forward, picked it up, and unsheathed the blade. Hearing the sound, the creature turned to face her. Athena leapt as high as she could and swung the sword with all her might.

The demon caught the sword in its left hand, the blade slicing through its palm all the way to the bone. At the same time, it caught Athena by the throat in its right hand. Everyone, friend and Dragon alike, froze. Athena choked as she writhed, trying to free either the sword or herself from the monster's grip. The creature tilted its head and looked deeply into Athena's eyes. It grinned.

Then it slid its palm down the blade toward the hilt, slicing even deeper into the bone, until it could wrap its fingers around Athena's hand, keeping her grip on the sword tight. It twisted the sword, wrenching Athena's shoulder, and drove it into its own abdomen. It continued to stare into Athena's eyes as it moved the blade sideways back and forth. In seconds, the demon weakened, its grip began to loosen, and Athena dropped to the floor, gasping.

The creature once again began to laugh as it collapsed. It uttered something in Japanese and instantly decayed into dust. A stiff breeze blew the ash through the open parlor door, and soon all traces of the oni were gone.

Athena looked up at the remaining Black Dragons. Two of them ran out of the room. The others, including the already wounded men, dropped their weapons and surrendered. Sydney handed Athena her gun, and together they held the men at gunpoint while Kono began securing them. Moments later, guardsmen from another post arrived and took over for Kono, taking the Dragons into custody.

Sydney turned to Athena and hugged her. This time, she allowed it. She couldn't tell which of them trembled harder. "Thank you, Athena," he said as he let her go, "for sending that creature back to hell. You saved us all."

"Not all," she said, looking down at Inukai's body, "and I didn't really do anything." She turned to Kono, who now sat on the sofa he had been hiding behind, looking ill. She asked, "What was that last thing it said?"

"Well…ah…well…"

"Come on, man, out with it," Sydney said.

"It said, 'I feed on death, and death surrounds you, Athena Voltaire. My feast has just begun.'"

Athena felt a chill run through her body. Somehow, she knew the demon was right.

A MAGICAL MURDER

Ryan Schrodt

Ellis Andrews always believed there were two types of women in this world—the ones that were worth any trouble you could face and the ones that would put you through it. Much of his youth had been spent confusing one kind for the other and paying the consequences of his mistakes. Finding feminine companionship had never been an issue for Ellis, but finding his way out of it had been his undoing more times than he cared to remember. When his boss at the Peavey Airfield informed Ellis and the other resident mechanics that they had been hired to work on planes for the traveling Keefauver Air Angels, Ellis was the only one who could not find excitement in the opportunity. Working on planes was his only escape from dames, and now even that was not safe.

Of course, his disgruntled disposition would not last once he had been assigned to repairs on the Jenny used for Keefauver's most spectacular act—an acrobatic wing-walking performance. While Ellis's interactions with the plane's young pilot were less than cordial (she insisted on telling him the plane's entire history and refused to let him work on it unless she was present), he was immediately enthralled by the act's true star—the beautiful Miss Ana Zaleski. He was certain, without question, that there was no trouble he could encounter that would not be worth a moment of attention from the 22 year-old acrobat who dazzled thousands of onlookers a year with her daring feats.

He was, in true Ellis Andrews fashion, completely wrong about that. But at the time he could not have known what trouble Ana would bring into his life.

Instead, Ellis spent the afternoon they met charming Miss Zaleski as best he could while still focusing on the task at hand. The two hit it off marvelously, just as Ellis had with countless women before, much to the chagrin of the pilot, who merely wanted to make sure her plane was in working order for the following day's performance before retiring to whatever low-rent accommodations Keefauver had arranged for them. With every flutter of Ana's eyelashes or giggle produced at Ellis's lame jokes, the pilot grew more and more frustrated.

Though she was not wholly immune to Ellis's charms, young Athena Voltaire had witnessed this scene at nearly every town the Keefauver Air Angels had visited since she joined their ranks earlier that year. She had a great fondness for Ana, and their friendship was strong—it would have to be in order for their dangerous act to be possible—but to Athena, the thrill of being in the air was far greater than the thrill of bedding random handsome mechanics throughout the Midwest. As long as their plane would fly the next day, Athena would do her best to ignore the routine romance building in the hangar.

"You know, Ellis, I was telling Athena earlier that there is a really great magician performing tonight, and the show isn't sold out. I don't suppose you'd want to join us, would you? I cannot think of anyone I'd rather have as our gentleman escort," Ana asked in her most playful, dollish voice. As expected, Ellis was hooked at the proposal.

"Sure thing, sweetheart. Just let me finish this up and we can get going. It won't take me long if you want to go freshen up," Ellis responded as he lit a cigarette and took a long, lazy draw. Athena was annoyed with the unsurprising air of cockiness that Ellis exhibited the moment he laid eyes on Ana. Had her performing partner not set foot in the hangar, it was likely that Athena and Ellis could have spent an enjoyable afternoon talking about their mutual love of aviation, but instead she found herself being unable to imagine wasting any more time with him than necessary.

A fog of cigarette smoke and idle conversation had already descended upon the club by the time that Athena had arrived with Ellis and Ana in tow. While her companions playfully flirted during the entire way there, Athena did her best to focus on her plans for the performance the next day. Since joining the Keefauver Air Angels, Athena had been very singularly focused on the aerial acrobatics that had made her one of the stars of the show. When she was grounded, she refused to let anything distract her from mentally preparing for her next flight, despite Ana's best efforts to keep her friend's focus out of the clouds. Unfortunately for Athena, that meant occasionally wafting through the acrid nicotine clouds in whatever nightclub or performance venue that Ana had dragged her.

"You know, Athena grew up around magicians," Ana told Ellis as she gripped his arm tightly in the entranceway. "She would probably be just as comfortable up on stage as she would in the sky."

"Is that right?" Ellis responded, barely acknowledging the conversation, instead remaining focused on the petite blonde on his arm. He wasn't the only one, though. Ana's black dress clung to her miniscule frame tightly—something every man in the building seemed to notice as they made their way to a table near the stage. Though she was far from jealous, Athena took notice of all the looks that lingered on her friend. Ana's natural beauty was accentuated by the simple, form-fitting dress and tasteful jewelry that fit perfectly with her delicate features. There was a simplicity and effortlessness to Ana's beauty that Athena had always admired.

"I wouldn't say that. There is no place I'd rather be than in the air," Athena responded, secretly hoping that her compatriots might actually want to talk about the upcoming air show. Instead they offered only indifferent but courteous nods and returned to their own playful banter.

Thankfully it would not be long before the house lights were dimmed and the stage curtain was drawn, revealing the Great Sandoz, an elderly magician whose glory days were clearly behind him. He wore a shabby, black cape over his purple tuxedo, though both were faded enough to qualify as shades of gray. His thin hands and long fingers looked as frail as the rest of him and shook wildly as he introduced himself, prompting Athena to wonder if he would even be dexterous enough to perform the simplest of tricks. She had wondered why the club had so few patrons and now she knew—it was unlikely that the Great Sandoz had been much of a draw since long before she was born.

Athena tried her best to enjoy the old man's performance, but his nervousness, combined with a disengaged audience, led to a rather disastrous act. Sandoz fumbled through trick after trick, often making mistakes and inadvertently revealing the secrets behind his "tricks" as he backpedaled his way through the set. The crowd noticed these errors about as much as they noticed his successes, which is to say that they barely noticed them at all. Much like Ellis and Ana, the other patrons were so entirely engrossed in their side conversations and drinks that they seemed only marginally aware that a magician was on stage. His skill was largely unimportant to them.

"For my final trick, I shall need a member of the audience," Sandoz announced, though what was left of the audience failed to hear him. "Any member will do, though it would warm my heart to have a beautiful young woman! Would any of you like to take part in this ultimate spectacle of illusion!"

"You should go up there," Ellis said, nudging Athena at the elbow. "I'd love to see how at home you are on the stage."

Athena responded politely, but quietly. Stage magicians loved to volunteer audience members that were being chided by their friends, so the last thing she wanted was to catch the attention of the Great Sandoz. "No, thanks. I'm not—"

"I'll do it!"

Athena and Ellis exchanged surprised looks as Ana shot out of her seat and headed towards the stage. Over the last hour she had shown absolutely no interest in any part of Sandoz's act, from his simple card tricks to his multiple attempts at corralling a dingy old dove that had escaped from his sleeve at the wrong time. And yet, the beautiful young wing-walker was making her way to the stage all the same. Ana had always moved with a certain energy and bounce, but her light-footedness was replaced with a determined stride that was shocking to Athena, though Ellis was far more concerned with watching the way her dress clung to her petite frame as she made her way up the steps to the stage.

"Ah! What a lovely specimen! I could not ask for a better assistant," Sandoz beamed. For the first time that evening, all attention was on the stage as Sandoz motioned Ana towards a large cabinet that was inlaid with intricate patterns of flowers and stars. It might have been the magnificent centerpiece of the act at one time, but the years had been unkind, leaving nothing more than a paint-chipped husk that creaked loudly as Sandoz opened the door. "For my final trick, I shall make this young woman disappear into the ether, only to bring her back again unharmed!"

Disappearing acts were often the final trick of a performance, and Athena had seen her fair share over the years. Sandoz's method was tried-and-true, though it was unlikely to elicit much amazement from the audience. It was possible that Ellis was the only person in the audience who was mesmerized, and that was only because he was faced with Ana being out of sight, albeit briefly. Ana smiled and gave him a wink as she stepped into the cabinet. Sandoz closed the door behind her.

"Klaatu! Verata! Niktu!"

With that incantation, Sandoz opened the door to reveal that Ana had vanished. Athena held back a groan as she stretched, knowing that the evening would be mercifully over the moment Ana reappeared. She resolved that her time was best served fetching their coats, freeing her from the misery of the old man's frail attempts at the wondrous illusions that she spent her childhood idolizing.

"And now, I shall pluck our brave, young volunteer out of the darkness and return her safely to our realm," Sandoz shouted wearily as he waved his wand at the cabinet. "Return to us, lovely maiden. Klaatu! Verata! Niktu!"

Athena was startled by the collective gasp as Sandoz opened the cabinet, though the real surprise came when she turned her gaze back to the stage. A scream escaped from her throat as she looked into the lifeless eyes of Ana. Blood trickled down her expressionless face onto the jewels adorning her necklace from where she had been shot by an unseen assailant. Sandoz had returned Ana to them, but she was not unharmed as promised. She was dead.

Those who remained in the club reacted with such panic and in such rapidity that Athena and Ellis were unable to fully assess the situation during the ensuing chaos. Athena immediately made for the stage, but Ellis grabbed her by the wrist and dragged her towards the exit. Athena grasped at the air in a futile attempt to reach her friend as Ellis pulled her into the mob that was moving en masse out of the club. As the crowd gathered around her, the last thing she saw was the Great Sandoz standing over Ana's body. Against the faded black cape, his skin was a ghastly shade of white, and Athena was certain she saw tears welling up in eyes.

They reached the street just as the police were arriving. "How could they get here so fast? That's impossible," Athena called out as Ellis dragged her into the street and away from the hysteria that was building in front of the club. Athena tried pulling back, but Ellis's grip was too strong and his resolve to get away from the scene was too unrelenting. "Ellis! Stop! We have to go back!" He offered no response.

Ellis finally came to a halt after they had rounded the corner at the end of the block. Athena wrenched her arm free and immediately used it to punch Ellis square in the jaw, putting him on one knee.

"What the hell was that for?"

"Are you kidding me? You nearly pulled my arm off dragging me halfway across Chicago! We need to go back and find out what happened to Ana."

Ellis rubbed his face, which stung from the sucker-punch. "We know exactly what happened to her. She was killed by that magician and the police have him. End of story. Your friend is dead."

"That old man wouldn't be able to hold a gun without shooting himself in the foot. Even if he wasn't in plain sight the entire time, there is no way he could have killed Ana." Athena's fist remained clenched. Not wanting to chance another punch, Ellis kept out of arm's reach. "I get it. You didn't know her, but she was my friend. I'm going back in there to find out what happened."

"You'll never get near the place. If you want to know the story, wait for the papers."

Athena frowned. She could not pinpoint why exactly, but she did not trust the police to handle this matter adequately. She knew that the Great Sandoz would be arrested for the murder—but would anyone bother to question it further? Athena had to know for her own piece of mind exactly what happened when Ana had "disappeared." She turned back towards the scene of the crime and left Ellis standing silently behind, still rubbing his jaw.

Knowing that it would take some time before the chaos at the club would die down, Athena ducked into a small café down the street, ordered herself a coffee and fought back her tears. She had only known Ana for a short time, but they worked incredibly well together and developed as close a bond as Athena had since she toured the world with Emily by her side. She knew that she should go back to the airfield and tell the others, but as the shock of the moment wore off, the last thing she wanted to do was relive the horrifying moment of Ana's murder—at least until she knew for certain why she was killed and by whom.

She was midway through her third cup when Ellis walked into the café and sat across from her. His trademark cocky grin had been replaced with a look of quiet contemplation. The two sat silently for a few moments, unsure of how best to move forward, given the events that had transpired that evening. As the tension began to boil over, Athena opened her mouth to deliver an apology for the sucker-punch that had left a large bruise on the side of the mechanic's face, but it was Ellis who spoke first.

"I think you might be right about what happened. There is a lot more going on than what we saw," he said meekly, without looking her in the eyes. "I'm sorry that I doubted you, but it all happened so fast." He paused, as if he expected some sort of response from Athena, but when she remained silent he continued. "I went back there and there were some men there, but they weren't the police. It looked suspicious."

"Why are you telling me this?"

"You said you were going back there, but I don't think it's safe. You shouldn't go alone."

"I can handle myself. I don't need you to look after me."

Ellis frowned. "I get it. You don't like me and you don't think I have any place in this, but I really liked Ana and I think we owe it to her to find out what happened. Let me help you."

"Fine," Athena responded with a cold authority before draining the last of her coffee and exiting the café.

When they arrived at the club, a single officer stood watch out front, though he was engaged in a conversation with two large, well-dressed men. Knowing that they could not use the main entrance, Athena and Ellis circled around the building to find alternate means. Thankfully a service door was left unlocked, allowing the duo to silently make their way inside.

"What exactly are we looking for?"

"Keep your voice down. And, honestly, I don't know."

"Then how will we know when we find it?"

As they made their way through the dark of the backstage area towards the main hall, Ellis found himself constantly crashing into things. The backstage was littered with scattered and overturned miscellany, making it difficult to navigate. "I said, how will we know when we find it?"

"I think we just did," Athena muttered as they found themselves facing the main hall, which had been completely ransacked. "I don't imagine the police did this."

Someone had clearly been looking for something after Sandoz had been arrested, though Athena and Ellis had no idea what that might be. They attempted to do their own investigation, though without knowing what it was they were looking for, it was all in vain. Given the disarray of the room, however, they were quite certain that whatever it was, it would be highly unlikely that it was found and extremely probable that it somehow factored into Ana's murder.

"Ellis, maybe we should just go to the police about this and explain our suspicions. What do you think?"

"I would advise against that, pretty lady," a voice that Athena did not know responded. She turned quickly, only to find herself staring down a gorilla of a man in an expensive suit, who also happened to have a gun pointed in her direction. She instantly recognized him as one of the men standing watch outside the club when they arrived. "You've found enough trouble for one night, Miss...?"

Athena refused to acknowledge his inquiry. Instead, she offered little more than clenched fists and a scowl.

"Very well then. Donny, would you be so kind as to subdue our nameless friend here?" Before Athena could respond, she felt a sharp pain in the back of her skull. As her consciousness faded, she remembered that there had been two men outside the club.

Athena awoke sometime later with the worst headache she had ever experienced. She heard voices, indistinguishable at first above the constant pounding in the back of her skull. She did her best to focus on anything but the pain and soon realized that she was bound at the wrists and ankles by a heavy rope. She was lying down, and the floor was cold. Her eyes were clearly blindfolded, but at least she wasn't gagged, though the more she considered it, the more she realized that there was no one she could call out to for help. She also heard voices.

"I'm tellin' ya, Sal, that dame looks familiar. I'm pretty sure she was at the same table as the dead one."

"But why would she come back to the club? You think she might know something about the goods?"

Goods? What are they talking about? Athena thought to herself as she tested the strength of her bonds as quietly as she could. Who do they think I am?

"What about him?"

"I searched him, too. He's clean."

"You find anything out about the dead girl?"

"O'Leary did some digging at the precinct. Turns out she's some airplane acrobat or something. Just in town for a few days. At least, that was her plan." The two voices chuckled heartily at their morbid joke.

"You wanna go get somethin' to eat? I'm starving."

"What about them?"

"I'm not buying them dinner," the other voice laughed. "They ain't going anywhere. We'll be back before they even wake up."

Athena heard the men push back their chairs, walk across the room, and open a heavy, creaking door. She counted to one hundred in her head from the moment the door closed and waited another thirty seconds silently to be certain there was no one else in the room. When she was absolutely convinced that she was alone, she made her first move.

"Ellis? Are you there?" she called out as loud as she could muster, though her throat was dry and her voice was hoarse. When there was no response, she called out another time. Again, she was met with only silence. Had they killed him? "ELLIS! PLEASE! ANSWER ME!"

This time her calls were met with a muffled grunt.

"Ellis, it's me. Wake up!"

There was another moment of silence, followed by something unintelligible.

"Damn it, Ellis!"

"A...Athena..." he responded weakly. Though she could barely understand him, and it was clear that he was in tremendous pain, the sound of his voice was the best thing she had heard in years. "Where are we?"

"I don't know, but I'm going to get us out of here," Athena responded as she strained against her bonds, doing her best to loosen them. Though she had not performed an escape routine in several years, she began working her wrists through the rope as if it were second nature to her. By the time she had wriggled free, she was filled with a sense of pride and nostalgia that momentarily overtook her sense of fear. That is, of course, until she removed her blindfold and was reminded of her current situation. She quickly untied the bonds around her ankles and made her way across the cold room to where Ellis lay. He remained barely conscious and was badly bruised and bloodied. "What on Earth did they do to you?"

"Nothing I can't handle after taking that right cross from you," he said with a laugh that turned to a pained cough. Athena took a survey of their location as she carefully untied Ellis. He was bound much tighter than she was (Athena silently took offense to being underestimated for her gender), but it only took a moment before he was free. They were in a large warehouse filled with broken and unusable sundries. The building had clearly not been used for its intended purpose for quite some time. The only light came through the broken windows, but it was bright enough to see where the concrete was stained with the blood of previous captives.

"How did you get free?"

"I did escape tricks in my father's act when I was growing up. It wasn't very hard. They were pretty careless when they tied me up," Athena responded with a smile.

"Magic, huh? Amazing." Ellis's left knee buckled the moment she helped him to his feet, and he cried out in sheer agony. Blood had soaked through his pants, and his lower leg was extending at an odd angle. She could only imagine the horrors they put him through. She helped him to a chair so that she could scout their location.

"I don't think we have much time left," she said as she hoisted herself up on a pile of crates to look out the window. "They only went to get something to eat, and I don't think they would leave us alone for long. Who knows what they'll do if they catch us." The outside of the warehouse looked to be as abandoned as the inside. None of the surrounding buildings looked to be occupied either. Finding someone to help them would be difficult, but far less dangerous than waiting for their assailants to return. "We have to go now," Athena said as she helped Ellis to his feet once again. This time she made sure to be on his left so that she could support his weight in place of his shattered knee.

The cool night air was tinged with the sour smell of the lake. Athena had no idea where exactly they were, though she knew they were much deeper into the heart of Chicago than they had been earlier that evening. The rows of warehouses on either side of the exit looked completely identical to Athena, making it impossible for her to determine which way to go. She arbitrarily chose a direction and began slowly working her way down the street, guided only by moonlight. Their pace was impossibly slow thanks to Ellis's injury.

They had only gone a few blocks when Athena saw a car approaching them. She knew it was a risk, but flagged the car down anyway. If it was the thugs, she was dead either way, but hopefully it would be someone that could take them to safety. Much to her surprise and delight, it was a police car.

"What brings ya out in such a scary place, Miss?" the officer asked with a thick Irish accent. "And what happened ta yer friend there?"

"We were taken, officer. He was beaten really badly and we have to get out of here before they get back." Athena's exhaustion made her borderline delirious as she delivered as much of the story as she could remember to the officer. "You have to help us, sir."

"Aye. I can help ya, missy. But only if you tell us what yer friend did with the jewels."

"Wha—"

"Don't play stupid. The pretty one was already killed. Ya want to live, ya gotta tell me what she did with them." The officer stepped out of his vehicle and walked around the car to where Athena stood, dumbfounded. Ellis remained slumped against her, too weak to intervene.

O'Leary. They said O'Leary did some sniffing around at the precinct.

"I don't want to hurt ye. I just want what's ours." O'Leary reached for the revolver at the holster on his hip.

"We don't have anything!" Ellis bellowed, still wincing in pain. O'Leary thumbed the revolver. "We just want to know why you killed our friend!"

"Aye, the pretty little one? She was just in the wrong place at the wrong time, I'd say." O'Leary smiled as his hand coiled around the gun. He was cheating towards Ellis. She would only have a split second to make a move.

"And what does that make us?"

"More o' the same," O'Leary sneered as he pulled the gun from the holster.

"GET DOWN!" Athena screamed as she tackled O'Leary into the side of his car. Just as she had hoped, the corrupt officer lost his grip on the gun, and it skittered across the pavement towards Ellis. "Pick it up, you idiot!" Athena bellowed as she delivered a stiff blow to O'Leary, who was too shocked to defend himself.

"I…I've never used one of these," Ellis stammered.

Athena pounced on O'Leary and delivered a series of wild strikes. "You don't have to," she said as she tried to catch her breath, "you just can't let him use it! Now get in the car!" O'Leary was conscious, but dazed from the flurry that Athena delivered. He had caught her with a few stray swings, but her knuckles took the most of the damage.

Headlights were shining upon them as Athena hopped into the car beside Ellis, shoving him into the driver's position. Ellis put the car in motion just as another car pulled up behind them and their captors stepped out. So much for speeding away unnoticed, Athena thought to herself as she watched the thugs pile into their car with the battered Officer O'Leary in tow.

"Can't this thing go any faster?"

"It would help if I knew where we were going—in this STOLEN police car, might I add!"

"Where is your sense of adventure, Ellis?" Athena smiled as she checked

O'Leary's gun for bullets. "They're gaining on us! Get us into the city. We can try to lose them there!" Athena leaned her head out the window to face their pursuers and was greeted by a wild gunshot that never came near her. "I don't think they want us to get away!"

Ellis tried to match her nervous laughter, but he was too focused on the road ahead and the weakness overtaking him. Adrenaline would only carry him so far, after which he was sure to succumb to the mix of exhaustion and pain that washed over him with every sharp turn and every bump in the road. As they made their way downtown, he felt himself grow weaker and weaker.

"Damn it Ellis, they are getting close!" Athena shook him back to reality as their tormentors fired another shot, this time catching the body of the vehicle. "Can you get us to a police station?"

"I...I think so. We aren't far..." Ellis stammered, never taking his eyes off the road.

Well, things can't get any worse, Athena thought as she leaned back out of the window and took aim at the pursuing vehicle. She squeezed the trigger and the bullet went exactly where she had intended, piercing the front passenger tire. That slowed them down, but it won't stop them.

"How much farther?" Athena asked as she opened the door to the car and tried to position herself for a better shot—standing halfway in and halfway out of the vehicle. She barely heard Ellis as she concentrated on her next shot, using the roof of the car to level her aim.

The second shot was even more precise, piercing the windshield and striking the driver in the shoulder. He lost control of the car immediately, and Athena knew they had gotten away. As she turned around to reenter the vehicle, however, she realized that Ellis too had lost control. She screamed as the rogue police car crashed into the wrought iron fence outside the police station. Then everything went black.

For the second time since arriving in Chicago, Athena woke up with a splitting headache and little knowledge of her surroundings. This time, however, she was pleased to feel a comfortable bed below her, though it did little to soothe the pain shooting through her body. As her eyes adjusted to the light, a figure came into focus at the edge of her bed.

"You are a very brave young woman," the old man said softly. "My granddaughter had great respect for you, and I can see why." He fidgeted with the cuff of his suit coat as he spoke. "You were a good friend to her. Perhaps a little reckless, but a good friend nonetheless."

"Who are you? Where am I?" Athena said weakly, not understanding how she ended up in the hospital bed.

"My name is Sandford Zaleski, but you would know me as The Great Sandoz. Ana was my granddaughter," he said with a forced smile. "And you, Miss Voltaire, are in the hospital. You took a nasty spill when your friend crashed the police car."

Athena opened her mouth to speak, but could not find the words. There were simply too many questions to ask.

"I was in a bad position, Miss Voltaire. I owed a lot of money to some very bad people." His voice was full of shame. "But my debts would be washed away if I could smuggle stolen jewels for the same very unsavory people. It's not something I'm very proud of, but I had no other choice." Tears began to well in his eyes, though his voice was calm and unwavering. "I wanted out, and so I went to the police and told them what I had done. They said I just had to get the jewels and testify. Ana was going to act as my courier. It was the only way to get the jewels to the police, but somehow they found out. All I needed was to get the jewels out of the club and I would have been free."

Athena thought back to the night of Ana's murder and remembered that when she emerged from the cabinet during the disappearing act, Ana's simple silver necklace had been replaced by one that was far more ornate. "That's why they killed her, isn't it?"

"She was my favorite, little Ana. Always so graceful and always so fearless." He could no longer hold back the tears and openly wept at the foot of Athena's bed. "I never should have asked for her help." He rose and walked out of the room before Athena could ask any more questions.

Ellis had already been discharged by the time that Athena had been released from the hospital. She made a brief statement to the police, but was told that the testimony of Sandoz and Ellis was more than enough to finalize the case against the men who killed her friend, including the corrupt Officer O'Leary, who pieced together and derailed the Great Sandoz's last shot at redemption.

Athena left Chicago angry and hurt, not understanding why someone so kind and so pure had to die for the mistakes of others. She mourned the loss of Ana in solitude, but dedicated every single performance with the Keefauver Air Angels that followed to her friend.

WELTSCHMERZ
(or "Athena Voltaire and The God of Flesh and Bone")
Dirk Manning

Standing in the warehouse, pistols in both hands, Athena Voltaire stared up into the face of a God.

Not a Norse God, like those she read about as a child... although the giant man(?) who stood before her could have easily stood side by side with any such mythological(?) legends. Standing nearly seven feet tall, with His pale blue eyes and equally pale blonde hair, it was easy to envision Him wielding a magic hammer, using it to crush the skulls of menacing ice trolls or hurling lightning bolts down upon hapless villagers from the clouds.

But He was not a Norse God.

Nor was He a Pacific Island God, the kind so often carved from volcanic rock and placed along the edges of beaches and temples alike, where they were paid homage by well-intentioned but simple-minded villagers who knew nothing of the technological advances that existed past their isolating island boundaries... although based on His chiseled form, barely contained under a skin-tight material Athena did not recognize, it would be easy to assume that He was indeed carved from rock – or perhaps even the side of a small mountain. Athena had known plenty of "strong men" in her day, whether friends, family, lovers or enemies (and sometimes a combination thereof), but none of them had the physique – if such a word even applied to such a borderline inhumanly muscular frame – of the man(?) who stood before her.

No… He was definitely not a Pacific Island God.

She was also fairly sure that He was not an Elder God, the kind whispered about as living beyond the stars by those who dedicated their lives to learning about the occult and the true magicks known only to those who sacrificed much of themselves – and oftentimes others – to gain arcane knowledge about the fabric of the universe. Hushed rumors muttered only in the darkest corners of existence stated that one could not see an Elder God without forfeiting one's sanity, and Athena herself had half-memories of partaking in such an experience – something concerning the disappearance of a young, rich woman in a fishing village the name of which she could not remember – and even now vestiges of the event (which may or may not have happened at all) flashed through her mind, because, looking up at the being before her, she knew that while He held the form of man, He could not possibly be real, much like the Elder God she once thought she saw could not have possibly been real, either.

Could it? Could He? Could any of this?

A low buzzing had begun to sound in Athena's head as she tried to remember the events that had led her to this moment, in hopes it would help her make better sense of what was now happening.

She had come here based on a tip from a trusted informant that this seemingly abandoned warehouse on the docks was actually a hotbed of nefarious Nazi activity, and a simple stakeout proved this to be the case. While she couldn't make out all the details of what exactly was going on within these walls from a simple stakeout, it was clear that numerous Nazi scientists and soldiers alike were all stationed here, working on… something.

After feeling fairly confident she had secured a proper headcount of how many of the rat-finks were there, it took little effort for Athena to let herself in and begin disposing of the cretins. While Athena was by no means a bloodthirsty vigilante, nor enamored with the idea of killing anyone – even Nazi scum – she was always willing to do whatever was necessary to thwart any insidious Nazi plots that she happened to stumble across or that otherwise came to her attention, and in these instances she would use whatever level of force necessary to keep the world safe from their unique brand of evil.

Within minutes she had cleared the room… or so she thought. Unbeknownst to her, two swastika-armband-clad goons were in a side room she somehow missed, and upon hearing the commotion caused by her entrance and the following assault die down, they left their unintended hiding place and crept towards her from behind…

Only to be stopped by Him.

Him… the being who was not a Norse God of legend come to life, nor a Pacific Island God somehow displaced in a dockside warehouse that doubled as a Nazi secret laboratory, nor an Elder God who – with a glance – could destroy the tenuous hold that allowed any thinking mortal mind to remain sane.

Looking at Him, her mind reeling, Athena knew that – whatever else He was or wasn't – He was a God.

A God of flesh and bone.

After studying her coolly for a moment (or was it more than that?), He smiled reassuringly, as if to indicate that, unlike the pair of fallen Nazis He had subdued – and in doing so, most likely saved her life – he was not a threat.

Finally, He spoke.

"I did not intend to intrude or intervene when I saw you arrive here, Fräulein." His booming yet gentle voice had an Anglo-German accent, and his tone was not unlike that of a loving father who, whispering to his newborn daughter, failed to realize he was doing so through a megaphone. His voice was everywhere at once, and it immediately made the buzzing in Athena's brain more disorienting.

"It is clear that you are a woman who can take care of herself…" He continued, squatting on impossibly thick legs to pick up the weapon of the fallen Nazi thug closest to him. "However, I feared, had I not interceded on your behalf, these two *schlägertyps* may have gotten the better of you. Strictly by chance, of course." His voice was humble, but still contained a deep-seated yet unflaunted power that was impossible to fail to notice. He motioned to the pair of unconscious men lying at his feet almost meekly, as if the roles were reversed and it was she, not He, who was the one worthy of worship.

"You are safe now, though, and these *verbrecher* will cause no more evil, allowing us both to part ways and carry on with what we must do." He spoke nonchalantly, crumbling the first Maschinenpistole 40 machine gun in his large hands with the same lack of effort a child showed when crumpling a candy-wrapper. He then slowly stepped down on the second one's weapon, a Walther P38m, effortlessly flattening it under his massive foot.

At this Athena's attention was pulled away from His eyes and to his shoes – if they could even be called shoes – and how they were made of the same sleek, skintight, unidentifiable fabric/substance that covered the rest of his body from the neck down, save his hands. It was only when he turned on his heels – did they even touch the ground? – that Athena's thoughts cleared enough for her to regain the power of speech.

"Wait!" she panted, sounding much more desperate than she wanted. His presence was suddenly like a drug that she feared she would not be able to live without. "Who are you? What are you doing here? Why did you save me?"

He turned to face her once more and smiled in a way that Athena would equate with bashfulness on any other man, although surely that couldn't be what it was, for a being such as He could not possibly have the same flawed emotions as mere mortals such as herself. Holding His sheepish grin, the stranger took a deep breath – which echoed like a M8 Greyhound rumbling down a cobblestone road – before speaking in slow, measured tones. "Who indeed? It is the question we *all* must ask ourselves, is it not?"

He paused for another moment before turning to face her once more, His massive frame filling the scope of her vision. "Do you care more about *WHO* I am, *WHAT* I am doing here or *WHY* I saved you, Fräulein? I fear I cannot stay long, but it would be rude of me to leave you without answering at least one of your questions before I depart… especially since it is of the greatest likelihood that you will never see me again."

The weight of that last statement stabbed at her heart deeper than it should have, and it prompted Athena to ask him a new, different question, one that had the most potential for an elongated answer: "What are you?"

He stared at her intently, and her thoughts started to become foggy and disorganized once more… but she did not care. All that mattered now was keeping Him in her presence. Near her. As close to her as she could manage to get Him.

Her knees buckled and she swayed momentarily when He began to speak again. "Very good, Fräulein, very good indeed." He smiled and nodded approvingly.

Athena swayed again before steadying herself on… something. She did not look to see what it was. She could not take her eyes off him. It was unnatural. All of this was unnatural. Her head was swimming and her thoughts continued to swirl and cloud. Had she been drugged? Of course not. It was… something else. Something irrelevant. He was there, looking at her, and that was all that mattered.

If Athena had the capacity to be worried she would have been terrified, but she didn't, and instead remained in her blissful, euphoric stupor, standing before a God.

She marveled at Him as His chest heaved several more times with equally loud and deep breaths. He pondered how to answer the small, prim woman's question before offering the best answer He was comfortable providing her. "I suppose, Fräulein, that I am not what I was made to be, but rather what I choose to be."

He inadvertently glanced down at the fallen Nazis at his feet as he said it. "Specifically, I am one who seeks to protect the world from those who would do it harm."

All that power… and He stalked Nazis in warehouses on U.S. soil? Even in her euphoric, haze-induced state it didn't make sense to Athena. Nor did how she felt. But that didn't matter. None of it mattered as long as she was near Him… in His presence."

"The world is broken, Fräulein – or at least very, very hurt. It is… *Weltschmerz*? Do you have that word in English?"

Why was he asking her such a strange question? Was He not speaking to her in English right now? She wanted to ask Him this – and respond – but couldn't. The whole warehouse was swaying now, making her nauseated. He, though, in all His grandeur, didn't seem to notice.

"This war between nations, it has done so much damage… to everything… it is causing… *WELTSCHMERZ*." He said the word one more time, this time with even more power and passion, as if by doing so the weight of the word would resonate enough to make her understand it. Staring at Him, she wanted to understand the word just as much as He wanted her to. She wanted to understand Him – to know Him – fully. Completely. Totally.

Athena's hands, now numb from how tightly she had been clutching her pistols from the moment she laid eyes on Him, were unable to do so for even a moment longer. She whimpered and dropped them. Unflinchingly, He continued. "Make no mistake… I recognize the power I have. I could easily tip the balance of the war towards whomever I would choose to align myself with –my makers or those who oppose them." He again looked down at the Nazi goons, this time deliberately sneering. "Some say that all that is necessary for the triumph of evil is for good men to do nothing, but I ask you: Cannot evil results also come from good men doing too much? Cannot the road to *Hölle* be paved just as easily with *good* intentions as it can be with those most vile?"

His massive shoulders seemed to sag lower and lower the more He spoke in this saddened tone. Athena wanted to comfort Him, but did not know how. Her voice had left her, and the room was swaying too much to risk stepping towards Him.

Besides… how could one hope to comfort a distraught, confused, and pleading God?

"I… wish to do more than this… but the truth is that I am afraid to do so, Fräulein. All my power – all this power, and all I can do…" He lifted his large hands, each one the size of a breadbox, into the open air and examined them with His cold, steely gaze. "The terrible responsibility that comes with this power is too much for any one man to bear."

Athena wanted to weep. To weep and to hold Him. Random colors began flashing before her eyes as the room around him began to flit in and out of focus.

"It is a terrible burden, Fräulein, to have so much power that you become powerless." He stood tall once more… and a new expression began to cross His face.

Anger.

"I thought, even before... *this*..." He motioned across His body, now, His face a visage of malice that frightened Athena. "I thought that I knew what true power was... but I was a fool! *Ein völliger Narr*! A *pappnase*! TRUE power is not the ability to impose your will on others – nor even reality. It is none of those petty things! *Tölpel*."

He was now in a rage, but at whom she did not have the capacity to fathom.

To Athena, the room began to smell of copper. And roses. And burning meat.

"True power is shown only in RESTRAINT! I know that now! I have shattered both men and mountains with my bare hands with equal ease! I have walked across the bottom of the ocean and the surface of the moon! I have moved so quickly time not only ceased to move, but once even moved backwards! I have done all these things – ALL OF THEM – and so many more things than I could ever reveal. So many more impossible things..."

His eyes glowed. He seemed taller. Athena's hair began to stand on end. She attempted to mouth words – any words – but could not.

"I am now capable of so much... but all I can do – all I DARE do – is *THIS*."

With little more than a twitch of His right foot He crushed one of the unconscious men underfoot. He acted with such speed that the motion would have remained completely unnoticed were it not for the quick popping noise followed by the squirt of red pulp splattering across the floor.

"I did not even need to touch them to subdue them, Fräulein! That is the extent of my power now... of what I am!" He looked up at her, again, His eyes now wide with rage.

The second thug suddenly awoke from unconsciousness and began shrieking in pain as his body contorted in grotesque and previously unimaginable fashions, his limbs, torso and neck all bending at angles and shapes unfound anywhere in nature.

Athena's stomach lurched, and its contents launched from her mouth in a vomitous pile, mixing with the gore at her feet.

"Look! LOOK! SEE HOW THESE VERMIN SQUIRM AT MY MEREST THOUGHTS!'"

Inexplicably, Athena's hands were now slipping in the mixture of bodily fluids that, only moments before, was at her feet.

"I COULD END THIS! I COULD END ALL OF THIS! This false Reich, the delusions of that petty man with his vile visions of the future! Did you know, Fräulein, that across Europe – not just in Germany – but across the whole continent – that he is creating death factories? Compounds the size of small villages, the whole purpose of which is torture and murder! *WELTSCHMERZ*."

He was screaming now, and Athena's ears were filled with both his booming voice and a high, tinny whine, as if she had stood too close to an exploding grenade.

"*WELTSCHMERZ! WELTSCHMERZ!*" He continued to scream. "THE WORLD IS BROKEN, YET I CANNOT DARE FIX IT!"

Athena felt something trickling across her upper lip and down her temples. She believed it was blood, but she could no longer control her arms enough to place her hands in either location to check. She felt as if the world had somehow completely turned on its side and that her bones were turning to rubber.

"I HAVE BEEN MADE IMPOTENT!" He was incensed, and she was now sure that His feet were not touching the ground.

She was equally sure that she was dying... dying at the feet on an angry, tortured, and oblivious God.

A God of flesh and bone... and rage.

So much rage.

"*I THOUGHT I WAS TO BE MADE A GOD... BUT NO! ALL I HAVE LEARNED IS THAT IF THERE IS A TRUE GOD, HE IS LAUGHING AT ME! LAUGHING AT HOW I HAVE ALL THE POTENTIAL TO RESHAPE THIS WORLD AS I SEE FIT, AS IT SHOULD BE, YET I –*"

"*please...*"

It was a small, whispering, female voice that uttered this single word, but it pierced the darkness like a gunshot. Athena heard it just beyond the ringing in her ears and His manic bellowing, but she could not pinpoint the alien source from which it originated.

He heard it too, and she saw Him look down at her – the anger instantly melting from His face. She wanted nothing more than to continue to hold His gaze, but she could not. Her eyelids were too heavy now, and the world faded to black, the remnants of His echoing voice rattling through both the warehouse and her own trembling skull.

When she opened her eyes again she found herself staring not into His eyes, but into the starry night sky. The world smelled not of flowers and burning meat, but of an urban waterfront. Her ears were no longer ringing, and instead she heard only the gentle lapping of waves against the dock upon which she was lying, motionless.

Groggy, she forced herself into a sitting position. She found that, despite a throbbing migraine, she could think clearly again, and this clarity of thought prompted her to reach for her guns, which rested in their holsters once more.

There was no present threat, though. She was completely alone.

In the distance she could see her plane, barely peeking out from behind a docked ship at the far end of the pier, exactly as she left it an unknown number of hours before.

Seeing that she was safe from any immediate danger and her means of escape was intact, she released her grip on her pistols and turned to face the warehouse…

But it was gone.

No… not gone. The word "gone" implied that it was once there, but was now missing. Rather, it was as if the warehouse had *never* existed, save in her own mind.

Carefully, Athena lifted herself to a standing position as she catalogued the memories of her time leading to now, including how she so carefully monitored the goings-on in the warehouse before entering it, dispatched the Nazi soldiers and scientists inside alike, and then met Him.

Him.

The God.

The sad, impotent, angry, and tortured God.

The God of flesh and bone.

Instinctively, Athena looked to the sky and scanned it in every direction, only to see – as she suspected she would – nothing.

She remembered then, reflexively, something He said to her earlier in the evening:

"*It is of the greatest likelihood that you will never see me again.*"

On weak legs, she turned and carefully began to make her way towards her plane.

Towards freedom.

Towards home.

In the coming days she would learn of many odd occurrences being reported from around the world that night: A flash flood hitting Clipperton Island. An earthquake in Australia. A volcanic eruption in Naples. A meteor shower seen only by residents of the uppermost regions of Austria.

These unusual events, and several more she would discover in the weeks, months, and years to come, happened all within the hours of her unconsciousness, and every time she learned of a new occurrence –through casual research or equally casual conversation – the same word crossed her mind:

"*Weltschmerz.*"

Finally, she understood it.

THE GUNS OF KERR

Marc Mason

Athena grasped both sides of the sink, taking a deep breath. While her initial inclination was to punch Emily in the face, that was not how the rules of polite society worked. Tonight she was stuck in polite society.

The telegram had arrived three days ago, and as Athena Voltaire read it she felt a rush of excitement. Her teenage years had been spent roaming the European continent on tramp steamers as her family's Wild West show toured the world, and it would have been a far lonelier existence without Emily Summers. The two were the inseparable yin and yang of the shipping lanes, ebony-haired daredevil Athena committing acts of rebellion on the ships' decks and masts, and Emily flashing a winsome smile and twirling her curly blonde hair to smooth over any trouble those stunts might cause.

Yet, the relationship was hardly one-sided. Emily's flirtatious nature led to more than one boy feeling burned and responding aggressively, and it was Athena's gifts for lethal right hooks and devastating kicks to the groin that saved the day for the duo. It was after one such incident that Athena held her friend close and swore that they would be "best friends forever."

Did such a proclamation still stand? Athena certainly believed so.

A- Saw an ad for your show in El Paso. Husband and I are living in Tucson. You simply must stop over and have dinner on your way to Los Angeles. See you soon! —Emily

"Married? I wonder what kind of sap she finally let get close to her?" Athena pondered. "Well, whoever he is, if he turns out to be a jerk I'll pummel him. Dinner... is on." The aviatrix lost herself in thought for the moment, and then realized that the idea wasn't all pleasant. "Damn. I'm going to have to shop."

Emily bounced with joy when she saw Athena walking across the tarmac from where she parked her plane. She quickly gave up waiting and ran to embrace her friend and begin to get reacquainted. "I can't believe how amazing you look," Emily said.

"Likewise, gorgeous!" Athena replied. "You're positively radiant!"

The pair released one another, and Emily held up her left hand, displaying a massive diamond ring set in a gold band. "It's marriage, I tell you. I've never felt so happy, so content, in all my life."

Athena examined the rock adorning her friend's hand. "Pretty impressive. Wow. How much did this thing cost?"

"No idea," Emily said with a smile, "but whatever the cost, Robert can afford it!"

Voltaire cocked an eyebrow. "Tell me about this... Robert," she said, and then let out a laugh.

The story flowed from Emily like a rushing river. Robert Randolph had spotted Emily at a party and it had been love at first sight (or so Emily believed, Athena found herself thinking). He came from one of Arizona's wealthiest ranching families, but was mostly focused on charity work. "Something near and dear to my heart," Emily noted. Their courtship was a brief one, and he had made an honest woman out of her quickly.

"So what are you doing now?" Athena asked. "Working on the charity stuff?"

Emily's eyes flickered. "Oh, God, no. Well, sometimes. Mostly, though, I go to parties, dinners, social functions... I mingle, make connections, take things back to Robert if they sound interesting."

Athena was puzzled. "You... aren't performing?"

The new Mrs. Randolph shook her head vehemently. "Never again."

"I don't understand. You used to love working when we were kids. Putting on a show was so important to you."

"Oh, God, Athena. We were kids! I got that stuff out of my system. I don't have to do it anymore. I'm going to relax, have a baby or two, and enjoy the rewards of my new life." Athena started to speak, but Emily cut her off. "And frankly, so should you. Still on the road? Still doing shows? Sweetie, why? You're in your prime and beautiful. Why not catch the right fish and enjoy your life a little?"

That was not why Athena wanted to punch Emily in the face.

After the two parted ways at the airport, Athena engaged in one of her least favorite activities, but one that in this case was a necessary evil: shopping. A flight suit was not acceptable eveningwear, and after a presentable dress was procured, she went back to change clothes and leave the pilot togs with the plane. Soon after, she arrived at the restaurant in a cab, tipping the driver handsomely and wondering not for the last time why she hadn't just gotten back into her plane and gone on to Los Angeles. But "best friends forever" kept rattling around her skull and she had no choice but to keep her commitment.

The greeters opened the doors wide and she entered with what she felt was a bit of flair, appealing to her inner show woman. Athena caught a glimpse of herself in the large, polished mirror that hung inside the vestibule and had to admit that her shopping had paid off. The black dress sparkled in the light, and the gloves were a nice touch, giving her a bit of glamour that she tended to deny herself. She indicated to the maître d that she was meeting the Randolph party, and he snapped for a waiter's attention. The waiter led her to Emily's table, and it was there that the night's long list of surprises began unfolding.

"Athena!" Emily cried out joyously. The blonde woman leapt from her chair and hugged her old friend. Breaking the embrace, she gestured towards the strikingly handsome man seated next to her. "Athena, I'd like to introduce you to my husband, Robert."

He stood and gently clasped her hand. "It's a great pleasure to meet you, Athena. Emily has told me a great deal about you."

"Most of it is probably even true," Athena said with a laugh.

"Indeed, I hope it is," he said, returning a smile. It was then that Athena realized there was someone else walking up behind her. "As for this gentleman, I'd like to introduce my friend Adam Beechler. Adam, this is Emily's friend, Ms. Athena Voltaire."

The young man reached out for Athena's hand. "Enchanted to meet you, Ms.

Voltaire."

Athena was too stunned to do anything but shake the man's hand and offer a brief greeting. The foursome sat down at the table and began perusing the menu. Voltaire did her best to focus, but her rising tide of anger kept getting the better of her. "A setup! I cannot believe she brought me here for a setup!" she thought. "I ought to… I ought to…!" She looked over the top of her menu and caught Emily sneaking a sly glance at her. In return, Athena gave Emily a look that she recognized all too well from their childhood. It was the look that said, "I ought to punch you in the face."

Instead, Athena said, "Please excuse me. I need to powder my nose. Alone."

Emily slid into the role of hostess. "So Adam, tell us what you do."

As the man cleared his throat, Athena took time to study him. He wasn't a bad-looking fellow; he was cute in a sort of tweedy way. His glasses slid forward on his nose whenever his head moved, meaning that he either wasn't rich enough to get a new pair that fit better or self-aware enough to realize that he needed them. Knowing that Emily had brought him here as a blind date, Athena settled on option two. He gestured gently with his hands as he spoke, marking him as someone that spoke in front of crowds with some frequency. Had Emily chosen an actor to try and introduce her to? Why on Earth would she do that? And why wasn't she actually listening to him speak so she could get some of these answers?

"An archivist, you say? Fascinating!" Emily squealed in delight. "What exactly are you working on right now?"

His hands and his smile both spread wide. "It's incredible stuff, really. The Pueblo Museum recently took delivery of a number of Navajo artifacts, and I've been working with the curator to write the materials for the upcoming exhibit. I did all of the research and have written the text that our patrons will read as they walk through the halls."

Robert's interest level rose. "What sorts of items will be on display?"

"We have painted art, pottery, maps… a few skeletons that date back a bit. Oh, and a couple of strange pieces, including one that is supposed to have," Adam altered his voice to try and sound spooky, "mystical powers!"

Athena leaned forward and prodded her would-be date. "Really, Mr. Archivist? You don't believe in mystical powers?"

He stuttered. "Umm, well… that isn't to say that I don't, mind you…"

Voltaire cut him off, putting the full weight of her annoyance into her words. "Because I assure you: there are things in this world that can't be readily explained by science or nature. I know. I've seen them. Maybe if you got out of the museum and into the world a little bit, your mind would be a bit more... expansive."

Across the table, the archivist attempted to speak, but no words came. Emily gave Athena a dagger-filled look and stepped in to break the awkward tension. "Interesting. Adam, would it be possible to go behind the scenes and see the exhibit?"

"Sure. When?" he said, trying to gather himself.

Emily winked at him. "How about after dessert?"

The foursome piled into Robert's car and drove away from the restaurant, Athena unable to deny her friend one last favor. Plus, she thought it was kind of fun poking at the archivist and seeing how it drove Emily crazy. "Must take life's pleasures where you can find them, after all. By the time this night is over, she'll never pull anything like this ever again." Just to be certain that the archivist got no ideas about her warming to him, she put as much distance between them in the back seat as possible.

As night had fallen and the museum was closed, Randolph had no trouble securing a parking spot right in front of the building's steps. The four climbed out of the car, Athena moving quickly so that no doors would be opened for her, and they walked the stairs to the museum's entrance with anticipation.

While Athena did not care for the archivist, she did happen to love museums. Her time in Europe had taught her to be respectful and intellectually curious about cultures and history. Much of that stemmed from moving from town to town and visiting each one's museum or other place of preservation. The history of the American Southwest was a sad one, and one that Athena felt she should know more about, so the visit to the Pueblo Museum did offer the chance for some enlightenment, a chance she hoped to use to its fullest.

The archivist unlocked the front door and herded the group in. There were still lights on for security purposes, making it easy for them to follow him as he began guiding them through the halls and towards his upcoming exhibit. The walk was brief, and as they approached a door at the end of a long hallway, he stopped and held up his hand.

"A few things I should tell you. As I mentioned, there are skeletons, fully put together. My bosses have insisted on putting them in garb and in giving them weapons."

"Were they actually warriors?" Athena asked.

He shook his head. "I don't know. Maybe." He opened the door and turned on the lights in the room. "But that isn't the real issue. Whoever brought us these materials disturbed a burial ground, which is forbidden."

"And culturally inappropriate," Athena said, cutting him off.

"Right," Beechler said with a sigh, and pushed his glasses up his nose. He gestured across the room and the group could see five fully articulated skeletons wearing armor and holding spears and knives. "We're expecting to have a bit of a row once this exhibit opens to the public, one that I think we'll have to back down on. So you all may be the only members of the public to ever see it."

"Lucky us," Athena muttered, causing Emily to elbow her in the ribs.

Robert walked across the room to take a closer look at the bodies, and Emily followed. That left Athena standing with Adam, a situation neither was comfortable with. After a few moments of quiet, she had an idea.

"So tell me, Mr. Beechler, where are the objects with 'mystical powers'?"

He brightened. "Right this way, Ms. Voltaire," he said, gesturing towards a table on the right side of the room. "I'll show you The Guns Of Kerr."

Athena cocked an eyebrow. "Guns? The mystical powers belong to a pair of guns?"

Adam stopped. "They aren't just any guns. Ms. Voltaire." He paused. "These guns are haunted."

"Or I should say, its bullets are."

The group gathered around Adam, anxious for an explanation. Absently pushing his glasses up his nose, he placed the glass case holding the guns on a nearby table and began telling a tale near to being lost.

"To understand the Guns, you have to understand some of the history of this region—the history of the Navajo, really. As you likely know, the Navajo have a reservation here in Arizona. They were moved there in the 1860s, and at first, it was pretty small. However, after some time passed, they were ceded more land, and that land did include some whites still living on it. Some of the whites got along with the Navajo just fine."

Robert shook his head. "And some didn't, of course."

Adam nodded. "Sadly so. The idea was, in order to keep the peace, that there would be peacekeepers from both sides that worked in conjunction to make the arrangement work."

"Did it?" Athena asked.

"For the most part, history seems to suggest that it did. As you might expect, some of the Army soldiers assigned to the task were fairer and more open-minded than others. One of those was a Captain named Kerr. These," he gestured at the case, "belonged to him."

The teenage girl that Athena remembered suddenly emerged from Emily. "I've seen a lot of guns, Mr. Beechler, and not much is distinctive about these. Except perhaps their age. I'd put them at forty, fifty years old at most."

Beechler coughed. "You have a good eye, Mrs. Randolph. They're forty-five years old. Pretty ordinary Colt revolvers on the surface. But the legend behind them is rather interesting. The story goes that Kerr was called to a shaman's home late one night, and the old Navajo was in a bad way. A couple of whites had come roaring through his camp and abducted a young girl. The shaman begged Kerr to find her before…" Adam paused, trying to find the words, and the trio nodded in understanding. "Well, Kerr rode off into the night, tracked the two men, and found them in a mountain pass drinking themselves stupid. The girl was tied up in a tent, and when Kerr had finished subduing the men, he discovered that he had arrived too late." Emily gasped. "Angered, and feeling bitter about not having found the men before they could do their evil deed, Kerr decided to eschew his own country's law, and took the pair back to the shaman so that the old man could deliver his own justice."

Athena found herself impressed. "Seems fair. And it couldn't have been an easy choice for Kerr."

"By all reports, it wasn't. But the shaman's decision was apparently quite simple. He was extremely grateful to Kerr for his efforts and for bringing the men back to the tribe for quiet retribution. So he asked for Kerr's guns, that he might place a blessing upon them. The legend says that it was more than a blessing. Kerr could load bullets, focus on a target, and the bullets would fly as 'ghosts', passing through rocks and walls until they were on top of their target, when they would return to solid form and do their bloody work."

Robert burst out laughing. "Ghost bullets! What a wonderful story!"

"You'd be surprised at how many people believe it. The documentation on this story was located only a few months ago, and already we've had an inquiry from someone seeking to reactivate the shaman's spell for his own use." Adam shook his head. "Imagine if it truly was real. No one would be safe from someone shooting these things."

Athena studied the guns closely. Unfortunately for her, she could imagine that all too well. There were numerous times such a gun could have come in handy were she wielding it; there were many more times that she would have lost her life had the guns been held in the hands of others. Such a power was ultimately best left unused, of that she was certain. "Well, Mr. Beechler," she said, tilting her head away from the case, "that is indeed quite a story. Will you be writing it up for the museum's patrons to read?"

"Not this one. The Guns will appear with a brief bio of Kerr in the section of the exhibit dedicated to life on the reservation and that's it." He took a handkerchief from his pocket and wiped some dust off of the glass. "I believe that the fewer people that we encourage to believe in magic guns, the better. History is the study of fact."

"Wise choice, Mr. Archivist," Athena said softly.

"Indeed," Emily added. "Hmm. I'm feeling a bit warm. Adam, where might I find a drinking fountain?"

He pointed down the hallway. "Go back the way we came, and you'll see one by the entrance."

Emily tugged on her husband's sleeve. "Come with me darling? Make sure I don't get lost?" Robert gave her his arm and the pair sauntered down the hallway, leaving Voltaire and her blind date alone in the exhibit. She found herself walking around the room and reading the text Beechler had written, and Athena had to admit that it was thorough and informative.

"Feel free to ask me any questions," he said, clearing his throat. "Odd thing, really. I have what they call a 'photographic memory'- I can memorize just about anything once I've read it. So if some of the text begs for more answers…"

Athena nodded and continued to read. She had no idea about such horrific things as the Long Walk, where nine thousand Navajo men, women and children were forced to walk over three hundred miles to the first "reservation" they were given, followed by a similar walk a few short years later that returned them to their own sacred grounds. She shuddered, thinking about the toll that had to have taken on those people.

"Are you cold?" he asked.

"Just appalled," she replied softly. "It feels like every bit of the history in this room is coated in blood and pain. I don't know how you stand it."

He shrugged his shoulders gently. "It isn't easy. But if I had chosen European history, it would have been no different. Crusades, inquisitions, the black plague… all parts of human history are coated in that blood and pain."

"Then why history?" Athena asked, finding herself curious.

"This may sound foolish, but I got into history because I'm an optimist." Athena cocked an eyebrow at him. "Seriously. I have always felt that if we understand the mistakes we have made along the way, we can prevent them from happening again."

She giggled. "That is optimistic! Have you noticed what's going on in Europe these days?"

"Unfortunately, I'm all too aware of it. This Hitler fellow… he frightens me. He's very clever. His political machinations feel like the beginning of something larger."

Athena began to wonder if she hadn't misjudged this man. He was smarter than he seemed, educated, and he genuinely seemed to think about the world. He was the exact opposite of what Emily had been suggesting she needed to find for herself. She began to get the idea that perhaps her childhood friend hadn't forgotten what kind of person Athena Voltaire really was, and that she had tried to do something nice for her as a make-up for their earlier conversation.

"Dammit," she whispered. "Now I'm going to have to apologize. Right after she apologizes to me, of course."

Adam cleared his throat. "Did I say something wrong, Ms. Voltaire?"

She felt herself smiling. "Not at all. And please: call me Athena."

He registered surprise. "Athena it is. Is there anything else I can tell you about the exhibit, Athena?"

Something at the edge of Athena's vision registered as wrong, and her head whipped around to the warrior exhibit. "Umm, yes, you can, Adam. Perhaps you can explain why the skeletons are moving!"

Their actions were slow as the skeletons struggled with their first movements in decades. But there was no question that what Athena had seen was absolutely true: the Navajo dead were shaking their dust off their bones (literally) and beginning to test their range of motion.

Adam's face was a canvas of awe, confusion, and terror. "Oh, my God! This is not possible!" His eyes grew wide. "What do we do?"

Athena was nonplussed. "I wish I knew. This is a new one, even for me." He shot Athena a questioning look. "Long story. Lots of long stories, really. Let's just say I have some experience with... odd things."

"Should we try and talk to them?"

She began to get a bad feeling about the situation. "I don't quite think they'll say anything back. No vocal cords. It might be best if we backed out of the room. No sudden moves."

Unfortunately, it was too late for that. Suddenly the skeletal horrors seemed to take notice of the pair. Had their faces still contained muscles, Athena was sure that the look they gave her and Adam would be one of rage. They shook off all accoutrements, holding on solely to the weapons that had been placed on exhibit with them.

"Adam," she said out of the side of her mouth. "I think we're in trouble." Before she could make a move, a bony arm drew back and a spear was launched at Athena and the archivist. It narrowly missed the pair, and they went sprawling to the ground, out of the line of fire.

"You think we're in trouble?!"

Athena slid across the floor towards the spear and took it in her hands. "This is such a bad idea," she muttered, but there was really no choice. Whatever was happening here, she had to protect Emily and the others. She kicked off her shoes then picked herself up off the floor and saw her foes advancing. Spotting Adam out of the corner of her eye, Athena put what passed for her plan in motion. "Run! Find the others and get help! I'll hold them here!"

The young aviatrix lifted the spear above her head and yelled, hoping that it might serve as a distraction as she ran towards them, but the long-dead warriors betrayed no emotion, instead raising their own weapons toward her. "Five against one isn't exactly a fair fight," she thought, "but maybe the fact that I'm still alive gives me an advantage." As the nearest of her opponents came into range, though, she came to a bittersweet realization. "Of course, that's only an advantage if I stay alive."

As the warrior thrust his spear at her, Athena parried the attack with her own and spun on her heel to deliver a blow to the midsection. Much to her surprise, though, she fell down as the spear passed through the skeleton's ribcage and all the way through the body without touching a single bone. Seeing her vulnerable on the ground, it raised its own weapon again and made to deliver a killing blow, but Athena kicked its legs out from under it, and it hit the floor with a loud crack. She leapt off the ground and attempted to drive her spear through the skull, but a second warrior blocked her stroke, using its tomahawk to catch her spear and yank it away from her.

Athena Voltaire was unarmed.

The tomahawk swung its way toward her torso, and she barely jumped backwards out of its way. The dead thing again reached back with its bony arm and swung its blade at her in a downward stroke. Athena dodged to the side, ramming herself into the wall. The skeleton pressed its advantage, bearing down on her, but as it reached back to swing its weapon, that gave her an opening. She reached up with both hands, grabbed the bony arm, and shifted her weight and turned. That slammed the warrior into the wall, and without warning it broke apart into dozens of pieces.

That was when her left shoulder exploded in pain. She attempted to move, but found she could not, and as she craned her neck to look back, she could see why: a spear was lodged in her shoulder, a spear in the hands of a skeletal foe that was pushing it forward. Athena was trapped against the wall, unable to leverage her way out, and a second warrior was approaching with a tomahawk. Her eyes opened wide as the debilitating pain began spreading through her body. She focused on the tomahawk, wondering how long it had been since it had been sharpened. How many men and animals had met their end from its blade?

How much… how long… was this going to hurt?

Suddenly she saw a blur, and the tomahawked warrior was gone from her view. The one holding the spear in her shoulder lost its concentration, which allowed Athena to take a step backward (which was excruciating) and then a step forward, which caused the spear to drop from her shoulder. As she turned herself fully around she saw Adam on the ground, wrestling the skeleton that had come so close to burying its tomahawk in her skull.

"Couldn't let you have all the fun!" he yelled at her, and at that moment the spear-carrier returned its focus to Athena. She was bleeding badly from her left arm, which was now useless, but her right one was working just fine. Athena took three quick steps and got too close for the warrior to do anything but swing his weapon like a primitive stick. She blocked its first strike with her forearm and spun through his movement, but the second swing got through, hitting her in the back just below her wound. She wanted to scream, but held the pain inside. She had fallen forward from the blow, and now her opponent was once again behind her with a clear view of her back and the blood dripping down it.

On instinct she dropped to the floor, and as she did the spear passed over her head and sparked against the wall. Athena reached up and grabbed hold of the spear, using it to brace herself and pull herself up. The warrior, caught off guard, attempted to regain its balance, but stumbled. That gave Voltaire the opening she needed. She shoved backward with the spear, adding to the creature's lack of balance, and it went tumbling to the floor. Without hesitation, she sprang forward to press the advantage, raising the spear high above her head and delivering a crushing blow to the skull. As it splintered into dozens of pieces on its own, the rest of the body followed.

Discovering herself to be without another foe, Athena turned back to check on Adam. She watched as he fought a bizarre duel with the dead on the floor of his museum. He landed an impressive head butt to the creature's jaw, which actually did seem to stagger it. As it reeled, Athena shouted for Adam and threw him the spear. Needing no instruction, he buried the weapon in the warrior's skull, causing the same sort of disintegration that had felled the other two. Adam gave a wan smile, then noticed the blood spreading down Athena's shoulder.

"Good lord! Are you okay?" He jumped from the floor and ran to Athena's side, checking out her wound. Adam took his jacket off and threw it aside, then began tearing strips off of his shirt and applying them to her shoulder.

"Hurts," she admitted. "Plus," she offered a smile through gritted teeth, "I just bought this dress."

"Well, if it makes you feel any better, I just bought this shirt," he said with a wink, tearing off another strip. "You know, you might be able to get the dress dry cleaned. Robert probably knows someone."

As he finished applying the makeshift bandages, her eyes flew open. "Robert! Emily! Adam- there were five skeletons! We stopped three!"

Adam knew what had happened even before he looked, but a quick glance at the table told him he was right. "The Guns... they're gone."

"We've got to get moving, right now!" she told him. "Maybe we can stop them before it's too late!"

The duo moved quickly through the museum hallways, making their way back towards the entrance. Once they reached the lobby, they discovered that they were indeed in time... and a little too late.

Tied up back-to-back, Robert and Emily were sitting in the middle of the floor, a figure standing over them. Athena guessed that he was in his early 40s; his brown hair was beginning to show signs of gray, and a slight paunch had developed around his midsection, something not well hidden by the flight suit he was wearing. The two remaining skeletal warriors stood at the man's side. Athena searched her memory of arriving at the airport earlier and felt a tingle of recognition.

"Ahh, Mr. Beechler. So good to see you again. As you can see, your museum's refusal to return my ancestor's Guns was simply not something I could accept. Thus, I must use other means to retrieve my property. My apologies for the damages caused to the rest of your exhibit, but if you want to make an omelet…"

Adam's voice was full of rage. "Chandler! Your property? Your Guns? How dare you, sir! Have you no sense of decency?"

The man's voice took on a cold tone. "Decency? Hardly required, I'd say. In fact, let's make this even more indecent." He reached into his clothing and produced a grenade. Beckoning to one of his undead assistants, a skeletal hand reached out and took the grenade from his hand. The man Adam had called Chandler then made sure the creature had a solid grasp and pulled the pin from the grenade while keeping the firing mechanism from reaching the "trigger" point. "There. Now we're truly indecent, Mr. Beechler. So here's what is going to happen. I'm going to leave. After I am gone, my little friend here is going to make sure that you and your date stay. After thirty minutes pass, he will walk outside, get the pin for this device, and replace it. Of course if you misbehave, he'll just drop it in the lap of one of these two, and this place will need plenty of repairs and a new paint job. Do I make myself clear?"

Athena and Adam nodded assent. "Quite clear," Adam said, his voice barely above a whisper.

As the door shut behind Chandler and the other skeletal warrior, Athena assessed their situation quickly. Adam started to move towards Robert and Emily, but she held her arm out and kept him in place. She needed a plan.

She found a memory.

"Emily?" Her friend's head jerked upward, her eyes meeting Athena's. "We've had so little time to reminisce since I've been here."

Robert fought back a choke. "This hardly seems the time."

Athena continued. "Never a bad time to remember fun with old friends. In fact, I was just thinking about our time in France when we were children. Do you remember all the fun we had, Em?" The blonde woman nodded, curious where Voltaire was leading her. "I think my favorite moment came when we were in Marseilles. You and I went to a market there, and that poor woman had her bag stolen by that rather unpleasant looking fellow…"

Recognition flooded Emily's face. "I do remember that. That was the day we had been playing soccer with those boys in the street. We learned some amazing moves from those boys. Those cute, cute boys…"

"The one with the freckles was mad for you, Em."

Emily watched as the skeleton holding the grenade ambled around her and her husband. "Oh, it wasn't so much that he fancied me for my looks." Robert strained to peer over his shoulder and give his wife an incredulous look. "I think it was more that he saw how I dealt with that thief."

"Robert, darling?" she said, anticipation rising within her. "Duck!"

He did as instructed, and her right leg swung out into a kick, toppling the skeletal warrior off his feet. As he fell, his grip on the grenade failed, and it dropped from his hand. Emily's left leg whipped upward, her foot catching the grenade in motion, and the kick sending the explosive flying over her husband's head and towards the bowels of the museum. Athena and Adam dove for the floor, and the four waited for the explosion.

It was quick in coming.

Metal and plaster shrapnel flew through the room and fell upon them. Adam could see that a small fire had broken out, and after he was able to right himself and make sure that his companions were okay, he set about finding the means to extinguish it. As he did, Athena slammed the remaining skeleton to the floor, destroying it, then freed Emily and Robert from their bonds.

"Oh, my goodness, Athena! What happened to your shoulder?" Emily asked, seeing the bloody rags wrapped around her friend's arm.

Athena managed a half-hearted smile through her pain. "These fellows," she said, gesturing to the bones on the floor "have a very rude way of getting their master's point across."

Robert looked a bit dazed, and Athena could see that he was reaching his limit for insanity that evening. She reached out with her good arm and placed her hand on his chest. "Are you injured?"

He waived her off. "Excellent!" Athena said, trying to be encouraging. "Neither is Emily, so the two of you did well in taking care of one another."

Randolph coughed and looked at Voltaire's arm. "Unfortunately, it seems the same cannot be said of Mr. Beechler."

Athena gave Robert a playful punch in the arm. "Please! He barely has a scratch on him, and I just have a little flesh wound. Heroes all around. But now we need to get moving, because this Chandler is getting away with the Guns."

"Do you have a plan?" Emily asked.

"Don't I always?" Athena said. "Robert, we're going to need your car keys. Oh, and to leave you behind to deal with the authorities. Sorry…"

"Adam!" Athena shouted louder than necessary. "Please do try and avoid the bumps!"

Beechler sat ramrod straight at the wheel of Robert Randolph's car, his foot pressed against the gas pedal, the gas pedal pressed against the floor. "Sorry!" he said, feeling a bit sheepish. "This is my first car chase." He paused, questioning his choice of words. "And I'm not even really chasing another car."

Sitting in the rear, Athena leaned forward, pressing her upper torso against the front seats and giving Emily the best possible access to her back. As Athena gripped her forearm with her jaw, her childhood friend once again began the task of sewing the wound in Voltaire's shoulder shut. Emily had cleaned it as best as possible while the vehicle careened through the streets of Tucson on the way to the airport, but it had to be closed now, or infection could easily set in.

"I can't believe I'm sewing you up again," Emily said, her voice tired, the evening's events weighing on her. "Thought we were done with this at our age, darling."

Athena unclenched from her arm and let her head rise a bit. A half-laugh, half-cough escaped her lips. "Are you joking? This is the second time this month I've gotten stitches. Of course, the first time it was because a screwdriver slipped while I was tightening an engine bolt, and it went halfway through my palm." Adam's eyes jerked sideways and she saw him looking at her in the rearview mirror. "You two really don't know how to have fun."

Voltaire gritted her teeth as Emily pulled a particularly tight stitch closed. "Oh, yes, I do. It's called 'a nice evening out with my husband, his oldest friend, and my oldest friend.'" She paused to examine her handiwork. "You'll notice," she said, finishing another closure, "that nowhere did I mention explosions, the occult, or sewing your arm back together."

Athena turned slightly, locking eyes with Emily and smiling warmly. "That," she said, "used to be our description of a very good Tuesday."

Emily put her hand against Athena's face and caressed her cheek, then quickly shoved the raven-haired woman's head back to facing forward and held it in place. "Just your luck, Athena," Emily said, dripping with sarcasm. "It's Monday."

Realizing that there was to be no placating Emily at that moment, Athena returned her attention to the man behind the wheel. "All right, Adam, we have some time. Who is this Chandler? Why does he want the Guns?"

Keeping focus on the road, the archivist began telling what he knew of their opponent. "Honestly, I thought he was a bit of a harmless fool. His name is Brian Chandler. A white, but he claims to be half Navajo, and that he has 'shamanic powers'. Has money- not hugely powerful money, but money. Originally wired the museum and offered a sum for the Guns. We denied him, of course. Then he came to town, wrangled a meeting with our director, made another offer, was rebuffed. Oh- here's the rub: he claims to be a distant relative of Kerr himself, and therefore the rightful owner of the Guns. But since he has never once supplied anything resembling proof, and we have water-tight paperwork that says Kerr had no descendants, none of us felt even the slightest twinge of sadness for denying his claims."

Athena furrowed her brow. "Shamanic powers?"

Adam took a deep breath. "Yeah. Who would have believed that?"

She smiled at him. "No one. That sort of thing sounds crazy."

"You seem to deal with crazy with some frequency, Ms. Voltaire."

"And I never really want to believe it. Not until I have to."

"Well, I believe Mr. Chandler now."

Athena gave him a rueful look. "Me, too. And that means we have to stop him before he can do the ritual that bonds the Guns to him. No telling what this man would do with them. He's clearly demonstrated that things like basic morality mean very little to him. Robberies, murders, assassinations… all on the table with those Guns." Suddenly she felt the tension in her left shoulder ease.

"All done," Emily said, using her fingernails to cut the thread and leave no excess strands flying away from the wound. "Good as… well, not new. But the scarring should be minimal, at least. And it's mostly straight."

Athena eased back in the seat next to Emily and turned to fix her friend with a serious look. "Thank you, Emily. For everything." She nodded her head towards the front of the car. "For everything. You have always done your best and tried your hardest for me. I want you to know how much I appreciate it."

Emily leaned forward and embraced Athena in a careful hug, avoiding the repaired left arm. "I just give back what you've always given me, Athena."

Adam's voice broke the pair's reverie. "Old Tucson Airfield. We're here."

"Chandler's flight plan said he was coming from the Grand Canyon area," Athena said, jogging back to her waiting plane and once again in her flight suit. "He's got about 30 minutes lead on us at this point, but the good news is that the kind of plane he's flying is slower than mine. We won't catch up to him completely, but I think we can cut that lead of his in half."

Emily looked pained. "I don't suppose I have to tell you, darling, that what you are proposing to do is ridiculously dangerous. Not to mention reckless. We can call the authorities and have them waiting on Chandler when he lands up north."

Athena shook her head. "That's assuming he lands at a regular airfield. My guess is that he won't. He'll want to set up the ritual in private and avoid any potential interference from the police. What we have in our favor is that he believes he has all the time he needs. That grenade was supposed to hold us off for a half hour, and then he probably thought we'd call the authorities. He won't be expecting anybody. And he doesn't know that Adam has... special help."

"Then good luck. See you next time you're in town?"

The weary pilot hugged her friend tight. "Count on it, Em." Releasing the embrace, she turned to Adam. "You ready?"

He gulped. "Have I mentioned that I don't like to fly?"

"Trust me- you're going to love it after this."

"Uh. Why?"

She gave him a playful punch in the shoulder. "Because I'm going to actually teach you to fly the plane. Best way to pass a long flight. It's going to be great!"

After a couple of hours in the air, Adam began to notice changes in the air temperature and smell. "Athena," he yelled, "we're getting close! The cold means we're approaching the area nearing the Canyon, and the pine means we're over the forest near the southern rim!"

She turned around in her seat as much as she could. "Okay! I'll start taking her down so we can start looking for lights and movement where it doesn't belong!"

The aviatrix maneuvered the stick and moved the plane into a gentle descent. It was now the middle of the night, something that Athena felt worked to their advantage. Larger camps and settlements would have a brighter profile. The odds favored Chandler having a smaller setup and perhaps even lights resembling a landing strip. If she and Adam were lucky, he might even be careless enough to forget to extinguish them.

After thirty minutes of gliding her way around the eighth wonder of the world, Athena spotted an unusual line of lights in the distance. She gestured to Adam, and he took out a pair of field binoculars that Athena had stashed under the passenger seat. He took a long look through the lenses and spotted what he believed to be a plane. Adam gave Athena a thumbs-up; fortune had favored them on their search.

Positive thoughts immediately left Adam's mind, however, as Athena made a sharp banking turn, veering the plane on a collision course for the lights in the distance and nearly causing Adam to lose the contents of his dinner. She cut her own lights, going dark and leaving only the sound of her engines to fill the air. The sound would announce her as she approached, but it was her hope that Chandler would be baffled by the absence of light and not realize how close she was until it was too late. Voltaire lowered her altitude, moving closer and closer to the ground, and as they approached, the pair could see Chandler bathed in the light of a bonfire.

Adam noted that the villain was dressed in traditional Navajo clothing from Kerr's era. "He's really taking this all the way," Adam thought. "Maybe he actually is Kerr's descendant." Beechler mentally slapped himself in the forehead. "What difference does it make? He's a madman and he has to be stopped. I only hope that I can do what Athena needs me to do when the time comes."

Chandler was stalking around the fire, feeling freer than he ever had in his life. At the entrance to his hogan sat the Guns upon an altar. The warmth of the blaze comforted him, as he found himself amused at how easy it had been to snatch them from the museum. The man and woman he had subdued in the foyer had gone down easy enough thanks to his undead warriors, and Beechler and his date had proved no more effective. Indeed, it was clear that the archivist's woman had been injured. That surely meant even more of a delay in the authorities being put on his trail. More than enough time to finish what he had started and bond the Guns to his own spirit.

Another circle around the fire and then he knelt down in front of the Guns and began speaking from a scroll in the tongue of his ancestors. With each passing word the cursed weapons began to glow, and as he approached the final words they were nearly incandescent. But as he began to speak the last of the spell, the noise he had been hearing in the distance began to grow louder. Louder. LOUDER! Suddenly confused, he shouted the next few words, and he began to wonder if the Guns needed to hear him clearly or if it was merely enough to speak the words.

Before he could discover the answer, Athena Voltaire and her plane burst forth from the darkness and passed mere feet over his head. Chandler threw himself upon the ground and let out an involuntary stream of cursing. Angered, he got up and reached for the paper containing the final words of the bonding ceremony. He heard the plane landing nearby and quickly turned his attention back to completing the spell. It was then that he loosed a mightier scream than he had ever put forth in his life. The Guns of Kerr were no longer glowing. They were inert. The words spoke in anger as the plane passed overhead disrupted the ceremony. He was going to have to start over. That woman... that pilot! She and Beechler were going to pay for what they had done. Of that much he was certain.

Athena checked to make sure that each chamber in her revolver was full, then turned to Adam. "You sure you're okay with the plan?"

He nodded. "It will be difficult, but I think I can do it. Fortunately, the thing is short."

"Great! Let's go!" She tugged his arm and broke into a sprint from the plane towards the fire which illuminated the enraged form of Chandler. She could see that he was rushing in and out of his hogan, finally running from its doorway and taking up a position on the far side of the fire. Athena looked to make sure that Adam was close behind her, then altered her path to intercept the madman.

As they approached, Athena left her gun in its holster. She would give Chandler an opportunity to surrender without bloodshed; "After all," she thought, "tonight is a night for polite society. It would be rude to simply shoot first." There was also the matter of whether or not Chandler was unaided in his nefarious deeds or if he had others backing him.

However, as Athena and Adam began to clearly see Chandler, they could see that he was alone. He also looked to be unarmed, holding only a small burlap sack in his left hand, his right one empty.

"Give it up, Chandler!" Adam demanded. "You have nowhere to run!"

The older man scoffed. "Run? Why would I run?"

Athena drew her gun. "You're outnumbered and outgunned!"

Chandler's lower jaw curled into an evil smile. "I believe you have that backwards," he said. He reached into the sack, produced a handful of dust and threw it into the air in a circular pattern. As he did, a smattering of Navajo words escaped his lips, and suddenly the ground behind Athena and Adam began to shake. The pair turned to see what was happening and looked on in astonishment as a dozen skeletal bodies exhumed themselves from the earth and rose up in defiance of death. Each was armed with the weapons they took to their graves.

"Oh, great. These guys again," Athena groaned, her shoulder suddenly beginning to throb. She looked at Adam, and it was clear that he was bewildered and more than a little frightened.

"As you can see, my dear Ms... whatever your name is…"

She cut him off. "Voltaire. Athena Voltaire."

"As you can see, Ms. Inconsequential, it is you that is outnumbered. It is you, Mr. Beechler, that has nowhere to run." Chandler turned his attention to the risen warriors. "The woman is yours. See to it she doesn't interfere. This one," he said, pointing to Adam, "is mine!"

Adam's eyes grew wide. He turned to Athena and whispered. "This was not how it was supposed to go!"

Athena winked at him. "Are you kidding? It's kind of refreshing. Normally the whackos see me as the biggest threat and try and kill me first. Having someone else as the target is a nice change." She slapped him on the back with her good arm. "Don't worry. I'll handle these guys and then come rescue you. Fair enough?" He nodded. "Then go get him, cowboy!"

Voltaire faced down the small army of the dead that Chandler had set upon her. "Twelve bad guys. Six bullets. Guess I'll have to pick up a weapon or two as I go." She aimed the revolver at the skull of the nearest opponent. Caressing the trigger, it spit fire and lead, and the bones that once held together a human head exploded into hundreds of pieces. The rest of the body crashed to the ground.

Now she had their attention. The undead began picking up energy and movement and making their way towards her. "One down, eleven to go," she thought briefly. Then her mind turned to other things, among them survival… and wishing she had more bullets.

Chandler's right cross landed squarely on the left side of Adam's jaw, and he went down hard. The older man drew his leg back to kick Beechler in the ribs, but he was distracted by the booming sound of Athena's gun going off. Seizing the advantage, Adam swept his legs through Chandler's, causing the shaman to lose his balance and crash to the ground. Adam attempted to elbow his foe in the throat, but Chandler rolled out of the way. Both men forced themselves off the dirt and heard the gun discharge again.

"Your girlfriend isn't going to last with a six-shooter, boy!" Chandler sneered.

The gun went off again. "She's tougher than you think," Adam replied, full of what he knew was false bravado. "And she's not my girlfriend!" Beechler ran at the older man and made to tackle him. However, as he did, the older man stepped aside and tripped him, sending him sliding through the dirt. As he lay there trying to regain his bearings, he looked to his left and saw the hogan. In front of the domicile sat the Guns Of Kerr, and in front of the Guns… was exactly what Adam was looking for. Before he could move, though, two things happened: Athena's gun went off again. And Chandler's foot landed squarely in Adam's ribcage, knocking the wind from him.

For the next few seconds, Adam was going to be helpless.

The nearest opponents were approaching Athena almost warily. "Apparently the dead aren't dumb," she thought. Two approached on her left, weapons raised. She steadied her aim and pulled the trigger twice in succession.

Chandler's next kick came in almost the same spot, and Adam felt what he was sure was the cracking of bones. That kick also had more force behind it. Adam felt himself lifted briefly from the ground, and he rolled over nearly twice. As his eyes adjusted, he looked up and saw that this had the effect of moving him closer to where he wanted to be anyway. The question became: how many more kicks would it take to get to the hogan, and would he be intact enough once he got there? Taking a chance, he attempted a roll on his own, and as he did, Chandler kicked at him again, this time only grazing him, aggravating the older man.

The shaman moved aggressively to stay with Adam's rolling body, and as his young foe came to a stop, he drew back his leg and kicked with all his might again. As he connected he heard the satisfying crunch of bone cracking under pressure and watched as Beechler's limp body rolled and flopped until he was facing away from Chandler and lying on his side.

Another shot rang out in the darkness, and Chandler decided it was time to administer the coup de grace. He reached beneath his clothing and pulled out a long knife, one that decades ago was used for skinning fresh game. The boy lying before him in the dirt? He was to be the freshest game of them all.

Adam could not see the knife, but every instinct in his body told him to get away. He took one more look to make certain he had gotten what he needed, then he rolled over to face the older man and gingerly began to push himself up from the ground.

"That's it, boy," Chandler sneered. "Better to see the end coming."

A sixth shot exploded from the darkness. The gun was empty.

Adam held up his hand in a stop gesture as he faced what he was sure was a certain death. "Just one thing, Chandler."

"What?"

"The ceremony." Chandler was alarmed to see that the younger man was holding the scroll in his hand. Beechler spit blood from the corner of his mouth. "Somehow I doubt you memorized it!" With all his remaining energy, Adam reached back and hurled the scroll into the blazing fire.

Chandler's face was a mask of anger and horror as he watched the ceremonial words descend into the fire and evaporate into ash. His head snapped back to Adam, watching as the smug look on the younger man's bloodied face went away quickly as he fell back to the ground. "You… you will die for that, boy, and die most unpleasantly!" He raised the knife over his head and prepared to bring it down upon Adam, but before he could, a tomahawk came flying from the darkness. The blunt end hit Chandler's hands, causing the shaman to drop the knife. Startled, both men looked through the fire to see Athena Voltaire standing with her hands on her hips.

"See? I told you I'd rescue you," she said with a hint of self-satisfaction.

The older man recovered his wits quickly, reaching down and scooping up the Guns in his hands and sprinting in the direction of his makeshift runway. Athena rounded the fire and rushed to Adam's side, intently watching Chandler run off into the darkness.

"You've gotta go," Adam rasped. "You can't let him get away."

"I won't," she said, sliding her right arm under Adam's left and bracing herself to lift him off the ground. "But I'm not leaving you here, either. No telling what other sorts of surprises he's left behind." They worked together, and after a gentle effort and a lot of pain in Adam's torso, he was on his feet. In the distance, Athena heard a plane engine roar to life. "Sounds like he's going to make a run for it in the air." Athena's face lit up. "Let's show him just how bad an idea that is, shall we?"

Athena held Adam upright as they crossed the dark and dusty ground, her plane nearly in sight. As they moved, she heard the distinct sound of a plane taxiing and soon enough the smooth purring of a bird in flight. There was a moment of dismay as she heard Chandler's plane moving away from her; tracking him in the dark by sound – and in a canyon no less – would be tricky. Suddenly, though, the shaman did her a favor.

"Adam! Look! He has some sort of light in his seat!"

His eyes flew open. "Oh, damn- what if he did memorize the ceremony?"

"We had better get on him quickly!" Athena replied.

As they reached her plane, Athena let Adam go and bade him to get himself into the aircraft while she revved up the engines. Seconds later the pair was back in the air. The plane gracefully took wing and gained altitude, sending a jolt of adrenalin through Athena. This was what she did; this is what she was meant for.

Peering over her shoulder, she saw Adam slumped in his seat, blood drying on his mouth and chin, black circles around his eyes. "Poor guy," she thought. "Not exactly the polite evening on the town he was expecting tonight." Athena shut off her own plane's lights. She'd catch up to Chandler by using the dark.

It wouldn't take long.

Chandler raged and fumed at the twists that fate had presented him. The scroll. "Gone! The ritual is gone!" He wracked his brain, trying his best to remember the entirety of the spell, but pieces of the text escaped his memory. Still, he was determined to succeed. The second seat held the last skeleton from his journey to Tucson, and as the older man spoke a command in Navajo, it took control of flying the plane.

The shaman placed the Guns in his lap and began speaking what he remembered of the ritual. "The mind is a tricky thing," he told himself. "If I start the ceremony, perhaps subconsciously I'll remember the correct words and be able to complete the bonding." The first few lines slipped off his tongue like honey, liquid and sweet. A feeling of confidence and awe overtook him. The Guns of Kerr had once again begun to glow. It was going to work! If only the plane's engines weren't so loud, so he could enjoy the moment.

It was then that it dawned on him: that was not the sound of his plane.

Athena slid out of her seat and gave Adam a slow nod. "I have to take the fight to him," she told him, assuring him that she wasn't completely insane. "It's the only way to recover the Guns." They were nearly on top of Chandler's plane, and the glow of the half-finished ceremony would illuminate them as well in a matter of moments. Their timing needed to be perfect, or Athena Voltaire was going to

be a permanent part of the Grand Canyon's landscape. She held up four fingers and slowly began dropping them in a countdown. As she reached one, then zero, Adam turned on their own plane's lights, setting the sky ablaze and temporarily blinding Chandler. Using that distraction, she made the jump from her plane to the top wing of his.

Chandler's vision slowly cleared, and he offered a brief prayer of thanks to the gods that the skeleton had no eyes to blind and that they were thusly still in the air. But as the black spots washed away from his eyes, he saw something that he initially felt shouldn't be possible. The woman, the one with Beechler, was sliding down off the top wing and into the space between the two. Somehow she had boarded his plane. That would not stand.

The older man reached into the skeleton's "lap" and dropped the Guns of Kerr, at the same time withdrawing its tomahawk. Seeing Athena moving toward the pilot's seat and Chandler himself, the shaman made to cut her off. He slid his body over the small windshield and into the small area between pilot and propeller and swung his legs over towards the wing, attempting to kick Athena. She dodged, but slid backward as the plane's balance, destroyed by having two humans on the right wing, tipped it precariously to the side.

Athena grabbed a wing strut with her good arm and held on for dear life as the undead creature at the stick worked to compensate. Overhead, Adam watched with no small sense of panic as a horrific thought came unbidden into his mind:

"Oh, God. She only taught me how to fly. She didn't teach me how to land."

Slowly and gently, Chandler's plane regained a sense of balance, and Athena once again moved to take on the older man. He saw her coming and took a roundhouse swipe at her with the Tomahawk, missing and clanking it against the wing strut. Taking advantage of the opening, she threw a strong right cross, connecting with the shaman's jaw, staggering him backward and back on top of the engine area. She attempted to press her advantage, but as she approached, he landed a solid kick to her midsection and she fell to her knees. Sensing what was coming, she grabbed once again for a wing strut, and the plane took a sharp turn to the right. "Not going to get rid of me that easily!" Voltaire yelled.

The plane leveled out again, and Athena looked up to see Chandler holding on to the upper wing and raising the tomahawk to take another swing at her. She quickly lashed out and kicked him in the knees. She heard a satisfying crunch and even above the whistling wind she could hear him cry out in pain. He staggered back, and once again took cover in the small space between the windshield and propeller.

"This is taking too long," Athena thought. "Just by being here I'm giving him too many opportunities. I need to try something… different." She scoured the sky for her own plane and saw Adam keeping a close but safe distance. Suddenly, the idea came to her. It was risky. "And stupid," her subconscious added. "But I have to try it."

Reaching out with her weakened left arm, she waived at Adam and spun her finger around in a circle.

Chandler watched as the woman kept her death-grip on the wing. "She can't hold on forever if we keep tipping," he thought. "Or I could throw the tomahawk at her. But if I missed, I could damage something important in the wing. Unacceptable." He watched as she began moving towards him once again, then he slid his body down so that he was standing on the wing as she approached. But a few feet away, she stopped and gestured at him to walk forward and fight her further out on the wing. The older man laughed at the ridiculousness of the challenge and shook his head. She once again gestured for him to walk out further and join her, and once again, he shook her off with a nasty laugh.

Behind him, unseen by Chandler as Athena egged him onward, the Guns Of Kerr began to glow.

Athena made one more gesture for Chandler to come out and fight her, but the shaman held his ground; the solid, safe ground. "Smart boy," she thought. "But just keep watching me." The older man held her gaze for an extra beat, and then Athena made her move. Reaching above her, she grabbed the top wing with both arms, ignoring the excruciating pain in her left shoulder, and swung her body around so that she was once again on the top wing. She began to quickly shimmy her way along the wing and was nearly atop the engine compartment when the tomahawk swung from below and almost took her hand off. She yanked it away, then slid towards the left side of the plane so that she could regain her footing. "One more trick," she said, crossing her fingers.

The Guns Of Kerr were glowing like a small sun.

Athena caught sight of the astonishing light and figured she only had seconds before Chandler realized what was happening. She crouched, bracing herself against the wind, and timed her jump from the wing so that she floated over the shaman and landed in the secondary seat of the plane, right in the undead warrior's lap. It crumbled beneath her, sending the Guns to the plane's floor. Athena turned herself back toward the front of the plane and saw a look of amazement on Chandler's face. She watched the older man's lips form the question "How?" and shrugged at him. The she picked up the Guns Of Kerr and held them in her hands.

Initially, Athena was afraid they would burn, even through her pilot's gloves, but their warmth was gentle, almost a caress. The glow from the Guns flowed out from their handles and across her body, enveloping her in their power. As it dissipated, the guns took on a new look, as if they had just rolled off the manufacturing line, and their weight increased, as if… loaded.

Chandler looked on in impotent rage. Some way… somehow… this woman had just bonded herself to the Guns Of Kerr. It took but a moment for him to realize how. "Beechler!" Chandler roared. He took in the sight of Athena's plane overhead. Reaching back with all of his might, he hurled the tomahawk in his hand at the focus of his hatred. Athena watched the weapon fly straight for Adam. Instinctively, she raised the Gun in her right hand and focused on the tomahawk as it twirled its deadly path through the air. She pulled the trigger, and a small white cloud burst forth as a ghostly bullet left the barrel.

It traveled a straight path, through the bottom left wing of Athena's plane, leaving no damage, and continued upward, striking the tomahawk mid-flight and splintering it into thousands of pieces. "I'll be damned," she smiled. "It really worked!"

Athena gestured for Adam to fly closer. As he did, he dropped a rope ladder down to her and she began climbing back to her own plane. Once she ascended the ladder, she gave Adam a gentle squeeze of the shoulders and then slid herself back into the pilot's seat. It was over.

Not to Chandler.

Below, the shaman had quickly made his way back to the pilot's seat and regained control of his plane. Only then did he realize the enormity of what had just happened. He had lost the scroll, the Guns, and if he was ever to return to civilization for other purposes, he was now a wanted man. "I have nothing left," he whispered to the clouds. "Nothing." A strong sense of determination came over him. "If I have nothing, then that's what they shall have as well!" He rolled his plane into a steep banking turn, noticing as he did that the woman was now taking the stick back from Beechler. He dove lower, hoping that they would ignore him for a few minutes - out of sight, out of mind.

They did just that.

From below, Chandler saw the other plane make a course change to the south. He then began a rapid climb, taking dead aim at Athena and Adam with his own plane, a collision course that would see them all dead and scattered amongst the vultures.

"I lost sight of him!" Adam shouted. Athena looked over her shoulder and scanned the horizon for Chandler, seeing nothing.

"I don't like it!" she yelled back. "He's out here somewhere!" Her mind raced back to her initial attack of the shaman's camp, and she knew what she had to do. "Listen – you have the stick. Hold it steady and don't panic, okay?!" He looked bewildered and worried. "Trust me!"

Athena reached down and cut the engines, sending her plane into a glide. From below she heard the sound of engines approaching at a high speed. With the speed of thought, she drew the guns and began firing bullet after bullet through the bottom of her plane, sending waves of mystical death in the direction of Chandler's plane. The fire, then explosion, that erupted beneath Voltaire's plane told her what she needed to know: she had found her target. She quickly restarted the engines and made a wide turn to make certain that the older man was no longer on their tail.

The fires from the wreckage below told her all she needed to know: the threat posed by Chandler was over.

The plane landed near a campsite along the Colorado River, and Athena helped Adam make his way back to the ground. "Are you sure you want to do this now?" she asked him. "You need a hospital."

He winced and nodded. "I know. But I can do this, then tell the rangers I had a hiking accident. They'll get me to a hospital soon enough." She pulled the Guns Of Kerr from her belt and held them in her hands one last time. "What does it feel like?" he asked.

"They feel alive. Like a part of me." She took a rueful pause. "Which is why I have to give them up." She handed them to Adam. "Hide them well, Adam." Athena reached out and tilted his chin until he was looking her in the eye. "You can never see me again. Just in case. I can never know, okay?"

Adam took off his shirt and wrapped it around the Guns. "I will. And I'm sorry."

Athena looked at the beaten and worn man across from her and felt a twinge of regret. "I'm sorry, too. For a lot of things." She gave him a coy smile. "You weren't the worst blind date ever."

He started to laugh, but stopped, the pain in his ribs too great. "I'd love to be able to say the same, Ms. Voltaire. But…"

She gave him a gentle punch in the shoulder and put up her fists as though she wanted to fight, then laughed. He smiled at her, then waived goodbye. "See you in the history books, Athena."

"I hope not," she replied. "You know how history tends to repeat itself. I'm not sure you could take the punishment!" Athena strode back to her waiting plane. As she slid into the cockpit, she saw Adam watching her and gave him a salute. The pull of the Guns weighed on her heavily, but the pull of her life weighed on her more. Los Angeles was waiting.

It was time to go home. Alone. Again.

THE KISTE, THE KASTE & THE KYKEON

October Crifasi

Athena sipped at her champagne. She felt herself being watched and lifted her eyes slowly. The brunette woman seated across the table held Athena's glance and smiled warmly, as if she were family. Athena nodded in return, but found the exchange odd. The first time she had met this woman was but a half hour ago. Even then Athena's grandparents had kept the introductions brief, with barely enough time to exchange pleasantries and to take a quick tour of their historic Grecian estate. Athena hadn't even been given the chance to change out of her flight gear. Now here they all sat gathered around the dinner table, waiting for the footmen to bring in the aperitif.

"You must excuse me for staring so," the mysterious woman spoke after a moment, her large brown eyes brimmed with tears, "I am ... so grateful to Anastasia and Achilles for taking me in. And for you-"

"Cora," Athena's grandmother interrupted gently, "it is our pleasure. We are grateful to have you with us." The silver-haired woman leaned forward and covered Cora's hand with her own. "You are safe now."

"For me?" Athena asked, somewhat surprised.

Two men dressed in the finest of black suit coats and trousers whisked into the room, their arms loaded with trays of sweet Grecian delicacies.

Athena's grandfather addressed his guest with a bright, wide smile as if Athena hadn't spoken a word. "Anastasia is right, Cora. We are thrilled to have you here. Please do not fret about Petros any longer. We have the best security in all of Greece. You work is safe here."

He raised his glass. "To long-time friends."

"What?" Athena said flatly. "Excuse me, grandfather, did you say Petros?"

She signaled to one of the footmen – she was going to need more champagne.

"I thought this weekend was supposed to be a vacation from my dealings with men like Petros?"

Anastasia glared at her husband from the opposite side of the table. The old man's smile faded as he paused to consider his answer.

"Clearly it is not for the 'R and R' as you promised."

"Wh-why, yes, of course it is, Athena," Anastasia spoke in his stead, "but Cora is a personal childhood friend, and when we received word–"

"No," Cora interrupted and silenced Anastasia with a wave of her hand, "My dear Stasia, it is all right. She has a right to be upset."

Athena noted the rings on the woman's hand as she spoke. Each finger was adorned with its own puzzle of silver figure eights and chunks of pink tourmaline. The same shapes echoed in brown, gold green and pink embroidery down the sleeves of her blouse.

"Do not be angry with your grandparents, Athena," Cora said. "It is not their fault. It is mine. I should never have involved them."

Achilles coughed into his hand and sat back into his chair. The footmen returned to the table to replenish empty water and champagne glasses. One in particular caught Athena's attention as he seemed to struggle with the most menial of tasks. He stood over six feet tall and wore black horn-rimmed glasses. His jacket was not as crisp and fine as the others, and he seemed particularly nervous when he had to be around her.

"I'm listening," Athena said, eyeing the young man as he made his exit.

"I have dedicated the last five years of my life to the excavation of what remains at the ruins of Rocca di Cerere in Sicilia," Cora began, "the Sanctuary of the Great Mother, Demeter.

"It is one of the larger temple ruins left in the area known as the Valley of the Gods in Enna. It has ties to the Eleusinian Mysteries, specifically the series of rituals believed to endow its initiates with the power and wisdom of the immortals."

"And now Petros wants that power," Athena sighed.

"Yes," Cora spat, "He bribed select members of the Sicilian government with promises of great riches and power should they allow him to come in and take over the ruins for his own private purposes."

"And?"

"And they did, to my surprise. Though the first I heard of the agreement was when Petros showed up with his men, his guns and his supposed High Priestess demanding access. Many of my staff were either killed immediately or were corralled as his servants against their will. My assistant and I barely had enough time to collect our findings and flee on foot."

The tall server returned to the room with a silver pot of coffee. Athena watched him nearly trip over his own feet and spill hot coffee on himself. She heard him swear under his breath with a thick Grecian accent. He left the room in a huff.

"What exactly did you leave with?" she asked.

"Why, the very ceremonial items described in Homer's account of the old rites. The Kiste, the Kaste and the sacred chalice of the Kykeon," Cora replied.

"Where are they now?"

Achilles Maragos leaned toward Athena and whispered, "I had a special safe built to keep such things. I will take you to it after dessert. It's a marvel to behold. Even you would have difficulty cracking its code. I had it built right into the walls of the study downstairs."

Athena shushed the old man before he could speak another word as the awkward waiter had made his return.

"What?" He laughed at her, "Are you worried about these men?" He indicated to the servers as they brought in more carafes of wine. "I hired each one myself after proper and lengthy investigation."

"Such faith you have in your old Pappous," he teased. "Really, Athena."

The dining room floor rumbled from what sounded like an explosion from the rooms below. Achilles and his guests sat in silence for a moment, their faces lit only by the dim glow of candles set in a line down the center of the table. Seconds later, a dissonant choir of men's voices cried out for Achilles, punctuated by the pop of gunfire.

Cora stood immediately and surprised them all as she grabbed up one of the serving knives from the table and fumbled her way from the room toward the sound of the commotion.

"Not this time," she hissed.

"Cora, come back!" Anastasia exclaimed and stood from the table.

Achilles snapped up one of the candles from the table and started after Cora, only to have Athena block him.

"No, I will handle this," she said firmly, "Get YaYa to safety."

The old man nodded his head and handed the candle to his granddaughter. One of Achilles' security men thundered into the room from the servant's entrance on the opposite side, a scratched up radio in one hand, the polished metal of a pistol in the other. "The perimeter has been compromised, sir," the man began.

"I can see that!" Achilles exclaimed.

"How many?" Athena demanded.

"We tracked four..."

Gunfire erupted from below them a second time and a woman cried out.

Anastasia ran to her husband, and he put his arm around her, "Please, Achilles," she pleaded.

"Get them out of here," Athena yelled at the security officer. She reached her free hand behind her and pulled the Remington Model 95 pistol from its hiding place at the small of her back. .

The hint of a smile flashed on Achilles' face.

"The best security in all of Greece," Athena said grimly and disappeared into the darkness.

The security officer grabbed Achilles by the arm. "Sir, madam, please..."

Athena moved slowly, allowing her eyes to adjust to the darkness. The large, black shape of one of the footmen's bodies lay dead across the top of the staircase, with another body splayed diagonally down the stairs a few feet away. She recognized him as the man who had just filled her champagne glass. She tiptoed over the bodies and moved quickly down the length of the stairway to the floor below.

The entrance to the study loomed large before her. She slipped into the room without a sound and blew out her candle as she did. She placed the candle on the floor and crouched low behind a large upholstered armchair. The silvery light from the waxing moon streamed through a large window onto the floor in front of her. She could hear the whimper of a woman from somewhere in the room.

She searched the room with her eyes: nothing but moonlight and bookshelves. The woman's cry grew louder. Athena slipped effortlessly from behind the cover of the chair toward the sound. A gloved hand immediately grabbed at her mouth and another one pressed the cool tip of a gun gently under her chin. "Drop the weapon," the faceless voice barked into her ear. Athena struggled against her captor, but he only pushed the barrel of the gun deeper into her skin. "NOW." She let the small pistol in her hand fall to the ground.

The man behind her held her fast as he pulled her backwards out of the room and into the hallway. He spoke fast in broken English, "You were not supposed to be here." Then he yelled to the room beside them, "Nikolas! You go."

The lights flickered back into life, and the figure of a tall man dashed out from the back of the room, carrying a small golden box. He sprinted for the back of the house and out into the gardens. Athena jammed her right elbow into the man's gut and pushed her left foot down the front of his shin hard. The man yelped and doubled over as she whirled around and landed a kick to the side of his head. He fell to the floor in a heap. His gun dropped and skidded within inches of Athena's feet. She picked it up and aimed it at his head. "Sorry to disappoint you."

She heard gunfire behind her on the stairs and the thud of someone falling to the ground. There was an additional exchange of gunfire and what sounded like the loud growl of a plane off in the distance. She heard her grandfather call out to her in Greek before the loud drone of a small cargo plane washed out all sound. Athena fixed her attention on the scene inside the room in front of her, the gun still pointed at the heap on the floor.

Books lay in tatters on the ground. Chunks of wood and plaster littered the floor in a wide semi-circle in front of the wall at the end of the room. A massive hole yawned out from the middle of what used to be bookshelves and nick nacks. The charred remains of the safe door dangled in precarious fashion at its edge.

Athena drew back her gun and ran into the room. She peered into the dark space in the wall and saw all that remained was a small square of yellowed paper. A catalog tag that read "Kiste, Kaste, Chalice, and Ceremonial Container, Rocca di Cerere, Sicily" in perfectly handwritten letters.

Achilles ran into the room and stopped behind her just as Athena spied Cora Sotera, lying crumpled in a ball on the floor on the opposite side of the room; her breath was slow and labored. A crimson stain spread slowly across the width of her hip.

The woman opened her eyes and reached out her hand toward Athena.

"Oh Cora, I am so terribly, terribly sorry," Achilles said, choking back tears.

Athena went to her side and knelt down. She took the woman's hand to check the strength of her pulse.

"Please," the woman rasped, her eyes locked on Athena, "you must not let them get away. Petros must not possess the sacred relics." Cora grabbed for the chain of the necklace hidden under the nape of her blouse. She pulled it free, revealing the silver amulet that hung from it. On one side was the shape of what looked like sheaf of wheat made of the smallest pieces of amber she'd ever seen.

"Take this," the woman said, "It will protect you."

Athena shook her head no.

With trembling hands, Cora fumbled for the clasp and let the chain fall from her neck, she put the chain and amulet into Athena's hand and closed her fingers around it. "You must…"

"Rest now," Athena said gently.

Achilles crouched down on the other side of the woman. "Yes, listen to Athena now, Cora," he said, wrapping an arm around her, "You just rest, now."

As the two lifted her slowly from the ground, Athena whispered with exasperation to her grandfather, "You owe me a vacation when this over, old man."

Petros Valdoros took a long drag from his cigarette and rocked back on the heels of his freshly polished shoes. He could hear the sound of the ocean as it crashed against the rocks around him. He exhaled. A smile covered his face as he felt the damp night air on his skin. He brought the cigarette back to his lips slowly, squeezing the thing between the flesh of his thumb and finger. For a moment, he almost forgot about the slender, white-haired woman that tapped her foot impatiently at his side.

She immediately snatched the thing from his lips and spat, "You not soil your body with this. Your body iss temple. You must keep it pure."

The shock of it caused him to almost fall from the wooden dock where they stood. He choked smoke from his nostrils and mouth.

"You see?" she exclaimed and wagged one of her long, gnarled fingers in front of his large, round face.

"I see. I see," he grumbled.

Petros looked sideways at her, doing his best to suppress his annoyance. Soon the destiny the old woman claimed was his would come to pass and he could be done with her. She had done nothing but nit-pick and nag him since he spared her life during the first temple raid in Athens.

A small ferry emerged from the fog in front of them as the old woman stomped the cigarette out with one of her sandaled feet. Petros pulled another one from the silver case in his trench coat pocket and placed it between his lips. She immediately snatched it away and stomped it into the dock. He muttered something indiscernible to no one in particular and contemplated the proper disposal for such a woman as this.

The boat approached the dock in slow fashion and landed against the end of it with a thump. Two of Petros' men ran to meet it, and Petros licked his lips. He could feel his pulse quicken. There was nothing to stop him now; he had everything the ancients called for, including the stinking pigs needed for sacrifices. The old stories the woman told him were true; he believed it to his core. He moved quickly towards the craft as a tall, young man with short, dark hair and black horn-rimmed glasses emerged from the back of the craft. The young man held a golden box in his arms. He secured the container nervously with his hands. Petros rushed to meet him.

"Yes. Ne. Nikolas. Good. " He grabbed for the box. "Give to me."

He snatched the box with its jewel-encrusted fasteners and ornately carved lid greedily from the younger man's arms and hugged it close to his chest. He closed his eyes and inhaled deeply. Behind him, the old woman pulled something from the deep pocket on the front of her gown and began to whisper in an indiscernible language.

Nikolas stared at his uncle with large, frightened eyes, his words quick and in broken Greek, "You said no trouble - no trouble."

"Yes," Petros crooned, his eyes still closed, "easy, weak security."

The old woman began to weave back and forth, her whispers seemed to double and triple in the air around them, like some unearthly and unseen choir had surrounded them.

Nikolas shifted his weight as his shoulders tensed. "There was a woman."

Petros' eyes flashed open. He could feel the heat of his anger rise into his cheeks.

"Voltaire."

The flight to Sicily was a short one, mercifully, Athena thought to herself. For the most part, it was a smooth one, too, outside of some chop just off the coast. Achilles promised her a competent crew once she arrived in Catania, but based on the events of the last twenty-four hours, Athena held little faith in her grandfather's connections. She had sent a few telegrams of her own prior to her departure.

The plane tilted to the left gently as it made its way over the city of Catania. The ground was alive with activity. What looked like military men and civilians flooded the streets and airport.

The plane continued past the heart of the city, and a few minutes later a dirt airstrip came into view. A small, white house and two large aircraft hangars sat at the end of it. A smattering of single-flyer planes sat pilotless in random order in front of the buildings. Two men stood outside the largest of the hangars with their faces directed up toward the sky.

Athena guided the plane down onto the airstrip with ease. The plane bounced a few times and then finally slowed to a complete stop just before the runway spilled out onto the hangar plaza. A short man with cropped hair the color of salt and pepper ran toward the plane as she gathered up her things and climbed down. The man sped to her side and extended his hand to help her.

"Signorina Athena!" he crooned.

She stepped down and he continued to hold her hand. He lifted it to his lips and kissed it. "It is always a pleasure to see you."

She smiled politely and took back her hand.

"Thank you, Dominic. I appreciate you accommodating me on such short notice."

"We are always happy to accommodate such a beautiful woman as yourself, Signorina," he said.

"And I always appreciate your discretion," she said.

"Of course," the man said, still smiling, "No one knows you are here. I have made sure of that."

He indicated the two men standing by the hangar doors. "We will be sure to have your plane fueled and ready for you upon your return." He smiled. "I will see to it personally."

Athena looked down at her watch and back up to the dirt road that stretched out behind the airstrip and off into the horizon.

"Grazie."

She spied the shape of a vehicle making its approach towards them. "Ah."

The sound of the jeep reached her long before the actual vehicle did. It sputtered and groaned as if its best days were long past it. Athena couldn't quite make out the person behind the wheel. She kept her hand poised above the Colt Peacemaker at her right hip, just in case it was not welcomed company.

The jeep bounced and popped its way into the hangar plaza and pulled up alongside Athena and Dominic. A dark-haired boy in his late teens sat at the helm. The sleeves of his white t-shirt were rolled up to his shoulders and his khaki pants were smeared with auto grease. His hair was disheveled and half of a cigarette dangled from his lips. He squinted at Athena through the smoke.

"You look lost, Signorina. You need a ride?"

Athena cocked an eyebrow at him.

"Do you know this man?" Dominic asked with concern and took a step toward the vehicle.

"Yes," Athena answered, her eyes on the young man in the jeep, "It's all right, Dominic, you may leave us."

Dominic bowed briefly and returned to the hangar.

"You're late." Athena addressed the young man, "I was beginning to think something had happened. Where is your father?"

The teen put the jeep into park and jumped out of the vehicle. He made his way to the passenger door and held it open for her.

"Yes, my cousin, it is good to see, you, too," he chided.

She gave him a hug begrudgingly before she climbed into the passenger side.

"Hello, Alex," she said matter-of-factly. "Now, answer me. Where is your father?"

Alex leapt back into the vehicle and started up the engine. "He is sick," he said.

"So he sent you?" she asked in disbelief.

"Not exactly," he said as he squashed out the cigarette on the dashboard, "I volunteered."

"Why does 'volunteered' sound like 'no one knows I'm here'?" she asked.

"Because you are smart, like me," he chortled.

The small truck sputtered forward as he shifted it into gear.

"This jeep is no good to me outside of the city," she yelled at him over the sound of the engine.

"Yes," the young man yelled back, "I know. I have other transport waiting for us once we leave the city limits."

Athena attempted to check the chambers of her Colts, but the vehicle bounced and jostled too much to do so with any accuracy.

"Did anyone see you on the way here?" she asked.

"Oooh," Alexander laughed, "You mean Petros?"

She nodded yes.

"That is why I picked you up late. I had to take the long way. They are almost everywhere, looking for you."

It was early. Too early for such things Petros thought to himself, but the old woman had insisted. Baptism in the lake where Hades has taken his queen, Persephone, was crucial to be received as an initiate. He had to bite his lip to keep his teeth from chattering as he stood partially naked in the frigid water.

Frona spoke words of the old language and held his arms up in the air. She scoured his skin with a sponge and oil that stank worse than the old woman herself. He wished Hades would come and steal her away.

"How much of this-this 'preparation' is necessary, old woman?!"

Frona stared deep into Petros' beady, green eyes.

"Initiate must be cleansed of all his impurity before he takes the Kiste."

She gathered up the bottle of oil and sponge and turned for the shore where Petros' men stood waiting for orders.

Cursed wretch, Petros thought to himself. He took a deep breath and composed himself.

"Please, forgive me," he demurred, "I know this."

The old woman turned to face him. She returned to his side with a grunt.

Once she finished the bathing ritual she led Petros to the shore, where Nikolas handed the old woman a crème-colored linen gown. She draped Petros in it, smoothing it gently with her hands. She looked him up and down and smiled.

"Yes," she said with pride.

She then leaned her face close to his. Her eyes narrowed.

"If I were you I would pray to Hades that he will find you clean and that Demeter finds you worthy," she growled.

She tapped one of her long fingernails on his chest. "Lit-tle-fat-man."

Petros' face flushed with anger.

She continued, "They alone are your judge. They alone decide if you shall know the ecstasy of the immortal or if you shall know the agony of an endless death."

"They will make me a God either way," he replied through gritted teeth, "You are alive because you promise me this. Or do you need reminder?"

Her expression relaxed and she smiled at him kindly again. "No. Of course they will. I do not lie."

"Good," Petros exclaimed and he grabbed his nephew by the elbow and walked him away from the woman.

"Voltaire is not stupid woman. I am sure she is already on her way. You get the men and search the hills; your brother has already taken to the old roads."

Nikolas smiled a stupid, toothy grin.

Petros grasped Nikolas' arm tighter. "Do not let me down."

Nikolas stopped smiling.

Petros released his arm with a push. "GO."

Nikolas nodded and headed off toward the group of men shivering in the early morning air.

Two motorcycles growled their way down the weatherworn path. The dirt road snaked its way through the Sicilian countryside, around clusters of eroded stone stairways and wide expanses of crimson and tangerine-colored poppy fields. The two riders said nothing to each other until they came to a break in the road. Alexander pointed to the broken paved trail that stretched out to their right.

"This way," he said.

Athena nodded in agreement, and the motorcycles climbed up the roughly hewn track as it stretched and curved through the hills. Trees stood tall and lush above them, providing apt cover and shade.

As they wove higher and higher, the road was punctuated by long-spindly shrubbery and the white-yellow crumble of walls and temples of a time long past.

Athena pulled ahead of her younger cousin and slowed her pace to a near crawl as they neared the Valley of the Gods. She signaled to Alex to follow. They were about to leave the cover of the trees and would be in clear sight of anyone travelling above or below them.

She scanned the hill. The road disappeared and then reappeared higher above them and off to the right. A cloud of dust and dirt still lingered in the air above it. She yelled back over her shoulder, "Alex! Stay close, we are about to have company."

The trio of black motorcycles appeared at the crest of the hill above them in an instant. Their riders were large, gruff looking men, their firearms strapped to the front of their jackets. The unmistakable silver insignia of Petros Valdoros gleamed on the tops of their helmets in the light of the late afternoon sun. The man on the bike in the middle hollered something at the other riders, and the pack lurched off the road and bore down the hill toward Athena and Alex with speed.

"Go! Go!" Athena yelled to Alex and she waved him forward. She kicked her bike from its standing position and sped off. It took her a few seconds to realize her cousin did not follow.

When she turned to look, she saw Alex struggling to get his motorcycle to move. She swung her cycle around in a spray of pebbles and dust and blazed back in Alex's direction. She stopped at his side. The engine would not turn over.

"Leave it!" Athena commanded.

Petros' men were almost on them.

"Get on!" She pointed to her seat. "I need to you drive."

Alex jumped off his bike and let it fall to the ground in a clatter. Athena already had her motorcycle in motion as Alex scrambled onto the seat in front of her and grasped for the handlebars.

"Keep it steady!" she barked at him.

"You sure you know what you're doing?!" Alex exclaimed.

"Don't you worry about me," she replied as the motorcycle lurched forward, "you worry about the road."

The duo sped off with Petros' pack of men in fast pursuit. The cycles zigged and zagged across the road, scattering gravel and debris as they went. The first man squeezed off two shots in a row. The bullets knocked the rear wheel cover with a loud ping. Athena took careful aim at her assailant and fired. His cycle careened to the left.

"Damn it, Alex," she exclaimed, "I said steady!"

The other cycle grew closer and closer to Athena's side. She took quick aim for its gas tank and fired. The bullet reached its target. Petros' man swore loudly just as the cycle exploded in a burst of flame. The bike in line behind him

swung to miss the explosion, but was unable to turn in time. It slammed into the burning cycle and threw its rider several feet into the air before it too exploded and landed in smoking pieces of metal and rubber on the ground.

"Did you nail the bastard?" Alexander yelled over his shoulder.

"The road. Just watch the road!" she exclaimed.

The remaining motorbike burst through the cloud of billowing smoke behind them, its driver with gritted teeth.

"Hold on!" Alexander called out, and the motorcycle jolted to the right.

Ahead of them, the road wrapped sharply as the hill dropped off to their left. As the last of Petros' men grew closer and closer, he pulled at the gun strapped across his chest and fired at them. The bullet pierced the front tire of Athena's motorcycle and flattened it instantly. The entire motorcycle jack-knifed high into the air.

Athena was jettisoned skyward and landed on the ground with a grunt. Alexander pitched forward from his seat and landed directly in the cycle's path. The bike flipped over on itself and landed with the rim of its front tire flat across his left leg. The snap of his shin could be heard from where Athena landed. She groggily pulled herself half up from the grass and fired at the remaining gunman's chopper as it sped towards them.

She did not miss. The driver slumped forward onto his handlebars. His motorcycle shot straight ahead and off the hillside where the road curved to the right. A few seconds later, the loud crash of its impact against the ground below echoed throughout the hillside.

Athena collapsed out of breath onto the ground. She took a moment to steady herself. No bones broken, but her legs and forearm throbbed with what she knew would be painful bruises. She heard the whimper of her younger cousin and pulled herself to a standing position. Alex!

She ran to his side and checked him for injury. He tried to sit up, but pain through his leg was too intense.

"Take it easy, Sailor," she said to him gently, "That leg is in bad shape."

He moaned with frustration.

"Can you feel the other one?" Athena asked him.

He nodded yes.

"Good."

Athena scanned their surroundings. Several feet behind them a tall tree had partially fallen to the ground at the side of the road.

"Put your arm around me," she directed, "I need to get you someplace safe for the time being."

He reached up his arm and placed it wearily around her shoulders. He cried out as she hoisted him up and wrapped her arm about his waist.

"You volunteered for this, remember?" she said with a slight smile. "Pretend you're Douglas Fairbanks on a new adventure."

Alex tried to laugh, but groaned in pain instead.

As they neared the downed tree, Athena could see its spidery branches angled down close to the earth with a slight opening in the middle. The branches of several other trees intermingled with the downed limb, creating a cave-like dwelling underneath.

"This will have to do."

The two ducked carefully into the makeshift shelter. Athena sat her cousin down with gentle care against a tangle of branches.

"Alex," she said gently, "I need you to promise me you'll stay put and be quiet until I come back."

"And where else would I go?" he asked.

"Please," she said.

She sat back on her heels and looked her cousin in the eyes.

"You promise me, Alex," she said. "No one should see you under here. Keep it that way until I come back."

"And what if they come?" Alexander asked as he shifted himself to a more comfortable position.

She thought for a moment then reached for the back of her neck. She unclasped the silver necklace Cora had given her and squatted down next to him.

"This," she said and clasped it around his neck, "is supposed to protect you."

"And what if it doesn't?"

She pulled one of the Peacemaker pistols strapped to her hip and put it into his right hand.

"Then you can always try this."

Petros was nowhere to be seen. Just over the ridge, Athena spied an outcrop of several large boulders. They fit together in a semi-circle with one long slab of marble along the top of them to form a cave. The dirt floor inside it extended several feet below ground level. In the middle of the stone sanctuary sat a large, flat slab of rock. Athena assumed this to be the altar Petros intended to use.

Athena crouched amidst the tall, green grass and spindles of shrubbery that grew at the ruin's edge. She pulled a small pair of binoculars from her breast pocket and peered through. On the western side of the altar, several small piglets grazed their way around a large circular pen. Women dressed in tunics of crème-colored linen with similar symbols to the one on Cora's charm appeared from behind the rocks to place candles and spread dried herbs around the perimeter of the cave's semi-circle.

She watched as an old woman also made her way to the altar. She held an ornately carved box in her hands. Behind her followed two attendants. One held what looked like two large golden snakes and a chalice; the other held a small woven basket.

"Ah ha," Athena said to herself with a smirk, "Gotcha."

A pungent odor assailed her nostrils. She froze.

"Yes," a male voice said behind her in broken English, "as you say –"

The man brought the handle of his gun down hard and fast against the back of her head. Her body fell to the ground.

"Gotcha."

Petros could hardly contain himself. *The time has come.* He thought he could feel the earth pulse beneath his feet. He could not stop licking his lips. Nikolas and the rest of his men stood stationed around the sanctuary in case of trouble, or in case something went wrong.

He watched as the old woman muttered to herself in the old language. She lifted a small bowl made of shell into the air above her head. The bittersweet smell of sage filled the air as she brought the bowl back down; white-grey smoke billowed out in waves as she placed it on the altar before her.

Frona's voice was rich, and the melody of the song she sang strange and disturbing. A young woman dressed in a cloth gown came to her side, bowed in silence and walked back to her place behind the altar. Petros watched the proceedings from bent knees in his assigned spot in front of the altar. Another woman bowed in silence, placed a goblet made of gold on the altar and returned to her assigned position. His eyes met with the woman before she placed her gift on the altar; there was fear in her eyes. Petros laughed out loud with pleasure. *Yes, you should be afraid.*

Frona stopped singing and her eyes flashed open.

"Continue," Petros said.

The old woman closed her eyes and raised her palms to the sky above.

Two of Petros' men appeared at the perimeter of the temple. They pulled between them a young man bound in ropes. He was wounded and unable to stand upright without some assistance.

Petros felt the anger rise within him at the sight of them.

"What are you doing? I said not to interrupt. We have begun! Get rid of him."

Frona opened her eyes and glared at the men. She squinted at the boy between them. After a grunt, she motioned to two of her attendants to bring the wounded man to her. Petros jumped to his feet as the attendants accompanied the young man to Frona's side.

Petros' men remained where they stood, behind the herbs and candles of the temple's perimeter. They seemed nervous and apprehensive of what they saw before them. The shorter of the two leaned forward and spoke first anyway, "We are sorry Petros. We found him hiding in trees outside grove."

He added with a shrug, "You said to bring."

Petros growled and was about to respond, but he stopped abruptly as Frona placed her hands on the wounded boy's cheek, a curious look on her face. She stared at the amulet around his neck. She grabbed it up in her hand.

Her eyes widened and a smug smile found its way onto her lips. "Well, well," she said and turned to address Petros.

"The Great Mother is pleased, Petros," she said, her eyes still on the amulet, "She has sent you the ultimate sacrifice for our work. He comes bearing the mark of our Mother's beloved daughter, Persephone."

She gestured quickly with her hands to the women behind the altar. "Quickly, he is hurt. Bring me the Kykeon."

A woman appeared at Frona's side, with the chalice from the box in her hand. She handed it to Frona and bowed her head. Frona took it graciously and lifted it gently to the wounded boy's lips.

"Drink," she said softly, "It is sacred mushroom of Demeter. It will make you strong."

The young man tried to resist, but did not have the strength to stop her. She poured the brown liquid into his mouth.

It was the pain that brought her back to consciousness, a lightning rod of heat that seared down her scalp to the base of her neck. She went to feel it with her hands and quickly realized her hands were bound together tightly behind her. She was surrounded by small circular snouts, each sniffing and slobbering up and down the length of her arms and legs. They were accompanied by grunts and squeals in the air around her head.

She stared face down into pile of dark brown sand. The sniffling moved up to her shoulders. She shook her head and kicked at her feet, but her ankles were bound as well. She kicked again and rolled herself over; squeals erupted around her, and the slobbering stopped. She stared up into the orange-pink of the early evening sky. Her view went black as the snouts and faces of countless plump and curious piglets crowded together, trying their best to get a smell of her.

"Ugh."

She shook herself back and forth in an attempt to shoo them away. It did not work. She took quick assessment of her situation. Thick, white ropes bound her hands, and her feet were bound just as fast. She was gagged and surrounded by at least twenty or more soft and snorting baby pigs. I've dealt with worse.

A young woman dressed in ceremonial garb appeared at the edge of the pigpen and poured what looked like an orange porridge into the trough a few feet from Athena's side. She smiled down at Athena and the pigs.

"You are blessed," she said with a thick Greek accent, "to be such sacrifice for Great Mother and her new King, Petros."

Athena squirmed in place until she was able to sit up and swore loudly behind her gag. The young woman bowed and then left. Athena looked around for a way out. She watched as her pen mates fought to eat from the low trough beside her. She pulled a few times at the ropes around her hands and feet to assess their strength; there was a slight give.

Really, Petros, rope? She felt around for the knots used and tested her boots. Slightly loose. She fell to her side in the dirt and got about the business of untying herself – the first trick her father ever taught her. She counted the passing seconds in her head as she pulled herself free, determined to break her father's record.

Her concentration was broken by the shout and the growl of an old woman's voice. She shifted herself back up to sitting so she could see. The temple sprawled out before her just over the pigpen. She maneuvered herself so she could see Petros clearly now. She'd recognize that annoying rasp anywhere. The stout, balding man wore a long crème gown and paced back and forth like a rabid dog in front of the rock outcrop Athena had spied earlier. There was a younger man being escorted out of the altar now, too. Someone she'd seen before. She had to shake her head and look again. Alexander.

Her cousin stood next to the old woman; his eyes glossed over. He was dressed in a cloth gown with serpents embroidered in gold down the front of it. Before them the dedication altar stood. The golden box was on it with its lid open. The woman pulled a long, curved knife from the belt at her waist. The old woman nodded to one of her male attendants and handed him the knife and a goblet.

"Bring the first gift to honor the God of the Underworld."

The young, blonde man headed towards Athena and the pen of pigs. She had not forgotten the task at hand. She shook her wrists, and the ropes fell free to the ground. She quickly untied the remains of rope on her feet. She pulled the gag from her mouth. The blonde priest leaned down to unlatch the gate and walked in. He grabbed Athena up from the ground to a standing position.

He looked down and saw Athena's free hands. He looked back up at her face with a confused look. Athena smiled.

"Didn't quite break my personal best, but it will do."

She elbowed the blonde smartly in the chin, and he fell backwards, dropping the sacrificial knife and goblet. Athena picked up the knife quickly and punched the man smartly in the face. He fell back into the pen with a thud, causing the door to swing open. Athena stomped her feet hard on the ground. "Shoo, shoo, shooo."

The pigs burst forth from the pen in a mad scatter. Petros turned to see what the noise was about. He rocked with fury as he watched Athena emerge from the pen gate, the glint of a knife in her hand. The pigs ran amuck into the temple grounds.

"No. No. No!!" Petros said, his volume increasing with each word.

Nikolas and his men watched in shock as Athena made her way through the chaos. She was to be Petros' first kill as an immortal. She was not supposed to escape. Athena made an attempt to free her way to the altar. Frona's attendants were quick to line up in a protective circle around Petros, Frona, the altar and her cousin.

Athena maneuvered her way through the animals and tried to get a better visual lock on Alex. The distraction caused her to trip over a piglet. She fell face down into the soil. The dagger flew out of her hand and landed on the ground a few inches from her face. She cursed. Nikolas dove into the perimeter and shot at her as she fell. The bullet just grazed her shoulder. He quickly zipped his way through the chaos and stood breathing heavily before her as she found her footing. In his hand he held the slim dagger.

"Here peegy, peegy, peegy…" he leered.

He lunged forward at her, and she hopped to the side. She grabbed up his arm and pulled it into her chest. Using both hands she twisted his arm, causing him to howl. She leveraged her body weight against him, and he fell to the ground. She slammed her arm against his wrist, and the dagger fell from his hand. She hit him in jaw, hard, and his head fell back to the ground. She grabbed the guns from the holsters on his chest.

She pumped the air with bullets as the remainder of Petros' forces bared down upon her. The pigs continued to run in every direction, knocking over cup and candle as they did. The dry grass around them caught flame. The young priests and priestesses broke their sacred positions and ran to shepherd what pigs they could back out of the area.

Frona watched in shock. "No, this is not right. We must stop."

Petros grabbed her by the shoulders and shook her.

"Continue you old hag. DO NOT STOP. "

"The blood. We only need one sacrifice, you told me so." He pulled a small knife from the sleeve of his gown.

"Kill him!" he ordered and pointed at Alex.

"No," she exclaimed, "This is not right. This is not—"

Petros lunged at Alex from across the altar and sliced his forearm. "Kill him!"

Alex winced in pain. "Wha-OW!"

Blood raced down his arm and onto the open box on top of the altar.

"ALEX!" Athena cried out.

The ground began to vibrate, and Frona threw her arms into the air, her eyes grey and her body stiff. She began to lift from the ground. A wind began to circle around the altar. Frona's women did their best to make a protective circle around her. Petros leapt at them, pushed the women out of the way. He kicked Alexander to the ground and out of the circle.

"Yes." he said gleefully. "YES. Great Hades I am here."

Frona's clouded eyes looked down at him curiously. She opened her mouth to speak and a deep male voice spilled forth.

"Come before me, Initiate."

Petros greedily drank from the chalice on the altar and then snapped up the two serpent-like cuffs from the box on the altar beside it. He positioned himself beneath the old woman as she hung suspended in the air.

"YES. I am here and I am ready, I have drunk of the Kykeon, and I have the Kiste and the Kaste. Now MAKE ME A GOD."

The woman's face twisted in a foul smile. She pulled the cuffs from his hands and held them together; white and gold light streamed from her hands, fusing the serpent cuffs together, and she then pulled them apart into two live, pulsing, golden serpents. Frona threw back her head and laughed a dark laugh.

"Let the judgment of Hades be upon you."

The old woman shoved a golden snake to each of Petros' arms.

All movement stopped. Even Athena stood speechless and watched, transfixed.

Petros groaned and threw his arms skyward. Frona continued to laugh as the serpents entwined on either arm came to life, their slim bodies circling Petros' limbs. They twisted and hissed, growing longer and larger. The serpents grew and grew in size until they had completely enveloped Petros' body.

The earth rumbled and shook. Petros' eyes rolled back into his head. "YYEEEESSS. All of Greece, all of the WORLD will call me Supreme…"

Athena dropped to the ground and crawled to Alex's side. She grabbed his right arm and shook.

"Alex?!"

He lifted his head; he stared at her in confusion. Frona shrieked from behind them, her voice human and terrified. She fell to the ground in a thump.

Nikolas groggily lifted his head from the ground a few feet away. He cried out when saw his uncle in the clutches of the golden snakes. He fired his gun haphazardly at the creatures' heads; the bullet ricocheted off the altar behind them. The earth continued to shake, and Frona's attendants ran from the altar in all directions.

The golden serpents squeezed together around Petros' body. They pulled tighter and tighter. Petros coughed and wheezed and tried with feeble hands to grab at the large serpent heads above him. Each serpent plunged amber-colored fangs into his shoulders. Petros screamed with pain.

From behind the altar a large form began to take shape. The form slowly became the shape of a man dressed in a black cloak and a spiked silver crown. His smoky eyes looked over the scene with an eerie calm.

The serpents pulled their fangs from Petros' skin, and he began to glow a dullish blue. His body grew in size and glow to match the serpents; he gasped no longer. Nikolas fell to his knees; tears streamed down his cheeks and steamed up the thick lenses of his glasses.

Petros continued to grow; his eyes glowed a strange green color. He turned his attention to Athena and smiled a large, wide, menacing smile.

"ALEX," Athena screamed, "If you can hear me – it is time to GO!"

Petros lumbered toward her.

The spirit behind the altar spoke, "This initiate is not worthy."

Another larger form appeared at his side, a beautiful woman with long, braided hair and a crown made of sheaves of wheat. The two of them cast their eyes down at the form of Frona as she shook and whimpered on the ground.

The soil beneath Frona began to shake and shift. A great hole began to form in the earth. The old woman screamed. The ground beneath the old woman gave way completely, and she disappeared in an instant. The young priests and priestesses that had remained ran out of the temple screaming, as did the few that remained of Petros' men. Athena scrambled to grab her cousin and move to safer ground.

"PETROS VALDOROS," the apparitions spoke in unison, "We find you unworthy of the sacred gifts of the Gods and condemn you to the form most befitting the life of the man you chose to be on this plane."

Petros froze in his place, fear shown in the green glow of his eyes. There was a great flash of light followed by a great squeal. When Athena turned to look, she saw the man once known as Petros now running around in circles on the grass, squealing and snorting as a baby pig. The golden serpents of the Kiste and Kaste fell to the ground and reverted back to their innate form of two golden, serpent-shaped cuffs.

The apparitions laughed. The woman with the long braids caught Athena's glance and smiled warmly at her before she disappeared in a gust of wind and the sweet smell of lavender. Athena stood with a confused look on her face. She recognized the expression.

She gently picked up the cuffs and brought them to the golden box on the altar. She placed them cautiously inside its silken interior and clasped it shut. She picked up the box and the chalice next to it and turned to attend to her cousin, but felt the barrel of a pistol pressed against the back of her head.

"No," Nikolas said, tears still wet on his cheeks. "No. You do not get to live."

A shot rang out, and Nikolas Valdoros fell to the ground at Athena's feet, dead.

"Yes," Alexander said with a slight smile, a small, black pistol still in his hand. "Yes, she does."

"I do not know how else to thank you, Signorina Voltaire."

Cora Sortera sat tall in her wheelchair, a brown and green blanket across her lap. She reached up for Athena's hand. Achilles and Anastasia Maragos stood behind her.

"No offense, Cora," Athena answered politely as she squeezed the woman's fingertips, "but next time could you call ahead?"

The older woman laughed. "I will see what I can do."

"I am grateful you chose to spend this particular vacation with family," the older woman said with a smile.

"Ahh, yes, well…" Athena gave her grandfather a stern look.

"Oh! I almost forgot," Athena reached for the back of her neck and unclasped the chain that hung there.

"No," Cora replied, "You keep it. I have a feeling you will need it in the days ahead."

"I can't let you leave here without proper protection," Athena said with concern.

"Oh don't worry about me," Cora said. She tugged on the handle of the dark green leather leash in her other hand. The small, fat piglet chained to the end of it squealed up at them in defiance.

"I think my new friend and I will be just fine."

LAND, SKY AND SEA

Elizabeth Amber Love

Sweat formed on his face and around the back of his neck. His hands were clammy and his heart raced. Phillip Richardson's slight, weak frame made him useless to the Army. He hated that he couldn't serve his country, as his father had in The Great War. His life buried in books and labs was evident. Phillip's nerves took over as he squatted outside the door. He never felt quite this way before. Exams seemed so irrelevant compared to this plan. His cockiness gave him some comfort. If anyone could steal from Princeton University's great Dr. Lyman Spitzer, it was him.

He wiped his palms on his trousers and dragged his sleeve across his forehead. Someday... someday his time would come. He'd get his payoff soon. Then he could be like other young men, spending time with girls and shiny new cars. It was in his grasp.

Phillip's mind started to close the walls in around him. He saw it and felt it as a dark miasma blocking all his peripheral sight. He paused. He needed to pull himself together and be a man about this. He needed to do it. He needed to make a better life for himself, and this was the path that presented itself. He was perfectly situated as Dr. Spitzer's post-graduate fellow for the sonar program. He was in the heart of Spitzer's research on thermoclines, revolutionary technology that would give Americans an edge in the war underwater.

Loyalty is something of a cornerstone during wartime, and America was fearless. For most people, nationalism steers allegiance. For a few others, it's the prospects of profiteering, and thus Phillip Richardson found himself in a unique position. Phillip breathed as best he could. He tried again and again until his lungs filled with more oxygen. Fainting was not an option.

Phillip's parents had seen him as a confused boy despite his high intelligence quotient. He would have been satisfied leading a group of young ne'er-do-wells for the rest of his life. But now he saw that his father was right. He could no longer accept his role as the boy lacking social skills and wealth. He had clawed his way into positions of leadership among social outcasts and troublemakers. Anyone with that kind of backbone had to be able to steal one ledger from an office and get out unnoticed.

He wiped the sweat from his hand again and got a better grasp of the key he had slipped from Spitzer's jacket. His fingers fondled the unique engraving on the end of the key. His thumb bumped over a skull as he inserted the shaft into the lock.

Phillip Richardson had to deal with the consequences of his latest bad decision. His blood pressure rose and his heart beat faster than the time his father caught him stealing his Lincoln. Within the walls of Dr. Spitzer's office, it had been the first time Phillip felt conflict within himself. Regret was not something with which he was familiar, and he hadn't enjoyed it one lousy bit.

Phillip had spent many months innocently exploring the office's nooks and shelves. Spitzer carried his current project notebook with him. It contained all of his notes and scribbles for working through problems. But a more pristine copy existed, and Phillip knew where it was stored. That leather bound notebook would be in the scientist's desk.

Phillip took the silver letter opener from the cylinder on the desk. The lock was child's play. It may have offered some confidence of security to Spitzer being inside an already locked office, but Phillip was able to make the drawer within seconds. He retrieved the ledger and dropped the key outside the door. It wouldn't be the first time Spitzer's key fell out of his own pocket.

Harrison Mathur entered Dr. Spitzer's office behind Athena. "Lyman, meet my old friend Athena Voltaire. She's the one I told you about."

Athena could smell the leather from the hundreds of thick books on the shelves. The aroma, mixed with the oils used to polish all the mahogany, created a thick air of masculine scents.

"I've anxiously awaited your arrival, Miss Voltaire," Spitzer said. "Thank you for traveling all the way to New Jersey for this. I... I didn't know what to do. I'm too scared to tell the FBI about what's happened." Athena noticed his hand slightly trembled when she shook it. He was an attractive young man that seemed much older than his twenty-four years. Thin blond hair was combed over his head, and he wore perfectly round glasses. She noticed the obvious signs of exhaustion: dark circles under his eyes, slumped shoulders, and a mug of coffee on the desk that had left ringed stains on the blotter.

"My pleasure, Dr. Spitzer," Athena said. She remained cautiously aware of the scientist while taking in the rest of the room. The shelves were lined with leather-bound books about physics, engineering and weaponry. Testaments to Spitzer's impressive achievements were elegantly framed and mounted, including a letter from the Secretary of Defense. It took a lot to impress the country's best aviatrix, but Lyman Spitzer managed to do it in just a few minutes.

There was no time for Spitzer to hide his cards. He had to lay everything out if he wanted Athena's help. He fussed nervously with a letter opener adorned with a ruby-eyed skull at the end. He spun the blade on fanned out papers from a file folder marked "CONFIDENTIAL." Athena took the opportunity to absorb the details of his office and got to know the man who sought her out.

"I'm developing advances in sonar technology for the United States military. I don't need to explain to you the level of importance this has for our nation," he said.

Athena turned her head to address him. "I'm familiar with your contributions, Dr. Spitzer."

He continued, "Do you have any idea how critical thermoclines are?"

"Certainly. They greatly advanced the technology for our submarines."

Athena shifted her gaze to her old friend Harry. He stood there smoking his imported cigarette while keeping his other hand occupied with his hat. Ol' Harry knew Athena's weaknesses. Among them were machines and the technology that makes them possible. He knew she could be one hell of an engineer if she were the corporate type. But not his old flame. Ever since they were teenagers, she'd had the free spirit of a bird on the wind, which is why her time with the Air Angels seemed like the sort of job she'd never leave.

Athena wrested the conversation's control from the nervous scientist.

"Dr. Spitzer, I understand very clearly that the global war is not just in the sky but under water, and it's only a matter of time before the United States is deeply entrenched in it."

Spitzer let his right hand linger on the fibrous manila folder containing the confidential documents. His unconscious movements drew in Athena's attention.

The red text was emblazoned across the cover like a warning beacon. She couldn't help but wonder about its contents.

She urged him further. Whatever he had to say, he was clearly fighting it.

He finally exhaled, and the words shot out of him like a bullet leaving a gun barrel. "The research on thermoclines has been stolen by my assistant."

Athena remained calm and refrained from showing any emotion. Her eyes looked up from the folder. Her brain had already deduced that it was probably correspondence about said research.

"It changes the game," he said. "The process of active sonar changes everything."

Harry and Athena exchanged silent glances.

"I can imagine it would. I'm still not convinced that the FBI should be left out of this," she said in a cool demeanor. "Doctor, why don't you tell us what happened, or what you think happened?"

"His name is Phillip Richardson. He's a brilliantly talented boy with an edge you don't often find in scientists," Spitzer explained. "He comes from hardworking parents in Rhode Island, an odd couple to be sure."

Harry inhaled a hit of his cigarette. His words flew through the spiraling exhale of smoke. "But really, Lyman, if national security is at stake, Athena would be risking her life. The FBI might be the safer choice here."

"I'm afraid to tell them. It was my mistake hiring him. He's a rogue member of the Skull and Keys organization," said the professor. His eyebrows lifted, showing concern, and his gaze was drawn to the unique letter opener twirling in his fingers. "Before this, he seemed like a juvenile delinquent, like his behavior was just acting out, but I'm honestly afraid that he's crossed a line that he can't cross back over."

Spitzer walked through the trails of Harry's cigarette smoke to one of the bookcases. There was an entire shelf devoted to Princeton University yearbooks. He pulled on the one marked "1936" and flipped open to a page showing the Skull and Keys group shot. He poked at the faces of six boys.

"When those boys splintered off from the original brotherhood, they were instantly into trouble. Vandalism. Mischief. Stealing cars. Each dare escalated. And each time their connections were able to get them off, if they were caught at all, which wasn't often.

"Phillip was the leader. His young age never mattered, much like me. He's bright but he's cunning to the point that it's alarming. At first I thought my feelings were melodramatic, but I'm being proven correct."

Athena took the yearbook from Spitzer's hands. She studied the faces and flipped through additional pages while he continued to speak. She found the portrait of Phillip Richardson and saw something in the lines of his face that looked like a portent of trouble. Harry looked on in silence, still holding his hat in one hand with his burning cigarette in the other.

"Look, Dr. Spitzer," Athena began, "I don't agree with you about leaving the FBI out of this, but I will help you. The Axis cannot get that data."

Harry joined in at last. "If anyone can get your data back, it's my Athena." His smile was beaming. His charm was endless. Harry's personality and romanticism wouldn't be squelched by a mere global crisis.

"Your Athena," she said with an eyebrow cocked in his direction, but there was still a smile. "I haven't been your Athena in over a decade."

Athena and Harry walked down the cold, lonely corridor to the stairs and made their way out of the grand building. They left behind the antique aromas for fresh air. The street was lined with bountiful dogwood trees covered in blossoms on a breezy spring day. Harry hailed a cab as Athena thought out loud.

"Harry, something feels off about this whole mess."

"What do you mean?"

"If Phillip Richardson is a rogue Skull, there's a chance they're trying to handle this internally, if you catch my meaning."

The wrinkles formed on Harry's brow as he thought about his friend Dr. Spitzer. The lines across his forehead aged him.

"Darling, I'm sure Lyman is just upset and he has reason to be. He's nervous. He's terrified that his own research could be in the hands of our enemies and that someone he trusted is to blame. I don't think Spitzer is the one we have to worry about here, but I'm not sure about the rest of the Skulls. We don't know much about Richardson or his connections," said Harry.

The taxi's windows were down halfway, allowing the wind to blow Athena's dark, wavy hair around at the ends playfully. Harry could smell the strawberry scent of her shampoo released by the breeze. He so hoped that they would have a reunion that wasn't life-threatening.

"Richardson is undoubtedly more of an idiot than your friend is willing to believe," Athena said. "He betrayed his friend, his employer and his country. He's put his life in danger and who knows how many other people's. He's gone from inconsiderate scoundrel to full-fledged terrorist."

Harry turned in the backseat. His hand reached up and brushed aside the hair blowing around Athena's cheek.

"We can do this, Rabbit. We can get that data back from Richardson before he sells it and turn him over to the proper authorities."

"Yes, Harry. I know I can." Her eyes conflicted with the smile on her face. "The fates have aligned for us today, but probably not in the way you were hoping. I'll drop you off in Lakehurst to meet your Aunt Margaret. Then I do my own recon on the base. It seems like it might be the perfect spot for Phillip to run with the files."

The cab let them off at a small private airfield where Athena had left her Grumman Goose. The cockpit was a cramped space that Athena was not used to sharing.

"Harry, I don't mind you tagging along but do me a favor," she said.

"Anything."

"Don't touch anything."

He held up his hands in surrender. Athena helped him with his seatbelt, then buckled herself in.

"All right. All right! But seriously, Athena, thank you for letting me hitch a ride to Lakehurst with you. It will be great to fly over New Jersey traffic rather than sit in it. I promised Aunt Margaret I'd try to be there when she landed. You know I'm her favorite nephew, right?"

"Harry, you're her only nephew."

Onboard the LZ 129 Hindenburg zeppelin, the pilot received instructions to kill time over Manhattan due to severe winds in New Jersey. Margaret Mathur tried to relax in a seat near a window. She accepted a cup of tea that had a hint of rosehips, perfect for calming the mind. The rains and wind swayed the giant dirigible. Margaret's nerves didn't want to respond. She just wanted her feet firmly on the ground and promised herself that her next trip would be by boat.

Back inside the Goose, Harry struck up more conversation. The flight would be short. There was more than revisiting the past behind his intention for the talk.

"Do you remember the last time you were in New Jersey?"

Athena had been focused on her mission, but the question made her snap back to a different time for a moment, a time before she started risking her life on a daily basis.

"Of course I remember," she replied.

On the blimp, Margaret and the other passengers were distracted from their late landing by a spectacular view of the eastern coast. They saw the tall buildings of New York City. They saw the bridges and the cars that looked like mere specks. The ship turned about and headed back down the New Jersey shoreline.

Newscaster Herbert Morrison was on the ground in Lakehurst, the airship capital of the world. The rain came down then stopped and then started again.

"They're jumping out the windows! Harry, we can get to them!" she shouted.

"Margaret!" he exclaimed with great fear choking his lungs as much as the smoke.

"Harry, listen to me. We can get them!" she firmly iterated.

Passengers and crew were climbing from the windows of the gondola. A middle-aged man stumbled in his attempt to find footing on the ground, which resulted in him landing on top of Harry. The fall actually helped shake Harry from his shock. He quickly assisted in righting the man then copied Athena's approach in reaching for people that would have dived from the windows and broken their necks. The heat could be felt and more explosions were likely. The gondola was quickly going to be destroyed. Margaret Mathur, Harry's doting aunt, was climbing through broken glass. Her skirt shredded and her jacket caught.

Athena spotted Margaret clinging for life to the broken window frame. Some curtains were dancing through broken windows as if they were also trying to escape. The country's best stunt aviatrix showed no fear. Her hands gripped for a loose bowline and she climbed up several feet.

Margaret's hair had been immaculately twisted up showing off her heirloom pearl earrings only five minutes before, but was now a mess of tendrils attacking her face. From inside the gondola, a stewardess helped release Margaret's caught clothing from the shards of glass. Margaret turned her head to see who was steadying her. She saw the bosom of a petite young woman. Margaret saw the customary uniform and a lapel pin that read "DIANA" in bold letters. The stranger held Margaret from under her shoulders as tightly as possible. The carrier was crashing down further as more of the hydrogen burned away. There was a massive jolt, and Diana lost her grip on Margaret. With her satchel around her and her pistol strapped to her leg, Athena Voltaire kicked off from the gondola's side and began sailing through the smoke.

Margaret's falling body thumped into something moving through the air, Athena swinging on that bowline, flying through the noxious smoke. She grasped the arm of Margaret in the nick of time. The strength Athena needed to heroically hang onto Margaret while swinging was a surge which she had never before felt. Above her head, a row of windows exploded in a fierce blast. Her right hand began to loosen the hold she had on the cable. They were descending and spinning. Athena's boot caught a bit of the framework, and she used her leg to steady them before pushing off like a rock climber and rappelling down the burning wreckage. All the while, Aunt Margaret let out several screams that could barely be heard over the noise of the fire.

When Athena's feet landed on the ground, she saw the stewardess above her on the same line. She had been along for that wild ride the whole time, and it was a good thing too; the gondola was about to be smothered in the collapsing

Morrison spoke into his microphone: "It's starting to rain again. The rain had slacked up a bit."

Athena managed to land her G-21 Goose during the lightest rainfall. She looped the strap of her durable flight bag over her head and across her body. She stepped out of the small cabin door and when her boots hit the ground they sloshed in the mud. Welcome to Lakehurst.

"The last time I was here, we were just kids and I was in my father's stage show." She looked up at Harry. "Atlantic City seemed so glamorous then."

They walked across the airfield and saw the base's military personnel and aircraft, along with the waiting public. The airship carrying Harry's Aunt Margaret was cleared for landing, and at twenty minutes past seven o'clock in the evening, Captain Max Pruss did his best against the spring winds. This was the most difficult landing he'd attempted with the blimp over the past fourteen months.

"The back motors of the ships are just holding it," newscaster Morrison continued. "...uh, just enough to keep it..."

Everyone's eyes were on the grand spectacle of the LZ-129 Hindenburg. Grey skies with dark clouds blanketed the area for miles.

"IT BURST INTO FLAMES!" Morrison shouted.

The gasbags contained hydrogen to give the ship its ability to defy gravity, but despite incidents warning of hydrogen's dangers, the engineering was never upgraded. It was only a matter of seconds before the entire ship was encompassed in flames. Black smoke billowed to the sky, darkening it even more, hiding the once charming spring day.

"It burst into flames. It's falling and crashing! ...It's a terrific crash, ladies and gentlemen..."

Their faces glowed from the flames as Athena and Harry watched the horror before them. Their eyes reflected the turbulent rhythms of the burning that released dark grey nebulae above the airbase. The sound of the fire muted the many screams cried out to God.

"It's smoke, and it's in flames now; and the frame is crashing to the ground, not quite to the mooring mast."

Athena charged toward the burning wreckage of the Hindenburg. Her actions often seemed like she didn't plan anything at all, but like a great chess master, she knew where she would be five steps ahead of the situation.

"Oh the humanity!" Morrison wailed. He wasn't alone. Tears and cries escaped the face of every onlooker.

"Athena!" Harry called out. She kept running, so he followed.

Another ruptured gasbag exploded. By instinct, they turned away and hunkered down. Athena saw Harry close to her now. The thermite coating of the bags gave off an odor of searing metal, suffocating everyone.

air bags.

Harrison was immediately next to them when they hit terra firma. He grabbed Margaret's arm and all of them ran as quickly as possible. Medics were arriving about three hundred yards away across the muddy field. Aunt Margaret's shoes were in a sad state, just like the rest of her JC Penney's outfit from New York City. She wasn't a rich woman, but she was a proud woman of standing. Now, all of them looked like a rag-tag bunch of street urchins that had raided a dumpster for filthy clothing merely to be covered in something. Harrison held his dear aunt tightly. She was distracted from the affection by staring back at the direction of the Hindenburg's heap, no longer recognizable.

"Harry, the ambulance is right over there," Athena said. "Take this woman with you when you go," she said while removing her comforting arm from Diana's shoulders.

Harry was confused. She was going to leave them. They should stick together and get to safety.

"Wait. Where do you think you're going?" he said. His eyes pleaded with her to stay.

Athena took his elbow and led him a few feet away from the other women who were consoling each other. The stewardess had mustered some composure and seemed to be back on duty, putting her own needs off and asking her customer if she was all right.

"Harry, what if this wasn't an accident?" Athena said. "Sure it could be, but the fact that we suspect an act of treason to be occurring right now, right in this very place? What are the odds?"

"You're thinking sabotage?"

"I can't be sure, but right now I have to find that little bastard from Princeton."

Athena's form soon disappeared completely in the smoky air and crowds of frantic people. She had remembered the layout of the base from the air. There was a bank of four nondescript buildings made of cinder blocks and bearing only a few markings of their designations. It was as if a sixth sense pulsed at that moment. Athena's protective common sense was fighting the ambition within her. She wanted to go forward. She knew she had to keep going. She felt the hackles on her neck raise, but she would not stop now. She could sense someone was nearby. If there was anything fortunate about the destruction across the field, it was that she was provided some cover.

She saw a man through the haze. He was close, but she was pretty sure he hadn't marked her as anyone other than a person caught in the chaos. Because she had studied the yearbook photo of Phillip Richardson, she knew it could be him. He was thin and his brown suit was tailored well to his form. He also appeared to be the right age. Everyone there at the base had some look of terror, but this one man also had a look that Athena read as suspicious. What made her more convinced was when she espied the top of a design on the leather cover of the ledger he carried and deduced it was a Skull and Keys fraternal order insignia. It had to be Spitzer's missing data.

Athena watched Phillip enter the nearest building. He opened the door slowly and paused to take a peek. Inside was dark and outside was smoky. His eyes were being tested this day. Athena ducked behind a trash bin just in time when Phillip gave one last look towards the landing fields. Then he resolved his mind to continue forward into the building. Athena quickly ran to the door in time to keep it from closing. She slid inside and immediately crouched down in a shadow to get a grasp of her surroundings.

Her eyes adjusted quickly, and she saw that she was between stacks of steel shelving holding crates of military supplies and mechanical parts. Odors of dust and oil blanketed the air. Athena also detected a heavy scent of metal. Not everyone would recognize that metal had a scent. It wasn't fragrant like wood but there was most definitely something apparent with different metals, whether it was dirty coins or a burning iron; the scent of metals was distinct. She assumed this must be more of a dumping ground for things that may have some salvageability. Phillip walked through the stacks with caution. Athena took a look at the door and saw that there was tape over the locking mechanism.

When Phillip approached a different set of shelving stacks in the huge warehouse, he paused again and looked all around the room, feeling an amateur thief's paranoia; an experienced one would have a better plan and a load of confidence. His feeling was justified. Athena remained obscured by the stacks, but she could see Spitzer's infamous leather journal in the crook of his arm.

Phillip had no idea that his delay gave Athena time to see past him. She used the same sort of stealth to continue to follow him and duck behind a crate further into the room without him noticing. There were four men inside the room already. She knew they would be Phillip's focus.

Three of the men were armed and suspiciously looked around. The fourth— the boss man—he stood there like a sequoia. Joseph Corzetti was an inch or two above six feet tall. He had a big barrel of a chest smoothed under his vest. The group looked like a strangely fashionable platoon in fedoras, sharp suits and pocket watches offering a minuscule dazzle through a haze of cigar and cigarette smoke.

One of the goons was sporting a new Beretta handgun in his right hand. His Sicilian dialect was easily recognizable. Athena knew enough to get by. She was curious about Phillip Richardson's education in foreign languages. He most likely knew Latin, she figured; he may be able to comprehend enough to learn what they are really planning to do with him and the data.

"Do you think this guy will show?" asked the pistol-wielding goon.

The boss replied in English. "Don't worry. There's enough cover. He'll be here."

"It would be suicide not to show," said one of the other gangsters.

Phillip finally crossed the aisle where Athena was. She moved quickly and quietly. She knew it was the last opportunity to stop him from selling the secrets and meeting an untimely death. Her hand reached around and covered his mouth.

"Shhh," she whispered in his ear.

Before he realized what was happening, Athena coldcocked him and rendered him barely conscious. He was dazed, but at least he was unable to scream with her hand over his mouth. She tried to reassure him that he was safer this way. "Trust me. Dealing with me would be better than dealing with them."

Phillip groaned as he slumped all the way to the floor.

"Did you hear something?" the first goon asked, still maintaining his native language.

The boss had the confidence to speak freely.

"Nah. It's just the chaos. This place ain't never seen destruction like this before."

"Sal, check by the door, just in case, would'ya?" pistol man asked of one of his comrades.

The journal was still in Phillip's arm resting against his chest. He had been holding onto it so tightly when Athena grabbed him.

The thug called Sal walked over to the side door, which was another exit from the building. He opened it and took a moment to surveil the commotion outside. The Hindenburg was gone. Completely. Things were noticeably more morose than twenty minutes ago.

Sal's head was leaning out through the open door when a solid fist across his jaw decked him. Harrison had followed Athena's footsteps after Diana assured him that she would look after Aunt Margaret. Harrison's college boxing days weren't so long ago that he couldn't remember his tricks of the sport. Plus, outside of the ring there were no rules.

The crack of Sal's jaw drew the attention of his boss and partners. The Sicilians rushed over to their associate. Harrison had the advantage of his eyes being adjusted to the outside light, dark as it was from the explosion. He grabbed a machine gun from a thug and bashed in the mobster's head, rendering him unconscious. The goon with the Beretta fired at Harrison, but missed the mark.

"Don't shoot!" yelled the boss. "You'll draw attention to us!"

Athena grabbed the journal from the delirious scientist. She tucked the book into a pouch and ran over to the door. Joseph Corzetti, the stalwart boss, was framed by the threshold. Athena landed a heavy boot to the back of one of his knees, sending a searing pain from his ligaments to the rest of his leg. He went down fast and hard. In a quick step she landed a side kick to the left side of his head. Corzetti had no idea what happened. He had neither seen nor heard her coming. But as he yelped in pain, his remaining minion pointed a gun right at her.

Harrison was busy in a boxing match with the other thug. Harry knocked the man's fedora clear off his head with a devastating right hook. It was time to forego those rules that Harry believed made boxing a gentleman's game. He planted his left foot and forced his right one down on his opponent's kneecap. Down he went.

Athena knew the man before her was a criminal through and through. He had undoubtedly killed, but at times there seemed to be a code of never harming women and children. Was he one of those types or was he simply a killing machine with no heart, no mercy? Her beauty was so angelic no matter how much grime and sweat was on her that it stunned the gunman long enough for her to close the gap. She locked his wrist from moving and cleanly disarmed him without so much as a breath.

Sal's listless body kept the door from closing. Harrison ran through the doorway to find Athena standing victorious over the other two incapacitated thugs. She tucked the gun into the pouch with Spitzer's journal. Harrison gathered up the other firearms and carried them away from the men. He followed Athena through the steel stacks until they stopped at the slumped body of Phillip Richardson.

"Is he..." Harrison's words trailed off, but his raised eyebrows finished his question for him.

"Harrison! No. He's fine," Athena said.

She crouched down in front of Phillip and took his lapels in her fists.

"Hey! Phillip!" she said firmly but not too loudly.

Harrison wedged the guns and rifle between a couple of crates on the shelves. He squatted down next to her to look at the face of the traitor.

Athena gave the boy a good smack right across the face. His bleary eyes looked at back at her.

"Can you hear me? Phillip? Can you walk?" she asked.

Phillip gurgled something that sounded like, "Guinkilme."

"Well, yes, they were going to kill you," she said. She felt guilty because a small part of her felt that he deserved it.

"I don't think you'll get anywhere with him, Rabbit. Let's just haul him up on his feet and muscle him out of here," Harrison suggested.

They did exactly that. Each of them wrapped one of Phillip's arms around their necks and they practically dragged him out of the building through the door Athena originally entered.

There were plenty of M.P.s around due to the horrific destruction of the blimp. In fact, when Athena and Harrison approached carrying Phillip, the officers thought it was a rescue from the explosion. Athena explained in full detail what had happened. She said Richardson was selling secrets but she didn't say how. She didn't mention that she now possessed the leather journal. Athena was originally hired to retrieve the book for Dr. Spitzer, and to her mission she would remain true. More soldiers were called over and ordered to the opposite side of the building to round up the Sicilians.

Athena and her dear friend Harry walked through the madness on the field and returned to the medic station.

"By the way," she said to him, "you do realize I detest when you call me 'Rabbit,' don't you?"

It was as if it was the first time he had ever smiled. The distress of the day had weighed down so heavily upon Harrison for hours that he couldn't remember when he last smiled. He wasn't aware of the effects a smile and laugh could bring him. Some of the tension melted off his shoulders and cascaded down his spine. The release felt good.

"I call you that because," he paused his steps and gently grabbed onto her arm, "because when I met you, you were part of your father's stage show. It was like you were one of his props."

"Well, I hate it," she said.

"Too bad," he said. "You were the most adorable of his props, if that helps at all."

They smiled at each other for the seconds they required. It was three deep breaths before they turned and continued their walk. They found Aunt Margaret and Diana resting as comfortably as possible on the tailgate of an ambulance.

Epilogue

Margaret Mathur's parlor was lavishly decorated with deep reds, magenta and gold embedded in dark brown woods. A small vase of fresh flowers sat in the center of the table set for afternoon tea. Margaret entered the room from the kitchen. She presented a plate of cookies to her nephew Harrison, his longtime friend Athena Voltaire and their special guest, Dr. Lyman Spitzer.

"Mrs. Mathur, these are the best tuna sandwiches I've ever tasted," Lyman raved. "I don't know how to thank you for your hospitality." Spitzer paused, then looked over at Athena and Harrison seated at the table. "And to you two, I really don't know how to thank you. You saved my hide, my life's work, and perhaps the country."

Harrison spoke up after a sip of the hot chrysanthemum tea. "You've thanked us enough." He looked up at his favorite aunt. "This is delicious, Aunt Margaret. But honestly, Athena must be used to this sort of challenge and adventure. For me, it was all new and exciting."

"Exciting?" Athena chimed in. "Lives were in danger. Including your own, you twit," she said with a sideways smile.

Lyman let out the deepest breath he had been able to take in a long time. He stared into his demitasse of tea and swirled the liquid around. The violet patterns on the porcelain began to mesmerize him. When he finally inhaled again, his conscious mind returned to the room.

"Phillip was my protégé. My assistant. And I thought he was my friend." Spitzer exhaled quickly. "The Mafia? I can't believe it."

Athena filled in the details about the connection. "It was the Sicilians, actually. They were trying to trade the data for weapons. Mussolini wanted that intel."

Margaret had the pleasant voice that reassured everyone that all would be well. She looked mostly like her old self, but the harrowing experience they went through the day before had taken its toll on her. She had a heavy feeling inside her middle-aged chest that no matter how well she moved back into her routines of life, she and the others would never be the same.

THE FORBIDDEN ISLAND

Michael May

Turns out, Errol wielded a fork and steak knife with as much flair as he did a rapier. If she was truthful about it, Athena enjoyed watching him eat. She liked his company a lot. In addition to his epicurean skills, he was funny, self-deprecating, full of great stories, and not at all difficult to look at. That's why she kept accepting his dinner invitations whenever they'd finish a fencing lesson.

There was also, of course, a reason why she never accepted more than that. He obviously wanted to sleep with her, but she wasn't interested in him that way. He was a great teacher and a fantastic friend, but he was also married and a troublemaker. She wanted nothing more from the relationship than she already had. But he wouldn't have been Errol Flynn if he hadn't tried for more.

"Athena, why don't we see more of each other?" It wasn't a request just a question. And one that he'd asked several times before during other dinners. It wasn't that he was forgetful. He'd just never accepted the answer she kept giving him.

She was opening her mouth to give it once more when she saw the two men approaching the table from the other side of the restaurant. They were out of Errol's line of sight, so he was still waiting patiently for her response. Grateful for the coming distraction, she smiled back at Errol and sipped her wine. By the time she'd finished, the men had arrived.

Athena could tell right away that they weren't autograph-hounds. The shorter one avoided eye contact like he might be about to ask something embarrassing, but the taller, white-haired man was on business. Athena knew his type. He was sharply dressed in a white suit with a flower in his lapel. His tiepin was 24 karat gold, and there was a fair amount of precious metal in his watch, too. Whatever he was after, it was a lot more valuable than an autograph, and he was intent on getting it.

He'd been looking at her all the way to the table, so she wasn't surprised when he addressed her instead of Errol. "Miss Voltaire." His voice was a hard, deep baritone. "Harry told me I'd find you here."

Of course he did, she thought. Harry Warner had no concept of other people's privacy. She didn't complain though, but smiled graciously at the man.

He extended his right hand. "My name is Arthur Lovelace. I'm a business associate of Harry's."

She shook his hand. "Nice to meet you, Mr. Lovelace. This is Errol Flynn."

Lovelace nodded politely at Errol, but couldn't have been less interested. Errol cocked an eyebrow at Athena and gave her an amused grin. He picked up his wineglass and leaned back in his chair to watch the show.

"I apologize for interrupting your dinner, Miss Voltaire, but it really is quite an urgent matter. Allow me to introduce my associate. This is Mr. Thomas Walton."

"Tom," the other man corrected. He held out his hand too. "Nice to meet you, Miss Voltaire." He shook Errol's, too. "Mr. Flynn."

Lovelace indicated the two empty chairs at the table. "Do you mind if we join you briefly?"

Athena already didn't like the man and this was really too much. "Actually, Mr. Flynn and I were just—"

"No, please," Errol interrupted, half standing. "Sit down. Some wine?"

Athena shot him a confused look, but he just kept on smiling. He was enjoying this. "I know Athena has an interesting business, but I've never had the opportunity to see her in action. I'd love to hear what you have to say, Arthur."

Lovelace took the chair that he was already standing over. Walton cleared his throat a little and went around to the other side of the table.

When they were all seated, Lovelace waved over a waiter and ordered a fresh bottle of wine for the table. "And Miss Voltaire and Mr. Flynn's dinner is on me tonight." The waiter nodded and turned to leave.

Athena was about to protest until she saw Errol. He was beaming; absolutely thrilled with Lovelace's presumptuousness. The actor saw her scowl and looked surprised. "What?"

Athena turned to the millionaire. "What can I do for you, Mr. Lovelace?"

"Mr. Walton and I are partners in a venture that requires a pilot of considerable skill. Harry tells me that's you."

"Where are you going?"

Lovelace paused, as if trying to decide how much he wanted to tell her. Tom Walton took the opportunity to jump in. "We're looking for my wife, Miss Voltaire. Like you, she's a pilot. Her plane went missing in the Pacific three weeks ago."

Athena noticed that Errol had stopped grinning. She leaned forward and looked hard at Walton. She was used to clients being dishonest with her, but if Walton was lying, he was brilliant at it. She hadn't noticed it before, but his eyes were bloodshot and had heavy bags under them. He wasn't crying or carrying on, but he looked miserable.

She wondered about Lovelace's involvement in this, but decided it wasn't the time to ask. Instead, she went after more immediate details. "What do the authorities say?"

Lovelace interrupted. "That's why we need you, Miss Voltaire. The government says that they can do nothing. Unfortunately, Mrs. Walton was flying over Japanese waters when she went down. Both we and the United States government have been forbidden to search the area."

Errol let out a slow whistle.

Athena kept her eyes on Walton. "Is there any chance she could have survived?"

"We're hopeful," Lovelace answered. "There's a small island in the vicinity of her last radio transmission. We'd like for you to take us there."

She couldn't hold back the burning question any more. She turned on Lovelace. "And what's your role in this?"

"Mr. Walton isn't in the position to fund such an expedition. I am."

She wanted so badly to ask him what he was getting out of it, but didn't want to give him the satisfaction of lying to her. She'd find out sooner or later, with or without his cooperation. That's when she realized that – in her head, at least – she'd already taken the job.

"We'll need a seaplane. Mine's not outfitted for this kind of job."

"Already taken care of." Lovelace smirked. "There's a Sikorsky S-39 waiting for us in Hong Kong."

With the S-39's range, they'd have to do some island hopping to refuel between Hong Kong and Japan, but it would do. "I'll need charts of the area, including a map of the island."

"Charts of the waters aren't a problem," he said, "and we can locate the island on them. But the island itself has never been mapped."

As much as she didn't like or trust Lovelace, at least he was prepared. They may not have been ideal preparations, but she'd worked with less. "Give me what you have," she said. "I'll be ready first thing in the morning."

Walton let out a long sigh. "Thank you so much, Miss Voltaire. I can't tell you how much this means to me."

Lovelace stood. "Very good. I have us booked on the six o'clock flight to San Francisco in the morning, then the Philippine Clipper from there to Hong Kong. We can go over the charts and other details on the trip." He extended his hand again and she shook it. "Thank you, Miss Voltaire." He dripped insincerity. "It means the world."

When he and Walton had gone, Errol pretended to pout, but the twinkle in his eyes gave him away. "Early morning, I suppose. No dessert, then?"

Athena speared a piece of steak with her fork, chomped it, and smiled sweetly at him as she chewed. "Not the kind you're thinking about."

She hated to admit it, but Lovelace's planning was impressive. He was as prepared as he possibly could be under the circumstances. In fact, some of the information he'd collected had to have been illegal. A lot of it was written in Japanese, but Lovelace had English translations for everything that needed it.

They spread out the maps and documents on the table of the deluxe stateroom Lovelace had reserved for them in the back of the Clipper. It would take them about a week to reach Hong Kong, and from there Athena planned out another couple of days in the S-39 to get to Musha Island, where Susan Walton had disappeared.

Getting there wasn't Athena's big concern though. By all accounts, Musha was the most forbidden of forbidden places. Not only was it deep in the territory of heavily militarized and expansionistic Japan, it was also off limits even to the local people. No fishing was allowed there and – if Lovelace's documents were accurate – the military kept a discrete distance as well.

It was that last part that gave Athena hope about reaching the place. None of the papers so much as hinted at what made the island taboo, but whatever it was, she figured that she could deal with it more easily than she could with warships and fighter planes. As long as she could fly her group in undetected, they had a good chance of not being caught while they were there.

On the other hand, Athena was growing less and less confident that they'd find Susan Walton alive when they got there. Whatever was on Musha, it had even the navy spooked, and that meant that there was more to the place than just local legends. Susan had been alone and unarmed. She sounded tough, but Athena didn't like her chances.

Walton was confident, though. He absolutely believed – without a hint of doubt – that his wife was alive on Musha Island and in need of rescue. Athena wasn't so sure, but she didn't try to convince him otherwise. Let him have his hope, she thought.

She was glad to be able to spend some time alone with him on the flight to China. The Philippine Clipper was a huge plane, and though she saw a lot more of Lovelace than she wanted to, the industrialist didn't make any special effort to always be around. In fact, he seemed to value his privacy as much as anyone and often went off by himself to read. That gave Athena a chance to talk to Walton by himself and get some answers to questions that had been bothering her.

"What was Susan doing in Japanese waters?" she asked him once over coffee in the dining lounge.

Walton looked uncomfortable. He glanced over her shoulder at the door to the back part of the plane.

She leaned forward and got his attention with her eyes. "Tom, I need to know what we're getting into. The more I know about Susan and the island, the better our chances of finding her and getting us all out of there."

He cleared his throat. "She was working for Lovelace."

"What?"

"He's looking for something. I don't know what it is, but he had Susan out searching for it. He believes it's on Musha Island."

"Something? Like what? Oil? Minerals?"

Walton shook his head and lowered his voice. "I don't know. I don't think it's any of those things though. He'd never be able to get rights to take stuff like that out. Not from the Japanese. Whatever it is, I think it's something small. Or at least portable."

That sent Athena's mind spinning. What the heck was on that island? "Do you have any guesses?" she asked. "What are his interests?"

"I don't know him that well. Neither did Susan. He just hired her out of the blue one day. Gave her a plane and a job. She couldn't turn him down."

Athena understood. There weren't a lot of jobs for female pilots. "She sounds like a remarkable woman."

"Bravest person I know," he said.

"We'll find her."

He nodded, but he looked terrible. "She's also the toughest person I know. I didn't realize how tough until she disappeared."

"What do you mean?"

"Lovelace," he said. "I only met him this week when I went to see him with the idea of going to look for her. Susan had never mentioned how horrible he is. He didn't seem to bother her."

"But he bothers you."

Walton was practically whispering; leaning forward so she could hear him. "I've never met a more selfish, greedy person. Whatever he thinks is on that island, you can believe that it's all he cares about. He certainly doesn't care about finding Susan."

"So why does he need you?"

"I've asked myself the same question. Honestly, I think I just came along at the right time. He would've figured out another way. Maybe it would've succeeded; maybe it wouldn't have. This way, he gets to come along and if anyone asks, he's just being philanthropic."

"Wait a minute. Does he know that you know he has an ulterior motive?"

Walton shrugged. "We've never talked about it, but he has to suspect."

"Then we have to be very careful," she said. Clients had burned her before once she'd helped them and they realized they didn't need her anymore. Lovelace reminded her a lot of those guys.

She brought the S-39 down in a small bay on the east side of Musha Island. She'd flown low to avoid being seen from the air, deciding that if they were going to be spotted she'd rather it be by a boat. Fortunately, they'd seen neither boats nor planes all morning, and she was confident that they'd arrived undetected. Whether they could leave the same way was a different matter, but at least they'd be able to make a run for it to China if someone tried to stop them on the way out.

She'd picked the bay for a couple of reasons. For one thing, it was one of the few accessible parts of the island. The south and west sides were all cliffs and the north was a long stretch of beach that the plane would be easily seen against. They had more cover in the bay, tucked behind the long arms of land that wrapped around it.

Another reason she liked the bay, though, was that it was a good place to begin searching for Susan. Their quick survey around the island's perimeter revealed no sign of her plane, but if she had survived the crash, the bay would be a natural place for her to make camp. A small stream fed into it from inland, which made it much more preferable to the empty, northern beach. There was also a lot more shade here.

Walton wasn't so sure, arguing that the north beach would give his wife a much clearer view of rescue craft. His opinion was that Susan would risk capture if it meant getting off the island, but the lack of any construction in that area brought him around to Athena's point of view. Susan obviously wasn't there, so they might as well check out the harder-to-see area around the bay.

Athena landed, and since there was enough room between the water and the thick tree line, she drove the plane up onto the beach. It was barely enough room – and one of the S-39's wheels never actually left the surf – but they were at least able to hop down onto dry land when they left the plane.

All three of them wore pistols, but Lovelace and Athena carried Winchesters too, just in case. Lovelace had brought a rifle for Walton as well, but Walton said he'd be no good with it. He didn't even really want the pistol, but saw the wisdom in carrying some kind of protection. Athena also had a large hunting knife strapped to her belt. Lovelace sneered at it, but she ignored him. Ammunition could run out.

Since Walton was light on weapons, he volunteered to carry the large backpack with food and other supplies. That meant that he was a little slower than the other two, but that probably would've been the case anyway. He'd told Athena on the Clipper that he was an accountant and he certainly had the speed of a man used to sitting behind a desk. But, it turned out, he also had a really great eye.

They were still on the beach, walking towards the stream, when he pointed to a spot in the trees about twenty yards away. "What's that?"

Athena didn't see what he was talking about at first, but then she noticed that some of the green in the brush was actually oxidized bronze. "Is that a gate?"

Lovelace broke away from the two of them to run over to it. Athena was right behind him, but he was already running his hands over it when she got there. "It is a gate," he said. "Look, there's a wall."

Sure enough, a long, ivy-covered, stone wall reached into the jungle from either side of the metal gate. Athena tried to look down the beach to see if it broke off at the stream, but she couldn't tell from where they were.

"What are those markings?" Walton asked, coming up to the gate.

Lovelace opened his mouth like he was about to answer, but he said nothing. They looked familiar to Athena, but she wasn't sure. "I don't know. They're some kind of hieroglyphs, but not like any I've ever seen." They reminded her a little of some she'd seen in Tibet, but that didn't make any sense.

Lovelace pressed on the gate. It didn't move, so he put his shoulder into it. Walton took a step back. "It won't budge," Lovelace grunted. Athena pushed too, but nothing. Whether it was locked or simply rusted shut, it wasn't opening.

"The wall's only seven feet high," Lovelace noticed. "We can get over it."

"I'd like to see what the stream does," Athena countered. "Maybe it goes inside the wall."

"All right," the millionaire said. "Let's check it out. We can go over the wall later if there's no other way in."

The stream didn't go inside the wall, but ran alongside it for a while before curving away, deeper into the jungle. Unfortunately, they saw no signs of a camp either on the beach or up the stream to the point where it left the wall. If Susan had been here, it had been a while and she had covered her tracks very well.

Walton wanted to follow the stream. "She'd want to stay close to fresh water and probably as far away from that wall as possible."

Lovelace couldn't take his eyes off the structure. "No," he said. "She's in there."

Athena watched him. The word that described him, she thought, was "entranced." "Why do you think that?" she asked.

The question broke him out of his spell. He coughed and tried to look nonchalant. "If she made it this far, she would have tried to complete the job I sent her on. That's behind this wall."

"What job is that, exactly?" Athena asked.

"It's none of your business, Miss Voltaire."

She looked at Walton, who appeared to want to say something, but kept his mouth shut. She was getting frustrated with his timidity. "What about him?" she asked Lovelace. "Is it none of his business what you hired his wife to do?"

Lovelace ignored Walton and glared at Athena. "It's between her and I," he said. "We're going over."

Athena looked at Walton. He couldn't take his eyes off the wall and he was sweating hard, though it wasn't that hot. She shook her head and swore under her breath. Walton's motive for wanting to explore upstream was as selfish as Lovelace's for wanting to see behind the wall. But in spite of that, both men had solid rationale for why Susan Walton may have made either decision.

It all came down to whether she was the kind of woman who wanted to survive or the kind of woman who wanted to complete her task. Walton had made her sound very brave on the plane, but she was also distrustful of Lovelace. Would she risk her own life to complete his mission? Right now, Walton was saying, "No," but the Susan he'd described on the Clipper sounded like a different person. Beside that, Athena was beginning to have ulterior motives of her own.

She was incredibly curious about whatever it was that Lovelace was after. If they went after it, it would not only satisfy that curiosity, but it might help Lovelace focus. She held up a finger to him and said, "Give us a minute."

She pulled Walton aside and lowered her voice. "Look, he's not going to be able to concentrate on finding Susan until we get whatever it is he's looking for. Once he has it, we'll have his full cooperation in locating her and getting off the island."

Walton looked upstream like it was a friendly fort in enemy territory.

"I know you're scared," she told him. "But I really think this is best for Susan. There's a good chance she went in there. I think if you're honest with yourself, you know that's true."

A tear streaked down his cheek.

"And even if she's not," Athena continued, "we'll have a better chance of finding her with Lovelace's help than without him. Agreed?"

Walton nodded.

Athena led him back to Lovelace. "Okay," she said. "We're ready."

They decided to cross where they were, but follow the inside of the wall back around to the gate to see if there was a road or path there that might lead somewhere interesting. They all agreed to each other that that's what Susan would have done, but they all knew that wasn't why they were doing it.

Lovelace gave Athena a hand to the top of the wall first. She straddled it to help him over and then Walton. Even from the outside of the wall, they could tell from the trees inside that there was more jungle there, but Athena was still disappointed that there wasn't also some kind of building or structure as an obvious destination within the enclosure. She didn't want to spend a lot of time on Lovelace's object. Going back to the gate felt more and more like the right thing to do.

Lovelace led them along the wall, followed by Walton and then Athena. As they walked, she noticed that the ground was squishy and moist, like the area had been flooded recently. There were a lot of earthworms, too, but they were a strange color. Sort of purple, but on the blue side.

That got her looking around for other animal life. She'd noticed some birds and tuft-eared squirrels outside of the wall, but inside it was much quieter. Not unnaturally so, but enough to be creepy.

They reached the gate before too long, but all that was there was a small path into the trees. It wasn't paved or even worn down very much. More of an animal path, though they'd seen no animals yet big enough to have made it. Lovelace didn't stop to discuss, but turned and went down the path, deeper into the jungle. Athena and Walton exchanged a look, but followed him.

The path began sloping downhill and the ground became even wetter. There were puddles everywhere and Athena finally called attention to them. "What do you make of this, Lovelace? It wasn't this wet outside the wall."

He didn't answer, but he stopped and knelt down to look closer at a puddle.

Walton and Athena caught up to him. "What are you looking at?" she asked. "Tracks."

She stepped past Walton, who looked around nervously. "What kind of tracks?"

"I don't know," Lovelace said. "I've never seen anything like it."

Athena had. Next to the puddle that she'd thought Lovelace was looking at was a set of prints going from right to left across the path. They were large and webbed. "Crocodile," she said.

Walton came up behind her. His voice cracked when he spoke. "They're enormous."

"Saltwater crocodiles," she said, adjusting her grip on her rifle. "They grow them big in this part of the world. Males get up to eleven feet long." She ignored Walton's gasp. "I saw one in Australia that..." but she broke off when she heard a twig snap in the bushes to the left. Lovelace raised his rifle as Walton got behind Athena.

"Get ready to run," Athena whispered. "They're fast, but they won't chase you that far. If you can stay ahead of it, it'll give up before long."

She was aiming towards the ground, expecting the crocodile to be down there, so she was startled by the snarl from much higher off the jungle floor. It was almost on level with her chest. She raised the barrel of her rifle. "That's no crocodile."

As if to confirm, the creature sprung from the bushes. Fortunately, Athena and Lovelace were both ready, and it went down with two bullets in its head.

Lovelace gave a long whistle. "What is that thing?"

Athena had been absolutely right. It not only wasn't a crocodile, it was like no other creature she'd ever seen before. It wasn't as big as she'd imagined and she wondered if it hadn't been standing on its hind legs when it had growled. It had crashed through the brush on all fours, though, and was only a little over three feet tall at its shoulder. But it wasn't a normal reptile.

It had scales, but it was as fish-like as it was reptilian. There were fins on its back and legs and on the stubby, little tail. Athena couldn't figure out that tail; it was all wrong for swimming. In fact, the creature's whole body was completely weird for a water-based animal. It was compact and stocky. The face had a short snout and a couple of small, blunt ears.

Lovelace was obviously freaked out and shot it in the head one more time just to be sure it was dead. "What is that?" he asked.

Athena nudged it with her boot. "I don't know."

When it didn't move, she slung her rifle over her shoulder. Then she knelt to get a better look at the animal. She touched its neck. "Are these gills?"

Lovelace got closer, but Walton wouldn't come near. From several feet back, he said, "You know what it looks like to me? Some kind of amphibious bear."

Athena laughed, but quickly stifled herself. He had a point. The body shape was kind of bear-like. But the gills, the fins, and the webbed feet... "That's impossible," she said. She stared at Lovelace, daring him to explain it.

"Don't look at me," he said. "I have no idea what that is."

They left it lying there in the path and continued downhill, deeper into the marshy hollow. Though it was around noon, the jungle got darker as they went. Not only were the trees thicker, but there was also a fog all around that grew more and more dense. The puddles were getting larger too, but they were shallow and the three of them were still able to walk pretty much wherever they wanted.

Athena continued speculating aloud about the creature they'd shot. Walton – who stuck very close to her – joined her, but Lovelace said nothing. To Athena's mind, that was all the evidence she needed that he knew something.

"Is it some kind of scientific experiment?" she wondered aloud. "Is that it, Lovelace? Are you here looking for some kind of gadget?" Nothing from the millionaire. "A weapon maybe?" He stopped and spun around to face her, but she never learned what he was about to say. Another fish-creature slammed into him and sent him flying into the mud. This one was different though.

There'd been no roar, screech, snarl, or any hint of warning from the beast. It had attacked quickly and silently, and by the time Athena got her rifle raised, it was already tangled up with Lovelace, throwing his weapon away and making it impossible for Athena to get a good shot at it.

She tried to get a bead, but it was too fast and kept moving Lovelace in between itself and Athena. It was similar in color and scale pattern to the one they'd shot, but that was the only similarity. It looked humanoid, for one thing, even rolling on the ground like it was.

"What is this place?" Walton screamed.

"Run!" she said. "Get in a tree!"

Lovelace held his own for almost a minute, but he was no match for the thing. The monster got on top of him and raised its webbed claws for a final blow, but that was all the opening Athena needed. She took the shot.

But the thing was quick. It must have heard something, because it spun to look at her almost as she was pulling the trigger. It stared into her soul with its large, black eyes for the fraction of a second it took the bullet to reach it. To Athena, it felt like minutes. Then there was blood and a cry of pain as the creature's head jerked back and it fell off of Lovelace.

Athena immediately aimed another shot, but the animal was already on its legs and running away. My God, is it fast, she thought.

She ran over to Lovelace, who lay still in the mud. He groaned, so he was alive, but she had a hard time telling how hurt he was with so much wet dirt covering his wounds. She ran her hands over him, feeling for open cuts, and was relieved that there weren't that many. His shirt was pretty shredded, but except for a nasty gouge on his cheek, his lacerations were superficial.

She stood up and wiped as much mud off her hands as she could. "Get up," she said. "You're going to be okay."

He groaned again and rolled over onto his stomach. "I know," he said. He got his legs under him and stood up with a grunt. "Just got the wind knocked out of me."

She cocked an eyebrow at him. "Seriously? You looked worse off than that."

He picked up his rifle. "I'm not that old, Miss Voltaire."

She still hated him, but she had to admit that she was impressed. He was that old, but he was also tough.

Lovelace looked around. "Where's Walton?"

"Up here!"

Athena got to be impressed again. Walton was no good in a fight, but he was one hell of a tree-climber.

They walked the path for another half-hour before reaching the bottom of the hollow. Athena believed that Lovelace knew more than he was letting on about the fish-creatures, but she didn't press him on it. She was more concerned about looking around them for signs that the humanoid one was coming back. She'd scared it off with a graze to its head, but if it was intent on hunting them, she wasn't sure she could hear it sneaking up. She hoped that she could, now that she knew it existed and how deadly it was, but it shook her that it had surprised them so easily before.

She was getting more and more frustrated with Walton, who was so frightened now that he crowded her for protection. She was trying to be compassionate, but he was getting in the way of her rifle if she had to suddenly swing it around. She finally had to lay down the law and make him walk ten paces in front of her.

At the base of the hollow they found their second sign of civilization after the wall. It was a large clearing with a dried up fountain sticking up in the middle of it. The ground was also firmer here, and Walton discovered that under a thick layer of mud, the floor of the clearing was paved with flat stones.

The fountain depicted a fish-like man – very similar to the creature that had fought Lovelace – holding a spear in his right hand and a huge, conical shell in his left. "Did you see this?" she asked Lovelace. But he was already past and didn't answer.

The fish-man held the shell as if he was pouring something out of it, undoubtedly where the water would have come from if the fountain were running. Around the edges of the pool were more hieroglyphs like the ones on the gate. Athena wished she had a camera so that she could study all of this later at her leisure. There was something important here, if she could just figure out what.

She and Walton were still studying the fountain when Lovelace called out from the other side of the clearing. "Over here!"

She walked towards him. "What is it?"

"A path. A paved one."

Sure enough, she could see a wide path through bare patches in the mud. It led up out of the hollow and was paved with the same kinds of stones that covered the clearing floor. "Looks like we're getting close," Athena said.

"To what?" asked Walton.

"To whatever he's looking for."

Lovelace just grunted and led the way.

In a few hundred yards, the slope they were walking got very steep and the path became steps. On either side of the foot of the stairs were large statues of dolphins, reared up and watching over the hollow with a serious, important air. Lovelace ignored them and started up.

"What is this place?" Walton asked.

"I don't know. It doesn't feel Japanese, but it doesn't really fit any kind of civilization I'm aware of. And that statue in the fountain…"

"It looks just like the thing that attacked us."

They followed Lovelace up the stairs. "It could be some kind of lost race," Athena suggested.

"Is that possible?"

She thought back to Tibet. "Oh, it's possible."

After about forty steps, they cleared the fog. The jungle was still thick on either side of them, but up ahead they could see a huge cliff looming. The steps ended at an opening in the cliff and Lovelace was just going inside. Athena hadn't realized how far ahead he'd gotten.

"Lovelace!" she called. But he didn't stop. "Come on," she said, as much to herself as to Walton, and she started to run.

At the top of the stairs, a short tunnel carved through the cliff and opened up on the other side. Even from the inner entrance to the tunnel, Athena could smell the sea air and hear waves crashing on rocks. Lovelace was nowhere to be seen.

She was in shape, but she still had to catch her breath. Walton was still coming up the steps, puffing and wheezing. "Hurry up, Tom!" She didn't wait.

At the end of the tunnel, the cave opened onto a beautiful, man-made lagoon. Maybe fish-man-made, she thought. There was a coral barrier 100 yards out, enclosing a circular area of the clearest, bluest water Athena had ever seen. Over to her right, built into the cliff-face, was the entrance to a magnificent temple.

She couldn't believe they'd missed it when they'd circled the island from the plane, but they'd been searching for potential places to land, not anything like this. Seeing nothing but cliffs on this side of the island, they hadn't looked that closely at the rocks themselves.

A wide causeway connected the tunnel entrance with the temple, and Lovelace was already two-thirds of the way to the other door. He was moving more slowly now and holding his side, winded from the stairs. "Lovelace!"

He stopped and turned to look at her. "Come on!" he called, and kept walking.

She caught up with him at the temple entrance. There was no door; just a twelve-foot arch set back under a portico with spiraled columns and a decorative roof. Inside, an enormous chamber was brightened only by sunlight that came in through small windows above the portico.

The chamber was paved with the same kind of stones they'd seen around the fountain in the hollow, but that wasn't the only similarity between the two places. The fountain itself was repeated, too. Only on this one, the fish-man figure wore a coral crown.

Lovelace immediately went toward the fountain, but Athena only noticed it briefly, distracted by a large, half-eaten carcass on the floor and the even bigger pile of bones against the wall. The bones were from animals of all sizes, but the carcass was from one of the fish-bear creatures they'd shot earlier.

She called after Lovelace. "Are you seeing this?" But he ignored her.

She watched him grumpily. He circled the fountain, looking for something, but not finding it. He looked around the chamber wildly, but except for the fountain and the dead animals, there wasn't anything to see.

"What are you looking for?"

"It's not here!"

"What's not here?"

He jerked his head toward her and stared.

"Lovelace, if you tell me what you're looking for, maybe I can help you find it."

He looked agitated; impatient with not finding the thing and with her just for being there. He kept fidgeting with his rifle. "It's a map."

"A map? Of what?"

He looked long and hard at her. Judging her, she felt. He must have decided she was okay. Or maybe he was just out of options. "Have you heard of the Naacal?"

"I'm not familiar, no."

He sighed. "Have you heard of Mu?"

"As in the lost continent? It's the Pacific's version of Atlantis."

"That's right. And the people who lived there were called the Naacal. They were the ancestors to both the Egyptians and the Mayans, and they were so advanced that not even the sinking of their continent destroyed them."

"So legend says."

"So this island says!" He held out his hands to indicate the chamber around them. "I believe this was an outpost of Mu."

It all clicked into place. "And the map leads there."

He smiled. "The map leads there."

"But you don't know there's a map. You heard about this place somehow, figured out that it might be this outpost, then... assumed there'd be a map?"

"There has to be! Why would they build an outpost to the surface world without any kind of reference to how to get home?"

She shook her head. "You're insane, Lovelace."

A voice behind her called to them. "Miss Voltaire! Mr. Lovelace! You should come see this!" She'd forgotten all about Walton.

Lovelace pushed past her and ran to the chamber entrance where Walton was standing. Athena followed.

Walton was pointing down the causeway in the opposite direction from the tunnel. Athena hadn't noticed before that the causeway actually continued a little past the temple entrance. She'd thought it was just a large gathering area in front of the portico, but at the end nearest to the ocean was a narrow set of stairs leading down. "There's some kind of tower down there," Walton said.

Lovelace raised his eyebrows at Athena then started down. She and Walton followed him. "You came down here by yourself?" she asked.

"I know it wasn't very smart, but I hoped I might find some sign of Susan. I peeked in at you and Lovelace and saw him searching that room. I realized how worked up he's become over this thing he's looking for. And then I realized that I haven't been as worked up over my wife. I felt ashamed."

Athena patted him on the back and smiled at him. "It was brave," she said. "Whatever that fish-creature is, I think it lives around here."

He stopped walking and the color drained from his face. "Are you sure?"

"Something around here has been hunting the local wildlife and eating it. The chamber up there is full of dead animals. That might be why we didn't see a lot more of them than we did. The fish-man has my vote as the most likely hunter."

"Oh, God," he said. "Susan."

She regretted her nonchalance. He'd toughened up a little and she'd immediately started poking his courage to see how deep it was. She should have known it wasn't very. "Don't worry," she said. "She's a resourceful woman. If she's around, she'll have made it to shelter. Maybe even in this tower. Did you explore the whole thing?" She started walking again down the last few steps to a small walkway. It ran along the cliff face a few feet above the crashing ocean, but there was a curve in the cliff wall and she couldn't see where the walkway went. Lovelace was already out of view.

Walton came too. "No," he answered. "I saw the tower and came right back to find you."

Well, she thought, it was still brave.

Like with the temple, Athena wondered how they'd missed seeing the tower from the air. And for the second time, she forgave herself. It was tall, but it was carved from the cliff face with only a large window at the top, overlooking the ocean. From a distance, it would look like part of the cliff.

At its bottom, the walkway they were on led them to an entrance. At one point there had been a door, but that was long since rotted away. Lovelace was already stepping over the decayed wood and into the darkness when Athena and Walton arrived.

Athena went next with Walton behind her. They were in a small chamber with an empty fireplace and more rotten wood on the floor; probably the remains of whatever furniture this place used to have. Lovelace looked around a little, but there was nothing to see. He quickly gave up and went towards the stone stairs leading to the next level.

The next level was fifty steps up and split into two sections by a wall of metal bars. In the back half, bolted into the walls, were thick chains with manacles. "A cell," said Walton. The place smelled like a prison, too. It stunk of feces and urine.

The cell door was open and in the cell Athena saw scattered piles of poop. "This isn't good. Something lives here." She looked around some more and saw little piles of bones too. Nothing as large as what was in the temple chamber, but something had the occasional dinner here as well. "We need to get out of here."

Walton agreed. He was standing near the stairs, looking up and down them. He was ready to bolt in either direction depending on which the cell's current tenant returned from.

Lovelace poked around a pile of nasty rags with his foot. "Wait. We haven't checked everywhere yet."

Athena unslung her rifle. "Why would the map be in the jail?"

"What's this?" He knelt down and pulled something from under the dirty strips of cloth. It was a leather satchel, just as filthy as everything else in the room. Lovelace looked like he'd found a billion dollars. Athena got closer and even Walton calmed down to watch Lovelace from the stairs.

Lovelace opened the bag and gasped as he looked inside. He pulled out some papers. "Maps! This is it!"

"Lovelace, what are you talking about? Those can't be more than a year or two old. They're probably not that old."

He looked at her like she'd just slapped a puppy, but he dropped the empty bag to examine the papers. She was right. They were new.

"That can't be..." He shook his head as he looked, getting more and more violent the more he saw. "No, no, NO!" He threw the papers across the room.

"What is it?" Walton asked. He knelt to pick up a sheet that landed near him.

Athena figured it out. "It's hers, isn't it? It's Susan Walton's."

Lovelace didn't answer. He had his hand over his mouth and his eyes darted from side to side as he thought.

Walton gave a strangled, little cry. "Susan?" He held out the paper in his hand. "This is yours, isn't it, Lovelace? It's your instructions to her!" He looked up the stairs and screamed his wife's name. "Susan! It's me, Tom! Where are you?!"

"Tom, stop!" Athena said. But he ignored her.

She knelt down and grabbed a handful of the rags at Lovelace's feet. They weren't just random bits of cloth. She saw a button; part of a stitched pocket. Her heart sank and she looked at Walton, still calling desperately for his wife.

She stood up. "Tom!"

Something in her voice got his attention. He looked at her; looked at what she was holding. His mouth moved, but no sound came out.

Athena took a step toward him, but he closed the distance himself. He hurried to her and touched the shredded clothing. He had tears in his eyes. "Susan..."

Athena felt like she might cry herself. "I'm so sorry, Tom."

He took the rags from her and sat down on the floor, staring at them, cradling them, and weeping.

She knelt down with him and touched his shoulder. "Tom. Let's get out of here."

"No!" Lovelace had been standing still, looking like he was in shock, but he broke out of that. "We haven't found it yet!"

"We found what we came to find," she said. She helped Walton to his feet. "We're getting out of here before that thing comes home."

Now Walton was back too, but he was sluggish. Dazed. "Yes. We have to leave." He dropped the rags, wiped his hands on his pants, and went back to the stairs.

"Not without the map!" Lovelace unslung his rifle.

Athena had been waiting for that. She high-kicked him in the chest and sent him flying into the wall. She was on him before he had a chance to get up. She took his rifle away and since her hands were full, she called for Walton. "Tom, get his pistol." She held her rifle on Lovelace until Walton completed the job.

Lovelace was furious and desperate, but he didn't move.

"Now," Athena told him, "Walton and I are leaving. If you want to come with us, you can. But if you want to stay here with that creature and look for a map that may not even exist, that's fine too."

"You can't leave! That's my plane!"

"Not anymore. If you come with us, you can have it back. But if you stay here, you'll never need it again. We're not even sure there's only one of those fish-men. If you stay here, you're never leaving."

"At least leave me a rifle!"

She thought about that. "Walton and I are going back downstairs. If you follow us, I'll shoot you. If you stay up here until we're gone, I'll leave a rifle in the room below. That's the only deal you're getting, so I don't even care what you decide. We're leaving; you do whatever you're going to do." She turned to go.

"No, wait! Wait!" He got to his feet. "I'm coming with you."

"I'm not giving you a weapon."

"It's okay. I'm coming with you."

"Fine." She took one step down the stairs, but stopped cold. Still carrying both rifles, she held up a hand to stop the two men. Once everyone had quit moving, she listened, trying to hear the sound again.

There was silence for half-a-minute, but then she heard it: a small scraping sound on the steps below, just behind the curve of the stairwell. The hairs on her arm stood straight up and she heard Walton quietly gasp behind her.

She slowly turned around and motioned them to the stairs going up. Walton went without a word, but Lovelace motioned for one of the rifles. Athena shook her head and waved the gun at the stairs. She mouthed the word, "Up."

He looked past her at the stairs where the creature was coming – because that's what they knew it was – and then booked it for the stairs, his boots pounding loudly on the floor. Athena swore in her head and turned to face the thing that was already skittering quickly up the stairs.

She dropped one of the rifles to give herself a better hold on the remaining one, but the thing was so fast that she missed it with her first shot. It jumped up the last few stairs at her and was on her before she could get off another round. As expected, it was the same fish-creature from the hollow. The graze wound still marked its large, scaly forehead.

To Athena's surprise, it didn't gut her. It knocked her down, but then leaped off again and went for the other stairs. Athena got up and ran after it.

It was faster than she was, so she could hear the screams before she could see what was going on. They were screams of anger though, not pain, from both Lovelace and Walton. She rounded a curve in the stairwell and found Lovelace holding two pistols, Walton's and the one that Walton had taken from him. The millionaire was using them to hold off the creature, but he hadn't fired yet. Maybe he wasn't sure the creature could be killed with the low caliber bullets of the handguns. Athena sure wasn't. But he'd made the creature nervous enough to stop it momentarily.

Walton was behind Lovelace, trying to get the pistols back, but Lovelace held him off with elbows and shoulders. Walton tried to lunge around, and Lovelace took advantage of the move to spin out of the way. Walton's momentum carried him past Lovelace and into the arms of the creature. Lovelace didn't even look back as he ran up the stairs.

Athena raised her rifle to shoot the creature in the back of the head before it could rip Walton apart, but she paused. The creature wasn't killing its victim. It just held onto Walton and stared at him. Athena couldn't see its face, but it cocked its head to the side as if it were trying to figure something out about the man.

Walton stared at it back, terrified at first, but then calming down and full of curiosity. Athena saw a question cross his face and he mouthed a word that Athena couldn't make out.

The creature pushed him aside and ran after Lovelace, taking the steps two and three at a time. Athena had relaxed her rifle as Walton and the creature had their moment, but she raised it again to get a shot before the monster rounded the next curve.

"No, wait!" Walton grabbed the barrel of the gun and pulled it down.

"What is it? What just happened there?"

"That creature. I think it's Susan."

"What? Why would you think that?"

"The way it looked at me. I don't know, but I saw her in there."

She tried to get her mind around it, but was distracted by the sound of gunfire above. "Come on," she said.

Before they got there, they heard screaming again, but this time it was pain. A lot of it. It went on for the couple of minutes it took them to climb the remaining stairs, and when they got to the top, Athena wasn't surprised to find the creature standing over Lovelace. The monster was bleeding from several gunshot wounds in its face and chest, but it wasn't in as bad a shape as the millionaire.

The room took up the entire top of the tower. A large window overlooked the ocean, but there was also a doorway with access to the top of the cliff. With all that daylight filling the room, Athena could see every gory detail as Lovelace lay motionless in a growing pool of his own blood. His chest was ripped to shreds and there were long gashes on his face and arms. He was breathing, but irregularly and with a gurgling sound. Athena knew he wouldn't be for long.

The creature sucked some of Lovelace's blood off its claws then turned to look at Athena and Walton. It looked at Walton calmly, drinking him in with its enormous black eyes. Then it looked at Athena and little ridges formed in its brow, like it was struggling to understand something.

Athena set down her rifle and raised her hands. "Mrs. Walton? We don't want to hurt you."

The furrow in its forehead got more pronounced and its eyes narrowed. It hissed at her.

Walton held out his hands to it. "Susan, please."

It lunged at Athena, fast as a striking cobra. She went for her pistol, but it was too late. She didn't even have it out of her holster before the monster was right there. Except fast as the creature was, Walton was faster.

He got in front of Athena, shielding her from the creature. "Susan, no!"

The creature stopped short. Its claws were less than an inch from Walton's chest. It looked at him gently, then back at Athena with a ferocious hiss.

Walton put his hands on its shoulders. On her shoulders, Athena decided. "Susan, no. Please. It's okay. She's a friend. She helped me find you."

The creature looked at him in a way that broke Athena's heart. She was trying to understand and her mouth opened and closed like she wanted to say something, but nothing came out except a pitiful choke. Walton moved his hands to her head, pulling her close to him. She wrapped her bloody arms around him and held him tight.

He looked back at Athena and whispered, "Go."

"What about you?"

"I'll be right behind you. Go."

She picked up her rifle and went to the door, keeping an eye on Walton and his wife the whole time.

Outside, the cliff was flat on top, forming a ridge between the ocean and the interior of the island. A narrow road went along the top of the ridge to God knew where, but that was fine with Athena. Anywhere but here. She wanted to call to Walton and make him follow her, but couldn't risk breaking the spell between him and Susan.

He saw her still watching him and motioned with his head for her to keep moving. She compromised by stepping around the side of the door to where Walton and his wife couldn't see her. Athena wasn't about to leave him, but she agreed that he couldn't just walk away with her either.

She knelt down next to the wall of the tower and listened; not eavesdropping, but ready to jump in with guns blazing if Susan turned on her husband. All she heard, though, were soft whispers, followed by an audible "I'm sorry." Then, finally, soft whimpering and the sound of something being dragged across the floor and down the stairs with a bump, bump, bump. Then Walton came outside.

He looked surprised when he saw her, but she didn't say a word. She peeked back inside to confirm that Susan was gone, with Lovelace. Even so, she made as little noise as possible as she moved to the road and didn't relax until they were far down it.

"Are you going to be okay?" she asked.

"Not for a very long time," he said.

She nodded and let the conversation sit there for a while.

"You think this will lead us back to the plane?" he asked.

Athena shrugged. "Eventually. It leads somewhere. Hopefully off this ridge; maybe to a village or something. If Lovelace was right about this place, we've only seen a little of the civilization that lived here."

"I've seen quite enough." He was crying. "I don't understand what happened to her."

"Lovelace thought this was some kind of outpost of an advanced, underwater civilization. Maybe there's something here that – I don't know – transforms people who stick around long enough. Maybe it prepares them for life under the ocean. Maybe that's why the Japanese don't come here."

"Horrible," was all he said.

She gave him a long look. "That was incredibly brave back there. You saved my life."

He wiped his eyes. "I wasn't thinking."

"No, you weren't thinking. You just acted. With courage." She put her arm around him and gave him a squeeze. "And I appreciate it."

She let him go, afraid he'd feel awkward, but he returned the brief hug, letting her know it was okay. They talked about Susan all the way back to the plane.

THE AUSTRIAN PRISONER

Ron Fortier

Austria 1932

Athena Voltaire ripped the radio headphones off her head and exclaimed, "We've got to get off the damn plane! There's a bomb hidden on it!"

Seated in the co-pilot's chair of the Vickers Type 163 heavy bomber, Captain Donald Gates was momentarily surprised into silence as the lovely American pilot's words sank into his mind. "What?" he finally blurted.

"That was one of your agents on the French border. Langdon called him ten minutes ago saying they caught a German spy trying to sneak off the base shortly after we took off. He confessed to planting a bomb on board."

"Damn it!" Gates began unbuckling from his seat. "Did he say how long we had?"

"Negative." Voltaire adjusted the controls, using a leather strap to hold them in place so the craft would continue on its present course. "All they got out of the spy was that we wouldn't reach our destination."

"Shit, shit, shit." Gates was up and moving back into the main cabin of the bomber, where his Royal Marines, their faces smeared with black shoe polish, were sitting under a red light, patiently waiting to reach their drop zone.

"Change of plans, lads," he informed them as he made his way to the rear and Weapons Sergeant Ian Tremayne. "We're jumping now!"

Sergeant Tremayne, a redheaded Irishman with a walrus mustache of the same color, sprang up, grabbed the fuselage door and pulled it open. Frosty air rushed into the cabin, instantly bringing the marines to full alertness. The men, parachutes on, weapons strapped to belts and bandoliers, took their places in line. Two thousand feet below was Austria, lost in the stygian blackness of a moonless night.

Captain Gates raised his voice above the constant drone of the four Rolls-Royce Kestrel V-12 engines. "We are twenty kilometers from our designated landing zone. Upon landing, each of you is to make your way east to the river. Then proceed south to a wooden bridge. That is our new point of rally. If anyone is not there by sunrise, we will proceed without you. Anyone injured or cut off is to make his way home as best he can."

Eight expressionless faces looked back at him. Each knew that any clandestine incursion on foreign soil would label them as a spy if captured. England would deny any knowledge of their actions, and they would be completely at the mercy of the Austrian government. His words were nothing new to them; every one of them had volunteered for the assignment.

"Good luck and Godspeed." Gates began putting on his own parachute rig as the unit began shuffling to the exit.

"That's it, lad, off you go." The big, burly sergeant with the dirty red mustache smiled as the first man put a boot on the door's frame and then plunged into the night headfirst. "Let's go, Murphy. Keep the line moving now."

Captain Gates was adjusting his parachute harness when Athena Voltaire came scrambling up the aisle, moving past the quickly disappearing line of marines.

"Got another one of those?" she grinned. He pulled a packed kit from an overhead bin and opened it for her.

"Have you ever jumped before?"

"Many times, Captain," she replied, lifting her legs through the leg straps and pulling the pack up to set it comfortably against her back. "Now let's the get hell out of here!"

"Indeed." Together they moved to the open portal, the wind tugging violently at their bodies. The last of the marines had dropped, and Sergeant Tremayne stood stoically awaiting them.

Gates leaned close to Voltaire and shouted. "You go first. I'll follow you. The sergeant will take up the rear, and we'll both try to keep you in sight on the way down. Watch out for the trees, and when you land, stay put. One of us will come to you."

Voltaire gave him a thumbs-up and shouted back, "Understood. Happy landings."

She nodded to the big non-com and then threw herself out of the plane.

An exhilarating thrill rushed through her veins as she tumbled through the air, the cool autumn temperature a welcome relief from the bomber's cramped and stuffy interior. Flipping end over end, she saw Gates and then Tremayne fall out of the plane as it continued on its journey eastward.

Having mentally counted to ten, Voltaire grabbed the metal ripcord and pulled it hard. There was a snapping sound behind her as the tightly packed silk parachute was released, caught the air and opened like a black flower behind her. She sensed the lines going taut and readied herself for the sharp jerk that halted her free-fall. Then she was floating feet first to the black earth below. She tried to spot the marines but could not, as their black dyed silk chutes made it impossible to see them against the backdrop of the still darker landscape below.

Suddenly a massive explosion tore through the sky, accompanied by a huge, bright, glaring fireball where the Vickers 163 had been. The 11,680-kilogram bomber had been instantly vaporized, and hundreds of pieces of shrapnel filled the surrounding space.

Voltaire felt tiny missiles rip at her chute and prayed it wouldn't be torn apart. She continued to fall at a slow and easy rate, the deafening echo of the blast slowly fading away. She momentarily wondered how far the loud boom had reverberated and what was the subsequent reaction, if any, of those living in the countryside beneath them.

So much for the element of surprise, she thought as she continued to fall.

Langdon Airbase – Two Days Earlier

"Please, come in," Wing Commander Jeffrey Sinclair invited, as Athena Voltaire walked into his office in the administration building of the Royal Air Force base. "The Captain and I have been anxious to meet you, Miss Voltaire."

The room was Spartan: a desk, lamp, several chairs and not much else. The two walls to either side were covered with photos of flying squadrons and their framed insignia patches, attesting to the Wing's proud history. Behind Sinclair was a single window through which the bright afternoon sun shone.

Voltaire, dressed in her comfortable dungarees and leather flying jacket, assessed both men, whom she was meeting for the first time. Sinclair was of average height, his body still military trim, with the kindly face of a school professor, his gray hair neatly trimmed with touches of white capping his temples. She removed

her gloves, extended her hand and smiled. "General Rawlings sends his regards."

"Ah, yes, old Chuck," Sinclair leaned over his desk to take her hand. "How is the old boy?"

"Getting ready for whatever happens next," she replied coyly. Sinclair nodded, appreciating her wit.

"Allow me to introduce Captain Donald Gates of Her Majesty's Royal Marines."

Voltaire turned to face the tall, rakishly handsome Gates, who candidly took in her statuesque loveliness without embarrassment. He had a rugged, tanned face indicative of an outdoor lifestyle, his body lean and yet possessed with a virile energy. His hair was a russet brown with reddish highlights, and she wondered if there was some Irish in his bloodline. His hand was calloused from hard labor, and she admired that.

"Miss Voltaire, this is an honor." His bass voice was smooth and friendly. "I've heard many stories about you over the years. I'd thought most of them fiction… until now."

"I'll do my best not to disappoint you."

"Please," Sinclair indicated the chairs. "Have a seat. Would you care for some tea or coffee?"

Voltaire took the chair nearest the desk, Captain Gates the other. She relaxed and crossed her legs. "No, thank you, Commander. I'm very curious as to what I'm doing here. General Rawlings' telegram was very cryptic."

"Well, it was our good fortune that you were here in England at all," Sinclair said as he sat in his own padded chair. "Most advantageous indeed."

"I take it you require my flying services?"

"That we do, Miss Voltaire, on a matter of topmost secrecy."

Athena Voltaire's face took on a puzzled expression. "But you have an entire airbase of pilots here. I'm afraid I don't get any of this."

"Allow me to start at the beginning, my dear." Sinclair sounded more like the teacher he appeared to be. "What do you know of the current political situation in Germany?"

"What I read in the papers like everyone else. There's been a lot of wrangling these past few months between the various parties. Some group calling themselves the Socialist Worker's Party seems to be stirring up a new brand of nationalism among the people."

"Very good. They're full name is the National Socialist German Worker's Party, and they are led by a clever fellow named Adolf Hitler. The German press calls them Nazis. Mr. Hitler is getting his country's industrialists excited about building a new military, which could make them millions and at the same time renew the Germans' self-respect."

"But I thought the provisions of Versailles forbade the Germans from rebuilding their army?"

"It does," the Wing Commander concurred. "Unfortunately the years have dulled the eyes of the world's governments into a false sense of security, believing the Germans would never travel that road again."

"But you believe they are."

"Yes, we do. Over the past year, several leading German manufactures have begun retooling their operations, and are now producing all manner of weapons, military aircraft and artillery. It is our belief that before the year is out, President Von Hindenburg will name Hitler as Chancellor of Germany, and once he's in that position of power, there will be no stopping the Germans' age-old lust for world conquering."

Voltaire pursed her lips and whistled softly. "You paint a grim picture, Commander. It sounds crazy."

"But all of it true," Gates added. "Our best foreign operatives have seen these plants up close, and we have the pictures to document everything."

"Alright, but what does all this have to do with me?"

Commander Sinclair reached for the pipe on the desk by his telephone before answering. "Well, my dear, in recent months many well known German artists, educators and scientists, aware of the coming social upheaval, have gone into voluntary exile, fleeing to whatever country will allow them safe refuge."

From his top drawer, Sinclair produced a pouch of tobacco and shoved the bowl of his pipe into it. "One of them was attempting to reach your country, at the invitation of your government, but was stopped while passing through Austria en route to France."

"Stopped? How do you mean?" Voltaire uncrossed her legs and sat straight, her attention riveted to Sinclair's tale.

"Apparently the Nazis learned of the gentleman's plans and had their colleagues in the Austrian National Socialist Party at the train station in Vienna. There they removed him and his wife, and took them to a nearby mountain chalet in Salzburg, where they have been kept incommunicado since."

"So, why haven't the Americans or you Brits cried foul?" Voltaire asked as Sinclair struck a match and held the flame over his pipe. He inhaled twice; the tobacco swallowed the fire and released a tiny whiff of white smoke.

"Rest assured, they did. But the Austrians maintained the couple were guests and not being held against their will. Which is pretty much how things now stand."

"I see. And who is so important that they have three countries butting heads over them?"

"Ah, well, I'm afraid I can't tell you that. Security protocols and such."

"Okay, but you still haven't told me where I fit into all this."

"Vickers-Armstrongs Limited informs us that you are certified to fly their new Vickers Type 163 bomber. Is that correct?"

"Yes, I was hired to test the prototype. Why?"

Commander Sinclair sat back in his chair and blew out a puff of smoke, then pointed to Captain Gates with his pipe.

"Because," the Marine officer continued, "we want you to fly me and a squadron of my men to Austria, where we will parachute into the countryside and affect the release of the target."

"What?" Voltaire looked at both men, getting more confused with each passing second. "And how exactly do you plan on getting out of there once you've achieved this ...ah, objective of yours?"

"After you've dropped us, you'll go on to an airfield in nearby Switzerland, where several of our agents have made arrangements with the Swiss. There you will refuel and remain for twenty-four hours, at which time you will then fly back into Austria to yet another rural, little-used airstrip where, if our mission is a success, we will be awaiting you with our guests."

Voltaire scratched her raven-hued hair. "Ha! Captain, I have to give it to you, you are one gutsy hombre."

"I'll take that as a compliment," Gates quipped.

"So what do you say?" Commander Sinclair asked. "Will you do it?"

"Commander, I'm still at a loss here. You must have dozens of skilled military pilots here under your command. Why recruit an outsider like me?"

"Because, Miss Voltaire, we suspect our ranks have been infiltrated by a German spy."

"Really?" Just when she thought things couldn't get weirder, they did. "And how do you know that?"

"Recently our London intelligence branch has intercepted several radio communiqués from this person to the Berlin military command. For the past few weeks, our people have been trying to hunt down the source of the transmissions, and have narrowed the search to this airbase.

"Thus, this mission has to be conducted with extra-special security measures. We simply don't know whom we can trust, and until the spy is caught, we have to suspect everyone, including our staff. You can see our dilemma."

Athena Voltaire bit her lower lip, her mind weighing the pros and cons of what was being asked of her. They wanted her to undertake a military mission into a foreign country. If anything went wrong, she would be imprisoned as a spy at best, at worst taken before a firing squad and shot. It could prove to be highly dangerous. As that particular thought entered her mind, she smiled inwardly at her own foolishness. When had she ever avoided the possibilities of action and adventure?

"So that's the whole of it, Miss Voltaire. What do you say?"

"Only this, when do we leave?"

Fifty Miles North of Salzburg

Athena Voltaire saw the vague contours of the earth as they rushed up to meet her. Tightening her legs, she gripped the parachute straps and prepared herself for the jolt. It wasn't the first time she'd made such a jump and she knew how to land properly, but that had been in daylight, where every rock and boulder was instantly visible. Now there were only blurry outlines of trees all around her, and she wondered how long she had before her chute was snagged by the branches of some massive oak. All this while she continued to plummet out of the sky.

Miraculously, she missed the trees. In the last seconds before impact, she sucked in a lungful of cool air and tensed. Her boots made contact hard. As she had been taught long ago, Voltaire continued to pitch forward and folded her knees as her shoulder went down on the ground, throwing herself into a roll. Bruised but unhurt, she wasted no time climbing to her feet and quickly enfolding the billowing black silk. Once it was caught as a bundle in her arms, she unhitched her harness and stepped out of it. She then proceeded to drag it and the folded parachute behind a clump of thick bushes. There she felt around on the ground for baseball-sized rocks, and set them on the hidden chute to keep it from blowing away in the next heavy wind gust.

Her eyes adjusted to the blackness around her. Leaving the bushes, she bent over, took another deep breath and thanked whatever lucky stars had been watching over her.

"Voltaire?" The soft calling voice came from her immediate front.

She went over to a big tree, stood behind it and drew one of her Colt pistols from its holster before responding. "Over here."

There were several footfalls, and then Captain Gates materialized before her, his own Webley pistol clutched in his hands. "Voltaire."

She stepped out from behind the tree, sliding the Colt back into its holster. "Right here, Captain."

"Thank God, you made it. Have you seen Sergeant Tremayne?"

"Right here, Captain," the big Irishman whispered as he emerged from the brush to their right. Voltaire noted he was clutching his lightweight ZB30 machine gun and was reminded these men were professional warriors. They left nothing to chance.

"Good to see you, Sergeant," Gates said.

"Likewise, sir." He turned and pointed back the way he had come. "The river's back there, maybe a quarter of a mile. I could hear it when I landed."

"Alright then, let's go. We haven't a moment to lose."

Without another word, the trio headed off into the woods, walking in single file. Sergeant Tremayne took the lead, Voltaire the middle and Captain Gates the rear.

For the next six hours, the three hiked through the Austrian countryside, keeping the swiftly flowing waters of the Amstun River to their left. The terrain consisted of mostly rocky fields, and Voltaire was glad their destination wasn't at a higher mountain elevation, where the temperatures were a lot cooler, even for late September.

The sun had just started to lighten the heavens when they reached the country bridge made of old, heavy timbers that was their rendezvous point. A dirt road wound its way from the bridge into a small valley. In the distance, the rooftops and cupolas of a small hamlet could be seen, including a church bell tower. As they neared the old structure under which the swiftly moving waters flowed, they spotted several shadows hiding beneath. Six of their companions were huddled together under the bridge's support beams on their side of the river.

"Are we glad to see you, sir," a young corporal named Olset piped up, as the men gathered around them.

"You're two men short, Corporal."

"Yes, sir. Dorkins here says he saw a piece of the plane's shrapnel hit Private Casey's chute and burn it up. He never had a chance."

"And Corporal Wickers?" Captain Gates knew all his men personally. "What happened to him?"

"More bad luck, sir," Olset continued. "He landed in a clump of trees near where I came down. Me and Nolan found him hanging upside down, his neck broke. When Riley showed up, the three of us cut him down and buried him there."

Athena Voltaire bit on her lower lip. First the sabotage and now two men lost. Perhaps the entire mission was jinxed.

"I see." Gates' voice was somber. "Not a very good start, is it lads?"

"What are we going to do now, Captain?" asked Corporal Dorkins, a short, beefy bulldog of a man.

"As I see it, we've only two options: either we abort the mission and make our way into Switzerland, or we can press on and do what we came here to do."

Sergeant Tremayne removed his knit cap and ran a hand through his thick hair. "Yes, sir. But if we do rescue the two civilians, how do we get them back to England? Without a plane to come get us, it would be rough going."

Silence fell on the group as the river continued to gurgle past them and birds chirped in the nearby trees. The marines looked to Gates for a solution, waiting for his decision.

"Then we find another airplane," Voltaire spoke up, surprising them all. "Look, this is a populated district. There must be several airfields in the area, both public and private."

"Yes," Gates agreed. "So what are you saying?"

"That once you've completed your mission, we find one and we borrow a ride home."

"But you don't know what kind of aircraft they have here," Tremayne said.

Athena Voltaire laughed. "Sergeant, if it's got wings and an engine, I can fly it."

No sooner had she uttered the word "engine" than they heard a coughing motor coming their way from out of the valley.

"Sounds like a truck?" Corporal Dorkins offered.

Gates tapped him on the shoulder. "You and Jenkins run down the road and confirm that. Hurry. I want to know what it is before it reaches us."

Both men nodded and took off running up the bank, across the wooden planks and off towards where the road turned into the trees. Gates and the others scrambled to find cover under the bridge.

"What do you think, Sergeant?"

"Well, sir, it's likely some farmer out here heard our plane explode this morning and called someone in authority to report it."

"And now they're sending someone to investigate."

"Yes, sir. That would be my guess."

Three minutes later, Dorkins and Jenkins came running back, gasping to catch their breath. "It's a quarter-ton truck with two military blokes in the cab," Dorkins hurriedly reported. "Would guess there's more of 'em in the back, but they got a canvas top so we couldn't see for sure."

Captain Gates knew he had only minutes to act. "What do you say, Sergeant?"

"Riding is lots better than walking," the big Irishman smiled.

"Exactly my thoughts," Gates grinned. "If Miss Voltaire would consider helping us once more?"

Athena Voltaire stood in the middle of the bridge, shielding her eyes from the sun with her right hand. She'd removed her jacket and pistol belt and unbuttoned the top of her shirt to expose a tanned neckline. Within seconds of taking her position, a lumbering, dirty gray truck belching oil fumes from its noisy tailpipe came into view. It was moving at a fast clip, and quickly ate up the short distance to the bridge. Voltaire made out the two men in the cab, and started waving her hands to get their attention.

The passenger, an older-looking man with a gray beard, yelled something to the driver, and as the vehicle drove onto the wooden surface of the bridge, its speed began to decrease until it came to a complete stop only ten yards away. Voltaire dropped her head slightly as if exhausted and then crumbled. She heard a door slam open and then rushing footsteps. She maneuvered her left hand, hidden by her body, to the small of her back, where she had put a Colt.

The Man approaching her called out in German, "Fraulein, what is wrong? Are you hurt?"

He dropped to one knee and gently reached out to take hold of her shoulder. Voltaire twisted onto her buttocks while whipping the Colt out and shoving the barrel under the man's chin. In her limited German, she said, "Yell and I shoot!" Startled, the man froze, his eyes going wide.

At the same time that she was the center of attention in front of the truck, Gates and his Royal Marines, who had earlier crossed the span to hide beneath the support tresses on the opposite shore, were now scampering up and onto the road, their weapons at the ready. From both sides, they converged on the back of the open transport, where ten Austrian soldiers were suddenly caught napping.

"No one move!" Gates ordered loudly, in fluent German. To add emphasis to his command, Sergeant Tremayne and his men raised their machine guns, aiming them at the now confused and frightened soldiers. Seated on wooden benches under the heavy tarp, most had their rifles standing between their legs. The marines had come upon them so quickly that not one had a chance to react.

"Now, all of you lower your rifles and jump out with your hands held up behind your heads!" Gates nodded to Tremayne, who then stepped up and unhitched the tailgate, allowing the soldiers inside to comply with the captain's order.

· Meanwhile, the driver, still behind the steering wheel, was getting antsy. His commander was still kneeling over the woman in front of him, and now there was a commotion coming from the back. He started to turn his head towards the suspended rearview mirror on his door when Corporal Dorkins suddenly yanked his door open and pulled him almost out of his seat.

The Brit pointed his weapon at the fellow and smiled jovially. "Sorry, mate, but this is where you get off."

Twenty minutes later, Dorkins—dressed in an Austrian militia uniform, his face washed clean—cranked the engine of the old quarter-ton beast and gave it some gas. Beside him, Captain Gates, similarly disguised, opened a small topographical map on his lap and studied its markings for several seconds before giving the corporal directions.

"Turn us around and head towards the village. The chalet we're looking for is located on the other side of the woods behind there. It's no more than three kilometers from the main square."

"Yes, sir."

Dorkins pulled off to the side of the road and began a slow, wide arc. He had to back up several times before completing the turn, as the dirt lane wasn't particularly wide. In the back of the truck, Athena Voltaire and the Royal Marines sat in silence, looking out at the surrounding countryside. When they rambled back over the river bridge, she wondered how the tied up Austrian troopers were doing below it. Gates had seen an opportunity and moved upon it swiftly. As they were not at war with Austria, and those men were simply country boys in the local militia, there was never any thought of harming them. Under Sergeant Tremayne's watchful eye, his squad had made sure to disarm the Austrians and then proceeded to tie them up with ropes found in the truck. All this after Gates had the commander and the driver swap clothes with himself and the corporal. Now they were speeding their way to the target in broad daylight, through hostile territory.

Voltaire leaned over to the Irish non-com and asked, "How long before those guys untie themselves back there?"

"Maybe thirty minutes, tops. Then they have another thirty-minute walk back to the town."

"So we've got about an hour before all hell breaks loose?"

Tremayne tugged at his red mustache and thought for a second. "Yes. If we're lucky."

For the next forty minutes Athena Voltaire and the marines sat quietly, watching the Austrian countryside diminish behind them as the old truck bumped up and down along the dirt road. Their maps provided them with a circuitous route around the small town's center, so they met very little traffic, just an occasional tractor from a nearby farm and a battered dairy truck making deliveries. Voltaire thought the landscape was beautiful and hoped someday she'd get the opportunity to revisit Austria under more normal circumstances.

Eventually they left what was the main road and turned onto a rutted way that led deeper into the thick woods that surrounded them. When the truck slowed to a stop, everyone in the back sat up straight, fully aware that things were about to get started. They heard Captain Gates jump out of the cab, and a second later he was looking up at them. "Alright, lads, we've reached our target. Everybody out."

Once on the ground, he explained the situation. "According to our map, the chalet we want is only around that bend ahead by several hundred yards. Sergeant

Tremayne, you will take half the men and cut through the trees and come in from behind the house. We'll give you a ten minute start, then roll in the front gate."

"Yes, sir. What kind of opposition do you expect us to encounter?"

"The last intelligence report we received said the Germans had a detail of ten men, most of them black-shirt professionals known as Gestapo. We're told they are merciless killers, so do not hesitate to shoot if they offer any resistance."

"Yes, sir, understood." The big sergeant took a step back and pointed to three men. "Jenkins, Olset and Riley with me. Let's go, and be quiet. We don't want those blokes knowing they have company coming."

With that, the four men jogged off the road into the woods and were soon lost from sight. Captain Gates looked at his watch, and then turned to the three men. "We are going to drive right up to the front door. When we come to a stop, that will be your signal to jump out and join me, weapons at ready. No one fires unless we have to, is that clear?"

"Yes, sir," Private Murphy answered. He was the youngest member of the squad, tall and gangly with sandy colored hair. Between him and Dorkins was Private Nolan, the squad's best marksman, a rugged looking fellow with thick, brown eyebrows and a broken nose.

"Good. Corporal Dorkins here will remain with the truck and keep the engine running while the rest of us subdue the Germans and secure our civilian targets. Once we have them, it's back in the truck and off we go."

"What about me, Captain?" Voltaire put her hands on her hips. "I take it I'm to simply stay in the back of the truck and out of the way." The expression on her lovely face was anything but pleasant.

"You are a civilian, Miss Voltaire." She started to speak, but Gates held up a hand and went on. "You are also our ride home, may I remind you. It would be foolish of me to jeopardize that by allowing you to get injured. Agreed?"

As much as she chafed to get into the action, she couldn't fault the captain's logic. "Agreed."

Gates glanced at his watch a second time and mentally calculated Sergeant Tremayne's progress. "Alright, lads, let's mount up." Then, as he and Corporal Dorkins went back to the cab, Private Murphy and Private Nolan jumped onto the open tailgate and together easily lifted Athena Voltaire aboard. They took their seats as the truck started up and moved forward.

Coming around the bend in the road, their target appeared at the end of a three hundred-yard straightaway. It was a massive, two-story chalet built in typical mountain fashion, with twin chimneys and a covered veranda. An open courtyard fronted the main entrance, at the center of which was a brick well. To the right of the main house was a stable, in front of which were parked several automobiles. Several people were moving about, some wearing official black uniforms.

"Park alongside the well," Captain Gates directed as they pulled into the compound. By now the German soldiers had seen them, and one of them immediately stepped forward to greet them. He was obviously an officer of some rank. Gates hefted his ZB30 onto his lap and whispered, "Kill the engine and get ready to move."

"I am Colonel Tenhauser," the Gestapo man said, coming up to the passenger door. "Who are you and what is your purpose here? This is a restricted area."

Captain Gates gave the colonel a friendly smile, opened his door and stepped out, leveling his weapon at the German. "Good afternoon, Colonel," the British commando answered in German. "If you would be so kind as to put your hands in the air."

"What is the meaning of this?" Instinctively Tenhauser began reaching for his sidearm, but Gates shoved the barrel of his machine gun into the man's chest.

"I said put your hands up!"

For a second the angry officer hesitated, and then raised both his hands. The rest of the troopers watching the confrontation had begun moving towards them.

"All of you, drop your weapons!" Captain Gates called out, again in German.

Corporal Dorkins rushed around the front of the truck to join Gates as Nolan and Murphy were dropping out of the back.

Colonel Tenhauser, a big man with a pallid complexion, was reddening noticeably. "Whoever you people are, you will pay for this outrage."

From the corner of his eye, Gates spotted a flash from the open stable door as a shot rang out. The bullet hit the top of the truck's hood, inches from Corporal Dorkins.

Startled, Gates turned his head. The Gestapo officer suddenly twisted his body and grabbed for the ZB30. Gates' finger jerked the trigger, and the weapon spit out a half-dozen rounds. Most hit the ground, but two caught one of the German soldiers in the legs, and he collapsed screaming.

Then all hell broke loose.

Seeing their comrade shot, the other Germans began firing wildly at Gates and his men. All the while, Gates continued to wrestle with the desperate Tenhauser. As hot lead filled the air around them, the marines quickly sought cover behind either the truck or the stone well. Stray bullets continued to hit the vehicle, one of them smashing through the glass windshield, raining down shards on a huddled Corporal Dorkins.

In the bed of the truck, Athena Voltaire hit the deck the second she heard the first shot. Cautiously she crawled to the open back and, rising up to one knee, poked her head around the side. There she saw the confusion of the battle playing itself out. Both Nolan and Murphy were crouched behind the stone well, firing, whenever they had a chance, at the Germans by the parked sedans.

She saw Gates in some kind of shoving match with a maddened German officer. Each was pulling at the captain's machine gun. Suddenly Gates brought his right knee up into the other man's groin and then savagely pulled his machine pistol loose. Folding up in pain, the colonel died on his feet as the ZB30 fired at point blank range into his stomach. He was pushed back, blood spraying out his back. With a look of total disbelief, he fell over dead.

Realizing he no longer had his enemy as a shield, Captain Gates turned and dove under the truck, while Murphy and Nolan provided him with cover fire. The civilians they had spotted earlier made themselves scarce when the fighting had erupted, not wanting to get caught in the crossfire between the two military groups. From his new position, Gates saw several of them hiding behind the corner of the house, frightened out of their wits. He prayed they would continue to stay out of the way, as the last thing he wanted to do was harm innocent Austrians.

While peeking over the well's lip to shoot, Murphy took a slug in his right shoulder and was knocked off his feet. Two Germans, seeing him go down, were emboldened and charged forward, guns blasting away. Nolan tried to return fire, but their withering volley kept him pinned down. Athena Voltaire witnessed all of this and realized the two Brits were in serious trouble. She pulled out a Colt, leaned out from behind the truck's canvas side, aimed and fired two quick shots. Her unerring aim took both men in the chest and dropped them in their tracks. Private Nolan looked back, saw her and offered her a small salute of thanks.

Gunfire erupted from inside the house, signaling Sergeant Tremayne's arrival into the fray. There were some shouts, followed by more gunshots, and then quiet. A few minutes later, the front door flew open and two German officers emerged, their hands clasped behind their heads. Behind them Sergeant Tremayne appeared, his machine gun pointing at their backs. At his urging, one of the captives barked out an order to the remaining fighters by the stable. "Throw down your weapons! All of you!"

Captain Gates scrambled to his feet, brushed dirt off his pants, and trained his ZB30 on the Germans, who were reluctantly complying with their commander's order. A thin haze of cordite smoke hung in the air. Tremayne and his prisoners descended the steps of the porch, followed by Corporal Olset and Private Jenkins. Corporal Dorkins hurried over to meet them, his weapon at the ready.

"Good work, Sergeant," Gates commended as they approached. "What about our guests?"

"They're fine, Captain. A little shaken up, but fit to travel. Riley is giving them a hand."

With the fighting over, Gates had his men herd the Germans back into the stable, where they were to be tied up. He realized that once they were gone there would be nothing to stop the Austrian servants from freeing the Germans, but he hoped they could at least get a decent head start in their escape.

Meanwhile, Athena Voltaire had gone to Private Murphy's assistance, and was helping him to his feet. The front of his shirt was smeared with blood, and he looked as if he were about to collapse. At the sight of them, an elderly Austrian couple came rushing out of the house.

"I am Bruno Schmitz," the man said in English, slipping Murphy's good arm over his shoulder and bearing his weight. "This is my wife, Rose. Please, let us help you."

"The bullet went clean through," Voltaire explained as they made their way slowly to the veranda. "If you could put some clean bandages on it—"

"Say no more, Fraulein. We will see to it."

Captain Gates joined them as they were laying the wounded marine on the wooden steps. "How is he?" he asked Voltaire.

"He'll live." She pointed to the Austrians. "These are the Schmitzes. I'm guessing this is their home."

"Ja, it is our home," Bruno Schmitz concurred. "When the authorities in Salzburg told the Germans we were old friends with Albert and Elsa, they brought them here. We had no choice but to go along with them. At least this way we could see to their welfare."

"Albert and Elsa?" Athena Voltaire looked at Gates, her left eyebrow arched.

At which point another couple walked out the front door and onto the scene, followed by Private Riley, who carried two heavy valises. The woman was small, with a tired face, her hair just turning a light gray. The man, dressed in a woolen coat, was also diminutive, with a round, chubby face and a trim mustache under two piercing, brown eyes. He wore a tan fedora to match his jacket.

Voltaire recognized him immediately as Captain Gates made the introductions. "Athena Voltaire, meet Mr. and Mrs. Albert Einstein."

Athena Voltaire turned the truck onto the main highway without slowing down. The heavy vehicle canted slightly, and everyone in the back was tossed to one side.

"Please, Miss Voltaire, try not to get us killed before we reach the airstrip," Captain Gates cautioned as she straightened out the wheel to follow the paved road. Voltaire had requested to drive once Herr Schmitz had given them directions to a small municipal field less than ten miles away. She'd argued that it would save them time, as once they reached the place, she would be able to direct them to the right aircraft for their needs immediately. She had also sworn to Gates that she could drive the quarter-ton beast.

"Well, Captain, the way you keep looking at your wristwatch, I'd assumed we were in a race."

He made a frown and tapped the chronometer. "As of now we are. Schmitz promised to wait fifteen minutes before freeing the Germans. That was two minutes ago."

"And you think they'll come after us?"

"But of course. We killed their commanding officer and took their prisoners. What worries me is how fast they get the word out about us."

"But you tore out the phone lines."

"Right. But what if they had a short-wave radio somewhere on the property? Perhaps in one of their autos?"

"Good point. Then I'd best keep this baby humming."

"Indeed, but do go a little slower on the turns. The Einsteins are scared enough as it is."

They had encountered very little traffic since leaving the chalet. Then, just as Voltaire was thinking things were finally going smoothly, a shrill siren began blaring from behind them. Both she and Captain Gates looked into the side mirrors bolted to each door and saw two Austrian police cars, each filled with uniformed men, racing up the road behind them. The whine of their twin sirens was almost deafening.

"What the hell?" the lovely pilot cursed as she floored the gas pedal. "How the bloody hell did they get on to us so damn fast?"

"I don't think it's the Germans," Gates offered, still looking back at the chasing autos. "Those are policemen. Most likely, our militia friends finally got loose and made it back to their headquarters."

The truck's speed rose as Voltaire sat up rigid and gripped the wheel tightly. "Well, like it or not, we've got a horse race now, Captain."

"No argument there. Just pray the airstrip isn't too far off. This old Nelly wasn't made for racing police cars."

With that, Gates twisted about and pulled open the small cab window. Behind it was a slit opening in the truck's covering tarp. He pushed this back with one hand and called out. "Tremayne!"

The sergeant's head popped up. "Yes, sir!"

"See if you can discourage our friends back there."

"Yes, sir. Gladly."

"Keep in mind they are Austrian nationals. Try not to injure them in the process."

"Understood, Captain. I'll handle it myself."

Sergeant Tremayne turned and made his way past his men and the Einsteins, who sat in the middle, clutching each other. Towards the rear, he crouched down, doing his best to maintain his balance. The springs on the truck were virtually non-existent, and even slight bumps in the road jolted the entire chassis. Grabbing the tip of the tailgate, he turned to Corporal Dorkins.

"Here, Dorkins, get down and peel back this canvas for me."

"Right away, Sergeant."

"Just keep your head down, lad."

"Roger that!" Dorkins, on hands and knees, reached up and pulled the tarp back. Now all of them could see the two black sedans from which emanated the ear-splitting wail. The lead vehicle was gaining on them.

Sergeant Tremayne went down on one knee, cocked his machine gun and fired a short burst at the ground in front of the auto. The driver, fearing Tremayne was actually trying to hit them, jerked the wheel and careened into the center of the road. Quickly adjusting, he brought the car back on their tail, only now the officer on the passenger side was leaning out the window with a gun in his hand.

"Look out!" Dorkins warned as the Austrian fired off several shots. Luckily his aim was off due to the motion of both vehicles, and the bullets came nowhere near them. "He's a feisty one, Sergeant."

"Yes, well, let's see if we can stop that kind of nasty behavior," laughed the big Irishman as he prepared to fire another salvo. Only this time, he let the big, black auto move in much closer before firing. He shot right into the exposed radiator grill and tore its front plate to shreds. Several of his shots hit vital areas of the engine, causing black smoke to begin rising up from beneath the bonnet.

The car began to swerve erratically as Dorkins and some of the others gave a loud cheer. Unable to control her, the driver desperately attempted to steer, but his suspension locked up and he drove off the highway and into a ditch, the front end crashing into a mound of dirt with a massive bang.

But that was only one down. The second chase car roared up to take its place, and the race continued.

Meanwhile, back in the cab, Athena Voltaire spotted a boxy control tower rising up over the treetops less then a quarter-mile ahead. She pointed it out to Gates and continued to keep the gas pedal flat. They had both heard the gunshots coming from behind them and the exuberant yell when the first patrol car went off the road. Now all they needed was a few more minutes.

The forest receded as the road ahead intersected a huge natural field on which the small airstrip had been constructed. Under clear blue skies, it spread out before them with two separate blacktopped runways and six hangars, three to either side of the strips.

Near the entrance gate was the control tower, affixed to a long building that Athena Voltaire deduced was the airfield's headquarters.

She sped past the brightly painted guard shack, smiling at the surprised young fellow stationed there. Despite the still-blaring siren, he began to yell at her, but stopped when he heard the gunshots coming from the chasing police sedan.

"Where to now?" Gates asked, his eyes trying to take in the foreign strip.

"I'm looking!" Voltaire snapped as she swerved onto one of the runways and drove along. There were a half-dozen single-engine airplanes scattered in front of the hangars, but none were what they needed. Then, approaching the third hangar on their side, she saw it: a German Junkers Ju 52 transport.

"Hot dog! We're in business," she exclaimed, turning the wheel and making for the big tri-motor aircraft. "It's an Iron Annie, their version of our Ford Tri-Motors."

"I take it you can fly her."

"In my sleep."

The Junkers was not unattended, and as they rolled up to her, several German soldiers and a few Austrian mechanics appeared out of the inky blackness of the hangar's interior. Hearing the wailing siren, they were curious as to the commotion descending upon them.

"Get aboard and start her up," Captain Gates ordered as Voltaire hit the brakes and killed the engine. "We'll take care of the rest."

"Right. Just don't take too long!"

As soon as the truck halted, Sergeant Tremayne and his marines exploded out of the back, several of them firing their machine guns at the remaining police car. It wisely pulled up behind a row of stacked rubber tires, affording some cover from the marines' salvo. At the same time that the Austrian coppers were climbing out of their automobile, several of the German soldiers by the plane were reaching for their rifles, while the unarmed mechanics ran for any shelter they could find in short notice.

"Freeze," Gates yelled, hoping to stop the Germans from starting another firefight. For a second, most of them—he counted eight—held up, and he thought he might get lucky after all. One of the Germans, a grizzled sergeant, continued to bring his rifle up, screaming at his men to do the same.

Within a heartbeat, bullets were flying everywhere in and out of the open hangar. Gates took out two of the enemy before ducking back behind several fuel drums. As he dropped behind them, he was joined by Sergeant Tremayne and Private Riley.

"Ah, not the best place to hide behind," Tremayne pointed out.

Meanwhile, Athena Voltaire had dodged several bullets to charge up the Junkers' short ladder and dive into it. She doubted the Germans would risk damaging their own aircraft, and once inside she was proven right. Getting to her feet, she started up the plane's center aisle, hoping it was deserted. She saw a shadow flicker in the cockpit and dove behind several seats just as the pilot appeared, firing a handgun. Pieces of the padding and wood rained down on her head, the shots missing her by mere inches. She was digging into her holster for her own gun when a loud bang rang out, followed by a grunt.

She raised her head to see the pilot slump over, the pistol falling from his grasp. She spun about and there, grinning ear-to-ear, stood Private Nolan, a smoking Webley in his hand. "You should be all clear now, Miss."

"Thanks." She stepped over the dead pilot and entered the cockpit.

Nolan went back to the door to help his mates get the Einsteins aboard.

From her seat in the cockpit, Athena Voltaire could see Gates and some of his men fighting desperately to give the others a chance to get aboard the plane. With the soldiers in the hangar and the Austrian police behind them, the Brits were in a really bad place. Still, Voltaire had seen them in action and drove dire thoughts out of her mind. She truly believed Captain Gates and his men would succeed, and she had to be ready when they did.

Quickly she began checking gauges and flipping switches. Her biggest worry had been the fuel supply, and she breathed an audible sigh of relief when the gauge indicated the tanks were full. She turned on the two Pratt and Whitney wing engines. Their drumming sound was music to her ears.

With bullets coming at them from every which way, Captain Gates, Sergeant Tremayne and the others were all but kissing the tarmac behind the gasoline drums.

Gates had ordered Corporal Olset and Private Nolan to get the Einsteins aboard the plane, and under the truck's body he'd seen them make their way to the ladder and carry out his order. Shortly after, the plane's motors came to life, and he knew Voltaire was fulfilling her end of the plan. Now it was time for him and the others to skedaddle while the getting was good.

"Sergeant, I think it's time we used these barrels to our advantage."

Tremayne fired a volley at the coppers, still behind the tire wall, before replying. "What have you got in mind, sir?"

"To leave these fellows with a hot farewell."

Sergeant Tremayne saw the look in his superior's eyes and laughed, even while bullets were buzzing all around. "A truly wonderful idea, sir."

"Then give me a hand with this one, will you?"

As the captain and the sergeant took hold of the heavy barrel and began to tilt it, the contents sloshed about inside. The other marines intensified their own firing to protect Gates and Tremayne, as they were momentarily exposed. The big fifty-gallon drum fell over with a clang and began rolling towards the hangar's interior.

At the sight of it, the German sergeant realized what they were planning and ordered his men to retreat. Gates and Tremayne watched the barrel roll farther into the huge, empty hangar, and just as it hit the back wall, they fired into it. The explosion rocked the entire structure, and instantly a geyser of flames gushed upward, splashing over the wooden wall. The building was soon engulfed, fire eating at it like a starving monster.

"Now!" Gates rose up and called out. "Everyone into the plane!"

The burning hangar had grabbed everyone's attention, and for a few minutes no one was shooting at the marines. Hurriedly, Gates and his men scrambled around the truck and made their way to the Junkers. As they started climbing into the aircraft, the nose engine coughed to life, and Gates looked up at the cockpit window to see Athena Voltaire smiling back at him with a thumbs-up sign.

Seconds later they were all aboard, and the Junkers Ju began moving. As the marines stumbled into the main cabin to take their seats, Captain Gates saw that Albert and Elsa Einstein were seated at the front of the plane. Corporal Olset was helping Private Nolan drag a dead body back to the doorway.

"Any problems here?" he asked, indicating the body.

"Bloke wanted to see our tickets," Nolan answered with a straight face. Gates couldn't help but laugh, and patted the man on the arm.

Athena Voltaire worked the throttle carefully and pointed the nose of the plane towards the horizon as it rolled along. The three engines were all purring like contented kittens, and the vibrations she felt were the sweetest sensations in the world. She was only truly ever happy when flying. As the craft continued to gain speed, Captain Gates entered the cockpit and dropped into the co-pilot's seat.

"Well, isn't this where we came in?"

"Yes it is, Captain." She watched the air speed indicator, felt the tug on the wings, and pulled back on the yoke. The nose rose upward, and like the elegant creature of the air she was, the Junkers Ju 52 climbed into the sky. Voltaire kept the ascent shallow and steady, keeping an eye on the gauges. Everything was reading fine. As they neared the edge of the tree line she continued to climb easily, and the airplane soared ever higher. Behind it a curling pall of black smoke rose into the clear skies.

Voltaire took a quick glance back, and seeing the black column, wondered at what storm was truly awaiting them in the weeks and months ahead. What foul thing was growing in the Rhineland that would soon engulf all of mankind as that fire below? And would they have the courage and strength to survive it?

"Take us home, Miss Voltaire," Gates instructed.

"With pleasure, Captain."

She pointed the nose westward towards the majestic peaks of the Swiss Alps, and they raced after the sun.

CULT FILM

Will Pfeifer

PART 1: PRE-PRODUCTION

Dec. 27, 1945, *Daily Variety:*
Athena Voltaire Set For Return to Silver Screen

"Warner Brothers announced Wednesday that filming will begin early next year on a new version of the life story of Athena Voltaire, the plucky adventuress and aviatrix best known for battling Hitler's stooges and getting tangled in all sorts of spooky and spine-tingling predicaments. Word is Harry Warner himself sees it as a perfect vehicle for either aging Oomph Girl Ann Sheridan or some lucky gal from the studio's ever-growing stable of would-be starlets. Budget said to be set at $500,000, and shooting is set to commence in February, possibly with Raoul Walsh behind the camera, five years after directing Miss Sheridan in 'They Drive By Night.'

"Warners tried this more than a decade ago with its much-ballyhooed production, 'The Adventures of Athena Voltaire,' but the picture proved a disappointment at the box office. Insiders say Harry views this as a property that still has plenty of potential – and it had better, too, with little brother Jack breathing down his neck."

March 13, 1946: Memo from Henry L. Blanke, producer, to Jack L. Warner, reprinted in *Warner Brothers Correspondence: 1931 to 1955*, edited by Gregory Cosgrove

"Jack,

"I have to say, I'm concerned about the 'Voltaire' project. Let's be honest -- horror hasn't hit in years (except for that no-budget stuff Lewton is doing over at RKO), and these days, the Nazi angle is more than a little played out. Maybe we could go with the romantic comedy angle? Better yet, sell the rights to one of the minors and move on. Maybe they can get Voltaire to do some publicity or script advising – god knows my team is having no luck with her. Hell, no one even seems to know where she is. Things were a lot easier ten years ago.

"Your call, as always. Meanwhile, I'm up to my neck in reshoots on the 'Of Human Bondage' remake.

"Best, Henry"

July 30, 1946, *Daily Variety:*
Voltaire Rights Switch to Pinnacle

"Sources say Pinnacle Pictures Corp., known for its chapter plays aimed at the kiddie audience, has nabbed the rights to the story of famed adventurix Athena Voltaire from Warner Brothers for an undisclosed sum. Budget for the picture, set to be the studio's first feature-length production, is said to be in the neighborhood of $125,000. Production is set to wrap by mid-August."

Aug. 2, 1946, Advertisement in *Daily Variety:*
HERE COMES ATHENA VOLTAIRE

"Pinnacle Pictures Corp., maker of popular chapter plays for nearly a decade, is proud to announce its first footstep into the world of feature productions. 'The New Adventures of Athena Voltaire,' based on the amazing exploits of the beloved adventuress, will star Dorothy Van Sloan as Miss Voltaire, with able support from Frank Clement, Jack C. Avery, Nora Stephens, Reed Stanley and Jackson Jones as the hilarious 'Cadillac.' Willis Arnold, best known for bringing 'The Bombardier' and 'The Bombardier Soars Again' to theater screens will direct, and the thrilling script is from the typewriters of Martin Lembeck and Allen Koenig. Special photographic effects will come courtesy of visual wizards Howard and Theodore Lydecker, and Henry Knox, making his American debut, will handle art direction chores."

Excerpt from German film journal *Das Kino Huete,* Nov. 1940 issue (translated into English)

"...Minister Josef Goebbels also announced the appointment of Heinrich Nacht, formerly employed in the art and production department of UFA, to the National Film Ministry, where his duties will include..."

Jan. 9, 1946, Joint Intelligence Operatives Agency Memo, partially declassified 1989

"Security Clearance pending for Henrich Frederick Nacht (b. 1899) as per [text deleted]; suggest relocation w/addition of revised personnel files, name, SSN [text deleted]. West Coast? Please advise."

Aug. 6, 1946, Daily Variety: "Production Begins on 'Athena Voltaire'"

"After years of delays and at least one transfer of rights, cameras finally began to roll Monday on Pinnacle's 'New Adventures of Athena Voltaire' in the Bronson Cavern area of Los Angeles' Griffith Park."

Aug. 7, 1946, *Daily Variety:* *Accident Halts Production on 'Athena Voltaire'*

"Problems continue to plague Pinnacle's 'New Adventures of Athena Voltaire' as one of the film's stars, Reed Stanley, last seen in Pinnacle's 1942 chapter play, 'Rancho Atlantis,' was injured when a portion of the film's Sinister Sanctum set collapsed on him. Stanley, 64, was listed in serious condition at Los Angeles Medical Center."

Aug. 14, 1946, *Daily Variety:* *'Athena' Actress Bows Out, Production to Continue*

"The latest mystery for 'New Adventures of Athena Voltaire' director Willis Arnold? How to complete shooting of the picture minus his leading lady. Claiming mental anguish and physical trauma, actress Dorothy Van Sloan has left the troubled production as of Tuesday. Arnold and the studio chiefs claim filming is almost done, and Miss Van Sloan's stunt double will be used for the necessary long shots remaining to be filmed."

From *Tinseltown Gomorrah* by Stephen Stark (Javelin Books, 1972)

"Delectable Dot Van Sloan remains one of Hollywood's most perplexing casualties, a victim of god-knows-what. Discovered Aug. 16, 1946, by one of Los Angeles' finest slumped behind the wheel of her roadster, she had been dead for hours—and, according to local lore—from a plethora of potential causes. Police supposedly found a pistol, a bloody knife, a pharmacy's worth of pills and a half-empty container of industrial-grade rat-killer in the seat beside her. Though it took the coroner weeks to figure out what finally finished off the former Princess of Poverty Row Pictures, the final answer was E – all of the above. Dot was a mere 27 years old."

PART 2: POST-PRODUCTION AND RELEASE

Aug. 18, 1946. *Daily Variety:*
Production Completed on 'Athena Voltaire' – Finally
"Pinnacle Pictures Corp. has announced that its troubled feature film, 'The New Adventures of Athena Voltaire,' has completed filming. Release is set for early October."

Oct. 1, 1946, Advertisement in *Daily Variety:*
AT LONG LAST – ATHENA VOLTAIRE
"Pinnacle Pictures Corp. is proud to announce its feature film debut, 'The New Adventures of Athena Voltaire,' will arrive in theaters Friday. The thrill-packed picture, based on the real-life exploits of the famed aviatrix, stars Frank Clement, Jack C. Avery, Nora Stephens and, as the title character, the late Dorothy Van Sloan in her last screen role."

Promotional copy from the movie poster of *The New Adventures of Athena Voltaire,* reprinted in *Serial Thrills: Movie Posters from the Golden Age* (Checker Press, 1994)
"SEE A LONE WOMAN BATTLE THE MYSTIC HORDES OF AN EVIL CULT…
"WATCH THE FORBIDDEN CEREMONY OF A LOST CIVILIZATION…
"GAZE UPON THE HYPNOTIC RUNES OF THE HIDDEN TEMPLE…
" … IF YOU DARE!"

Oct. 7, 1946, *Los Angeles Times:*
Police Close Theater After Disturbance
"LOS ANGELES – Police announced Saturday that the Tivoli Cinema located on Hollywood Blvd. will be closed until further notice. What officers referred to as 'a riot' in the theater on Friday night caused extensive damage to the structure and resulted in a number of arrests."

Oct. 9, 1946, *Los Angeles Mirror:*
Movie House Standoff Ends in Suicide
"EL MONTE – Roger Willroy, employed as a projectionist at the DreamLand Theatre, held sheriff's deputies at bay for more than three hours Sunday night before turning the pistol on himself."

From *Picture Palaces: The Glory Days of Moviegoing* by Carl Salisbury (Delcy Press, 1978)
"Though not as famed as other, larger houses in southern California, San Gabriel's Oriental Theatre had been a fixture at the corner of Central Street and First Avenue since the days of silent pictures. It burned to the ground on Oct. 13, 1946. Officials interviewed at the time refused to speculate on the cause of the blaze."

Oct. 17, 1946, *Your Sho-biz Spy* column in *Hollywood Reporter:*
Pinnacle Pulls 'Athena' Prints
"Seems like the troubles aren't over for Pinnacle's would-be entrée into the world of feature films, 'The New Adventures of Athena Voltaire.' Word is the studio is pulling the remaining prints of the picture – minus at least one lost in a fire in San Gabriel – for some extensive retooling. Studio reps remained mum about the reasons for the recall, claiming that director Willis 'One Take' Arnold is a 'perfectionist' who wants the problematic pic to 'be the best it can possibly be.' In other words, Your Spy sez stay tuned."

From *Poverty Row Productions: The Forgotten Studios of Hollywood's Golden Age* by Jerry Wahls (Switzer Books, 1982)
"Pinnacle Production Corp. remains the most enigmatic of the old bottom-tier movie studios. After several years of success with low-budget serials (see Appendix C, pp. 405-407), Pinnacle closed its doors for good in 1947 after producing a single feature film, 'The New Adventures of Athena Voltaire.' Apparently based on the exploits of an actual woman, the film remains – like Stroheim's original

cut of 'Greed' and Welles' original cut of 'The Magnificent Ambersons' – lost to cinema history."

Dec. 23, 1946, *Los Angeles Herald Express:*
Police Investigate Break-in at Shuttered Studio

"Los Angeles Police are investigating an apparent burglary Saturday night at the recently closed Pinnacle Pictures Corp. on Sunrise Drive. Among the items missing are prints of the studio's last film, 'The New Adventures of Athena Voltaire.' A security guard reports seeing a woman in her late 30s or early 40s near the studio at the time of the robbery. Anyone with information is asked to contact the police."

PART 3: THE LOST YEARS

July 28, 1967, Advertisement in *Los Angeles Times*

"PUBLIC AUCTION! Studio Assets – Furniture, Props, Sets, Memorabilia and Much Much More. Must See to Believe. All Will Be Sold to Highest Bidder. Former Site of Pinnacle Pictures Corp. Studio Lot. PUBLIC WELCOME! DON'T MISS THIS ONE! BUY A PIECE OF HOLLYWOOD HISTORY!"

Nov. 1, 1967, *Los Angeles Times:*
Seven Found Dead in Mulholland Dr. Mansion

"Police are investigating what sources are referring to as a 'mass murder scene' at the Mulholland Drive home of developer Jonathan Meisner. According to police, the bodies of Meisner and six others were found Tuesday in the home's living room. Police refused to speculate about the cause of death, and identities of the other victims were being withheld pending notice of their families."

Nov. 2, 1967, *L.A. Mid-Nite Informer:*
KULT KILLINGS IN LA-LA LAND!

"Mulholland was the scene of murder and mayhem Tuesday when a gang of crazed cultists rampaged through the swanky digs of Jonathan 'Johnny' Meisner, L.A. bigwig and well-known movie memorabilia maven. The police have their mouth shut on this one, but your plugged-in source here at the Informer hears that 'Johnny' was hosting a big movie bash that got way out of hand way fast. Word is that the party was an excuse for 'Johnny' to show off his swag from a recent auction, but a bit of set decoration from a forgotten 1946 flick drove some local loonies over the edge. Good thing he didn't show the whole movie, right Informed Readers? Right – and Right On!"

From *Tinseltown Gomorrah* by Stephen Stark (Javelin Books, 1972)

"And it's not just the stars themselves that flame out dramatically, taking everyone with them. Just a few years ago, well-heeled film fan Jonathan Meisner was murdered during one of his legendary showbiz soirees. A man as rich as Mister Meisner could afford more than just the pricey movie memorabilia that filled his home – he could afford to keep secrets. And just how he died – along with a half-dozen other local notables – is one he took straight to the grave."

Interview excerpt with art historian Dr. Lawrence Bergerac from *ArtTalk Journal* (Fall 2001 issue)

"Q: You claim that the Third Reich's experiments with psychological warfare extended to the arts?

"Bergerac: Certainly. It's obvious they were masters of the image, of propaganda, of taking a 3,000-year-old religion symbol and turning it into an icon of evil. Is it any surprise this artistic bent – and I use the term advisedly – was combined with certain occult tendencies among the elite to provoke a strong reaction to artwork, be it painting, sculpture or even the sets of a play?

"Q: Even the painted backdrop of a play, something the audience might not notice, could have an effect on their minds, causing them to act out?

"Bergerac: Of course. It's the art we barely notice that has the strongest impact on us. There are reports in German papers of the day of theatergoers charging the stage for reasons they couldn't later explain.

"Q: Then given how obsessed Goebbels was with the art of cinema, were these techniques ever used in films? The potential impact would have been…

"Bergerac: Film? No, of course not. Props and sets would only be glimpsed for a moment. It couldn't work.

From *The Encyclopedia Cult-Filmica* by Weldon Michaels (Serpentine Books, 1983)

"'The New Adventures of Athena Voltaire,' 1946, Pinnacle Pictures Corp. Director: Willis Arnold Cast: Dorothy Van Sloan, Frank Clement, Jack Avery, Nora Stephens, Jackson "Cadillac" Jones. Little-seen (ever seen?) low-budgeter based (loosely, I'm guessing) on a real-life celeb of the thirties and forties. Not to be confused with the Warner Bros. bomb a decade earlier. This one was barely released, barely screened, then yanked from theaters by the studio. Good luck laying your eyes on it. Too bad, too, because the production design was supposed to have been something to see."

PART 4: RE-RELEASE

Oct. 31, 1995, Obituary in *Los Angeles Times*
"Henry Frederic Knox, 96, died of natural causes Monday at St. Sebastian Home for the Aged in Los Angeles. Born in 1899 in Berlin, Germany, he was employed in that country's film industry until moving to the United States after World War II, where he found work as an art director in Hollywood. He leaves no survivors."

Nov. 17 to Nov. 19, 1995, posts on the *Lost Film Lovers* Online Message Board
"SShivers: Friend of mine taking class at UCLA film school sez everyone goin nuts about some big movie discovery. Film cans brought in, profs verrrrry excited. Anyone know what this is all about? Greed? AMBERSONS????"

"CarlDenham33: I dunno what movie it is but your right – everyone here crazy about it. My prof – not too connected – says he heard it was found in storage locker owned by some guy who died. Old guy – special effects maybe? Art director?"

"SShivers: Never mind. Got the scoop. Not GREED or AMBERSONS but still sounds cool. Posters all over campus now. Screening set for next week. IM THERE!!!!"

Xeroxed flyer found on UCLA Campus Nov. 20, 1995
"THE NEW ADVENTURES OF ATHENA VOLTAIRE
"One-time ONLY screening of LOST 1946 film
"In the days after World War II, an upstart studio trying to compete with the majors bet everything on a movie about a real-life feminist icon – and LOST! After a few troubled screenings, the film was pulled from theaters and all prints were considered lost – UNTIL NOW!
"Don't miss this LANDMARK EVENT!
"8 P.M. FRIDAY, NOV. 24, STECKLER HALL
"FREE ADMISSION WITH STUDENT I.D."

Nov. 23, 1995, *Los Angeles Times:*
Movie Theft Stumps Campus Cops

"Security officers at the University of California at Los Angeles are still puzzling over a break-in at the school's film department, where several canisters of film were stolen – apparently by an old woman.

"According to Henry Joseph, head of UCLA Campus Security, the theft took place early Wednesday morning when the school's Melnitz Hall was empty. Five canisters containing the 1946 film 'The New Adventures of Athena Voltaire' were among the items missing, and their location remains unknown.

"'Those old film cans can be pretty heavy,' Joseph said, 'which makes stealing them a chore for anyone. The fact that our security footage seems to show an elderly woman – and I mean a very elderly woman – walking across the roof with them just makes this whole crime even stranger.'

"Joseph said anyone with information about the theft should contact campus security. A scheduled screening of the film has been cancelled until further notice."

Nov. 27 1995, post on the *Lost Film Lovers*
Online Message Board

"SShivers: Anyone know whats up with ATHENA VOLTAR movie? Who stole it? Anyone find it? Been reading up on this movie and it sounds GREAT. Plus all sorts of weird stuff happens whenever its ben shown. I NEED TO SEE IT. Any info AT ALL????"

Nov. 28 1995, post on the Lost Film Lovers Online Message Board
"SShivers: HELLO? ANYONE?"

Nov. 29 1995, post on the Lost Film Lovers Online Message Board
[POST REMOVED BY SYSTEM ADMINISTRATOR]

PART 5: GOING VIRAL

9:14 p.m. CST May 30, 2018: Twitter post from @Filmfiend2727

"Any1 hear of athena voltar movie? From 1946? Big news coming soon. BIG NEWS"

4:55 p.m. CST June 3, 2018: Twitter post from @Filmfiend2727

"Cant say how but I got copy of athena voltar movie. Anyone in San Gabriel area know where I can get VHS drive w USB connection?"

11:36 p.m. CST June 6, 2018: Twitter post from @Filmfiend2727
"Special thanx to @errolflynnfan44. VHS drive hummin away as I type"

1:07 a.m. CST June 7, 2018: Twitter post from @Filmfiend2727
"SUCCESS! Good thing too – tape broke when I took it out of machine. But who cares? ALL DIGITAL NOW BABY!"

3:30 a.m. CST June 7, 2018: Twitter post from @FilmFiend2727
"DONE. Movie on youtube, Facebook, every torrent you can name. ATHENA VOLTAR IS HEADED FOR A SCREEN NEAR YOU!!"

3:31 a.m. CST June 7, 2018: Twitter post from @FilmFiend2727
"Ready or not, here it comes."

AFTERWORD
(or A Rambling Reminiscence About Making This Book)
Steve Bryant

This project had its origin at Athena's original publisher, Ape Entertainment. Ape co-publisher Brent Erwin suggested it to me as an in-btween release. I was intrigued by the idea, and even mentioned it on the Comic Geek Speak podcast.

I'd met Chris Murrin through the Comic Geek Speak forums and eventually started hanging out with him at San Diego Comic-Con each year. He was the second author attached to this collection, having offered his services via direct message on the CGS forums. Chris turned in his first draft of *Hakkō Ichiu* on July 13, 2008.

The book was going along slowly, as I was prepping a soft relaunch of the AV comic. At the San Diego Comic-Con the following year, Chris offered to edit the book, which didn't have a title at the time. We kept calling it the "Athena Voltaire Prose Book."

Bringing Chis on board was easily one of the smartest things I've done in my life. In the last decade, he's become an invaluable editor on *Athena Voltaire, Ghoul Scouts*, and other comics of mine, a frequent collaborator, and one of my best friends—which is weird, considering we live 2,000 miles away and see each other once a year. But that's life in the internet age, right?

I detailed the bumpy road to AV's relaunch in my Afterword for the *Athena Voltaire Compendium*, and it's not worth rehashing here. It was long, I overthought things way too much, blah, blah, blah, yadda, yadda, yadda...you can go read the painful details in that book.

There were some cool things that happened due to the delays, though. At the onset, I knew exactly one prose author, Brad Keefauver. As production on the book continued, I met more and more of my future collaborators.

The coolest part about inviting so many other creators into your sandbox? Your world expands. Sure, I knew the many wrinkles I'd like to add over the course of multiple Athena Voltaire stories: elements of film noir, screwball comedy, historical figures and events, etc. But this was genuine proof-of-concept taking place before my eyes. Athena's world was big enough to include all of these elements.

And just answering authors' questions expanded the world, too. Athena's family, her timeline, and her relationship to historical figures were all carefully considered when responding.

When I sat down to illustrate this book, I was delighted to reread all of these stories, and those extra wrinkles were apparent. It's a delight to see how so many talented collaborators took this character and ran in so many exciting, inventive directions. The cherry on top, for me, is that I was able to illustrate every story.

And that's the one hidden disappointment of this book. My first instinct is to illustrate the climax of each story. But I know how things work with illustrated books—you sometimes flip through and check out the artwork before reading. My responsibility as illustrator is to entice the reader, but not to spoil the stories. Historical figure reveal? Yeah, drawing that person blows the story. Reveal the identity of the killer or monster? Then I'm the jerk that ruined a cool story by someone I admire.

Not on my watch.

Speaking of the art…

When *Athena Voltaire Pulp Tales* was conceived, I was still illustrating everything traditionally with a brush and ink on paper. Since that time, I've switched to working digitally. For this project, I planned to revisit a few black-and-white techniques I hadn't used since I worked in the roleplaying game industry in the '90s. I explored ways to digitally emulate drybrush, greasepencil, zip-a-tone, and DuoShade. For context, feel free to Google those terms. I'll wait.

With about two-thirds of the illos completed, I shared the work-in-progress with a group of art pals that I meet up with every few months. Jim Nelson, Jason Millet, Jim Heffron, and I share what we're working on, pass new art books around, and generally critique and kibitz about one another's work. It's a great way to keep the creative fire burning.

At our most recent meetup, the guys overwhelmingly liked the digital DuoShade work more than any of my other illos for this book. It wasn't even close. With that in mind, I went back to the digital drawing board and began reworking all of the illustrations to reflect this stylistic approach.

With each piece that I completed in this vein, I got more excited. A coherent look for the book was coming into focus—and it was a look that was consistent with the existing AV comic art, but was also specifically designed to exploit the fact that the book would be printed in black-and-white.

Of course, I can point out a dozen flaws with any drawing in the book—every artist can pick their own work apart. But the nature of deadlines necessitate letting the work go at some point, and I've made my peace with these ~~flaws~~ nuances. And I've kind of fallen in love with black-and-white illustration all over again.

I'd be remiss if I didn't mention the amazing Jason Millet, one of the aforementioned art pals. Jason's a frequent collaborator, and is currently the colorist on the covers for the ongoing Athena Voltaire comic, as well as contributing to couple of books I write: coloring Mark Stegbauer's brilliant line art on *Ghoul Scouts*, and providing jaw-droppingly great painted art on *Undead or Alive*. I sent Jason my pencil drawing for *Athena Voltaire Pulp Tales* and asked him to give it a "Robert McGinnis crossed with Drew Struzan" vibe. He succeeded beyond my wildest expectations.

So yeah, that's the history of the book in a babbling, rambling nutshell. It took forever, but without that long gestation period, who knows which collaborators wouldn't be in the book? Who knows what form the look of the art would have taken? In the end, I'm glad for the winding path, because it gave Chris, Corinna, Gabriel, October, Ron, Brad, Tom, Amber, Dirk, Paul, Marc, Michael, Jason, Caleb, Mike, Genevieve, Will, Ryan, Eric, and me the chance to make the book you hold in your hands.

—Steve Bryant
the suburban wilds of central Illinois

P.S. Let's hope this books sells like crazy, because I've met a bunch more writers would would love to join the fun if we make a second volume.

SteveBryantComics.com | @SteveBryantArt | @AthenaVoltaire | like Athena Voltaire on Facebook

CONTRIBUTORS

CORINNA BECHKO is a New York Times bestselling author who has been writing both comics and prose since her horror graphic novel *Heathentown* was published by Image/Shadowline in 2009. She has worked for numerous publishers including Marvel, DC, Dynamite, Dark Horse, and Sideshow on titles such as *Star Wars: Legacy, Savage Hulk, Angel, Once Upon a Time, Court of the Dead: The Chronicle of the Underworld* and the Hugo nominated series *Invisible Republic*, which she co-writes with Gabriel Hardman. Her background is in zoology and it usually shows. She lives in Los Angeles with her husband Gabriel Hardman and a small menagerie.

STEVE BRYANT is the Eisner, Manning, and Harvey Award-nominated creator/ writer/artist of *Athena Voltaire* from Action Lab Entertainment, and the writer/co-creator of *Ghoul Scouts*, also published by Action Lab. He has also completed projects for Dark Horse Comics, IDW, Boom! Studios, Ape Entertainment, and others, as well as extensive work in the roleplaying game industry. Steve lives in the suburban wilds of Central Illinois with his son, girlfriend, and companion animals.

OCTOBER CRIFASI is a writer and musician living in Los Angeles with six guitars, two cats, and a pet dragon named Scorch. Her work includes *"Stagecoach Mary"* from the Eisner-nominated *Outlaw Territory Vol. 3* from Image Comics and several columns for *Acoustic Guitar* and *Classical Guitar* magazines. When not writing comics, October leads a parallel life as a music journalist and overall music nerd. More of her work can be discovered at www.rocktober.org and also in the forthcoming anthology, *Somewhere Beyond the Heavens: Exploring Battlestar Galactica* from Sequart publishing.

RON FORTIER – Comics and pulps writer/editor best known for his work on the *Green Hornet* comic series and *Terminator – Burning Earth* with Alex Ross. He won the Pulp Factory Award for Best Pulp Short Story of 2011 for *"Vengeance Is Mine,"* which appeared in Moonstone's *The Avenger – Justice Inc.* and in 2012 for *"The Ghoul,"* from the anthology *Monster Aces.* He is the Managing Editor of Airship 27 Productions, a New Pulp Fiction publisher and writes the continuing adventures of both his own character, *Brother Bones – the Undead Avenger* and the classic pulp hero, *Captain Hazzard – Champion of Justice.* (www.airship27.com)

GABRIEL HARDMAN is the co-writer and artist of the Hugo nominated sci-fi series *Invisible Republic* and *Green Lantern: Earth One,* as well as writer/artist of *Kinski* and *The Belfry.* He also co-wrote *Star Wars: Legacy, Planet of the Apes, Savage Hulk,* and *Sensation Comics featuring Wonder Woman* with Corinna Bechko. He has drawn *Hulk, Secret Avengers,* and *Agents of Atlas* as well as the OGN *Heathentown.* Hardman is an accomplished storyboard artist having worked on movies such at *Logan, Interstellar, Inception* and *Tropic Thunder.* He lives with his wife, writer Corinna Bechko, in Los Angeles.

BRAD KEEFAUVER is a longtime writer on the subject of Sherlock Holmes whose work includes his book exploring Holmes's methods titled *The Elementary Methods of Sherlock Holmes,* regular blogging under the title *"Sherlock Peoria,"* and a fictional conspiracy podcast called *"Sherlock Holmes is Real."* Chronicling an adventure of Athena Voltaire is one of his rare excursions outside of Sherlockian topics.

TOM KING is the Eisner award winning writer of *Batman, The Vision,* and T*he Sheriff of Babylon.* He currently lives in DC with his wife and three children.

ELIZABETH AMBER LOVE is the author of *The Farrah Wethers Mysteries: "Cardiac Arrest," "Full Body Manslaughter,"* and *"Miscarriage of Justice."* Love had a short story in the Anthony Award nominated *Protect volume 2, Protectors: Heroes.* She hosts the *Vodka O'Clock* podcast where she interviews writers, artists, actors, filmmakers and other interesting people. She blogs and covers news for her website AmberUnmasked.com. She's written comic book short stories in *The December Project, Shelter,* and Red Stylo Media's *Shakespeare Shaken* anthology; a future comic short story is in the works for Action Lab's *Stray* universe. Love has also had essays published at *Femsplain* and the Eisner Award nominated website, *Women Write About Comics.* She's a figure model when time permits during her life in New Jersey with an exceptionally spoiled cat named Detective Inspector Guster Nabu.

Official site: AmberUnmasked.com

Patreon.com/amberunmasked

Social media: https://about.me/amberlove

DIRK MANNING is best known as the writer/creator of comic series such as the "Cthulhu Noir" *Tales Of Mr. Rhee* and the enthralling horror anthology series *Nightmare World* and *Love Stories (To Die For),* all released by Devil's Due Publishing. Dirk is also the author of the ongoing inspirational column/book collection *Write or Wrong: A Writer's Guide to Creating Comics* (Caliber/Bleeding Cool). More of Dirk's gripping and exciting stories can be read in comic titles such as *Twiztid: Haunted High-Ons* (Source Point Press), *The Legend Of Oz: The Wicked West* (Aspen/Big Dog Ink), *Dia De Los Muertos* (Image Comics/Shadowline) among various other anthologies. Pre-releases of his comics on the crowdfunding platform Kickstarter have surpassed $100,000 (and counting), and he is quickly gaining a reputation as one of the best independent horror writers in comics. When not on the road Dirk lives on the Internet and can be found online at www.DirkManning. com as well as at Facebook, Twitter, Instagram, and Tumblr @dirkmanning.

MARC MASON is the author of *Schism: Out of the Shadows, Battery: The Arrival, Schism: Shadow Terrors, Red Sonja: Raven, Red Sonja: Sanctuary, The Secret World: Traveling Abroad for the First Time at 40, The Joker's Advocate,* and *The Aisle Seat: Life on the Edge of Popular Culture.* He is a librarian and professor at Arizona State University in Tempe, Arizona where he resides with his beloved wife Sophie and their children. You can find him online at MarcMason.com and on Twitter as @marcmason

MICHAEL MAY is the writer and co-creator (with artist Jason Copland) of *Kill All Monsters,* a graphic novel from Dark Horse Comics featuring giant robots fighting giant monsters in a post-apocalyptic world. He's also a prolific podcaster with a current slate of eight monthly shows. You can find links to all of them - and to his writing - at http://www. michaelmay.online/. Or follow him on Twitter at https://twitter.com/michaelmaycomix. Michael lives in Saint Paul, Minnesota with his wife Diane, his teenaged son (and frequent podcast co-host) David, and a big yellow dog named Luke Skywalker.

JASON MILLET is an illustrator, storyboard artist, comic artist/colorist. He provides working storyboards and conceptual art for NBC-Universal's One Chicago franchise as well as for many other television series and movies. He has also produced a wide range of artwork for a long list of advertising clientele and publishers.

He resides in Chicago with his beloved wife and daughter and their merely-tolerated cat.

CALEB MONROE is the writer of such comics as *Peanuts, Batman, Cloaks, Dawn of the Planet of the Apes, Ice Age, Steed & Mrs. Peel* and *Hunter's Fortune*. He lives and works in LA, but can be visited at calebmonroe.com from anywhere.

CHRIS MURRIN has been writing and editing comics and prose for over fifteen years. In addition to working with Steve Bryant on both *Athena Voltaire* and *Ghoul Scouts* for Action Lab, Chris edits numerous titles for both Arch Blue and LawDog Comics. When he's not pestering authors with his notes, Chris works with the marketing team at FX Networks, editing promos for both movie presentations and shows such as *Archer, It's Always Sunny in Philadelphia, The Simpsons*, and *You're the Worst*. You've probably seen his work go by in a pixelated blur on your DVR. You can follow Chris and @reply him with accolades via Twitter @ChrisMurrin.

MIKE OLIVERI is a writer, martial artist, cigar aficionado, motorcyclist, and family man, but not necessarily in that order. His short work has appeared in a number of comic and prose anthologies, and his first novel, *Deadliest of the Species*, won a Bram Stoker Award. His werewolf thriller series *The Pack* has been produced in both comic miniseries and prose novel formats. You can keep up with Mike and his work at www.mikeoliveri.com or @MikeOliveri on Twitter.

Having collected action figures and comic books from a young age, **GENEVIEVE PEARSON** always dreamed of being an action hero. When she grew up, she decided writing about them would be the next best thing. This was enough to get her on the show *King of the Nerds* on TBS, where she took second place and was named by the *New York Times* as the contestant who came "closest to being genuinely funny."

She now lives in the San Fernando Valley in Southern California and works in reality TV. She still hopes one day to have a room big enough to show off all of her Batman toys. Please visit her website, www.genevievepearson.com to find out more about her latest projects and connect with her socially.

WILL PFEIFER got his literary start as a child, when he wrote a spec script for the then-current cop drama *Starsky & Hutch*. (Sadly, it was never submitted.) He followed that achievement with several issues of various hand-made comic books in junior high and high school, then continued with several issues of various self-published comic books in college, which he sold through the mail, at comic book conventions and through various other illicit channels. Pfeifer's actual writing career (meaning, of course, the one he got paid for) began at the turn of the century with the publication of *Finals*, a four-issue satirical mini-series co-created with artist Jill Thompson and published by Vertigo, the not-for-kids imprint of DC Comics. Since then, he's written various adventures of *Catwoman*, the *Teen Titans, Aquaman, Captain Atom, Iron Man, Hellboy*, the *Spirit*, the *Demon, Wonder Woman, Supergirl*, the *Blue Beetle* and a certain guy in a bat costume. He's also the co-creator of DC's *H.E.R.O*, a much-beloved comic book that was cancelled after 22 issues but which Pfeifer prefers to think of as an unusually long mini-series.

When he's not consuming pop culture, Pfeifer likes to watch too many weird movies, replay too many episodes of *Kojak* and not write enough on his blog, XraySpex.blogspot. com. He's the co-host of the comic book podcast *Pictures Within Pictures* and former co-host of the former movie podcast *Out of Theaters*. You can follow him on Twitter @ willpfeifer and on Facebook under that same, difficult to pronounce name.

In his spare time, Pfeifer works a full-time job and spends his evenings with his beautiful wife and lovely daughter. But really, that's not the sort of thing anyone cares about in a bio like this, is it?

RYAN L. SCHRODT is a Harvey Award nominated writer from the great state of Iowa. He is best known for his surreal comedic webcomic *Dear Dinosaur*, but has also written for Image Comics, Titan Books, Action Lab, Red Stylo, and more. His debut illustrated children's books, *The Singing Sasquatch* and *S is for Suplex* will be released in early 2018.

ERIC TRAUTMANN has written for roleplaying games (notably West End Games' *Star Wars* roleplaying game), videogames (including *Halo: Combat Evolved* and *Crimson Skies* for Microsoft), and comics (including DC Comics' *Checkmate, Final Crisis: Resist*, and *JSA vs. Kobra: Engines of Faith*, as well as long runs on Dynamite Entertainment's *Red Sonja, Vampirella*, and *Flash Gordon* series. He co-wrote (with Brandon Jerwa) the 2013 PRISM Award-winning DC/Vertigo graphic novel, *Shooters*, illustrated by Steve Lieber. Currently, he is the series graphic designer for the Image Comics titles *Lazarus, The Old Guard*, and *Black Magick* and has contributed design to several forthcoming *Atomic Robo* collections for Tesladyne LLC. Trautmann recently returned to dice-and-paper gaming, serving as "minister without portfolio" for transmedia company Adamant Entertainment, tackling various production, branding design, book layout, and illustration chores for that company's various lines (including the Savage Worlds-compatible *Thrilling Tales* series of pulp adventure gaming products). He can be found online at www.erictrautmann.us, on Facebook, and on Twitter (@mercuryeric, where he swears too much).